RITE JUDGEMENT

DADA DETECTIVE AGENCY BOOK 2

PETE ADAMS

HEADS ROLL – CORPSES DANCE

PRAISE FOR PETE ADAMS

"*Pete Adams is the Salvador Dali of thriller writers*"
– *John Broughton*

A politically correct / incorrect, risqué, mischievous,
irreverent and,
ever so naughty, crime mystery thriller.
A real / surreal novel where life imitates art in *The
Rite of Spring*
Yes, a very British revolution.

———

The semblance of truth:
You've got to accentuate the narrative
Eliminate the unprovocative
Latch on to the imaginative
Don't mess with Mister Verisimilitude

You've got to spread hope up to the maximum
Bring hate down to the minimum
Have faith in pandemonium
And walk the talk with attitude

Original song, Accentuate the Positive:
Sung by Byng Crosby, songwriters Johnny Mercer /
Harold Arlen

"The imaginary is what tends to become real." –
André Breton

BOOKS BY PETE ADAMS:

To Carl Clauson, Director of the Hampshire County Youth Orchestra – in 2013 he staged a magnificent performance of The Rite of Spring, joining local dancers with the very accomplished youth orchestra. It made my mind buzz. I wrote notes throughout.

The Rite of Spring – the metaphor – at the end of this book I set out how I read the metaphor – but, for now, I leave the reader to draw their own conclusions (no peeking).

AUTHOR'S NOTE

This novel may shock you. If it doesn't, I apologise. In parts, it may offend and, yes, I apologise...? There is a cavalier attitude to religion, exaggerated caricatures, but what would you expect of a real / surreal story. Is there a happy ending? That depends on your point of view, but, there is hope...

St Winifrede – *Wikipedia* According to legend, Winifrede was the daughter of a Welsh nobleman; her mother was a sister of St Beuno. When Winifrede decided to become a

nun, her suitor, Caradog, was enraged and decapitated her. A healing spring appeared

where her head fell. Winifrede's head was subsequently re-joined to her body, thanks to the efforts of Saint Beuno, and she was restored to life.

The DaDa Detective Agency – Police Detective Jack (nicknamed Jane) Austin and his wife, Detective Superintendent Amanda Austin, retired and formed the agency. In his Oft-deluded parallel existence, Jack declared that his wife would henceforth be known as

Duck, and himself as Dick. Now, Amanda Austin is a strong woman indeed and, at any time can disarm her dipstick husband, but occasionally, she allowed his follies to remain unchallenged, confident that the anticipated train crash would derail any of Jack's pig-sty thinking (we think he meant big sky, but then again...). And, in this case, nervous that in retirement they would both become bored, she thought a low-profile detective agency would be quite fulfilling. All she needed to do was persuade her errant husband to select a new name, not being totally enamoured of the Dick and Duck Austin (DaDa), Detective Agency name, principally because she was a woman and not a bird and, if she had to be a bird, then why a fucking duck? She did, however, think her husband was a dick and so left that half of the nom d'agence, unchallenged. Maybe she could be Dorothy, a gift from God, or Daisy? Perhaps Dianna? Oh God, not Dee Dee. But she was lumbered with Duck and, DaDa. Maybe LaLa had a more appropriate ring to it?

Dada – *Wikipedia* – A European artistic and literary movement (1916-1923) that flouted conventional aesthetic and cultural values by producing works marked by nonsense, travesty and incongruity. Dada rejected reason and logic, prizing nonsense, irrationality and intuition. *Maybe it helps to understand matters if we make a nonsense of them? This is what the DaDa series of novels seeks to achieve.*

Umble Pie – A mediaeval pie made from the heart and entrails of a deer. If you upset the lord of the manor, you were sent to a lower table, where the fare was of poorer quality, and, made to eat umble pie (not humble – although this is the modern day derivation).

Ooh La Lovelies – a name inspired by Portsmouth fashion designer, Michelle Louise Finnerty and her company, *On La Lovelies*, producing beautiful haute couture, inspired from the fifties *elegance* mode – Michelle has kindly given me consent to use the name.

Illuminati – *Wikipedia* – The Illuminati are often alleged to conspire to control world affairs, contriving situations, infiltrating governments and corporations, in order to gain political power and influence and to establish a new world order.

Illusionati – Not very much is known of them, as you might expect.

"*Every word that is spoken and sung here represents at least this one thing: that this humiliating age has not succeeded in winning our respect.*"

Hugo Ball, referring to the Cabaret Voltaire. and it is equally relevant today.

INTRODUCTION

At the conclusion of the *Kind Hearts and Martinets* series and the immediate sequel, *Road Kill – The Duchess of Frisian Tun*, there was *nothing*. Just two stories evolving, one fleetingly surreal, but potent, the other very real and edgy and, they had begun to intertwine, like a DNA spiral. Was this an opportunity for change, or punishment for what has preceded us and, will continue in another guise, or maybe both? And what strand will succeed; *The People* or *The System*? A new birth? Not a rebirth.

Martin Heidegger said: *"There is no such thing as nothing."* – *"Das Nichts"*, the nothing. So, there is something? But, if it is not the right something, if it is a something that ignores the essence of reality, *"authenticity"* and, commits the vast majority of people into subjugation, *"theyselves and not themselves (ourselves)"* for the profit of the very few, then that something needs to change. But who can we reasonably look to lead the way? *The state? The establishment?* They are a part of the problem, no? *The church?* Other religious faiths? They have their own power-base agenda, yes? Is it even possible to turn this juggernaut of nothingness, of denial of a real something, around? And what is authenticity?

Kurt Vonnegut said: *"There is no reason why good cannot triumph as often as evil. The triumph of anything is a matter of organisation. If there are such things as angels, I hope that they are organised along the lines of the Mafia"*

Well, it turns out the angels were organising, but could they combat not only the evil outside, but also, the evil within? Read on and find out...

PROLOGUE

THERE HAD BEEN THE ARAB SPRING. WELL, what was called the Arab Spring, but there had been a spring, first in Tunisia, then Egypt, Libya, Yemen, Bahrain and Syria, Morocco and Jordan – all springs of varying degrees of success and all aimed at overturning an oppressive regime, or what at least was deemed to be oppressive, but had, in the course of time, been shown to be *benign* dictatorships, if that is possible?

To say that Britain faced, or needed a *spring*, might be pushing the analogy too far, but certainly the people felt oppressed by the establishment, comprised of the government, civil servants, banks and financial institutions, corporations, as well as wealthy individuals, all perceived to be in the grip and control of the elite; the one per cent. The people felt and were, in reality, disenfranchised. The elite, the Eton bunch, the old-money privileged, felt they had a God-given right to rule. A divine arrogance, established through generations of the same families, all moneyed, and all convinced they knew best. The plebs?

Well, they should be grateful for what they got. The crumbs off their table.

To say Britain needed a *spring* would also depend on which side of the fence you sat, silver spoon in a *bouche raffinee*, or a rusty nail stuck up your arse. But, something was brewing, and it looked as if it was not just letters to the newspaper, tuts at coffee mornings and grumbles in the working-men's clubs. This was different, there was a groundswell that was germinating, flourishing and growing in momentum. It had the hallmarks of a peasants' revolt, led not by an uneducated Wat Tyler, but some more powerful and influential persons and organisations supporting the movement, goading it even, some for altruistic reasons, but others saw that a dystopian society made for more opportunities to make smash-and-grab raids on the country's family silver. These unscrupulous institutions could do very well indeed, provided it went their way, which it was anticipated to do. As it had always done. But would it this time? They played a dangerous game and so what of the risks? The people would not see them until it would be too late.

On the other hand, would the power of the people be enough to overcome? And what was it they had to overcome? The enemy was nebulous and this had always been the way. Who are you fighting? Certainly in some cultures, as proven in the Arab Spring, the people had a known enemy that generally did not shield itself behind the pretence of a democracy and, the people had the will and the spirit; never say die. But did the British? The Brits had to be up for work in the morning, of course, but that was becoming less of an issue as jobs disappeared or people were slammed into zero-hours contracts. They would be up, but then a phone call; no work today. Idle hands? Maybe not, there might be something good on the telly, though this had been manipulated as much as it could with diverting news, often made up, of gung-ho sporting fixtures, jingoistic headlines, anything to distract the plebs, but even that interest was waning as people started to become aware of their cruel circumstances. It is hard to ignore hunger.

There were rumblings of discontent. The whiff of revolt in the air. A gathering storm, the big *Mo*. The established order was being challenged on several fronts and many of the traditional barriers, proven successful in the past, like starving the poor, disabled and sick, were being charged down. Revolution was being nurtured, but would it be a bloodless coup and, most of all, would it succeed? Read on...

PART ONE
THE DANCERS, THE PLAYERS...

ONE

Leonard Bernstein said, "If there is no one to play second fiddle, there is no harmony," and it is reliably thought he did not refer to the brand of hairspray of that name. But, in this instance, may his words have been misconstrued?

However, it is true that if an orchestra is to have a long and successful life, the leader of the second violins needs to be a player of the utmost capability; though often it is considered the player sent to lead the second violins is sacrificed on the conductor's altar, much like a virgin would be walled up by mediaeval builders, or the Romans sacrificed a bull and drank its blood; for the greater good. Should it therefore have come as a surprise that the second fiddle player, leader of the second violins, in the celebrated St Winifrede's Convent Orchestra, *The Nuns' Orchestra*, Sister Winifrede, who also taught geography at the St Winifrede's Roman Catholic Convent School in Portsmouth, sat in a pool of sacrificial blood. The ensanguined floor, a crimson pool, was highlighted by a brilliantly intense shaft of light that seemingly had no terrestrial electrical source.

The nun had been decapitated, her body posed on a chair in her position as leader of the second violins. She was playing the violin, except there was no chin present to tuck the violin under. Regardless, she gave a peerless and chinless recital, playing a beautiful and celestially haunting tune, *The Lark Ascending*.

The decollated head of Sister Winifrede had been placed on the conductor's desk, atop the score for Stravinsky's *Rite of Spring*. Her wimple was missing and the nun's hair, previously savagely cropped, had been superbly coiffed; she had the serene look of an Audrey Hepburn in her heyday.

It was June the twenty second, sixteen days after the Portsmouth celebrations of the seventieth anniversary of D-Day and the not so much celebrated, though thoroughly acknowledged in the newspapers, partial destruction of Frisian Tun, a previously enchanting middle class street in pretentious, so some say, middle-class Southsea (See *Road Kill – The Duchess of Frisian Tun*). An English idyll within the City of Portsmouth, a strategically important naval and commercial port on the south coast of England and, to pile conundrum upon Gordian Knot, this was just a few days after the revelation that the Duchess of Frisian Tun was none other than the notorious London transvestite gangster and socialite, Mad Frankie the axeman.

The social mores were all asunder. Unusual? Not really. So much was happening that was inexplicable? A collision of catastrophic events, too numerous to list. Something in the stars? Certainly the past few weeks had the pundits running panic stricken for their copy of *Nostradamus*, their *Old Moore's Al-*

maniac, but they should have waited for the revelation from Crumpet and Pimple, investigative journalists, as even more was to be exposed; something would need to be done.

And now there was Umble Pie.

Orchestra practice was at lunchtime... would it go ahead, if you pardon the pun?

———

To say Ernest, the caretaker at St Winifrede's, was odd might be an understatement, though the degrading aspects of his job suited his purpose; he sought only promotion within his Order and, sacrifices had to be made.

Ernest sloped his head and cupped a hand to his ear as he drifted, broom in hand, toward the school hall, as if drawn by the tantalising scent of *Bisto* gravy, sniffing out an inspirational audio trail, not a mouthwatering aromatic fragrance, but a spooky melodic emanation. The elegiac chords bountifully suffused the corridors with an evanescent life, supplanting the ordinarily insensate passageways during lesson time, much as the gravy would enrich even the dullest roast meat.

Ernest tracked the haunting sound and soon arrived outside the school hall, the source of the music. He tipped on to his toes, for he had the appearance of an insignificant short man, which to all intents, he was. He was short and cultivated his insignificance, which actually came naturally to him and, if he had stopped to think about it, he might have realised this was why he was still lowly within the Order. He peeked into the hall through the porthole window in one of the double doors. He didn't know about the importance of a second fiddle, or harmony, but he did know that orchestra practice would likely not go ahead later that morning.

The hall was a terrible mess and this would mean trouble. He would be blamed; he always was. He took in a panoramic view of the assembly room, a gloomy ambience to what was ordinarily a light and bright auditorium now seemingly subjected to an artificially created darkness, daylight mysteriously occluded. His comprehension of a gloom-saturated disarray was, however, short-lived and only cursory, as his focus was drawn to the body of the decapitated nun captured in an extraordinarily bright laser like beam, its illuminating journey picking up fairies dancing to the music; agitated dust motes, moving as if dancing a ballet to the tune being played, *A bird going up*, he thought. A minor distraction from the macabre scene.

Ernest stepped through the doors and into the hall. He was not nervous, he was buoyed with an excitement that would be inexplicable to a casual observer. He had seen scenes like this in books and read about such apparitions in the Order's pamphlets. Was this his blinding light? A clarion call to arms, his calling? If it was, then Ernest was ready, up to the task and, as he thought this, so his body inflated with Holy Caretaking spirits. He stood erect as he filled his lungs with air to puff out his pigeon chest, the consequence of which was he got a nostril full of the sickly ferrous scent of blood, and the accompanying sensitivity of death and its incumbent fear tingled along his spine. His ersatz though righteous bravado fading rapidly, Ernest's naturally occurring simpering cowardice reasserted itself.

Overcoming his pusillanimity, his faith instilling him with spurious bravado, Ernest approached the orchestra practice area, the chairs and spindly music stands set out like skeletons waiting to be given body and soul through musicians in habits with their musical scores. He was attracted not to the fiddling headless nun, but to the conductor's rostrum, where a second ethereal sunbeam spotlighted a head atop the conductor's table and, as he focused his stare, he could see that the score had been annotated with a scrawled note in red. Blood? He closed in for a better look. The scrawl tailed away to the bottom of the page where the red *ink* oozing from the ragged neck end painfully slowly dripped off the desk to the floor, forming a gathering of tiny splash marks outside a blackening, congealing pool. Ernest polished his bottle-end glasses and read the score annotation in handwriting that appeared similar to the Stravinsky notation above the title, it read: *Give us a sign, oh Lord. The reckoning is yours – £73, plus tip.* Ernie had not a clue what that lot meant and only now he thought he might have misinterpreted the tableau? This was not a call to arms for him but the fucking Druids, always troublesome at times of apostasy. Well, they would not disrupt his plans. His plans. Not this time.

Ernest Pugh was considered several picnics short of a shilling and he did nothing to dissuade people of this image – he encouraged it. But in this guise, he did make a fair caretaker at St Winifrede's, which was a religious establishment considered lowly in his *Order of Caretakers*. His sister, Gladys Pugh, was the lay school secretary and she had arranged for her *simple*, oft-delusional, brother to get the job, where she could keep an eye on him. Although Gladys was not a nun, she did have empathy for the strict religious order and this was respected by the Mother Superior, encouraged even, but what would the head nun do if she was aware that Gladys reported back to the sainted, and much feared, *Holy Barbaras*? Hell hath no fury like a ratted-out Mother Superior, and then there would be the reaction from the *Barbaras*.

Kids can be cruel and the school children called the caretaker, a man in their view, diminished in stature and lacking in perceived mental faculties, "Hair Ernie", and not because he had twenty three cross-combed hairs plastered across his bald top pate, giving the semblance of the railway track confluence at Clapham Junction, but because he had a toothbrush black moustache, very much in the mode of Herr Hitler. Or, they called him Blind Pugh, as a consequence of the bottle-end glasses he wore, which meant he could not reliably see beyond his politically questionable moustache and once, while cleaning the floor of the staff ladies lavatory, he cleaned rather too thoroughly the intimate regions of the headmistress, also the convent's mother superior, as she bent down to pull up her gigantic knickers. They remain friends, the headmistress and the mop.

Blind Pugh he might be called, but Hair Ernie had a black spot or two up his sleeve and he sensed it was getting close to the time when he would be called upon to play his hand, which was at the end of the sleeve of his beige caretaker's coat, the top pocket of which sported an emblem in a tawny fawn, with cream and pastel blue highlights – *The Order of Christ's Caretakers*.

It was Hair Ernie's task, as school caretaker, to

make sure all was shipshape for the orchestra rehearsal and he discussed with himself and, a largely unresponsive nun, the mess around the second violin sister, who had now stopped playing; presumably distracted by Ernie's interrogation. The caretaker eventually realised that his conversation was somewhat one-sided, albeit the answers lyrically sounded in the ether, much as he would expect of a vision. Turning to the conductor's rostrum, he became aware that it was Sister Winifrede's head, sans coif, who was conversing in reply, though geographically relocated. He did think she looked gorgeous with her new hairstyle. She had a beatific visage, especially glowing in the pencil beam of such high-ordered brilliance; Joan of Arc light, like.

He ceased his conversation with the speaking head in order to clean up the mess beside a violinist whom he did not recognise. In fact, he knew only that the nun was a violinist as she had a violin in her hands and he wondered now if it had in fact been her playing that beautiful tune? Were his eyes and ears deceiving him? What he did know for certain was there was a God-awful mess of what looked like ketchup. So he brought his new mop into use; the headmistress had confiscated the old one and she had jovially said to Gladys, one day in passing, that she had the cleanest pelvic floor in the school.

And so Ernie set to cleaning, but there was gallons of the gelatinous stuff, a veritable lake. Gradually he began to realise, as he talked to himself, that both this new nun and sister Winifrede, were likely one of the same penguin and one part, the head bit, no longer conversed and, the complementary part, the body bit, no longer played. In fact, there was an eerie silence in the hall, so much so that Ernie could hear his ragged breathing. He took a drag on his inhaler, for he was an asthmatic, and scanned the orchestral mirage as he pictured in his mind the nuns playing, a vision so real in this eerie silence. Were they asleep in this vision? Ernie was aware that nuns got up in the middle of the night to attend to their scooters, but slowly it dawned on the simpleton caretaker that both nuns were not sleepy Vespa enthusiasts, but were now indeed dead and that this might, in actual fact be, just one nun, albeit separated and in different places and the mirage of the full somnolent orchestra faded slowly along with the lark, which had ascended and buggered off.

After running on the spot for several minutes, Ernie felt a call of nature beckoning, but remembering his sister's words about photographing any high jinks or merry japes that the kids got up to, in order to protect himself, he took his phone from his leather utility belt and photographed the scene. Ernie had been given a leather builder's belt for Christmas by his sister and he wore this all the time, the loops and pockets containing a sink plunger, an unsavoury toilet brush, light sabre, handkerchief for blowing his nose and for storing bogeys, his spam sandwiches, a bottle of water, a bottle of *Domestos* bleach, his inhaler, and of course his phone. There were two further leather loops that secured the broom and mop so these tools, the religious symbols of his trade, dragged behind him as he toured the school, redolent of *Clint Eastwood* in *The Good the Bad and the Ugly*, at least Ernest thought so. Well, he certainly had the ugly bit.

He photographed the scene and went to see his sister, the school secretary, to report his find, adding first of all an apology that he was ever so sorry that he had not got the hall ready for orchestra practice and that it wasn't him, honest.

The headmistress with her supersonic, mother-superior bat ears, overheard the conversation and stepped into the school secretary's office and joined Gladys with her brother in a one-sided conversation. Eventually sense prevailed and the mum penguin suggested they go to see what the fuss was all about and she stomped off in the direction of the school hall, the floorboards vibrating from the not inconsiderable weight and determined manner of the big mum penguin's deliberate step. It was said that the novices knew when the mother superior was approaching during periods of contemplative, enforced silence, by putting an ear, in the manner of deep and sincere prayer, to the floor, and like an approaching train, the novices would be alerted at their heavenly station and, were thus able to take up a more traditional angelic prayer-like stance in readiness of the approaching *Thunderbolt Express*.

When the mother, Gladys, and Ernie, reached the hall, there was still the lake of blood, a trail of size-thirteen bloody boot prints leading in the direction of the corridor, but no body and certainly no head on the rostrum, though the front page of the conductor's score was soaked a claret red and defaced, if you pardon the heady pun. The mother superior launched forth a raucous guffaw, which caused Ernie to hide behind his sister's voluminous skirts, while proffering his phone that still displayed the photograph.

After a moment or two of collective sounds of mirth, all at the expense of poor Ernie, the mother looked at the picture and then to the floor and the red lake. She lowered herself, which took several more minutes, at the same time giving poor Ernie disturbing lavatorial flashbacks and, by and by, she stuck her index finger, the one she uses to stir the communion wine, into the red viscous liquid, fully expecting to scoop up some tomato ketchup deposited by naughty children and, after a moment or two of holding in her mid-morning doughnuts, she suggested this might indeed be blood and that the police should be called and they were.

The police soon arrived. They did not know what to make of the situation, but did agree it was blood and, something horrible must have happened. After a cup of tea out of the convent's best bone china, with digestive biscuits, for the mother superior never shared her doughnuts, they cordoned off a crime scene and orchestra practice was postponed.

TWO

THE NEWS DESK AT THE *PORTSMOUTH EVENING News* received a message for either Cecelia Crumpet or Everard Pimple, the newly formed dynamic-duo reporting team, who had scooped exclusively and were now currently writing up in depth, following their banner headline splash of a week ago, a news item that had all government departments in a spin. Already there had been a flurry of resignations at senior civil-service levels, Mandarins nervously gripping their bottoms, the whiff of government ministerial, laxative-induced reshuffles in the offing, not to mention powerful corporate magnates stunned into eating what was being described by journalists, inaccurately as it transpired, as *Humble Pie*.

The message reported a civilised furore at the Roman Catholic Convent school of St Winifrede's. A violinist in the famous Nuns' Orchestra had been decapitated, the body and head having now disappeared, or so it was proclaimed. The note was passed on to the journalists, who were currently staying with the Austins at number 5 Frisian Tun, the Austins being the source of their scoop and a lot more besides.

17

To the uninitiated, the Austins were believed to have retired from their senior police jobs and their se-cret-squirrel positions in MI5 and had set up, in their new retirement personas, *Ooh La Lovelies, DaDa* – the Dick and Duck Austin Detective Agency. Jack Austin being Dashing Dick, he having allocated his long-suffering (over a relatively short period of time) wife, the soubriquet, with no additional superlative epithet, Duck. And those who knew the fairly re-cently dubbed Mrs Amanda Austin, likely as far back as when she was Detective Superintendent Amanda Bruce, would know that this strong woman, ordinarily a pillar of patience and understanding, would go along with her new title, (pretty much as she went along with being the wife of a well-known dipstick detective), allowing for the fact, should the occasion arise, as it most surely would, where Dick exceeded the bounds of her patience, which, as most also knew came with quite clear limitations as far as her new husband was concerned, she could slap him back into place. She would then say sorry, say that Duck loved Dick and then everything would be okay. Except it would start all over again – but isn't this the way with prima donna dipstick detective men?

She did love the fifties fashions, though, espe-cially the *Ooh La Lovelies* dresses, not that these suited Dick particularly, especially the scalloped necklines, though he did like the V-shaped deep cut to some of his wife's dresses as this provided him with the occasional surreptitious opportunity for a "butch-er's hook" (Dick was a cockney) at his wife's "Bristol Cities". His notion of what he perceived as surrepti-tious was, though, pretty much blatant, his eyes out on stalks being a big giveaway to Duck, not that she minded, she loved the idiot, which led to many suggestions she get herself off to Specsavers and then a brain doctor. However, Dick did love the fifties lashings of ginger beer, except he didn't like ginger, so he just had the beer. He did like the ginger-nut biscuits, though, which he dunked into his *Dog's Bollox* ale. He was a tickler for *Famous Five* accuracy, he erroneously thought to himself and thus, broadcast to everyone, as he was prone to speaking his thoughts, a bit like the manner in which he would read, following a guiding finger; he spoke out loud reading as well. So you could see why it was necessary, every now and then, for Amanda to clump her dipstick. Life could be confusingly difficult at times for the reportedly retired detective chief inspector, though, we suspect, not as much as it was for the retired superintendent. And then, were they retired coppers or even retired spies?

———

That same day, nearly time for elevenses, which would have made it eleven o'clock in the morning, there or thereabouts, as it can sometimes take a while for the kettle to boil and the tea to brew, the conductor of the Nuns' Orchestra, Beatrice Flat, not a nun, did not respond to Wanda Linley-Cloud's repeated knock at her bedsit room door.

Coincidentally and curiously, for it is said she was long overdue a visit to Specsavers, Bea Flat was also the girlfriend of Aedd Murphy, who was a geography teacher at St Winifrede's and brother to Sister Winifrede, leader of the second violins. Wanda had in mind sharing elevenses of camomile tea and Viennese whirls with Bea and talking through the planned orchestra rehearsal. Wanda, who was a member of the orchestra having once been a nun but left to get some and become a part-time window cleaner, was concerned that Bea was not ready for practice. This was unusual for a woman who had more than an authoritarian and controlling manner about her, although this could be diminished in effective power by the distinct nasal twang of her Midlands accent that people struggled not to laugh at.

After getting no response from her repeated rapping on the door and, seeking to preserve some skin to her knuckles as this could irritate when she dipped her hands in the bucket of water, in order to soak and wring out her chamois leather to clean windows, Wanda rattled the door. It was locked. She lowered herself to the keyhole, there was no key, which offered an unrestricted, though mini-porthole view into the room. Captured in an intense spotlight, she could see the body of Bea Flat, dressed beautifully in a bunched chiffon flowery-print dress, tulips we understand though flowers and agricultural crops in general are not my strong point, but the conductor was beautifully attired in a dress of some vegetation, but prone and also minus one head. The dress really suited the lady maestro of the Nuns' Orchestra, even if she was a little on the chubby side.

Not able to gain entry, the room being locked from within, Wanda went out to the back garden and, collecting her double extending ladder that she always kept beside the dustbins, she scaled the wall to have a look in through the first-floor window of Bea's modest bedsit room. The window was secured shut. Peeking through the window that she noticed could do with a clean, the scene she had espied through the keyhole was affirmed to her. The conductor's body lay prostrate, arms stretched out as if in supplication at a church altar and it was highlighted in a pencil thin shaft of intense light. Bea was face down, except there was no face. The head was detached and similarly illuminated upon the bedside table. Wanda could not resist; she took a picture with her phone before she called the police and, after she returned to the ground and replaced the ladder, for she was most particular about a tidy back garden, she called the mother superior to suggest they call off orchestra practice. Wanda was then informed that rehearsal had already been postponed and so she relaxed and went back to her room for her camomile tea and Viennese whirls to await a visit from the cops.

The additional conundrum, which was to later fox the police, but not the Ooh La Lovelies, DaDa team, well Dick at least and it seemed that Everard Pimple concurred, was that the conductor's body was locked within the room, secured from the inside. But later on, it had to be said, and after careful consideration of the photographs, Bea Flat's hair, highlighted in the second beam of bright light, looked gorgeous. The new hairdo made the previously average-looking Rubenesque woman, attired as she was in a sumptuously dazzling floricultural dress, bunched with starched crippling petticoats (that might have been Crimplene), looked like a generously proportioned, nineteen fifties movie star. Well, she would have, had the head not been removed from the conductor's comfortably plump body and placed on the bed stand with a conductor's baton stuck up her nose. The head had been deliberately placed beside the bedside lamp, which was in the shape of a bust of Beethoven, whereupon it was easy to make the comparison as Bea had a strikingly similar hairdo as the composer. And beside both was a discarded nun's wimple, which, upon later inspection, was found to have a note scribbled upon it, in red, blood. It said: *Give us a sign, oh Lord. The reckoning is yours – with additional rinse and Composer set, £103.76 plus tip.*

THREE

MEANWHILE, BACK IN FRIESIAN TUN, THE feelings of Pimple Minor, (for he was a minor as he had an older brother, Pimple Major, who was a *Something in the City*, though of diminished intellectual credentials, but exceptionally useful contacts), ran amok. This was not an extraordinary sensation for this dim-witted and fully inbred member of the British aristocracy; Pimple was the Honourable Viscount Everard Pimple, the fourth degree of rank and dignity in the British peerage, though people ordinarily called him Pimple. He was uncomfortable being called, "My Lord," as would be his entitlement. Generally the family Pimple understated their rank. The mother, a fearful moose of a woman, was often referred to as just plain ordinary Dame Pimple and she allowed this, especially when she shopped in Lidl. Life was less complicated that way, not that you would know this, as the plebs lived in awe of the dame and generally were cast aside in her substantial bow wave, clearing the checkout aisle of the disabled-persons' till, in order to accommodate the girth of the more than comfortably buxom dame.

Running amok, as were currently the feelings of this overly sheltered and naive nitwit son of the Pimple long line of inbreeds, was not unusual, as his lordship's feelings were rarely under control. Not because he was now central to the disclosure of such an enormous conspiracy that had already rocked the establishment; his establishment, if he actually stopped to think about it, which he hadn't, of course. And, it was not because a nun had been beheaded, for he knew that this would be all right in the end. No, these sensations were of a particularly unique source of elation, generating in the posh dimwit a sort of reflective reverie and in particular, a saucy sexual reverie of the kind Pimple had only ever read about in his top-shelf magazines, for Pimple was ardently and most passionately in love with a beautiful woman and remarkably, this woman reciprocated these feelings, though in a more experienced, intelligent, and pragmatic way.

Over the past few weeks or so, Pimple had examined his luck and wondered often if it was just a dream, which would sum up his luck to date. This would not be unusual for the twenty eight year-old Lord of sadly diminished brain cells, as Pimple had lived, up until quite recently, in virginal ignorance. But now he was in love. And amazingly, it appeared that the glorious goddess of his dreams, the love of his life, loved him in return and this was way beyond Pimple's wildest dreams. But she did, and had whispered these terms of affirmed affection in the Pimple taxi-door earholes and, not just once, but frequently through the past few nights of lust and love. Not only did she assure him he was the love of her life, she did not get irritated, well, not much, when he giggled as she whispered these sentiments of dewy affection into his ear, because her urgently hot, moist and asthmatic breath tickled. She must love him, or at the very least be challenged in the brain department equally as much as Lord Pimple. But, and here was the mind-boggler that was to confuse all onlookers, as the relationship became known, this woman was not only a sex siren, she was also of above-ordinary levels of intelligence and ability, being an investigative journalist of rare talent. How could this be?

There would of course always be, in the crevices of the limited Pimple brainbox, the lingering sense of doubt, which was more a sense of maternal dread, a much-accustomed and familiar sensation, for Pimple's mother, the formidable Dame Pimple, had up until these past few days controlled him for all of his twenty eight, reluctantly celibate years. But now, the crunchy peanut butter, a cunningly clever device conjured by the dame to keep the floozies away from her son, had been well and truly removed from behind Pimple's sensitive ears and thus the lanky aristocratic beanpole gent with prominent, almost straight, front teeth and a short-sighted look, corrected with black-framed gogglebox spectacles, was fair game for any passing floozy. Not that anyone would call Cecelia Crumpet a floozy, passing or stationary. Well, not in earshot of the vivaciously gorgeous reporter, though if she happened to be passing, I would recommend a quick glance at her rather alluring bum. See how it gyrates in a siren sense; *nee nah, nee nah; hubba, hubba.*

Pimple had a note from his mother excusing his absence. So, why would his collywobbles department be energised? Fear for his life? But of course this could just be a lingering afterburn of having been

25

well and truly shackled to the not-insubstantial bosoms of his moose mater for so long and now released,
and subsequent to a few weeks of awakenings, having
savoured the feminine nectar of not just the goddess
Cecelia, but just prior to this wondrous launch of cou-
plings with the vamp of the Portsmouth news desks,
Pimple had been inducted into the world of female
sexual wiles by the Shirley Temple-like seductress,
the dearest lovely Georgiana Lovebody. Ms Lovebody
was a synchronised swimming instructor of the parish
of Southsea and, in particular, she resided within the
cosy, though now battle-scarred, middle-class street of
Friesian Tun, albeit the dearest loveliest Georgiana
residence was the pied-à-terre within a large Victorian manse that, had you read the book, *Road Kill –
The Duchess of Friesian Tun*, you would know should
never have been granted planning consent to be converted to flats.

So what was it, Pimple thought to himself? What
was the genus of this current sensation of edginess?
Mummy had said he could have a sleepover with Cecelia and so he had, even though he had no pyjamas.
Was it because that sleepover had substantially extended to more than the one sumptuous night, albeit
within the Austin household, central physically in
Frisian Tun and, one might boldly presume, though
proof would be scant, central to all of the preceding
violent shenanigans. This is how Jack Jane Austin,
sorry, Dick, described the actual combat carnage of
this decorous middle-class street, as if it were just a
Blue Peter moment in a children's fantasy that left
Friesian Tun, not so much a leafy idyll, which it previously had been, but more a meandering lane resem-
bling a street in a devastated Beirut suburb. Maybe it

was his lack of pyjamas? Or was Pimple now a part of the Ooh La Lovelies, DaDa, and if he was, what would this mean? Was he scared? Would Cecelia look after him? Pimple shivered. Pimple's nerves, not the sexual ones, but the scaredy-cat ones, which so naturally resided close to the surface of the Pimple elongated and skinny frame, were actually in a state of trembling red alert, because of what he and Cecelia had done and, not just in the bedroom department, though this carnal reflection frequently dominated the generally inadequate Pimple brainbox.

Cecelia Crumpet had great hopes of expanding Pimple's grey-matter capacity, believing that his brain had just inexorably shut down due to years of crushing dominance from his mother, an excess of crunchy peanut butter behind Pimple's posh, *World Cup Willie* earholes and of course, the continual company of inbred socialites, all of equally diminished brain accommodation, complemented with an excess of divine aristocratic arrogance.

Cecelia would make sure Pimple grew in experience, saw something of the world, just as soon as he stopped ogling her body, not that this particularly bothered her. She had seen the potential in Pimple's mind with some of his naïve, it has to be said, insights into their current news report. She had also had her eye on this chap for some time and knew him. Indeed, extraordinary as it may sound, she truly loved him.

Together, and over the past few weeks, Cecelia and Pimple had written the account of a dastardly conspiracy. It was so uncommonly dastardly that when they went to bed, which was often in these past days, they were almost always mentally exhausted, though it might be construed there was more than insightful investigative journalism contributing to this malaise of exhaustion. But, and this was novel for Everard Pimple, he was now experiencing for the first time a combination of energetic sexual wellbeing, combined with a happiness of having achieved a serious piece of reporting and, despite his very recent virginal awakening and, despite sleeping next to the most gorgeous woman he had ever viewed from a distance or on a centrefold, Pimple slept, for he was well and truly knackered.

And so, when they awoke that morning, Cecelia and Pimple set to work again, subsequent to a brief coupling, for it was sadly brief in that the dearest lovely Georgiana had not fully completed her lessons in swimming trunkless synchronisation and Cecelia recognised that this task would now fall to her, if she were, as she had every intention of doing, going to spend the rest of her life with Pimple. She loved this dozy posh man, still to be moulded into a man. He had a beautiful innocence that appealed to the raunchy reporter and she was also convinced, the silly cow, that there resided somewhere within the moronic inbred shell, a deeper intelligence. Such is love?

Cecelia had shared this relationship experience, or lack of current experience as far as Pimple was concerned, with Amanda Austin, who imparted that it had taken her some time to train her husband, Jane. This was the nickname of Jack Austin, believed by many to be an elderly, ugly, retired detective chief inspector of the Portsmouth Community Policing Unit, but who was, in point of also presumed fact, a retired spook. He was, though, most definitely ugly; that was irrefutable. The points of fact in this case would generally be dulled, not because this is the nature of the spook world, but generally because of the nature of Jack (Jane) Austin, now calling himself Dick, who was without any doubt of blurred fuzziness (if you pardon the colloquial *nom-de-cop*) a natural-born twat. Being a twat came naturally to the man, as anyone who knew Jack Austin would tell you, though generally out of earshot, which was not normally that far away as he was also a celebrated deaf twat. He was a deaf twat who refused to wear deaf aids in case he looked a twat and, all of this from a generously overweight, tall and particularly ugly man. He was unmistakably and most definitely, an ugly, gigantic, deaf twat. Oh, and he had only one eye, so add to that a half-blind twat.

Those observant enough, especially those of a feminine disposition, would see in this case a certain similarity between Dick Austin and Everard Pimple, insomuch as they shared a masculine twatdom. But, whereas Pimple was handsome and suave in a superficially groomed way and was truly an upper-class-twit twat, Dick, the elderly cockney, barrow boy, spook filth twat, had a street savviness that had allowed him and, some would express this in an unfortunate manner, to survive many scrapes.

Scrapes is also how Austin would describe his many and varied life experiences, or occasionally they were shenanigans, though it was generally thought by others to be a wafer-thin survival of not just himself, but of all mankind, from an apocalyptic chain of events, many of which were now being reported on by the newly formed dynamic journalistic duo of Crumpet and Pimple, soon to be Pimple and Pimple, if Cecelia had her way. She also looked forward to switching her name. Crumpet had been an ant in her knickers all of her life and she now looked forward to becoming a Pimple. And who, knowing both the strength of Cecelia and the current cotton-candy persona of the posh knob Pimple, would not imagine this marital event becoming a reality and sooner rather than later. Cecelia had, with the left-footed assistance of the dearest lovely Georgiana, of course, even tamed the moose, for it is said that Dame Pimple bore a remarkable resemblance to the Canadian tundra beast and, one whose temper was often born of a devilish cloven hoof origin. But the dame did have a soft spot for the ladies and, an especially particular penchant for damsels who had the appearance, passing or otherwise, of *Shirley Temple*, and blow me down if Dearest Georgiana Lovebody, synchronised swimming instructor, looked like the child prodigy film star of the old movies.

Cecelia Crumpet was, in the parlance of a previous, politically incorrect era, circa nineteen fifties, say, a tall and curvy sex bomb in the Marilyn Monroe mould and image, though Cecelia's hair was jet-black and bobbed in a saucy manner, at least Pimple thought so, and it flicked across her china-white cheeks to direct the masculine gaze upon two flaring azure-blue eyes, a deceptively cherubic face, set on fire by a slash of crimson, dynamite lipstick. Of a comparative age to Pimple, Cecelia, sometimes called Ceeley, was formerly the gossip columnist at the Evening News, though Sir Wendy, Pimple's uncle and proprietor of the newspaper and other journals, had yet to be informed of her resignation from that post and this was also to be accompanied by the formation of the new freelance writing duo, comprising, his up-until-quite-recently court correspondent, sad drip of a nephew.

Cecelia and Pimple had now also joined themselves to Ooh La Lovelies, DaDa (not that Pimple was fully aware as yet, but Cecelia had enrolled him on his behalf – clearly she would be admin in the relationship) and set themselves up as independent commentators on current affairs and news items of serious import. Well, Cecelia had and she had insisted Pimple follow her and he had, and who wouldn't? (I think I mentioned earlier the naturally occurring gyrations of Cecelia's bottom department?) And together they were focused on their current task, to record the events of the past year or so that had seen the appearance of a comfortable, to all appearances, democratic lifestyle in Britain, decimated. And, something else was afoot, though Dick (Jack Jane Austin, keep up) said it was ahand and, a sleight of ahand at that, not that anyone understood what he meant, except extraordinarily, Pimple did, being one who enjoyed the various shenanigans of illusionists, when leisure time and his mother would permit.

There was an affinity there, Amanda Austin thought, thinking of her husband and Pimple, and how the chalk-and-cheese pair got on. Maybe it was just a shared twatdom? She relaxed. Yes, that would be it, she thought. She was not happy being called Duck but, went along with it, for now.

For Cecelia, her long-term plan to settle with Everard Pimple had to be put on hold, as the story they had written together and just finished was probably the most important news item she and Everard would ever write. It was probably the most incendiary and devastatingly explosive exposé the world had seen for decades and was likely to set quite a few of the established power potentates back on to their fat backsides. It would likely make the country, indeed the world, sit up and cry out: "*Enough.*" It was time for change. People would question their previously blind acceptance of a faux democracy. Question all of the systems that so poorly served the populace. But if it didn't, then the conspiracy was deeper than anyone realised and then their course would be set to carry on, to expose the depths of corruption and this is what worried Cecelia as she looked at her Pimple, who just grinned inanely back at her, like the natural-born upper-class twit he was, but now with a semblance of an emerging backbone?

It is also what worried Jack Austin and his wife Amanda.

Pimple could see, or at least sense, something, but his mind turned to more exciting thoughts just after Cecelia punched the send button, making the story now electronically available for the entire world to see. It would be picked up and read by the establishment, secular and religious, and it would be the reactions that would constitute the conclusion to the story. *This story.*

———

And so, simultaneously, the churches and religious orders received holy orders. Umble Pie was active and this alerted the counter-intelligence services, agencies with orders within the religious orders of the world, who, in turn, sent out their own call to action. The cults, the minority but extreme and reactionary factions reacted, as they were expected to do and as they were briefed to do and had prepared for and, for which VI6 and the other church and religious house intelligencers expected and watched for. The Spanish Inquisition and allied clans, radical and reactionary wings. This time, they were all anticipated.

The angelic Mafia was ready.

This was it. Not only did Umble Pie threaten the mainstream religious orders, the spiritual power behind the throne, so to speak, but the plan threatened the corporate and banking world that was integral to the controlling influence of whatever doctrine dominated in whatever country. The power behind the throne, in the guise of spiritual guidance, never to be questioned, in other words; The *Deity of Mammon Incarnate*, real and deadly if disturbed.

The angels of mercy of altruistic beneficence had to be ready, they had to be prepared and the best way to be ready was to be proactive, to go on the attack. Umble Pie was a serious threat to the establishment. Big guns were needed to defeat big guns, whichever side you were on.

FOUR

TWEET, TWEET, IN LONDON'S STWEETS

A NIGHTINGALE SANG IN BERKELEY SQUARE. Well, not ordinarily, but occasionally in the square. More regularly it would tweet in a Salon du Coiffeur in a back street off the square. Well, not a nightingale, but a hairdresser and a not particularly tuneful or lyrical one, either. But he was, no doubt, a famous bird. And, when after work he walked to his Mayfair Club, he would walk, or mince might be a more accurate description, birdlike and tweet tunelessly as he stepped in a light-footed manner through Berkeley Square. Very often this would be to the annoyance of many who were partaking of a casual moment within the beautiful gardens, as the heat of the day's late-summer sun cooled to make it a most tolerable and pleasant experience. Some picnicked with glasses of chilled Chablis, smoked salmon, cheese footballs, and soggy prawn-cocktail vol-au-vents, because they were posh, or they thought they were.

Regulars at this spot all knew Twink and tolerated his squeaky passage as a part of the eccentric character of this chic and particularly la-dee-da English enclave of the West End of London. Others, less tolerant, second-banana people and less familiar with the ways of the world, which would include the passing acceptance of the Olde English eccentricities, shouted for Twink to: "Shut the fuck up." Twink studiously ignored all vociferated abuse, naturally, in the manner of all good genteel English eccentrics.

Twink, short for Twinkle Friseur, was a celebrated hairdresser. He was the grandson of the famous nineteen sixties hair designer and stylist to the famed and fabulous, Easypeasy Reg. However, in his bloated head, which curiously and astonishingly, accommodated an atrocious straggly wig upon a totally bald pate, Twink imagined himself a cross between a celebrated ballet dancer and an opera singer. Twink had, in his marginally less corpulent youth, tried out for the *Royal Opera Company*, without success. And, the remarks from the audition panel at the *Ballet Camembert*, were still indelibly stained in his psyche. "Monsieur Friseur, while we found your audition... curiously amusing, we would suggest that if you wish to pursue a career in classical dance that you not audition in old plimsolls." It was a sad fact that Twink had bad feet that not only were arranged at a quarter to three, they struggled to be shod in any normal shoe and alas, they were also decidedly dodgy aromatically, registering at Ponte L'Eveque levels on the fromage scale of magnitude, far out-ponging even the ripest of Camembert, coincidentally, regardless of the fact he bathed once a week, sometimes twice if he felt he required it and changed his stockings fortnightly.

"We suggest you wear looser pants, Monsieur Friseur... or take the cardboard out." A scathing remark from a chuckling Head of the Opera House audition panel when he referred to the squeaky high-pitched nature of Twink's voice, a voice that Twink considered had a naturally resonating high register; delicate and quite unique. Add to this the sad fact that nature had blessed Twink, or maybe lumbered would be a more appropriate term, with a big bum. Sadly also, this arse had been cultivated beyond naturally occurring levels with the injudicious, upon reflection, over indulgence of a love for croissants and other délicieuses pâtisseries. The consequent visual effect that a cheese-footballing picnicker would therefore witness, would be of a dominant derrière, exaggerated by Twink's mode of perambulation and especially accentuated by his sartorial preference for city-boy striped trousers that ballooned, obviously, in the bottom area and then subsequently tapered tightly, to grip the spindly dancer ankles of the celebrated hairdresser.

Twink was a sight to behold and it could take years of expert counselling to remove that indelible image. It did, though, make him an easy person to follow. And, totally oblivious as he twinkled along, Twink was followed.

And so this was the picture of the twiddly-dee, dumb, in a dozy sense, hairdresser, as he pranced and squeaked across Berkeley Square. An amusing sight, yes, but not to Twink and you would be well advised to keep all opinions of his appearance and manner of movement to yourself, as the man, for he was a man despite countless arguments to the contrary, had a fearful artistic temper. Twink was a temperamental bloated coiffeur who had a small chain of exclusive and *très* expensive salons in these salubrious parts of London and his mannerisms and appearance were all accepted as a quirky and, some would say, amusing side-effect of being a talented hairdresser, all of which was considered to be a part of the entertainment for those clients who could afford to visit the lavishly overpriced tonsariums.

And then there was Twink's entourage of cheer-leaders, dedicated and identically idiotically attired assistant hairdressers. Disciples some said they were and these apostles styled and coiffed and preached to the rich and famous, though Twink's business was predicted to dwindly-dee as his stock-in-trade rich, famous and, powerfully influential people, had recently been forced to eat, what had become known in the tabloid press, as Humble Pie. Again, this term had been erroneously ascribed, but the effect had been marked. Many of Twink's clients had been forced to admit to, or had their parts exposed, if you pardon the expression, in the conspiracy of avarice now being called *Mammon*, which had brought Britain to its knees. Well, ninety nine per cent of the British knees that is, as the one percent, the bees-knees set, who in London at least made up the Easypeasy's Boutiques of Unisex Hair Creations clientele, had been caught with their hair down, or was it their city boy trousers, down, and around their ankles, with a crusty Umble Pie shoved down their Y-fronts?

But, and this might well confound the ordinary observer, Twink was unmoved by the drop-off in trade and some might, and did, observe, that the very fact energised the celebrated hairdresser, for he knew what to do; he had a plan. God was on his side, after all, and who did not relish a crusade or two in their dull, humdrum lives. At least when victory was certain. God was, of course, first and foremost, a hair-dresser, although it is often thought that the son of

God's hair needed a good seeing to, but without question, God was on the side of this righteous hairdressing crusade.

———

Extraordinary, when you think about it, but contemporaneously, many other factions, noble organisations, the crème de la crème in religious sects and conclaves and of course, the top-knob corporations, all believed that God was saddled fair and square to their particular horse and no other. It was this knowledge of divine certainty, some said divine arrogance, which lent weight and assuredness to their vera causa and justified the use of all means at their disposal for their evangelistic, or commercial, or political, cause to succeed. Right would win, it was just a matter of which right would win. Their right, obviously, as God was no fool. And, isn't this the history of all wars, crusades, jihads; battles of irony, right against right? Sociopath or psychopath, the martinet line is fine and frequently in history, and now in these current times of civil tumult, our "betters" will step back and forth across that line like the skipping rope of dystopian belief.

———

This downturn in the big-knob haircut trade had been marked following the news of the passing few weeks and Twink was yet to learn of the Crumpet and Pimple, in-depth exposé, now in the electronic portals. However, the consequential fallout might coincidentally assist his *Council of God's Hairdressers'* diabolical plans. It was not acceptable for people of his clientele's stature to have to humble themselves publicly, to apologise and promise to mend their ways. The hierarchy of the established church had subtly changed over recent times but fortunately there were those traditional establishment organisations ready and prepared to drag it back on to the *righteous path*.

The Twink clientele were the elite. The power-brokers, the magnates, the aristocracy of their chosen sphere of influence, and they needed protection. They needed to have their path cleared in order to carry out the work of the order. That is the various orders, all dedicated to such a communal reactionary cause and, if big businesses, corporations, insisted on humbling themselves, so be it, the consequences would be dire. The cornerstones of obscurantist establishment, the ultraconservatives, needed to be reinforced in this period of vulnerability. Counter-revolutionary sects needed to act and they would.

An infamous banker, Justin Thyme of Bellands had learned that ultimate lesson. (*See Dead No More – Rhubarb in the Mammon*). The populace, and in particular the sects, were unaware, naturally, of the real cause of his perceived demise, which had sent shock waves through corporate and banking Britain, the prevailing thought being that the offside angels were playing hardball and this required a reaction.

Some of Twink's regulars at the salon and at Poncenbey's, the exclusive Mayfair gentlemen's club that gentlemen of a certain persuasion, though not all had to be persuaded to be hairdressers as it was a natural profession for them, attended, were definitely edgy. They expected *their* pie. It was just a matter of time and their *Council*, along with their affiliate *Brethren of Christ's Caretakers* and other allied Orders, were ready to act and would do so very soon. It had to be soon. The sands in the ancient and revered time glass of the *Fishers of Men*, (an organisation that did exactly what it said on the can) slowly drained and would not stand to be reversed another time, not yet.

The tabloid press rather appropriately called it, "squeaky-bum time" for the one per cent and for those who attended to the one per cent's hair or were caretakers for their buildings. The establishment could see it was time for action and, most importantly, a time of opportunity to reassert the norms that had to most people, almost imperceptibly, bit by bit, been marginalised. The people needed to be sat back down again and instructed on the realities of their lives, which was one of subliminal subjugation; TV, sport, distracting celebrity stories in the mainstream media, and so on. However, for those steeped in the history of a right to rule, of societies established to maintain the status quo, the lessening of their grip on the reins of power, finance and the steering of the moral ship, for the plebs that is, this Humble Pie nonsense, was simply not acceptable and they would act; were acting.

The thing was, who was already acting? And, who had done the hair of the nun and conductor, now being covered in all of the newspapers and on the TV news? There were clear boundaries, and the sects had survived and prospered by maintaining their own sphere of influence and, recognising those of the other factions; a tenuous, though successful, mutual bond of survival existed. The intelligence of these events had caused the calling of this extraordinary meeting of the Council. All seven high-priest hairdressers would attend The Poncenbey Club, consult Claudio, and make their plans. Such high-order meetings were taking place also in other sects, all over the unknown, secret, world.

So Twink swished his way to Poncenbey's on a mission. Having passed relatively unmolested through Berkeley Square, he fiddled and sashayed his way within the network of Mayfair streets, twirling his completely unnecessary accoutrement of a furled umbrella and slapping his thigh rhythmically, but out of synchronisation with his vocal ejaculations, with an immaculately folded copy of the Times newspaper. After a short trot, he turned into Shepherd Market, a cutesy bustling backstreet Mayfair village of lubbly-jubbly pubs and restaurants, nestled within a closed society of swanky stately townhouse mansions. More important, though, and generally unknown, was that Shepherd Market was the centre for the *Good Shepherd*. Not a person, not a herdsman, but a caretaking concept. This was a construct that had grown over centuries and the various Orders and Sects had established themselves in Shepherd Market as the centre of the reactionary, counter-revolutionary, right-wing religious organisations. Except, that is, for the Holy Barbaras of Seville. Nobody liked the Barbaras. Everybody was scared of the Barbaras, and preferred it if they stayed in Spain; the pavements were too uneven in London for their roller skates anyway and they were deliberately maintained as such, despite the efforts of the Greater London Council to repair them. Nobody wanted another Spanish Inquisition, and bumpy pavements were the capital's first line of religious defence.

Over the next few days, Shepherd Market would be buzzing with meetings in the various informal headquarter buildings of the various important sects, all with a common guiding light and, each secure in the knowledge they were better than any of the others. Except for the Caretakers of course; they were generally better organised and their toilets worked better and if anyone could stand up to the Holy Barbaras it would be the Caretakers, or maybe the Order of Bricklayers; they weren't bad either. And, they had Christ's Holy Hod (A brick-carrying device a bit like a bucket on the end of a stick), the most revered relic after the Holy Grail, which nobody had and it was generally thought that the caretakers had flushed that down a loo in St Pancras station. *The Hod of God* was now the most powerful religious relic in existence and it resided in Shepherd Market.

"Oooh ooh," Twink called to a group of tarts sitting at an outside cafe table, displaying their wares, none of which took the fancy of Twink. "Oooh ooh," the good-time girls called back, in a comfortably familiar manner; most people knew Twink in and around Shepherd Market. Twink stopped beside a group of young men drinking outside *Ye Grapes* pub and he air kissed a couple of them. They responded with ribald comments enjoyed by all and which, by coincidence, titillated Twink as he pranced on into White Horse Street and up to a substantial townhouse of Regency proportions, fronting close on to the pavement. Advancing up a short flight of stone steps to a black gloss-painted door, set in a masonry frame, he delicately rapped the brass knocker. While he awaited a response, Twink twirled his umbrella and pointed and twisted his incongruously shod feet, the plimsolls almost with a life of their own and all in the manner of a good solid member of the corp (short for corpulent) du ballet.

The door opened. "M'waah, M'waah." Twink air-kissed a greeting to the Poncenbey's Club steward, dressed, despite the fact that the club had no swimming pool, in his tight navy-blue Speedos with a casual lemon cheesecloth shirt draped across his shoulders, offering no cover for the steward's hairless chest – gone were the days of the hairs and Grace's, strict dress code, though some members still wore dresses, especially Grace and he had at one time been quite hirsute and, most certainly strict.

As Twink stepped into the club the steward M'waahed back, as was expected, and he closed the wide and heavy, glossy black door, on to the bustling noisy street.

"Are we all here, Dewek?" Twink asked of the steward, reinforcing his effected speech disorder that he was convinced people found attractive, not realising it was a source of great amusement behind his back. Twink handed his umbrella to Derek, who looped it on to the series of hooks that lined the entrance lobby. There were already six identical umbrellas hanging in serried rank; the *Magnificent Seven*, which is how these Poncenbey barbers referred to themselves. The members of the *Council of Christ's Hairdressers* were now all present.

'The others are in the club room, sir, awaiting your arrival,' the steward replied in an effected swanky, butlery manner. To all intents, he was a stiff, *Jeeves*, albeit inappropriately attired for the butlering he was expected to do in the club, as well as the cleaning, cooking and fucking washing up. He often told the members he could stick a broom up his arse and sweep up while he was doing everything else around 'ere, but this seemed to result more in brimming leering grins, rather than the anticipated response of sympathetic concern for the overworked rough-trade staff.

'Bollocks to the lot of yer,' Derek said under his breath as he watched Twink turn, in a fairy military manner, a casually flicked Angelina-ballerina leg and thence into the Club room. He heard immediately the, "Oooh oohs," and the, "M'waaa, m'waaa's," as the members greeted the arrival of their informally appointed number one, though it would likely be more appropriate to call Twink their number two. He was their *Grand Poo-bah*.

Someone of a dispassionate, or at least disinterested, disposition would no doubt view Poncenbey's as a local club of self-interested, well-placed men. A sort of gay Masons, which was ironic as Derek the steward had been a bricklayer before he decided he wanted to come in from the cold, though definitely not out from the closet, not that you would know this. Needs must and his loyalties were to *The British Order of Orthodox Bricklayers* (Boobs – the true masons, the original Masonic Lodge. The other lot, although more commonly known and quite powerful, were just a bunch of Tits compared to the grand and historic Magnificent Boobs) needed him in place, he supposed, as he minced himself into the lounge to take up his place behind the Cutty Sark, the old tea-clipper bar.

Derek bided his time. Although uncomfortable out of his ceremonial bricklaying leather lederhosen and hat shaped like a brick with a feather sticking out the side, needs must. He knew his task and he had agreed. He was now a Knight of Christ, a *Brick-slayer,* a highly ranked soldier for the cause of all the *Boobs* and had sworn the oath of all *Brickies,* as they were known, at the altar of Canterbury Cathedral, at midnight, on the eve of the day Thomas Beckett had been martyred.

The Council of Christ's Hairdressers were unaware that Derek watched them and that he was a *Brickie.* Well, they knew he was a bricklayer, but not that he had a full leather lederhosen with a badge on the bib. His regalia remained hidden at home. Hidden, because his wife was not aware of her husband's religious affiliations. She just baked, a recent fascination that to Derek bordered on obsession and this irritated Derek. How could he stop his wife baking? He cursed *Mary Berry,* but it was now a job and blimey did they need the money.

'Dewek, dwinks all wound, we have cause to celebwate,' Twink's casual order thrown in the direction of the club steward as he took up his position behind the ship bar, removing his lemon cheesecloth shirt, and draping a skimpy sailor boy's top across his shoulders and finally, setting his saucy matelot's cap at a jaunty angle.

Derek had a set of highly inappropriate attire for whatever function he was called upon to carry out within the club. A sailor's top for the Cutty Sark bar, a bar fashioned much in the manner of the old tea clipper, with even a seedy parrot, known as Claudio, swinging from a perch and calling out highly inappropriate and politically incorrect curses and comments, often in Italian and many, the English ones, taught by Derek. But, the resultant screeches amused the *Magnificent Seven Barbers of Christ,* when they were not listening intently to what the parrot had to say. Claudio was akin to a master of ceremonies in this club. Extraordinary, people often thought, but Claudio was no ordinary parrot and certainly no stool pigeon and, most certainly not a *Caretaker* or *Brickie* bird. He was, in point of fact, quite the opposite. You could say he was incognito, though he was definitely a parrot, the colourful if somewhat flea-bitten plumage being a dead giveaway. No, Claudio was VI6, Secret Bird Division. An Italian intelligencer.

When stepping out to serve drinks, Derek had a frilled and dainty maid's slip-on top, which also served for when he was obliged to use the feather duster to dust away at the intimate parts of some of the members, as was their particular bent. And, in the kitchen, he was obliged to wear a rubber, gaudily coloured apron, whose imprinted graphic gave the impression Derek was wearing suspenders and stockings on an image of a sexually excited Michael Angelo's David. All the time, Derek was duty bound to wear the not-particularly concealing *Speedo,* budgie (not parrot) smugglers. It had been humiliating at first but, as Derek had explained to his wife once, as she removed his make-up before bed, it was a job and it paid well, but his wife wondered what her husband had to do to earn such fabulous tips? She wondered also, at her husband's increasingly strange behaviour. He had increased his number of trips to the club's local church, not so much a church as a chapel, incongruously also, in Shepherd Market, it being at first floor and spanning across the entrance alleyway and had formerly been the Steering Wheel Club, but the Brickies had displaced them. She did not like that it was an all-male conclave and felt the priest, dressed incongruously in lederhosen and dog collar, had a power over Derek, not realising that it was in fact the other way around. The *Bricklayers* were the radical foot soldiers and Derek was a knight of the Order, and this Order was presently sounding the clarion. A call to arms, and legs, in every church across the capital, for it was written that there would come a dancing nun and she would gather the multitudes to her cause and the temples would fall and The Brickies would take up their arms (and legs) and behind their standard, the Holy Hod of God, they would destroy the factions and sects to establish a new world order, for the people, run by the people, in God's name.

———

It was the proclamation that the appearance of the Holy Dancing Nun was imminent that had got the Caretakers, the Hairdressers, the Barbaras, and of course the Brickies, and all of the other, not quite so important, sects energised. For the religious jungle drums were reporting that a nun had been decapitated in Portsmouth, the holy city from whence Richard the Lionheart had set out on his holy crusades. And now it is reported her holy body and holy loaf of bread (head, but as the East End of London cockney bible describes it), which reportedly had had a lovely holy hairdo, had holy well disappeared.

It was one holy mess. Even the newspapers were suggesting that it was "A Sign" and the people, the plebeian masses, had become fascinated and this fascination was to become even more energised, for the scriptures also predicted that the dancing nun would lead the people to pastures new. To a better life, over-

turning the temples of Mammon and casting out the money lenders, the bankers (money hoarders), power mongers and magnates. It was to be a revolution of ark-like proportions and it was predicted to start in the City of Mammon, often considered to be London. So the sects were on guard, alert.

However, Babs, Derek's wife, tucked her concerns aside as they had two small children and in a few months, they expected to be in a position to move out of their squalid one-bed flat, in one of the few remaining squalid parts of the East End of London that had not been done up for the poncy rich tarts, after kicking out the locals. Derek and his wife would get themselves a decent flat. She had refused the offer of the steward's accommodation at the club but sometimes Derek had to stay over. She tried not to think about that, but the members were very well connected and clearly liked Derek and they had offered to help them relocate very soon. She hoped and prayed for that day to be not too long away and that, when it came, it would come with only a few strings attached.

Derek seemed confident and told her not to worry, that everything was about to change and for the better and this worried Babs more. Derek was energised like never before. In the mean time she went back to her pastry and her *Funny Haddock* recipe book, open at the page on how to make offal pie; *schtum*, she asked no questions. Needs must.

FIVE

Pimple and Cecelia sat around the dining table with Jack and Amanda Austin. They chatted amiably about this and that, though Jack wanted to talk more about this rather than that, but Amanda insisted they talk about that, and that was that.

The telephone rang.

Jack looked at Amanda and it was clear by the look in his wife's eyes that, although he was considered to have retired, it would fall upon him to answer the phone. By the time this overly acted, silent-movie contretemps, carried out in facial gestures with the occasional shoulder shrug, had been played out by the loving, elderly couple of ex-coppers and ex-spooks, now Dick and Duck gumshoes, the phone had ceased ringing. Jack looked relieved, he never did like admin and just as he had settled back to his Girl Grey tea, which had been blown on by his wife to reduce it to the correct temperature for sipping and dunking biscuits, so the phone rang again, not unreasonably irritating him.

Mandy looked at her husband. 'Shall I get that?'

she asked sarcastically, with not so much disgruntlement as a loving acceptance that, as far as their relationship was concerned, retired or not, as Dick and Duck or not, she was admin and just about everything else. Jack considered himself a prima donna and beyond admin tasks and had the bumps on his head to prove it. He nodded his executive order, yes. His mouth was full of soggy ginger nut biscuit but, before he could speak, Mandy had put up her hand to acknowledge she would answer the phone. She placed a delicate finger to his mouth, to assert that it was okay and, to suggest also he should not order her around, but probably more importantly, she wanted to prevent an eruption of partially consumed soggy biscuit, very much in the way Vesuvius covered Pompeii in ginger nut lava. They were after all, in Pompey (the colloquial term used to refer to the City of Portsmouth).

The phone stopped ringing.

Both Austins again looked relieved and they would have noticed an expression of curiosity on the Pimple and Cecelia faces if they didn't have such loving eyes for each other. Jack and Amanda had recently married. It was a love that had grown over a period of time that Mandy could not begin to identify, though she knew for Jack, it was nurtured through an extended and very deep period of mourning following the death of his first wife, Kate, nearly four years ago.

Jack had said once he had loved Mandy since he first set his eye on her in a lift at the police station where they had both worked. She took that with a pinch of salt, considering it all a bit of eyewash to elaborate on the image he had in his mind, but she liked it. Eye, though, this was indeed the correct expression as he had only one eye. Some thirteen years back, Jack had fought with a serial rapist at the Camber Docks in Old Portsmouth. The struggle caused them to fall from the dock on to the deck of a trawler where the man struck with a boat hook, removing Jack's right eye and leaving a vertical scar that ran from his forehead to an inch or so on to his wrinkled ugly cheeks. As if to compound the already unsightly face, Jack Austin wore this resultant damage of sunken wrinkled skin into the redundant eye socket and raised silvery scarring with a perverted pride, not comprehending that this hideous injury could be seriously off-putting for most people. But for Amanda, she loved her ugly, overweight twerp and rarely noticed the horrendous scarring from the ancient injury.

The phone rang again and this time the Vesuvius gob erupted. Soggy ginger nuts were expelled from Mount Austinus across the Pompey table and a little on to the lacy trim of the blousy bosoms of Cecelia, which Pimple immediately lapped at with his tongue, intuitively knowing it was the gentlemanly thing to do. Mandy left the phone to ring while she indulged in a jolly good laugh at her husband's dilemma and the knowing fact that she had been omniscient where her husband was concerned, a fact never acknowledged by the dozy spouse, of course, as he could not see it. Well, he did have only one eye.

In the meantime, as Mandy brought herself under control, while multitasking a survey of the damage and assessing whether she should make Jack clean it up, or just do it herself, now, rather than later, after he had made an even greater mess, the phone stopped ringing. It was again a blessed relief.

Peace reigned for a short while as Jack pushed ginger nut residue around the table, glancing every now and then at his wife and when she looked away, he put some into his mouth. Waste not, want not as they used to say in Pompeii, only in Latin of course: *'Non vis non profundant,'* Centurion Jack said, least this is what it sounded like to Mandy, as Jack had now refilled his sizeable mouth with a Herculaneum amount of table debris.

'I saw that,' Mandy said, and Jack shivered at the possible consequences, at least this is what Mandy thought, but Jack was just a tad cold and resolved to put on his Fair Isle sleeveless sweater, which he did, and made a fuss about that, too.

The door knocker banged, resounding in an echoing Gothic manner as it filled the house with Gothic dread; a portent of bad news of Gothic proportions?

Admin raised herself from the soggy ginger nut mess and Jack Austin, taking advantage of his wife's distraction, prodded, pushed and poked at the debris with his best index finger, the one he always used for pointing, and he gathered a small mountain of residue ginger lava, which he then hoovered up with his mouth.

Mandy stepped into the hall to answer the door, a confusion of thoughts, who could it be banging so insistently on the brass Spirit of Liffy, knocker, and revulsion at the horrible sucking noise behind her. A passing thought: "Will Jack clean up his mess, or was he doing that already?" No, he would not do that, so she focused on the door, which opened upon a distressed Aedd Murphy, the geography teacher from across the road.

The lanky streak of Irish, Welsh, piss, out of Bristol, with traces of Scandinavia, who taught at St Winifrede's Roman Catholic School, blurted out to the maternal and loving Amanda, 'It's Bea and Winifrede, isn't it,' he began in his Welsh accent. 'They've had their heads chopped off, an all, an all...' an Irish lilt, and the wire wool ginger mop (apparently Scandinavian, though many considered it to be of Celtic derivation), atop the six-foot-six-inch, lanky streak of urine whizz quivered, and made Amanda think only of the ginger nuts before they became soggy, rather than any Viking marauding heritage or Norse cookie.

Amanda hugged the geography teacher, her arms easily able to grasp fully around Aedd's skinny frame, lent just a small degree of substance from the thick woolly cardigan he wore that depicted a bobbly woolly Norwegian Fjord; the football buttons pressed into Amanda, so she adjusted her hug to grasp Aedd's shoulders at arm's length. 'You had better come in,' she said, tugging the man of dubious ancestry, who put up no resistance and entered with no pillaging intent.

Aedd Murphy had crossed Frisian Tun from his ground floor flat, in the same converted Victorian manse that accommodated the synchronised swimming beauty in the pied-à-terre below him, to consult with Dick, Jack Jane Austin and, seek solace from Amanda Austin Duck, herself a tall person, and a handsome woman, though of dubious tastes and eyesight, as she had married Jack Austin; maybe she needed to go to Specsavers.

Oh God. What if she did? What would happen then? No more stories.

Aedd knew the senior couple well. He knew that, although thought to have retired from the police, Amanda having been a detective superintendent and an eminently sensible copper and woman, except in her perception of the man she loved and had married, Aedd knew they were still active in something. You could never be sure what the current status of the couple was, except Jack Austin had formed, by way of a retirement hobby and a swerve in sartorial style, a nineteen fifties fashioned private detective agency.

Those who knew Jack Austin knew also that this had disaster written all over it, as did many of the hare-brained schemes he came up with. But had he retired, either as an inept detective chief inspector or as a high-ranked spook? Who could tell, as the man was a self-confessed enema? At least this is what he said, but his long-suffering, over a short period, partner, now wife, would explain that as Mr Malacopperism, he frequently got his words wrong and used expressions incorrectly and inappropriately applied and in this instance, he probably meant to say he was an enigma, though, upon deeper thought, she would also explain her husband did speak a load of shite, so?

However, Jack had moved on from being an enema and was now calling himself Dick Dashing Austin. Mandy believed her husband may have been thinking of *Dick Barton* or *Flash Gordon*, but knew it never served to dwell upon the origins of her husband's thinking as it would generally change to suit the circumstances of the time and, more often than not, to extricate himself from trouble. And so, as Dick Dashing, he announced recently he was forming, along with his wife, who had no elaboration of her soubriquet Duck, *Ooh La lovelies, DaDa*, the nineteen fifties styled Dick and Duck Austin Detective Agency and this is why, Aedd called Jack, Dick, and Mandy, Duck, being a friend and neighbour and more importantly, a trusted confidant and thus, in the know, least he thought he was, but who knows?

SIX

AND SO IT WAS THAT AEDD SAT AT THE DINING
table and calmed himself, though you wouldn't know
it as the cardigan fjords looked like they were still in
the middle of a rough Atlantic storm, the waves
breaching the football buttons to ravage the pasty pale
face of the ginger Welsh, Irish geography teacher. He
raised his arms and with both hands out as if he was
ready to flap his wings and take off, he pinched finger
and thumbs and hummed rhythmically; meditating?
And then he looked agitated as he mentioned Burma
and seemed to be seeking a map somewhere? Yeah, I
think he was meditating, they do that sort of thing in
Burma, or is that Birmingham? Yes, it would more
than likely be Birmingham, because Bea Flat, his recently decapitated conductor girlfriend, was from that
Middle England city.

Mandy said she knew where Burma and Birmingham were and didn't need a map and Aedd looked
relieved he was talking to people with some experience of geography. And of course, Dick and Duck did
have this relative experience as they had been instru-

mental in the destruction of the world in Aedd's living room only a short time ago.

Mandy prompted the geographer again with a poke of her beautifully elegant finger and Jack felt jealous. That finger should be reserved for poking him and Mandy explained that there was plenty of time for poking later and further suggested Jack might like to shut up, the subliminal suggestion being that shutting up was a prerequisite to any poking to come. He did so, with an expression and hand gesture that suggested he was zipping his mouth, or he may have been poking himself? It is sometimes difficult to tell when faced with an enema with a face that looked like a wrinkled bottom on a senior citizen and one that was a dose or two short of *Diocalm*, which could erupt at any time in true Pompey fashion.

Mandy offered that Aedd might like to explain himself and suggested also, in a lovely way, she was getting fed up waiting and might be a tad irritated because of the phone calls and of course, she still had to poke her husband.

Aedd turned to face the still tight-lipped Dick. Aedd was a bit nervous of Mandy, he knew of her volatile nature as Dick had told him once and then he'd seen it manifest itself when Duck had one time overheard Dick explaining to Aedd about women; he had not heard her creep up (I think I mentioned he was a deaf twat). So Aedd explained himself to Dick who, in his fifties character, wore loose-fitting flannel trousers, which had probably consumed all the cloth available in the world at the time of their manufacture in order to cover the substantial Dick bottom. Though he liked these trousers because he could also use them to wipe his face and hands when needed and praised those clever scientists who had invented the flannel material you could wear and ablute with. And these ablutionary flannel trousers were *nipped-in* at the waist, in a very fashionable Japanese style, by an out-sized sumo wrestler belt that secured them just below his developing, though some argued they might already have developed, man breasts, leaving just a few inches of a powder blue shirt with a fly-away collar with rounded tips, visible beneath the Fair Isle jumper that just might have shrunk in the wash.

To add authenticity to his look, he chewed and sucked on and pointed with an empty briar pipe. Jack Austin did not smoke, he didn't want to stunt his growth, though Mandy secretly wished he would light up every now and then. And, if smoking dulled his appetite, she thought it would save on the budget for biscuits and cakes that Jack took responsibility for buying during the grocery shop, that and the fish, of course, as Jack was a seafood man; he saw food and he ate it. He had appointed Mandy as victualler general for the Austin ship, except for ship's biscuits and fish, as it was well known she would not buy many biscuits or fishes and, what she did buy (except for the fish) could not match in calorific value the desired intake need for her husband, in biscuits, that is, not fish as they have a lot fewer calories than say, a chocolate *Hob-nob*, though more importantly, the quantity of biscuits she would buy would run out within a day or two; Jack took shopping most seriously.

Duck (Mandy, *keep up*), on the other hand, was the picture of gorgeous nineteen fifties sophistication, in an elegant silky blouse with blowy-out bluebirds over Dover, flared skirt with stiff petticoats below, all of which she loved, but she refused to wear the bobby socks and plimsolls. Dick knew that his wife, Duck, had an autistic (he might mean artistic, though occasionally this was arctic) temperament, and he, as an understanding, all-knowing Alfred-male (he might mean alpha) enema (I think that bit is correct), had to accommodate his wife's moody penchants as part of his active role in matrimonial bliss, and he had the bumps on his head to prove that as well, which is why he now only thought these thoughts. However, alas, he was also prone to speaking his thoughts and so Mandy clumped him. She often clumped him anyway, just in case he had managed to control speaking his thoughts. She was after all, omniscient, as well as gorgeous, in a nineteen fifties *Sophia Loren* way.

Pimple took notes of the meeting, as instructed by the truly dazzling and ravishing Cecelia, herself radiant in her fifties French navy blue chiffon dress with a coffee coloured lacy trim to her conically prominent bosoms department, recently hoovered of soggy ginger nut. Aedd reported that the constable who had responded to the emergency call to Bea's bedsit, had forced the door for entry and been shocked at his findings.

'What were these findings, Aedd?' Cecelia asked calmly.

'Yeah, Aedd?' Pimple asked looking up from his notebook.

'I'll ask the questions for now Pimple darling,' Cecelia smouldered and Pimple quivered his acknowledgement of the admonition from his beauty.

'What?' Aedd was lost.

Cecelia repeated her enquiry. 'What did the constable say?'

'Oh, he said he was sorry for my loss.'

Cecelia sighed, 'Of course, as are we. However, did he describe what he found?'

'Yeah Aedd, what did he say he found...?' And Jack's query petered out, responding to a glance from his Duck. 'Carry on Ceeley sweet'art,' and he beamed an innocent smile at his wife who was not taken in, even if it was his Pride and Prejudice smile.

'As I said, the door was locked so he had to smash it in...'

'Smash, Aedd?' And Cecelia raised her glorious this eyebrows like two trained slugs; the effect was mesmerising for Pimple who remained quiet and hadn't even taken any notes.

'The policeman forced the door and he said he found a pool of blood on the floor and a red mess mixed with green snot on the bedside table. There was no body and no head.' Aedd elaborated that Bea, prior to being decapitated, had had a particularly persistent cold. He repeated what he had been told that, according to photographs taken by the bassoon playing neighbour, Wanda, (she was after all a Wanda window cleaner by profession, so the bassoon was a logical instrument to take up) in the next bedsit, of his adorable Beatrice's bedsit, Bea's body had lain in a pool of blood on the floor, her head having been removed and given a beautifully coiffed hairstyle in the manner of a conducting Beethoven, mid-symphony, before being placed on the bedroom nightstand, the image spoiled only by the conducting baton stuck up her nose. Aedd pointed out also that Bea often had trouble with clogged nasal passages even before she had contracted this nasty cold, not comprehending that this was the nasal conversational dialect of the Birmingham accent, the Midland's city from whence Bea Flat haled.

Dick reflected for a few seconds, though he said he was deflecting, which in the context of his considered argument was more than likely correct. He looked again at the emailed photo that had been taken by Wanda and then announced his conclusions that he dared refuting with a fixed grimace that only the practiced would notice. The grimace being concealed amid the ugly facial fixtures that were rapidly aging and compounding the problem. He expounded that there had in fact been no intruder of murderous or hairdressing intent as he could think of in those few seconds of arguable brilliance, which offered no explanation as to how the non-intruding perpetrator could have gained access to the room to have carried out the foul deed and, subsequently depart undetected, leaving the bedroom seemingly as though secured from the inside. And finally, the police had reported that the head and body had disappeared?

Aedd confirmed there were no secret doors or floor traps; it was a first floor bedsit room in a converted Victorian pile in Southsea.

In the meantime, Mandy had telephoned the police station and spoken to the team leading the investigation and they had emailed the crime scene photos to the former detective superintendent. There was no evidence of a hole in the ceiling, the photo showed just a lake of blood, a pile of old hair grips, some rollers on the Persian styled rug, and a can of *Har-*

mony hairspray beside the bed. There was no body and no head, though there was still a glutinous green mess on the conductor's baton, which now lay, sans-nasally, upon the pink flowery bedspread; they were hyacinths Aedd explained, and Jack nodded sage and onionly, in his characteristically vegetable manner. Aedd explained further, there was no stopping him as eye contact was useless as he scoured the Austin living room for a map, or if that were not available, an atlas.

'The common garden hyacinth,' Aedd had started, '*Hyacinth orientalis*, originated in Anatolia and was brought to Europe in the 16th century. The hyacinth bulb produces a dense, compact spike of flowers, six to twelve inches tall, and has highly fragrant, bell-shaped flowers with reflexed petals. The waxy, densely packed florets come in shades of white, peach, orange, salmon, yellow, pink, red, purple, lavender and blue...'

Aedd stopped, interrupted by Dick and for once everyone was pleased, but that soon changed to vexatious frustration as Jack asked: 'Where the fuck is Anatolia?'

Aedd looked completely made up and he might even, for the time being, have forgotten that his nun sister and buxom conductress girlfriend had been beheaded.

'I'm glad you asked me that,' he said, scouring the room nervously, responding to a collective and audible sigh. 'Anatolia, or should I say, Turkish Anadolu...' and Aedd chuckled timidly at his geographical faux pas, '... is also sometimes called Asia Minor. It's a peninsula of land and, next to archipelagos, I love peninsulas...' Aedd digressed and

Mandy booted his ankle and he regressed in agony but did restart. 'Today, this peninsula,' and he smiled in appreciation, rubbing his ankle, 'constitutes the Asian portion of Turkey and, because of its location at the point where the continents of Asia and Europe meet...' and Aedd looked as if he either desperately sought a map or was considering, with a degree of urgency, a poo? But Aedd was a geography stalwart and he continued: 'Anatolia was, from the beginnings of civilization, a crossroads for numerous peoples migrating or conquering from either continent, you see.'

They didn't, but said they did, if only to stop Aedd, and Mandy showing just how desperate she was, asked Jack to explain his theory, such that it was.

See, told you she was desperate and geography teachers can have this effect on people, it's a well-known fact; look it up and you will see, and Google also mentions their jumpers, or cardigans with football buttons, frequently depicting knitted geographical tableaux.

And so super-sleuth Austin puffed out his chest and half lifted from his chair and spake unto them, pointing with his briar pipe. Mandy pushed him back into the chair, 'Okay feckin' Moses, cut the theatrics,' she said, and so he did and, I venture to suggest so would you. It was the sickly-sweet meaningful smile that Mandy applied, the one she applies before sending out her death star tractor beam.

'It's Dick, not Moses,' Jack said, marvelling at how his wife could be so silly at times. But before Mandy could issue her angelic thunderbolt, Jack recommenced his reasoned explanation on behalf of the Ooh La lovelies, DaDa team. 'Suicide,' he said, rubbing his chin like Sherlock Holmes needing a shave might and then stood, bowed, sat back down and smiled beatifically. He thought, then leaned forward to the table top and looked studiously, in a caring Nightingale way, at Aedd, 'Don't worry, old son, she'll get better,' he said and carried on sporting his victory smirk, born of a certainty that only messengers of God could carry off. He then offered more words handed down from upon high, 'I don't doubt that...'

He was fortuitously interrupted by Cecelia, tipping her head towards Aedd who appeared speechless and was gagging in a bereft and bereaved manner, which Jack found quite distracting and certainly did not need Cecelia to point this out to him. And so he made like he was frustrated by the interruption, as if he had not been allowed to finish all that he had to say, which fortuitously afforded him time to think of additional insightful information, to pad out his prescient brainwave.

Amanda, however, did the real interrupting, so Dick, knowing his Alfred male place, remained schtum and Aedd, still choking on his shock and patent misery, had no chance. 'Suicide? Get better?' Amanda responded rather more vehemently than she intended, knowing her husband was a dipstick and it was no better than she should have expected, but she was also trying to be considerate of Aedd's feelings of shock and grief.

Jack loved the way his wife understood immediately the gist of whatever he was saying, it was what made him think they were soulmates.

'Arsole mates, maybe, mate.' Mandy reacted, even more intensely, to Jack's outspoken thoughts, a natural characteristic of her man and one that amused most people, most of the time, Jack thought, though not always, as he felt at the bumps on his head, coincidentally taking the opportunity to tell his own fortune, which looked good in the long term, but a bit iffy immediately.

Jack did wonder at Mandy's reactive outburst of contention to what he considered to be a reasonable theory, especially when you consider he had no real time to consider a considered theory. He thought maybe his wife was a little cold. The morning air did have a chill to it. 'Did you put your vest on this morning, sweet'art?' he asked, not unreasonably, also showing his concern for his wife's well being.

But Mandy was to be further taken aback as Pimple supported Jack. "Yes, it is chilly this morning. I put a vest on, didn't I, dearest lovely,' and he looked at his gorgeous partner. 'Though Cecelia did not put on her liberty bodice this morning, did you, darling?' And Pimple looked quite chuffed he had once again demonstrated his observational skills and growing understanding of lady underwears.

Mandy remained speechless, quite a rare occasion, I can tell you, and Cecelia joined Mandy in this recherché strained feminine hush as Pimple continued. 'Yes, Dick, I agree,' and turning to Aedd, he added: 'And, Aedd, I have no doubt things will be okay.' Pimple said this in a naturally assured manner that came as a consequence of posh-knob inbreeding within the aristocracy, the right to rule, a divine arrogance, which was about the only confidence Pimple had, if you excluded his now sound knowledge of ladies' under garments, and of course embroidery. 'Though she will probably disappear in the meantime,' Pimple added, not realising the body and head already had disappeared and that he should listen more carefully. 'And, I would get a plumber in if I were you, just in case the floor springs a leak, so to speak,' Pimple continued, unaware of the gaping looks from his exquisite Cecelia, the beautiful Amanda and, indeed, the distraught, lanky Aedd.

Jack nodded agreement. 'Yes, a plumber,' he mumbled, pointing with his pipe in the general direction of the kitchen sink, wishing he had thought of that, though if he was honest with himself, it was only a minor part of his theory and this consoling thought consoled him.

'A leak?' Cecelia asked, in an atom-bomb manner, still shocked that Pimple would think she should wear a vest or a liberty bodice and that he had agreed with the ideas of Jack Austin, whom she already knew was as daft as a brush, but she never expected to hear such things from her own intended. She knew that Pimple Minor (not Asia Minor as that would be Anatolia, or should I say, *chuckle*, Turkish Anadolu) was a bit dipsy in the grey cells department. It was, however, not like Pimple to be so insensitive to someone, especially to Aedd, in his current moment of grief.

But Pimple was insensitive to Cecelia's unsubtle censure and continued his discourse to Aedd, aware he was fully supported in his hypothesis of events by none other than Dick Dashing, whom Pimple considered among the elite of police officers and spooks, retired of course. But now, and even better in Pimple's view, Dick was a celebrated gumshoe. They had gone the previous night to C&A's (the Crown and Anchor pub) to celebrate their new personas of great brilliance and he knew this because Jack Austin had told him so, and it was further agreed that they would be henceforth known as gumshoes, a bit like wellingtons,

Jack Dick, had said and Mandy had galoshed him one. Mandy could be temperamental, especially if she had mixed her salt and vinegar and cheese and onion crisps.

Pimple continued his reassurance of Aedd, 'And, before you know it, your dearest chubby Bea Flat will be back conducting the Nuns' Orchestra and, I might add, I am also confident it will be complete with a revived and refreshed leader of the second violins, namely your sisterly nun, Winifrede. There,' and Pimple leaned back and shared a victory smirk with his gumshoe host, only Pimple had a handsome, though more dimwittedly vacant face than Jack Austin, whose face was as probably equally dimwitted and vacant, but it would be impossible to divine, except maybe by the experienced BBC uglywatch team. He had a naturally occurring ugliness a scientist had once explained to Mandy. This boffin had gone on to say he was however, completely dumbfounded at Mandy, who in his view as a specialist in the human countenance, was a woman of outstanding beauty, in a mature *Sophia Loren* way, they queried how such a woman of rare exquisiteness could attach herself to Mr Ugly personified? He passed on the contact details of a local *Specsavers* and, to be fair, Mandy did consider a consultation, but would she be able to withstand the shock of clear vision?

Answers on a postcard.

'She's not chubby, she's Rubenesque, boyo,' Aedd managed to say in his Welsh accent before Cecelia got in her two penn'orth, 'and she has disappeared. So how did you know that? I hadn't said,' he continued.

Ignoring Aedd, Cecelia questioned Pimple. 'Pimple, what on earth are you talking about?' Barely disguising her incredulity, as she looked deep into the Pimple blue eyes that radiated back a ritzy plonker look and, unusual for Pimple, she thought, a rare assurance that he was right. Was her Pimple becoming a man? Cecelia dismissed this thought as ridiculous, but Pimple often had the ability to amaze her with his perception. Not often, but sometimes he did. It was one of the things that had attracted her to him. Well, there had to be something, though he was passing handsome, if you were passing and not hanging around for too long and then screwed your eyes up, taking care not to bump into a lamppost, which was likely, as Pimple's body was notably akin to a street lighting standard which had not yet been switched on, or the bulb had blown.

Jack thought he should support Pimple who looked as if he would succumb under the withering gaze from Cecelia Crumpet, and he further thought it was time he put Pimple straight in the ways of women and how to deal with their various moods, in which subject, Jack considered himself a connosser.

'You? Understand women?' Amanda said, jumping in again, 'And I think you mean connoisseur?' Jack Austin also spoke his thoughts in his inimitable Mr Malacopperism manner.

Jack ignored his wife's *Barbie* comments as one would, when confident of oneself in both a theoretical and Alfred-male manner. He looked to Amanda to expand on his hypothesis, but she interrupted him again.

'Do you mean barbed?' And she tittered, along with Cecelia.

He did not appreciate his wife's interruption when he felt his considered theory was getting some traction, though he did consider modifying his earlier conclusions in order to get in even more tractors; he considered himself quite agricultural now, since learning all about hyacinths. 'Temporary suicide, then,' he said, though pulling a face that suggested he was uncertain in a meek mouse like way, which he expertly concealed with energetic staccato laughing. 'What d'yer fink luv?' Jack asked of his wife, who knew he always would slip into his coarse natural cockney manner of conversing when struggling to get traction, or even into tractors, as he could not do a country accent. Jack, however, knew his wife truly was a good detective and had been seconded to MI5 as she became close to, and then married, Jack Austin. So they were literally in it together.

Jack was never really a policeman, and not really a spook and, in fact was not truthfully anything, except as a cockney barrow boy he had an uncanny ability that allowed people to think he understood situations, which, funnily enough, he was able to do. He had an innate ability to dissemble facts, think laterally, and solve conundrums – except again, it was later found he didn't do a lot of that either. He used a local lad, Sebastian Sexton, who had Asperger syndrome, on the autistic spectrum, and worked for MI5 from a shed in a cemetery, not that many people knew that, either. Jack (Jane) Austin, Dick, was though a very good actress; a character actress it has to be said, as he did not have the face for a screen goddess.

'Temporary suicide?' Mandy reacted, leaning back, amazed and trying hard to disguise a titter of incredulity so as not to hurt Aedd further. She was a woman of consummate acting skills, who could most certainly be a screen goddess, though of maturing age and she said, not quite so vehemently, (she was used to idiotic statements from her ugly cockney-eejit husband, but this latest pronouncement did take her back). 'So, she cut her own fucking head off did she... thinking she might put it back again later, after dinner...?'

Aedd flinched, they all noticed.

Amanda calmed and put her hand on Aedd's bony shoulder to comfort him. She thought a little deeper. She was not so confident, her final query had tailed off – did her husband know something? Had he already spoken to Seb in his cemetery shed? Might he have used the phone while she was in the bathroom this morning? She had lingered over her ablutions longer than was normal, knowing it was foolish to leave Jack unattended for too long, but she discarded this thought as he always asked her to dial for him, to save his finger, which was frequently preserved in order to better pick his nose and for pointing, though these days, more often than not, if Mandy's fingers were not available, he used his briar pipe to point and pick his nose, which is why when he offered her a suck, she always declined.

It is also a sad fact that Jack Austin had memory and energy lapses from time to time. Mandy did worry her husband might be going senile, as opposed to doolally, which he had been his entire life, of course. Mandy had taken Jack to see the doctor and asked about a test for Alzheimer's, but Jack had assured Dr Borodin he was fine and got up to leave. "It's Dr Brynn," the doctor said to Jack's departing enormous frame as it turned sideways to get through the door, seeing no significance in the memory lapse with his name, as Jack Austin got the doctor's name wrong every time. The doctor also saw nothing amiss with Jack's welfare and behaviour, considering this an amusing quirk that both the doctor and Jack knew women liked. "Men should always have amusing quirks in order to amuse women, you see", Jack Austin often remarked and he had those bumps as well. Mandy resolved that at the next visit she would make sure Jack saw the female doctor so she would get a sensible diagnosis, but then she forgot.

Jack pondered Mandy's question for a minute. He was good at pondering, but the effect on his already ugly boatrace (face – he was nervous and always thought in cockney when agitated or scared. I think I have mentioned that, although a truly lovely woman, Mandy could be volatile and Jack tried never to be around when that happened, which is why he practiced his running away a lot). He tapped his finger, the pointy one, on the table, in the manner of all good Dicks. He made it rhythmic, 'What's this tune?' he asked.

'Fucking Doctor Who, it's always Doctor Who,' Mandy replied, now irritated that the theme tune was going through her head, but suggested her husband might like to continue or she would, *annihilate, annihilate*, him.

Jack did. 'I can see why you might question the temporary suicide, my love...' he said as he pondered the ceiling while offering her his reasonable face (no different from the normal ugly one). 'What do you think, then? Pro tem murder, momentary manslaughter? A passing deathness?'

'Fugacious death?' Pimple added, not wishing to be left out and also demonstrating his poshness.

'Mushrooms?' Jack asked back, in an intelligent

way. 'Are you thinking deaf by toadstool? Squashed in their ears? Clever.'

Mandy and Cecelia looked at each other, Mandy knowing that her dipstick had confused fungi and fugacious, and the two women just about controlled their mirth. Aedd cried some more, irritating Jack some more. He responded to Mandy, reinforcing his understanding face; still no difference, still ugly, and more importantly, still no change in Mandy's demeanour. Jack thought he might need to rethink his facial gesture and so gurneyed a little.

'You think a passing death?' Mandy replied with a slight chuckle at her husband's *let's-amuse-women-face*, him not realising that it was even uglier, which was, by coincidence, quite amusing. She carried on interrogating and simultaneously frightening her husband, 'And, temporary death, how so?' She queried, and Jack was temporarily encouraged, he liked it when his wife spoke Japanese, though it was to be a short-lived rapture of cosy respite and, it might be she was not speaking Japanese after all. Jack resolved to learn more about women and their various languages, but then forgot, in French.

'Tu as oublié? You forgot?' Mandy replied to her husband's outspoken Continental forgetfulness. 'How can you have temporary murder or even suicide?'

Mandy shook her head in wonderment. She loved her husband. He was a lovely man and she even batted back the many suggestions she should have gone to a brain doctor, whether made by friends or scientists, but sometimes he could be a gigantic overweight whale of a feckin' eejit, she thought, and not for the first time. So she applied her looking-at-kittens smile in order to relax Jack and then asked her questions in a more reasonable manner, in order to wrong foot him (a particularly cunning female tactic – I point this out for the naïve men among us, not me of course, and I have the bumps to prove it).

'Supposing...' she started off, lyrical and lovely, '...it was not temporary suicide?' She suggested, by way of a possible alternative theory, waving her arms, which had hands on the end, to reinforce the casual nature of her inquiry, 'And the second fiddle nun, say, and now Bea Flat, were in fact permanently murdered? How did the killer effect his escape from the school and especially from Bea Flat's flat and leave the room as though it was locked from the inside? And now we understand both bodies have disappeared, how did that happen, eh?'

Jack had fallen for the oldest trick in the women's handbook and relaxed. He realised it too late, of course, but thought he should counter this with more reasoned argument, as though he were describing puppies to a lady. It was a technique he was developing and thought he would give it a test run. He replied, 'And their heads,' correcting his wife in an amusing manner, realising she did not have his *eye* for detail. Jack looked at his wife with his knowing eye, the only one he had, to see how the ploy had faired. He loved her with a passion. She was his *Sophia Loren* of Portsea Island, he always said, and it was true, Mandy was a handsome woman and the *Oooh La Lovelies* fashions really suited her. She even had that olive complexion like *Sophia Loren*, except Jack didn't like olives, but was prepared to lick them on his wife's skin. Quite generous he thought, not that Mandy seemed to appreciate it and so he did mention the last time she should appreciate his licking her face, after all, he could poke her with his pipe, and we all know where that has been. Yes, in his pocket, and you don't want to go there, especially if it was his handkerchief pocket.

Mandy had shiny, slinky, black hair, and she had, much to Jack's approval, a full hourglass figure much like the Italian film star. She was beautifully tall, shapely, mature and womanly, but she also thought her husband talked a load of old bollocks. At a push, she could see that maybe she was handsome, maybe attractive, but she always thought her nose too big, but what do you know, Jack Austin said that her "fire-man's hose" was one of the things he truly loved about her, and her legs of course, he liked them, but they were not on her face, least they weren't the last time he licked.

Jack sighed and rubbed his head, his wife was giving nothing away, 'So, the second fiddle player has disappeared as well?' He looked smug, but unsure as he tapped his fingers on the table. Mandy didn't ask, she already knew the tune was Dr Who, it always was. Jack looked across to the mirror, yep he was smug but that morphed into unsure, with just a hint of smug. 'Oooh, it's too 'ard,' he murmured to himself, then, turning to his lubbly jubbly wife in the mirror, 'let's go back to bed," he reflected to Mandy's re-flected image, and he agreed with himself in the mirror and coincidentally the image also nodded agreement that he was a good-looking fella, though Mandy's reflection seemed not so sure.

So they did, Mandy suggesting that the reflected image was as dozy as the real self. Jack Austin ignored the feminine rhetoric, he was on a mission. He considered that he needed regular sexual sustenance in order to maintain his brilliantly incisive thinking. Mandy thought he just loved being cuddled and stroked by her and she acknowledged to herself that sometimes this was the only way to stop her husband's dozy incisive thinking.

SEVEN

IN THE MEANTIME, THE LOCAL POLICE WERE LEFT pondering, having telephoned Amanda just before she went upstairs; Jack had gone running ahead, excited like a kid at Christmas, though he did halt at the landing, realising his wife was no longer stroking his bum. After thanking them for the crime-scene photos, Mandy informed the community policing department, the department she used to run, of Jack's theories, sensing she could make a fool of herself, but also aware that, if Jack had spoken to Seb in his shed, there might be more to his theories than just total twaddle.

Was the community policing team still run by Superintendent Amanda Austin and DCI Jack Austin? And if it was, how come it was considered by many to be an elite squad, boasting a reputation for solving the most obscure of crimes? Reputed even to have solved the reasons for the credit crunch, the million-dip recession, and the country's economy, whereas the murder of a conductor and second fiddle player, and subsequent disappearance of the bodies, was just a bit too hard? And what did the superintendent mean when she reported that the former DCI, Austin, had reassured Aedd, telling him not to worry, that it would be alright?

The community policing department was left wondering, while Jack remained standing on the landing, to listen to Mandy on the telephone and, satisfied she supported him in his theories, he allowed her to guide him up the rest of the wooden hill to their bedroom, Mandy gently smoothing his substantial bottom, a task she knew soothed him and also enabled her to steer him to the bedroom, in case he forgot where it was.

He expressed mild confusion as she mumbled the conundrum of the fiddle player and conductor under her breath. This is what had her confused, she already knew that Jack's bum was big and knew why. But Jack Austin, who was a deaf twat and so could not hear everything his wife was muttering, did answer her questioning looks with a better questioning look, which he considered would teach her a lesson; giving him questioning looks, indeed. He was really good at questioning looks and so he and his wife temporarily retired from the scene of the conundrum of a temporarily decapitated orchestra conductor and second fiddle nun, intent on a bit of rumpy-pumpy in the bedroom department, conundrums being too hard for the time being, especially as far as conductors went. Jack Austin didn't like buses anyway, 'Ding, ding,' Jack's whispered foreplay aside to his very attractive, though olive tasting, wife; he certainly knew a lot about what to whisper to a lady when making love to her.

'Was that a bus conductor?' Mandy asked as she lost herself in the moment, after she had shown Jack the way, of course; he was busy collecting fares.

———

Aedd Murphy was left alone at the table as Pimple and Cecelia decided also to head to the bedroom for some incisive sex and so, a tad disgruntled, he returned to his flat in order to mope; he was, after all, mourning a double loss. His sister, very much on the Welsh side and formerly named Dyliss, was Sister Winifrede and she also taught geography, as did Aedd, at St Winifrede's Convent school.

They were a geography family. His mother, Blodwyn the Canary, a very fine bird, taught geography to the miners in the valley where they lived. The miners learned precious little as it was dark underground, but this did not dim her enthusiasm and it is said she spent a lot of time with the roughty-toughty men, making sure they grasped the basics, so to speak. His maternal granddad, however, was the dark side of the family and not much is said of him. He was the black sheep because he was not a geography miner and it was thought he deliberately covered himself, head to toe in coal dust, in order to spend as much time as possible with the other miners in the showers after a shift.

Anyway, as a consequence of the subject matter, geography, that the whole family were absorbed in, apart from Granddad who specialised in masculine hygiene, not many people knew the family existed. Even in the Welsh valleys. However, Aedd's sister had become well known as the principle second violin in the celebrated Nuns' Orchestra and now she had been beheaded, whether temporarily or permanent, Aedd was not sure. He was confused about that as well and, not unreasonably, upset. He felt he needed to cuddle up to a mountain, or wallow in an Ox-bow lake, some of the things he liked to do when he was feeling miserable and today, he felt wretched.

Wretched he felt, and even more so because he was unsure if he was also seriously mourning Bea Flat, the Nuns' Orchestra conductor and his girl-friend, though of a short duration? Yes, he was in a way, and he acknowledged that he felt even in such a short period, he had connected with Bea. She seemed to understand him. She liked geography, least he thought she did and, she remembered his name most of the time. But most of all, he simply loved to look at her bottom when she conducted the orchestra. Her fulsome bottom cheeks moved like shifting and sliding tectonic plates as she gyrated rhythmically in time with the music; mesmerising for anyone who had a passion for geography.

Aedd scratched his head, no mean feat to get through the ginger wire wool mop to claw at his scalp, but he did have skinny fingers, and he reflected that, in his way, he did love Bea. He sought comfort for his loss. He looked at the map to the Midlands, in partic-ular Birmingham, Bea's home city, pasted on the wall of his living room that he was wont to call his *salon du monde*, because he liked mondes and also, always thought had he not gone into geography, he would have loved to have been a hairdresser, with his own salon, like his grandfather in the mines. However, his current salon, of substantial plan area and volume, was battle-scarred following the altercation, as Jack Austin had put it to the authorities, but was in fact the blasting out of the large Georgian window that faced on to Frisian Tun. Bad enough, you would think, but subsequent to the demise of the huge Georgian-paned sash window, the duchess stormed the world and machine gunned the salon, leaving the wall-mounted maps and various related geological charts in tatters. There was also some structural damage, but this was of less concern to the wire-wooled, ginger mopped geography teacher. His maps and charts, though, were everything to him. It was his comfort, his passion, his world, so to speak, and it had been his life's love that had been plastered across the walls to be cut to ribbons, along with his heart, by a Kalashnikov.

Just prior to the storming of Aedd's flat by Lady Blanche Teapot, whom it later transpired was the transvestite London gangster, Mad Frankie White from Hither Green, Aedd had his spacious Victorian living room layered in maps of the world, complemented by geological charts relating to the various zones depicted. On the ceiling had been a dramatic modelling of Cape Trafalgar, the blue sea scene set with the English and French fleets, and even this singular military success of the Ye Olde British Navy had been decimated by the machine gunfire.

The insurance company had said they would replace the ceiling but were buggered if they were paying for someone to recreate the Battle of Trafalgar and the defeat of Napoleon's fleet, as important a moment as this had been in English history. The original ceiling scene paid geographical lip service to the mighty implications of the Cape and its relationship to Spain and Europe in general. The Philistine insurers had said they would only paint the ceiling blue. Aedd would have to add the waves and the copperplate title block himself.

And so it was, upon the bullet riddled, unsteady sixties coffee table, the top of which was glazed with new glass, below which a picture depicted a Canadian lake and, beside a collection of cotton wool puffs of canon discharge stood a growing armada of tiny paper model ships of both Nelson's and Admiral Villeneuve's line, painstakingly being remade by Aedd. He had already painted some of the waves on to the ceiling of the Cape Trafalgar Sea, replaced the charts and maps of the world on the walls, and the room was starting to feel, once again, a home from geographical home.

Aedd pondered his lot as he stood and absorbed the comforting sensations that his living room gave him. He fingered his rusty, wire wool hair, still unsure if the ginger was Scandinavian or of Celtic origin and he swung his gaze to the Rock of Cashel in Ireland and the ancestral home of his father's family. He was descended, so he said to anyone not able to get away, from the great Kings of Old Ireland and he allowed himself a brief glimpse to Tara, just up from Dublin and to the left, before swivelling his gaze to Swansea in Wales. He was also aristocratically descended, on his mother's side, from a long line of Swansea Joneses. He could trace his line back to Grufyyd Ap Llewelyn the Geography Jones, who did the maps for Owen Glendower, back in the day, Aedd would tell anyone who could stay awake long enough in his presence. Aedd was a geography teacher and that is all the explanation you should need. Just ask the Welsh and they will tell you that it is widely believed that the Welsh mining industry sank into a deep malaise due to a growing interest in geography and masculine hygiene, but that would be anthropology and will need to be comprehended in another book, other than to say, if Aedd's ancestors, on the

Welsh side, had not been so interested in geography and cleaning men's bodies, Wales would be a completely different place now; coal tar and carbolically speaking.

Aedd settled his bony bottom into a curvilinear leather armchair, redolent, he thought, of the rolling hills of the Downs of Central Southern England, and he incongruously looked at Birmingham, the city and its environs, as well as the adjacent chart depicting the City's geological structure. Beatrice Flat, missing and now considerably shorter, was one of the few women he had ever known who understood his passion for geography and she came from England's second city. He was thinking of Bea when the Irish bozzer to his flat, bozzed.

Aedd stepped to the door intercom, adjacent to the Mergui Archipelago in Burma, a casual thought about his earlier meditating on the geological marvels that were archipelagos, isthmuses and so on, and that Britain was itself an archipelago and how much he loved this geographical quirk of nature, possibly even more than peninsulas. An archipelago was a chain of islands adjacent to a large land mass and he was sad that he had not managed to pass on his love of archipelagos to his dearest Bea Flat. He thought one time, after she had finished conducting a concerto, the subject archipelagos was up for deep discussion while they shared a kebab and a jug of cider, and Aedd had pointed to Greece and Turkey, set to expand on the geological formation of that area of Europe, but, it wasn't to be. Bea was talking about arpeggios, whatever that was. It was a sad moment, but Aedd had got over his disappointment after a couple of weeks.

'How's yer, who's it on moy bozzer, so it is?' he

said into the door intercom, in his Irish accent, Dublin, just a bit to the north and left a bit.

'It's moy, Aedd.' It was a Birmingham twang, dead centre, Aedd thought, amusing himself as he recognised the accent before the identity of the caller.

'Bea? Whose coat is that jacket... so,' Aedd said in a Welsh and then Irish manner. He was thrown and as a consequence, he blended his Welsh and Irish but pressed the bozzer to open the front door made of Canadian Western Red cedar to withstand the salty sea air in Portsmouth. It was in this confused state that he leaned his head to the wall and cooled his forehead in the Adaman Sea, just off the western shore of the Malay Peninsula. Aedd was thrown off balance in humour and sensitivity and, through his forehead, he was sensible to a cooling effect and microscopic pin pricks from the eight hundred tiny islands that made up this wondrous archipelago. It was his favourite and, as he conjured the picture of the islands in more detail, there was a rap at the flat entrance door.

'Aedd, open up please... it's moy.'

It was definitely Bea's voice. But how could this be? He wondered as he offered a quick glance to where Birmingham was in the living room, before he passed into the hall and released the door latch. He could hardly tear his sight away from the Midlands of England, via the open salon du monde porte as it closed steadily on its spring. But curiosity won out, encouraged by a stinging prod from a conductor's arm, almost knocking Aedd from his rostrum of disbelief and, his back against the wall of no geographical significance, Aedd looked on in astonishment as Bea Flat barged by and he could not stop himself admiring the shifting tectonic plates of her wondrously Rubenesque bottom. Oh, how he wanted to fondle her substructure, even if it were only spectral.

'What is it, Aedd?' She asked, turning back, perplexed herself. It had been a difficult morning, but she knew how much Aedd liked looking at her geographical bottom. He had mentioned something about the African continent before and its unstable geological constructs and, if she was honest, she was certainly in the mood for him to go looking for Livingstone in her darkest African erogenous zones.

'Wer, wer...' Aedd was almost coherent, as he stepped ahead to hold the map room door for the ghost of his girlfriend, shaking his head when he realised she could just walk through it but he was first and foremost, a gentleman geographer.

Bea barged past the dumbfounded cartographical scholar and Aedd managed to let her know she had just passed the Mergui Archipelago, as if she didn't already know this? But, what she didn't know, as Aedd was still in the early days of courting the curvy music teacher from St Winifrede's Roman Catholic school, a woman whose body was very South Downs-like, was the origin of the term archipelago. Aedd's enthusiasm to impart this knowledge to what can only be his phantasmal sweetheart, caused him to miss the nasal request for hot lemon and honey and then a shag. Bea declared she had a sore throat and an itch and she couldn't give a flying fuck about archipelagos.

As if?

Musicians eh?

EIGHT

IT IS OFTEN THOUGHT THAT THE INTELLIGENCE services were discreet. Well, clearly Jack Austin could never be discreet. In point of fact, he was so indiscreet, with his overtly proclaimed socialist views, nobody would comprehend he was, or had been, a bit of a brains trust in MI5, but he had been, or was. Maybe he still was, but now in his cunning guise as Dick, in the Ooh La Lovelies, DaDa Detective Agency.

It is also widely believed that the secret services are the tool of the establishment and therefore, by their very nature, they were thought to be an elite *closed* group. That they would select its members from similarly elite structures, institutions or even government, in order to carry out tasks not necessarily open, or even voted for by a blindly naïve electorate and generally, this might be the case. However, in the secret services there were some people, like Jack Austin, who had a rigid sense of right and wrong and, in their guise of assisting the government, the establishment and by way of diversionary tactics, they strove to reveal to the world what was really going on. Unfortunately, though, the world, in its total naïve denial, did not always accept what was being shown to them. Most people preferred the cuddly cotton candy TV news that they found more readily digestible and often sugar coated by the right wing press, which is when they are not conveniently diverted by mind-numbingly dumb TV programmes.

Jack Austin could not see the irony of his indiscreet discreet service to the country, many considering him a socialist establishment in his own right or left. However, there were people in discreet high places who looked to make sure democracy prevailed, that the underhand was rooted out. A fulltime job it was and it always will be.

Among those highly placed individuals would be Olive Doyle of VI6. And then there was Dr Jim Samuels, to all intents and purposes a Harley Street psychiatrist. But he was in fact a major factotum in MI5. Factotum being a misnomer in this case as Samuels headed a serious section in MI5 and within the service he was viewed as someone who did a lot of jobs for anyone in the know or the establishment but that would be completely and erroneously to underestimate the man and his core beliefs.

Olive Doyle, Mother of VI6 (Vatican Intelligence, Foreign Desk), Bong, Father Mike O'Brien and Samuels met in Westminster Cathedral, as they had done many times and these meetings grew in frequency as Umble Pie grew in activity and their collaborative missions combined in shared ultimate goals.

'I believe in Jack Austin, as much as you do, Father Mike,' Jim Samuels said, across the table of Olive's modest office at the back of the cathedral.

Ben Diamond, known as Bong because he was as

tall as Big Ben, looked on. Jim Samuels had been briefed about Diamond long ago by his operative Grace Church and they already had Bong earmarked for services for them, but clearly Olive Doyle had sequestered the man and Jim accepted this might work just as well. He did, however, have his reservations about the personal relationship blossoming between Olive and Bong, but that may just have been his general discomfort around any overt show of affection, especially if this came with indiscreet fondling. (See *Dead No More – Rhubarb in the Mammon*.)

'I have read the files on Jack Austin. Bit of a cowboy maverick, don't you think?' Olive answered, waving a file that was presumably her report on the man known as Jane – she'd not got to Dick yet, Bong excluded of course.

Bong intervened. 'Barrow Boy, dearest...' he trailed off in response to the frigid stare from Olive, which melted to a warm smile when she saw her giant of a man cower.

'And you know him, how, Bong darling?'

'I have heard a little about him from Grace and learned more in my chats with Father Mike. It seems he has complete faith in the man, although I did catch him with his fingers crossed,' and Bong crossed his fingers to show Olive what he meant.

She smiled her understanding and returned her attention to Samuels. 'Okay, I do know of Jack Austin, but Jim, will you keep him under control, please? This is too big an operation for a *barrow boy*...' and she continued, looking at Bong, who smiled back, Olive had accepted his description of the maverick I-spy man, '...to ruin it, running amuck.'

Jim agreed but Bong noticed he had his fingers crossed.

The Mother Superior was headmistress of St Winifrede's school, though more importantly to her, she was Mutter Oberin, Sturmbannführer of the convent and, she wore the shoulder boards depicting the hand of God reaching out from a cumulonimbus cloud, of her rank, atop her penguin outfit to prove it. The mother superior was a cold and calculating nun. She was currently preoccupied with the deficit in the orchestra's second violins, an organisation that, if it did not bring in such large revenues for the convent and consequent high repute, she would not care for at all. She would prefer St Winifrede's to be a silent order, which was not possible of course as they had to talk to each other and, then there were the children who needed to be taught and that required talking, unfortunately.

There was a knock on the hefty solid oak door to her convent office. She called out, "Enter," gruffly. She was irritated by the death of a key player, but mainly the disturbance of her routines.

The Major Mutter was a stout woman who took no prisoners and, ironically, had a face only a Mutter would love. Her cold eyes, set into a pumpkin head, were pinched, from whom nobody knew, but the visual consequence was akin to a manic hog who had sucked on a lemon concealed within her bloated cheeks. The resultant effect was that she wore on top of the haughty drawn-in cheeks of a sourpuss a permanently fixed frown, but that face morphed to incredulity as she saw standing before her, Sister Winifrede. The previously dead nun was dressed in her nun's habit where the skirts had been pulled up and tucked into the top of her navy blue, flannelette knickers, with some additional securing string. Sticking out proud from the nun's hips, she was skirted in a stiff pink netting, frilly tutu, her chest was adorned with a matching pink, generously cupped brassiere, all atop the habit, which completed her ensemble, apart from her pink ballet plimsolls.

'Bless me, St Beuno, Holy Mary and bleedin' Joseph, Sister Winifrede?'

Was this a vision, she thought? The mother superior had always wanted to have a real vision. In her line, nunnery, it helped in the promotion stakes if you had a celestial vision or two, and she should know. She had already invented several, which had helped her to rise to her current lofty status in the Catholic Church and more especially, within the St Winifrede's Convent hierarchy, which was attached to the St Winifrede's School, not that she cared about the fucking school. The kids were a bleedin' nuisance (when her guard was down, the mother superior betrayed her Hanoverian Essex origins).

Sister Winifrede twirled and pranced to an unsteady halt in front of the large mahogany desk, said to have been carved from an orange box that St Peter himself had sat on beside the edge of the Sea of Galilee, just before he went fishing for men. This was, apparently, a penchant of his, but probably he meant pêcheur. The prima-ballerina nun marked time in a military *danseuse* fashion, while stretching her neck, hunching and relaxing her shoulders and, finally pointing her toes and then squashing her feet together at an unnatural angle, as though she had broken ankles. She flounced her hands and arms like a pink frilly bird struggling in flight and took in the dark ambience of the room, as if for the first time becoming aware that the office of this powerful mother penguin was blessed with beautiful stained glass windows, designed to twinkle joyfully, though reluctantly, in the presence of the dominating *dementor* mother. The coloured glass, in this instance, conspired with the powerful nun in making the room even more gloomy than the face of the mother superior, which, as has already been hinted at, looked like it had been slapped with a soggy haddock (pêcheur, blimey, keep up, I'm not your mother superior) and consequently would also not bear close aromatic scrutiny (you always have a lemon with fish – if you are posh that is, otherwise it's salt and vinegar liberally dosed on your chips as well).

The mother superior considered telephoning the *Barbaras of Seville*, the fascist nun sect, who maintained that the strict orthodoxy of the Catholic Church should be reinforced, and then, be strictly enforced. The mother always wanted to join the Barbaras and this miracle could be her passport into the modern-day Spanish Inquisition, nun department (SI-9 – whatever the number is, or it may be nun). She made a mental note to telephone them, when miraculously, the telephone rang. 'Holy Mary,' she said to the phone, but the inanimate old-fashioned Bakelite device replied only with more urgent ringing.

The mother superior signalled to Sister Winifrede, to hold her ballerina horses, and picked up the phone. 'Ja, ja, Top Mum here,' she said in a squeaky voice that irritated her more and she put this down to her surprise at seeing the ghost of Sister Winifrede, though she often worried she had something wrong with her voice box. She picked up the can of WD-40, she always kept on her desk, sprayed her throat, and repeated, 'Ja, Top Mum," to her superior, deeper in tone voice ensued, a hint of Germanic Essex, which she corrected to Spanish; it would be as well she practised, just in case. 'Hola,' She was now excited, her stare transfixed on the miracle. A resurrected nun, albeit dressed as a baller-fucking-rina, sans wimple, hair still savagely cropped, but now coiffed as though it was a glamorous *Audrey Hepburn* in the Hollywood film, *The Bells of St Winifrede's*, prancing and twirling before her.

The mother's thoughts raced, speculation of a place in the Vatican if the Barbaras were full. Books. Visiting lectureships and as a consequence, she did not really comprehend the message being relayed to her by Herr Ernie, gabbling on the phone, trying to tell her about the burst pipe in the auditorium and in particular, a gushing spring, where the leader of the second violins would ordinarily sit.

'Whoopah!' the mother superior said in Greek. 'A spring?' Immediately her mind gushed with even headier thoughts of the origination of the name of the convent and the school, St Winifrede's. Her mind was now a TV screen and she saw displayed like a running breaking news strapline before her eyes the miracle of St Winifrede's and she immediately resolved to get Ernie off the phone and telephone the newspapers.

The mother gawped at Sister Winifrede, who now leaned a straightened arm on the substantial desk, which still gave off the aroma of the zest of an orange and with one steadying hand, she gracefully stuck her leg out (a ballet term) horizontally, and then back in, a picture of choreographed innocence and virtue, as had been the original Winifrede, who reportedly had been beheaded by one Caradog when she refused to submit to him. Her head had been restored to her by her brother Beuno, who later became a saint. The mother superior thought it should have been Winifrede who was beatified (she later was of course because the nuns went on and on and so the Pope, back then, reportedly beatified her for a bit of peace and quiet), but it was a man's world then and was still, except the Barbaras were about changing that and, she would help them if she could get in and ironically, Winifrede could be her entry fee. Today was also the twenty second of June, the same date in ancient history when the original Welsh ballerina, Winifrede, is supposed to have met her fate.

The mother put the phone down on a still gabbling Ernie and signalled for Sister Winifrede to stop bloody dancing and to sit while she stood. Winifrede continued dancing, which was annoying, but the mother suppressed her anger and in a surreptitious manner, she circled the recently reheaded nun to look for evidence of decapitation and, although Winifrede continued to dance and the nun's neck was a little blurred, the mother saw none, though she was sorely tempted with a dying swan thought. She was not sure what she expected to see? A scar circumnavigating Winifrede's swan-like neck? A chain dotted line? But already she had in mind concocting a story, envisioning the installation of a holy well on the site of the chair for the leader of the second violins. The orchestra could go and play somewhere else. She couldn't give a toss about them, not now she had a genuine saintly vision.

Her thoughts strayed to a picture of endless visits by pilgrims, imagining herself counting the money as the convent coffers began to overspill, all of which she could use to help fund her installation into the Barbaras. They notoriously loved the holy spondulics and maybe she could buy herself a new set of roller skates? She had been practising on an old pair of rusty *Jackos* that squeaked down the corridor of the convent, a bit like her voice before she used the 3-*IN*-*ONE* or *WD-40*. And then there was the possibility of a new feast day installed in the Catholic Church calendar? Worldwide fame. And maybe she could save money on the skates and just squirt the *Jackos* with *WD-40*? Surely the Holy Barbaras would accept that?

Mother superior gave out a contented sigh as she regained her seat; did the stained glass brighten? She picked up the phone, relieved not to hear Ernie's blithering tone and dialled the Evening News, sat back, asked for the news desk and waited. 'Will you stop fucking dancing, for Christ's sake.'

Winifrede didn't, and she wouldn't, because she couldn't, and so she spun and twirled, stepped gaily to the door and jete'd out.

NINE

Inspector Josephine Wild, nicknamed Jo Jums, or Ma'amsie, a derivative of mumsy, which described her mumsy, plump image, of the Portsmouth Community Policing department, had just finished a meeting with the station commander, reporting that the two beheaded bodies had mysteriously disappeared from the crime scenes. Since this was a weird occurrence, she reported she would telephone, again, her former bosses Jack and Amanda Austin, still not sure if they had retired or not, but she often sought their advice on tricky issues.

Jack, feeling a post-coastal (as he would express post-coital) sense of well-being and a generosity of spirit that encouraged him to forgo his accustomed reticence to step into the world of administration and electronic communication, picked up the telephone beside the bed. 'Jo Jums, what light from yonder window breaks?'

Jo, inured to Jack's inanities and disguising her disappointment Mandy had not answered her call so she might get some sense, told Jack what had been reported.

'Well that's all right, then,' he said, still feeling quite well. "I knew this already and, as I said, not to worry, it will all turn out okay,' and he hung up the phone and went back to cuddling his wife; he loved a post-coastal cuddle.

'Was that Jo?' Mandy asked, rather unsubtly digging for more information, the cuddle becoming more of a frustration, a smothering of blancmange rather than *Angel Delight*.

'Yeah, the bodies are gone, which we already knew. Don't worry though, sweet'art, everything will be okay.' Jack knew in his heart this would be likely to need further explanation because, as previously laboured, Jack knew women, except the bit where they got fed up. He never quite understood that bit, but just now he wanted to enjoy his post-coastal slumber.

'Coital, its post-coital, you dozy sod, and what did Jo mean when she said the bodies had disappeared? I thought you were joking about that? Have you spoken to Seb? And, if so, it would help if you told me what he has said.'

Jack pretended to be sound asleep, making a slumbering note to himself to get someone to Google fed-up women when he got up, but his land of nodding repose and even faux snoring would not fool Mandy. He was coastally cuddling a very astute woman.

'Jack?'

'Hmmm?'

'Answer me.' The tone of her voice caused Jack to switch to Fred Alert. He sounded his klaxon and instantly made ready to dive or to make a run for it, or fake a fit, all tried and tested methods for Jack. 'You stay where you are and tell me.' Mandy reacted to his outspoken thoughts. She was familiar with his tried and tested failure tactics following his sounding of the klaxon.

Jack was let off as the telephone rang again and Mandy made a mental note to get the phone moved to her side of the bed, but Jack had it put beside him because he loved it when she had to lean over him to answer it. Jack answered, generously, 'Aedd? She has? Oh lovely. Told yer. She has? Oh, never mind, add some whisky with that. See yer,' and Jack replaced the phone and closed his eyes. He knew he was in the middle of a conversation with Mandy, but for the life of him he could not remember what it was about. Probably nothing important, he thought and wondered if he should throw a fit as a contingency measure, but settled in the end for a dive. He sounded the klaxon so Mandy would be aware of what was happening.

'Oi, surface now,' she said like a number one in control of the periscope. 'We were talking about the bodies disappearing and what did Aedd want?'

Now this did have Jack in a quandary. What question should he answer first and then, what was the original question? What had she seen in her periscope? And if he answered the wrong one first, would Mandy get fed up? He decided to go with the most recent phone call. He lived life on the hedge, which he found arboriculturally exciting, he always told people.

'Bea has just turned up. Bit of a sore throat, but otherwise okay. He was going to make her a cup of lemon and honey. I said put some whisky in it and then they were going to have shag, in the Maldives I think he said? Where's that?

'By the bedroom door,' Mandy answered, before she realised she was being a dipstick.

'There, see, told you everything would be okay,' and Jack closed his eyes again, intent on more beside-the-seaside slumbering, but he inadvertently muttered, 'I wonder if it was temporary suicide or pro tem murder? Or maybe it was an impermanent fatal accident?'

That did it and Mandy sat up in bed. Jack now knew it would be impossible to ignore her, or to sleep, as he would have to look upon his wife's glorious breasts as they swung before his one eye. He had been amazed about how these superb mammary orbs, not small, nor overly large, were just right for his artist's hands. It was as if Mandy and he were made for each other, Jack thought and as a consequence spoke.

Mandy derred and then agreed that she and Jack were soulmates and, were also made for each other. Jack smiled. Lumbered with each other was more likely the case, she thought, but knew she had to give to receive with Jack.

'So, you said Bea has turned up, fit and well?'

Jack smiled at Mandy, she could be such an eejit at times and, she never listened to what he had to say. 'No,' he answered.

'No?' she replied, getting irritated, as he never heard anything she said, which had just been irrefutably proven. 'I thought you just said Bea had just turned up?'

'Yes, but not fit and well. She had a sore throat, dinlo.' Cor blimey, he thought, girls, they never listen.

Mandy sighed, got up, leaving Jack floundering post-coastally, and went for a shower. They would have to get involved, she just knew, and if she was honest, she was quite captivated by the thought. The first real *Ooh La Lovelies, DaDa Detective Agency* serious case, if you didn't count the death and destruction of Frisian Tun and the machine gunning duchess, and she wondered what dress she would wear as she tapped on the bedroom door to raise Pimple and Cecelia.

————

The knock on the door made Pimple jump and as a consequence, Pimple made Cecelia jump. So she shouted at him, 'Oi, you bleedin' wuss,' she said, rather more aggressively than she meant.

Pimple gazed adoringly into Cecelia's deep azure eyes and told her that he loved it when she spoke sweet nothings to him. Cecelia looked up to the ceiling, which was not difficult as she was lying in bed, but her sigh was audible. Amazingly this seemed to excite her Pimple, who mistook the hiss of expelled air as an indication of sexual desire. He had a lot to learn, but this was in fact a natural default position of all men, so, seen in a prudential light, Pimple was making progress.

'I would most certainly make love to you again, dearest darling,' he said with all of the sensual gravitas Jack had taught him, 'but it sounded like Mandy wanted us downstairs.'

Cecelia sighed again and so Pimple planted a soggy kiss on to her luscious lips in order at least to give her something physical to hold on to. 'There, that will have to do until we come back to bed tonight, my darling love,' and he looked at his woman's face, convinced he had done the right thing. He was eternally grateful Jack Austin had taken the time to fill him in on the ways of a woman.

Cecelia sighed, yet again and thought Pimple may have caught the speaking of his thoughts from Jack Austin and, was not worried about that so much as him being advised by Jack on the ways of a woman. She would need to sort that one and pronto-tonto. Maybe check if Pimple had been sharing Jack's bath water. Mandy had told Cecelia that sometimes she spoke her thoughts immediately after Jack and she had shared a bath. She looked at Pimple as he began to pull on his gigantic boxer shorts which made him look like a flagpole with the flag of surrender at half-mast and she thought she needed to buy him some proper underwear, but that could wait.

'Pimple dear,' and she waited while he stood on one leg trying to extricate his left foot from the right leg hole in order to respond to her. He did not manage this, as it required the ability to multitask, which clearly Pimple did not have; he fell over.

Cecelia chuckled and waited for him to get himself up and to hop over to the bed. She smoothed his smooth cheek, still awaiting a few robust bristles, comforted herself, he was only twenty eight and there was time and said what had been bothering her for a few days. 'My love,' she began and Pimple grinned like a Cheshire cat, melting Cecelia's heart some more, 'I want you to be very careful. We are probably going to be doing stuff with Jack and Mandy that will be...' she stopped, because Pimple put up his stop-the-traffic hand that Jack had taught him and she was already fed up with that, and would have to get Mandy to talk to Jack to talk to Pimple. Cecelia's head hurt, so she carried on.

'What is it, precious?' She responded, gritting her teeth.

'Dick and Duck, darling. You got their names wrong,' and Pimple smiled his beatific, totally innocent smile that she just loved, and then he lolled his tongue from the side of his mouth, which she didn't like, but it was something Pimple had erroneously thought women loved. (You need to read *Road Kill – The Duchess of Frisian Tun* and all will be explained and if you have read it, but can't remember, then get a checkup for Alzheimer's. I can recommend Dr Borodin, Jack's GP. Was it Borodin?)

Cecelia smiled and Pimple's concept of what facial gestures attracted a woman to a man was reinforced and stored in the limited memory bank for later, but he had to forget that as Cecelia was going on about something else and he had missed it. He put his hand up again and asked if she could repeat what she had said. He was ready now.

Cecelia patiently obliged, 'I want you to be careful in the next few days, darling. We are likely to be getting into some difficult situations and I don't want you to get hurt.' She placed both her hands on to Pimple's red cheeks, squashed them so his lips pursed, she giggled at the sight and then kissed them to stop him being offended and carried on. 'Jack gets into all sorts of difficult situations...' She paused in thought. 'And so does Mandy, come to think of it and you do not have what it takes to get yourself out of these sorts of scrapes and I will worry about you. So promise me you will be good and keep safe, please.' And then she kissed him again so that it would stick in the Pimple memory banks, aware there was limited space and secretly hoping it would push out the tongue lolling information. It looked as though she had got her self-preservation point through to Pimple. However, she still worried. She had seen that Pimple, in reaction to an innate desire to protect her, was wont to throw himself into the face of danger. He had done so protecting both Mandy and her when Lady Blanche Teapot had sprayed Aedd's map room with machine gun fire. A stupid, though brave, move and frankly Pimple had no street savvy or reserves of malice, or anger, to call upon to assist him out on the street. He had never tangled with life, let alone life's dangerous misfits.

Pimple rose from her embrace and stood erect, in a standing sense, although he was still naked, apart from one leg in the wrong leg hole of his pants and was feeling amorous. He gave her a *Benny Hill* salute. Jack had taught him that one as well, and then lolled his tongue and said in a lisp, 'Yeth Miss.' She laughed but did wonder if this was her lot now, worrying about her dipstick man?

PART TWO

THE UMBLE PIES THICKEN

TEN

DR JIM SAMUELS HAD MOVED ON FROM Westminster Roman Catholic Cathedral to Downing Street and now addressed an extraordinary meeting. It was a rapidly arranged affair, but needs must as Umble Pie gathered momentum. Sitting around the table were the prime minister, deputy PM, senior cabinet ministers, the heads of the most important ministries and their permanent secretaries, known as Whitehall mandarins. It was unusual for them to be present, but Samuels' request had been more like a demand.

The prime minister called the gathering to order and nodded to Samuels. Each and every person around the table had not a clue what the meeting was about, including the prime minister himself, but they knew Samuels headed up a special division of domestic covert operations for MI5; this would be serious. As a psychiatrist, still with a practice in Harley Street, Samuels knew the type of people now sitting in front of him expectant, curious, and knew exactly how to deal with them.

He had their attention. A nervous tension was in

the air and Samuels played on this, drawing out the intrigue. It was what he was good at, his benign and soft, elderly face, topped with white Mr Whippy bouncy hair, defied the serious persona of this man who exuded control, a demand to be listened to, or there would be trouble and it would not be pretty.

When he felt he had the attendees in his grasp, Samuels started. 'You have each been sent a gift, marked perishable, collectively sent from the leaders of the world's religious groups. The Pope, the Archbishop of Canterbury and the Numpti of Cairo.' He paused to allow the verbal diarrhea of the PM to intervene, aware that a politician not talking would feel they were out of control, no longer loved, whereas in Samuels' line of work, secrets and psychiatry, it was the opposite; sit and listen, give others the space to talk, or in this case, the rope to hang themselves and he did this very well.

'The Pope and the Archbishop of Canterbury have sent me a package marked perishable?' Mackeroon, the prime minister, asked, looking around the table at his colleagues, hardly able to stave off a smarmy superior grin, which Samuels saw as the need for the PM to comfort himself, a need to seek and display self-assurance; it did not fool Samuels. 'I thought this would be serious and who is this Numpti chap?' And again Mackeroon chuckled along with his sycophantic posh school chums, each metaphorically slapping themselves on their comfortably well-off backs at a well served rebuke by their hero, to the master intelligencer.

Ah, Dr Samuels thought sarcastically, what an acutely incisive political mind the PM has, but didn't say, lest it betray his true sentiment. Instead he replied, 'You each have received a gift, sent jointly from the Pope, the Archbishop and the Numpti,' he repeated in order to reinforce what he wanted them to take seriously, 'and, the contents of each gift is indeed perishable. The message on the delivery card is clear and distinct, it says, "You..." and here Samuels drew out the news as he scanned the people present, so that it might best be comprehended in the individual, though shared, sense, "...are perishable".' That was it and the senior MI5 man sat down, only to stand again immediately, 'It also says we are to expect a sign. Well, it actually says, "Give us a sign, oh Lord", which we take to mean we should expect a sign.' Samuels smiled, he was enjoying himself. He loved it when career politicians became scared. When they realised there was more to their job than power, personal avarice and, future cushty job opportunities. Realisation that there might be a risk to life and limb, not in the collective national sense, militarily and so on, for that offered additional opportunities for making even more money, but namely, their own life and limb.

'A sign?' It was Dai Zeeze (pronounced Die Zeesay - see *Merde and Mandarins*), the relatively new smarmy home secretary, floundering as usual and looking to his permanent secretary to explain everything for him, but at least beginning to take this matter seriously, as his position in government demanded. His mandarin, Amlodd Jones, gave him a sideways look, not so much derision as disdain. Amlodd knew what was happening. He knew Samuels well and he knew people from VI6, had met Olive Doyle on a number of occasions

'In the Biblical sense we believe, quite appropriately,' Samuels responded, economic with his words, as was his manner. He cleared his throat, an affectation that indicated he was about to impart serious news. 'I am receiving reports that we may now have this sign, though I need a bit of time before I can confirm this and then I will report to you and hope to Christ, if you pardon the analogy, it does not capture the public imagination.' This is what he said, but in reality he was doing all he could, along with others, to spread the word. He wanted the public engaged.

'Should I telephone the Archbishop? Should I call the Pope, though I have never spoken to the Pope before and this Numpti fellow?' Mackeroon asked, looking to be told what to do.

Typical, Samuels thought to himself. A floundering, overstuffed, self-interested, cold fish. 'I would do nothing for the time being, Prime Minister,' Samuels replied and perused the table again before he added, 'just, be vigilant. We have stepped up security where we can. Where we have the resources.' Samuels could not resist the dig at the vicious cutbacks this government had instigated and were still implementing, in the name of austerity, despite it being previously proven beyond doubt that the measures were not working. Samuels knew there was another agenda for these politicians and, some mandarins, and this was the logic for the targeting ethos of Umble Pie at the government and civil service, as well as the corporations that held the country to ransom.

'Well, maybe we can raise a little extra funding?' the chancellor suggested, his sphincter reporting personal danger.

'We would not want to disrupt the government's fiscal policy, Sir,' Samuels responded with a grin.

'What would be said if it were later revealed we found money for your own safety, but nothing for social security, the NHS, Education, the Armed Forces and so on?' Samuels knew Olive Doyle and Jack Austin would have enjoyed that and he resolved to tell them, for he intended returning to VI6 directly following this meeting to debrief with Olive and then a trip to Portsmouth. He needed to get the *Old* team (Ooh la-Lovelies, DaDa) moving if they were to catch up. He had already received intelligence from VI6 that the Holy Barbaras were on the move, the ominous rumble of devotional roller skates across bumpy pavements now being heard across Spain. The Illuminati still eluded identification by the intelligence services, but it would be reasonable to expect they would be reacting and VI6 had their eye on those members of the *Orders of Caretakers, Hairdressers* and *Bricklayers* known to the Vatican secret services. Samuels found it interesting also that nobody around this table had asked exactly what had been sent to them.

Olive Doyle had explained the Church's concept that the pies were intended to be also a challenge to Christian and all other religious norms, ancient rites and rituals, expected forms of behaviour and censure. There would be other reactionary special interest groups as well and VI6 had reported the *Council of Jesuit Hairdressers,* as well as the *Barbaras* and the *COPS,* were unusually active. The *COPS* particularly so as the Numpti was in town.

'Do we not have security contingency funds?' the prime minister asked, looking first to the chancellor and then to a taciturn Samuels, who allowed his analytical thoughts to deliberate while he looked into the dead eyes of the PM, who, in turn, struggled to maintain the visual exchange. Mackeroon's cheeks and lips quivered. 'What do the Pope and the Archbishop have to say, and this Numpti, why would they send gifts to us... did they actually send them? What was it they sent, anyway?'

Ah, Samuels thought, now they ask, and well they might, as pretty soon their corporate chums will be on the phones asking for action, if they had not already, for this is not truthfully a specifically religious issue, but a moral one. Can the two matters be exclusive? Well, in history they have been artificially detached, but as Samuels had learned from Olive Doyle, this new Pope had released the moral cat among the overly stuffed establishment pigeons.

Straight lipped, a clenched jaw securing a fixed grin, Samuels answered, 'We have not spoken to the Pope as yet. He declined my call. His aide said he was busy praying and had a lot to get through. The arch-bishop was apparently breaking bread, by which col-loquial expression we assumed he was breakfasting and then he was going out on his bike, but I have people on this.' He chuckled, 'Not on his bike, you understand,' and Samuels fractured his face in order to squeeze out a subsequent chortle; it was not amus-ing, it was menacing and everyone around the table knew this. 'The Numpti is currently in London and we will meet with him soon. I also suggest that you, Mr. Mackeroon and Mr. Blogg, as deputy PM, dis-creetly meet with him also, as heads of our govern-ment. I will set it up.'

'Yes, yes, we will meet him, but the gift?' The PM pressed, 'What is it we have each received and you are holding on to?'

'Umble Pie,' Samuels replied.

'Humble Pie?' the chancellor questioned, knowing intuitively he would not have a clue as to what it felt like to eat humble pie and, he certainly had no intention of dining on such a humiliating dish.

'No, Sir, umble pie.' Samuels responded, emphasising the dropped *H*. 'It is a pie made from offal and entrails.' Samuels observed the *yuk* reaction followed by speedily composed cabinet faces of vacant stares and spurious intelligent interest and so, he elucidated. 'In mediaeval times, if you were out of favour with your lord, you were not allowed the better cuts of meat and were forced to eat the umble pie at a lower table, with the plebs, if you pardon the expression now popularised by your ministers. It was a form of public humiliation. A sign that you should have to answer to a higher power. In this case, we believe the implication is that the higher power is the Public... the People,' Samuels thought for a moment, raised lengthy arched white eyebrows and added, '... or maybe the Church? In its more caring guise?'

Samuels was careful to mark that it was the benign side of the church, as he was aware the reactionary sects were mobilising. Frankly this worried him more than the pies or the public rising up, though he thought it was the appearance of the pies that had been the catalyst to generate this reaction within the factional fundamentalists and now, there was a report of a dancing nun, miraculously raised from the dead. This is what he thought DaDa should monitor, namely, Jack Austin, heaven help them all, he thought; Samuels refused to call Jack, Dick, or even Jane, for that matter.

'The reasoning... we presume...' Samuels continued to expand languorously to the open mouths of the cabinet and their Aides, '... is that you have got your policies... err, disastrously wrong... and, you are, if you pardon the expression... crucifying the people for your own particularly selfish agenda.' Now Samuels did enjoy that and so he continued to rub salt into the newly opened wound, before denial could close it. 'I understand this gesture is the derivative of what we now call, and as you previously observed, "Having to eat Humble Pie"'.

'Humble pie!' A collective and easily anticipated false bravado of arrogant rejection resounded around the table.

The prime minister stepped in to cool the outrage. 'Are you saying, Mr Samuels, the church believes we have overstepped the mark? We have got things wrong? That we should admit to this publicly and change our ways? Apologise to the people? Is this what you are saying, Mr Samuels?'

'Yes,' Samuels replied, matter of fact. 'Though we still need to establish that the Pope, Archbishop and Numpti did indeed send the packages (he knew they had, but had to suggest he did not), but no holy smoke without fire is the MI5 motto in these cases.' It wasn't, but Samuels thought it quite apt and, within himself, he chuckled some more, while externally he maintained his appearance of cold and calculating alertness, which he reinforced with an applied stern visage. It was what they expected of him and he wasn't about to disappoint.

There was a palpable silence in the room, which did not last long, as you would expect with career politicians and pretty soon this changed to one of, ironically, righteous indignation, expressed no more fervently than by the deputy prime minister, Mr Blogg, 'How dare the church censure us!'

Samuels waited before responding, allowing the gathered power men and women to join with the deputy prime minister's sentiment. As the hubbub subsided, Samuels reacted. 'First off, as I said...' and he offered an accompanying audible sigh, expressing a degree of frustration that the politicians around the table heard only what they wanted to hear, '...'First off,' he repeated, 'we are not sure if this is the church. But, the sentiment expressed by the humble-pie metaphor is one that is popularly shared. It is something we in MI5 monitor closely, as you would expect of us, despite our much dwindled resources. And, if I might be so bold, your concerns about radicalised Muslims may be just a mild irritant, a convenient holy smoke screen, compared to an all-encompassing sense of disquiet throughout the populace, yet to be collectively expressed. But, we expect it. Despite the renowned temperament of tolerance and the easygoing nature of the British people, this will break and probably soon and, as I have said, we certainly expect it. And, when it does...?'

Samuels drew out the final statement and left it hanging in the ether, in order to emphasise something that MI5 considered a definite risk, almost a reality and that the public reaction, when it finally came, would be violent and widespread. You can only push the British people so far. Admittedly, Samuels knew that the British could be pushed further than most nations' peoples, but the reaction, when it came, would be proportionally larger in scale and come as a greater surprise, as the volatility would appear almost out of the blue. MI5 expected it. Well, they would, as they were also engineering it. They had their own agenda to getting the country back to a more balanced form of governance, knowing you cannot keep taking and never give. The people had been bled dry by an arrogance that defied comprehension by any well-balanced, ordinary man or woman.

The PM made to intervene, he was not pleased being spoken to like this, but before he could get going, Samuels halted him with a look that would be admired by any headmaster directed to an errant boy. 'And, if I might be even bolder,' Samuels continued, intending to be quite bold indeed, 'you have disdainfully ignored the fact that the ordinary man and woman in the street has suffered diabolically under your austerity measures. Measures brought in to deal with problems that they, truthfully and reasonably, see as no fault of their own. Add to this the fact that the economic solution to this catastrophic failure of the monetary system was so neatly presented to you recently and yet, after just a few months, you reverted to your previous self-interested policies. In short, you have learned nothing or, you have, for presumably personal and selfish reasons, chosen to ignore it. This is what we are dealing with now; the *Day of Judgment*, you might say... is here.'

Samuels paused and scanned the culpable, greedy, naughty children, all that is except Amlodd Jones, who Samuels knew was off his own hymn sheet or, if he was honest, he was off Jack Austin's sheet of Welsh hymns and arias. Amlodd was their source. Their man in the ministry and, as permanent secretary to the Home Office, although he had been lumbered with the sleaze ball, Dai Zeeze as home secretary, whom he could, at least, steer how he

wanted. Amlodd was second only to the Cabinet Secretary. He was a powerful mandarin and very useful
indeed.

Confident he had their full attention again,
Samuels continued. 'In short, you are facing a peasants' revolt, if you forgive the Wat Tyler analogy,' and
then Samuels sat back down and reclined in his seat,
folded his arms across his chest, gripping the lapels of
his finely tailored Saville Row jacket, giving the appearance of a relaxed comfort, but in reality he was
coiled, ready to spring. He had been trying to convey
this message for some time, aware people like these
sitting in front of him, Amlodd excepted, found it
nigh on impossible to see around themselves or their
own personal agendas. They found it impossible to
comprehend what was actually happening in the
country. Happening to normal people. The suffering
of the people, and this was especially difficult when
they had their noses back in the trough. It would
blow, Samuels was certain of that. The metaphorical
messages from the church might be just the catalyst
that a revolution could, and probably would, engen-
der, and the powers that be would look to him and
MI5 to sort out the mess and reestablish the old order,
of course. It has always been the way, the state needed
to keep the plebs down. MI5 was needed to enforce
the *Riot Act*. This was more easily achieved when it
was the natural order of things, but these were no
longer the good old Victorian times. The people had
tasted life outside of the gutters and runnels and they
would not go back to where they were currently being
herded. There would also not be a compliant police
service as they had been devalued and reduced in
strength and with morale at rock bottom. The fear

was that they would join the insurrection when it came.

The art and mettle of the MI5 man would be profoundly tested. He had in the past tried many methods to achieve a balance in society but it had not worked and sometimes, every now and then, every culture needed a revolution. It would come and Samuels considered it his task to control it as best he could and, to make it as effective and yet as safe as he could. He and VI6 had the plan and it might just work with a minimal body count. He hoped, but had no way of knowing for sure, once the blue touch paper had been lit. The problem was that Samuels thought that Pandora's Box had been well and truly opened and now there would be no way of closing the lid and, furthermore, he was not sure he wanted it closed. Things needed to change and maybe this was the impetus that many had been waiting for? Ironic it should come from the church, he thought, though he was still not convinced. Not convinced that the church could think of such an idea, despite Olive Doyle's reassurance this Pope was behind all of the moves, for he was convinced they had bought into it, but Samuels had decided not to push too hard. The means maybe justifying the end? Who knows? Olive Doyle certainly knew more than she was letting on, but it was a hypothesis Samuels kept foremost in his mind and, not for the first time, he wondered about this amazing volte-face of the mainstream church. What caused this to happen? And, as he expected, his little lecture had had no effect whatsoever on the cocksure, egotistical tosspots seated around the table.

'Well, what is MI5 doing about this?' the prime minister demanded, standing, already fed up the meeting had gone on longer than he wanted and happy to pass the buck. 'Liaise with the Home Office Mr Samuels,' the PM said nodding to Amlodd, 'and Zeeze will keep me briefed.' The PM made to leave the room as the home secretary reacted to being called into action.

'Who do you have on this?' Zeeze asked, as a schooled sycophant automaton, albeit in a *Bella figura* slick, Italianate intonation, his dark hooded eyes bullying and menacing, obscuring the coward behind.

'The best I have,' Samuels responded, knowing that his revelation was about to cause a serious stir and he settled to enjoy the reaction.

'Can you tell us?' the home secretary pressed, miffed at what he considered a supercilious grin on the MI5 man, who had pressed ahead and not consulted with him.

'I will be briefing the OLD team,' he replied and the grin widened to a full on cheesy smile.

'The OLD team?' The deputy prime minister inquired forcefully, demanding an explanation, but with a hint he might have made a fool of himself and that he should know what this was.

'The *Ooh La-Lovelies, DaDa,*' Samuels replied, equally forcefully, concealing any hint of hesitation or indeed the nervousness he always felt when he sent Jack Austin on a mission.

There was a rattling collective drawing-in of breath, a sort of inverse death rattle, some knowledgeable and concerned looks, some expertly masked confused faces, as to the meaning of this *Can-Can* terminology. People were aware that some secret mission codenames were as mystifying as the missions they named and not everyone around the table had full security clearance. The PM stopped in his tracks. He knew the name. He returned to his seat and lowered himself slowly, while some of the cabinet ministers repeated under their breath, "Ooh La-Lovelies, DaDa? The OLD team, shite." The intonation an indication that things were serious and there was a contagious, dubiously shared knowledge. Nobody wanted to be seen as outside of the loop.

Mackeroon seemed to wind himself up as the full impact of the suggestion and his knowledge of the implications registered. 'What?' The PM lifted himself from his seat as he spoke, the formation of the Ooh La-Lovelies, DaDa and their induction into the MI5 ranks, had been drifted past his desk and he had signed off on the proposal as it was MI5, even though he did not really understand it. He rarely understood anything he was asked to sign, but he did know of whom constituted the team and more especially, who would lead it; Jack Austin. To emphasise his clear displeasure as well as a comprehensive misunderstanding of State affairs, the PM suggested. 'Should we not call a meeting of Cobra (the UK Government crisis management committee) before we rush into things?' the prime minister asked, thudding back into his seat, trying to look relaxed and in control, though clearly still lathered.

Samuels answered, clear and direct, cold and emotionally detached, even though the PM's outburst had vexed him. 'We will need to call Cobra into action, certainly, when we know what is happening and we need the state to rule on appropriate action,' and under his breath Samuels muttered, 'Heaven help us.' He continued, 'However, things have already gone too far and we, MI5 that is, need to act now. You, gentlemen, ladies, you need to accept my decisions on this, for the time being at least and, I have decided. Oh, and be careful, despite what I have said, we will step up your security for the time being.'

Samuels stood, 'Mr Zeeze,' he spoke directly to the home secretary, with a cursory nod to Amlodd Jones, who already knew what was happening. Amlodd was *Chapel*, and was already alerted to murmurings that the reactionary *Welsh Caretakers* were energised. Brooms, mops and buckets, had been heard rattling in cupboards up and down the hills and the valleys of Wales. Samuels continued to address the startled Italianate home secretary, 'We will speak later this afternoon, when I expect to know more. In the meantime, I do not imagine anyone of you will partake of your Umble Pie,' and he departed the room, gurgling in amusement, picturing the government choking on their humble pie, though, he was truly worried.

Following all of the shenanigans of the financial crash and its subsequent effect on the ordinary person and, the still confidential intelligence learned recently of Bellands, a *Something in the City* power-broking company that had ruthlessly manipulated the markets and life generally, and all to their own advantage, Samuels was aware that the hierarchy of the Catholic and Protestant churches, and indeed the Coptic church in Egypt, had long been claiming that the world had descended into a devilish chaos. Though rarely combined in joint protest, the churches had recently been sharing a platform that conveyed the message that we now lived in a world so corrupt and dystopian that, if people had not been so hell-bent on survival, keeping their heads above an artificially created saturation of national and personal debt, the people would see just how the perceived mockery of democracy had duped everyone.

Things would blow and he needed to steer the explosion and ameliorate the damage. Samuels knew that this country, this Europe, this world, the churches had jointly declared, was no longer a nurturing, civilised society as the people had been educated to believe, it had evolved into a humiliating Age. A fact that the church, in all of its guises, seemed intent on pointing out to the people, believing that once the respect of the Church's credentials, lost, some say since the end of the First World War, had been re-established, then a firm moral control could be taken back on the country's tiller and then, who knows where that could lead?

Samuels saw all of this and had talked it through with Jack Austin, Olive Doyle and Father Mike O'Brien and they had called in Sebastian Sexton, who even now was working away analysing and promulgating suggestions from within his cemetery shed. Indeed it was he who had suggested a *Rite of Spring* to the Pope, apparently. Although Seb rarely left his shed in the cemetery, he did like a bit of ballet, as did Jack Austin, of course. And then the penny dropped. Jack Jane Austin, ballet, *Rite of Spring* – so Austin had not retired, he just pulled strings from the sidelines as an intensely motivated socialist and now Dadaist.

Of course, there was self-interest for the churches. Samuels could not ignore that and surely Jack Austin would have thought of this? The greater good, or God, and all of that, Samuels thought to himself and then wondered just how much Jack knew, or Olive Doyle knew, for that matter. He needed to speak with DaDa and Jack in particular. If he was not mistaken, he would not have to tempt the *OLD* team out of retirement. The *Ooh La-Lovelies, DaDa* were already on the case. Weren't they? He felt quite energised, he also enjoyed the fifties fashions, not that he would indulge, and his mind drifted to the *Just William* books. When younger, he had had a secret crush on *Violet Elizabeth Bott*; there was something about a girl with a lisp and he thought of Twink and cringed.

ELEVEN

MEANWHILE, IN THE SCHOOL ASSEMBLY HALL, Winifrede danced joyously around the new Holy Spring. Mother Superior was becoming increasingly annoyed and so she left the hall and the twirling, leaping, ballerina nun, to go back to her office to put a call through, first to the Barbaras, they needed to be here and then, to the Vatican, hedging her bets. And afterwards it was meet the press. All moves that had been anticipated.

———

Jonathan Pemble was CEO of *Godzilla Resource and Asset Businesses,* or GRAB as they were known in the City. They were the company set to frack the bajeezers out of the UK. Parliament had not voted on fracking, had not approved the proposals and the current government had no mandate from the people to undertake such a significantly intrusive and inherently risky operation. None of this bothered the government and a sense of social responsibility did not even appear on the radar of the companies with a vested interest. There was filthy lucre to be had, if not initially with the shale gas, then later on when they stuffed the hole full of nuclear waste. Not that anyone knew this yet, but that was the big profit centre; the *futures*.

Pemble, though, had received and eaten of his Umble Pie and deep down somewhere, in the bowels of his corporate persona, lay a decency that had lain dormant, submerged by a career-long lake of megalomaniacal bile. Pemble found, immersed in this swamp of malignance, a semblance of social fairness, a social conscience and he decided he would raise this in a news conference just prior to the board meeting where he would announce Godzilla's withdrawal from fracking. They would commence a policy of whole-hearted investment into passive and green energy systems. He would talk about how he intended to steer his company to consider what they were doing before they marched ahead. They would consider all of the implications and, if it was considered that fracking would damage the country, pollute the water for the people and cause geological mayhem, then they would not proceed. He knew this already, but it was essential the shareholders heard the background to the decision he was about to announce, which was to include divesting the company of their interests in the disposal of nuclear waste.

Pemble stood in the classically proportioned and marble columned shiny vestibule of his company's headquarters in the City of London. The press gathered before him had already been tipped off about the statement and the TV crews were there to capture this momentous announcement. He leaned on a pillar and casually flicked his recently trimmed blond locks.

He was a good looking *Tarzan* of a man and he knew it; he traded on it. He set about revealing his soul and unburdening himself to the national media, informing them that the reported earthquakes, where they, *Grab* plc, had been fracking, would be looked into and that he was sorry, on behalf of his company and, he would conclude with an apology to the country as he set out Grab's new direction.

He was not joined in this thinking and, not just by his fellow directors and shareholders, there were some who did not like the idea of his baring his soul. Passing strange when you think there was more than a tacit link to the churches, Godzilla's institutional investors, but it was not this soul that the *Caretakers of Christ* wanted baring. It was not what they wanted to happen. Their *Order* preserved the old order. They did not want the souls of the people freed. They needed the people just where they currently had them, browbeaten and eventually, once again, cowed to the teachings of Christ. This was how they perceived them, anyway, and oppressed penury assisted in achieving that.

Pemble was interrupted before he got further into his speech, the building caretaker, in his light tan overall coat, passed him by and waved a salute; farewell? Pemble was confused, but dismissed it as something ordinary people did and he continued, spreading his arms in supplication and, as he resumed his *mea-culpa* act, so he was illuminated by an intense light beam. Pemble's eyes screwed, as if blinded by a laser. There was a cracking sound that reverberated off the polished marble walls. The press jittered, then ran. Pemble stood his ground, confident in himself, unaware of what was going on around him. This was not supposed to happen. He expected the beam of enlightenment, which had been in the note attached to his pie, but this was not right. The pillar cracked some more, leaned in and then fell and this corporate Samson was crushed.

———

A Sign? But whose sign?

TWELVE

The Portsmouth News ran with the following headline that evening:

MIRACLE AT ST WINIFREDE'S
Beheaded nun back from the dead and with head

The article was short and sensationally written. Short on detail, because the police were revealing nothing. All of the information had come from the mother superior who claimed also that there was now a holy spring in the school assembly hall, promising that, "After the bluebottles had scarpered" she would be opening it as a site of pilgrimage, of homage for the people. "God has spoken," the mother had said.

The papers had not learned about the ballet dancing as yet. Mother hoped to stop that load of old shite as soon as possible. She had though mentioned it to Father Mike, Priest in charge of nuns, or at least he had said he was, when he telephoned her and of course, as planned, he released the news of the dancing nun anonymously, and the later editions amended their headline to:

MIRACLE OF REHEADED DANCING NUN AT ST WINIFREDE'S

And, pretty soon the nationals were running the story and clamouring for more information to feed the public's desire to feast on this story of *hope*. This was the first shred of hope they had had since the financial meltdown and, eight years of stringent and crippling austerity.

———

St Winifrede's Convent and Roman Catholic School was in the Portsmouth Diocese, their parish church being St John's RC Cathedral and it was from here that the diocesan business was conducted. Lay people, deacons, priests, a pastor in charge of the priests and, the odd monsignor or two popped in and, of course, the bishop; top dog, at least the bishop thought so.

The bishop had received a message from the Cardinal of Westminster that irritated him. He had never been particularly happy that he had been compelled by the cardinal to take on Father Mike O'Brien, generally thought to have assumed the role of pastor in charge of the priests and nuns but, aside from the odd mass, very odd indeed, the bishop considered, Mike O'Brien was very much an independent priest who determined his own course. A priest without portfolio, he had once explained to the bishop in a bulletproof, smarmy, angelic gobshite manner. And, despite regular rebukes from his bishop, Mike always seemed to get off scot free. Missives passed down from authorities hinted at Father Mike being beyond even the cardinal and to leave the mysterious priest to his own devices.

Of course, only a few people knew that Mike, although truly an ordained priest, was in fact MI5. Maybe he was even VI6, the Vatican Intelligence network. It was Mike's role, and had been for many years, to act as conduit for his long standing spook pal, Jack Austin, feeding back to MI5 but after that, beyond that even, nobody knew. Whereas Jack Austin considered himself an enema, Father Mike truly was an enigma. And this explained Mike O'Brien's presence in Portsmouth, his fingers into everything and also his *Teflon* capabilities, having followed Jack down to the city when the country needed specialist intelligence resources in this key naval, military and commercial port and whatever the Church needed, of course.

Samuels left Downing Street and, after a brief meeting with Olive Doyle, which included a wry exchange regarding their appreciation of the Portsmouth News article and how this had been taken up already by the national papers, he was driven to Portsmouth, where he was to meet Jack and Amanda Austin, Father Mike, Pimple and Cecelia, at the headquarters of *Ooh La-Lovelies, Dada,* namely the *OLD*, Austin's house centrally situated within battle-scarred Frisian Tun.

The MI5 Jaguar pulled up outside number five. The streets had now been cleared of rubble and the detritus of armed conflict (see *Road Kill – The Duchess of Frisian Tun*). Council workers and private contractors were beginning the restoration process to return this middle-class street back to its previous imperial glory, the garden walls, such an elemental part in emphasising the serpentine nature of this narrow lane, were progressively being rebuilt with reclaimed bricks, the footpaths restored and the tank track ruts in the road filled and new setts and cobbles built in. It was no longer a weathered beautiful scene, but it would soon settle down and nature would blend once again. The Victorian villa, the former residence of the duchess, still remained as a bullet-riddled, empty stucco shell, like a molar that had lost its filling. A for-sale sign was prominent on the site safety hoarding; the property being assessed for reconstruction. It was anticipated that the duchess would spend the remaining years of her/his life residing at the pleasure of Her Majesty and, a few other inmates with refined tastes, presumably.

Mandy, as her admin role dictated, held the front door open and watched the head of her MI5 division stride purposefully across the short forecourt. She bid him welcome with a light peck on the cheek and this threw Samuels. He was not usually greeted in this manner, but then this was not a normal household. As he stepped inside to shake hands with everyone, his mind was still on Mandy, whom he had come to know well over the past year or so, as she became closer to Jack Austin. He considered her a beneficial newly acquired asset and, although it may not have seemed it, she had had a calming influence on Jack. Really? On the other hand, Jack was, along with Father Mike as his conduit in MI5, a long standing spook, though Mike O'Brien and Jack preferred sitting, neither men being standing action-man spooks. Jack was a definite liability if he stood up and most certainly if he stood up in the field, not that he enjoyed the country, it smelled funny but, and heaven help everybody, he was an exceptional back-room analyst. A skill for which he was particularly able, as it transpired.

However, Pimple and Cecelia Crumpet were new to the fold and background work was still being carried out on them, Cecelia having a rather racy history, as was slowly being revealed, but an experience that MI5 considered fitting; eminently suitable, even. Pimple, however, well, background research on him had revealed that, up until the past week or so, he had been just that, the background, an aristocratic toff, a posh dope, a constituent part, by accident of birth, of the *beau monde* and considered by all, except the aristocracy, as a waste of space. But, Samuels was aware, incongruously, that Jack Austin saw something in Pimple and so did Cecelia, obviously, but he still needed to be convinced. However, experience told him that the opinions of both Austins, and especially Jack's, were not to be discounted, although this came with a degree of nervy trepidation. Not unusual, and the MI5 man was accustomed to this.

He courteously declined tea or coffee and knew Jack would not offer him any of his biscuits; he was set for immediate business. Samuels was another tall man, same height as Jack and Father Mike, six-four, though a lot slimmer, the hint of a life spent with health and longevity in mind, whereas Mike had the look of overindulgence in the communion wine, as a beetroot nose could testify if the pot belly had you flummoxed. And Jack Austin, well, it appeared that his raison d'être was one of careless abandonment. Mandy was slowly reining this in, but sometimes Jack got away from her. Elephant seals can be slippery customers at times and, uncanny for a sea mammal, he had a sixth sense as to where the biscuit tin had been hidden. Pimple was also tall, but in significant contrast, he was awkwardly gangly. A lanky set of posh skin and bones, much the same frame as Aedd Murphy, except Aedd wasn't posh, none of his accents could be considered refined.

Despite Pimple's nervous lack of self-esteem, slowly being attended to by the glorious Cecelia, he carried what he had (some said precious little), a nice-but-dim persona, with all of the grace that a socially advantageous, though incongruous, background provided. He carried his unfortunate features off with an innate aplomb that defied his natural dimwit disposition. He had a natural carriage that Jack said he acquired at a finishing school, although he also said, Pimple had left before they had finished and, it was more like a horse and cart (fart) in the wind, than a carriage. Jack laughed, nobody else did and he put this down to cockney rhyming slang not being taught in schools, like wot it should an' that.

Samuels indicated for everyone to sit. There was no need for extended welcomes, talk of bonhomie and definitely not Jack's shite jokes. It was to be a short meeting, down to business then away back to London. Samuels had that natural persona that exuded command. Jack had mentioned to Mandy once this was something that he and their head of MI5 division shared. It had taken Mandy some time before she had been able to stop laughing and Jack, a little longer to get over the implied insult from his wife, who was supposed to know him well. Mandy had insisted she did know him well, which enabled him eventually to relax, for he knew his wife enjoyed a laugh and so she had laughed again, proving both his and her own point. For the life of him, Jack was not sure he would ever understand women, but then he thought perhaps he did? Was he not consommé in all of the life skills and once again he was self-reassured and, clearly Mandy had enjoyed this as well, though she had had to go outside into the garden to laugh at that one.

Samuels took control and immediately summarised the cabinet meeting, his discussions with Olive Doyle, whom Father Mike knew well and Jack thought he did but wasn't sure, but the others didn't. The MI5 section head highlighted, in a jovial way, the reaction of the senior government ministers and officials to the gifts purportedly sent from the Pope, the Archbishop of Canterbury and the Numpti of Cairo, something that had been more than hinted at by Olive Doyle, but the extent of which was still unknown to Samuels, although it appeared that Jack knew. Why did this not surprise him? Samuels thought.

And then, reverting to a serious headmasterly tone, giving a demonstrable sideways glance towards Jack so that Mandy could see and later interrogate her husband, he set about revealing the crushing death of the CEO of *Godzilla*, the fracking company, news of which still had to hit the media. The implication being, what other signs could they expect and, what did the signs mean? *Godzilla* was not their sign and then there was the apparent, as yet to be confirmed, disappearance of the Pope? Samuels was not able to explain that and he suspected Olive had held back on some intelligence. Then there was the media coverage of the dancing, reheaded nun. How would that play out? The TV news teams were now camped outside the convent school. Currently thus far, an intriguing story, but one that was due to be elaborated upon by Father Mike, naturally, because the press needed feeding, as did the country.

Jack was visibly distressed, which had Mandy confused until he said he liked fucking and liked it even more with tremors and occasionally earthquakes. She shook her head in wonderment at the fracking eejit she'd married.

Pimple laughed out loud and Cecelia playfully punched his arm, to indicate this was not appropriate behaviour. Pimple fell off his chair.

'I say, Ceeley sweet'ums, that's a tad rum,' Pimple said, looking up from the floor.

Cecelia either did not know her own strength or Pimple was a bigger wimp than anyone had previously given him credit for. In the end, it was considered to be a little bit of both. Pimple, after he had retaken his seat, was inexcusably, and confusingly, still laughing and, after he had examined his arm for a fracture, he was able to explain the source of his mirth, the strength of which had withstood a right hook from his beloved. He was laughing at the church, he said, which irritated Mike, but Pimple carried on regardless of the risk to his health on so many fronts. He elucidated, saying this was not unusual behaviour for his Uncle Poopey, whose reputation, in the wag aristocratic and ecclesiastic, and very English eccentric world, was one of being *a bit of a card*.

Samuels was taken aback and he was quickly followed up by Amanda and Cecelia. Jack seemed unmoved, aback or forwards. 'How is Poopey these days Pimple, old chum,' Jack asked, speaking posh. He could not help it, where accents and mannerisms were concerned, Jack considered himself a bit of a comedian.

Mandy corrected him for the benefit of everyone else, explaining she thought Jack meant chameleon. Well of course he did, but he did go on to say, covering his dipstick tracks, that he thought it was his natural sense of humour that made him an exceptional spook and this had the whole table in hysterics, to which Jack took a piqued exception.

Samuels brought himself under control and viewed Pimple with intense eyes and, in a new and potentially useful light. 'You know the Archbishop of Canterbury?'

'Uncle Poopey? Yes, of course,' Pimple responded, serenely oblivious of the picture of amazement on the faces of the people surrounding him. Except for Jack.

'I've not seen Poopey for some time, I think it was at the synod a few years back now, something or other... the spring of twenty twelve. How is he?' Jack asked.

While the rest of the table switched their flabbergasted gaze to Jack, wondering what on earth he had been doing at a Church of England synod, Pimple was able, in a continuing conversational manner, to convey that Uncle Poopey was generally well, though still suffered quite badly with his piles, which, as Pimple further explained, was why Poopey had been pleased to get the Archbishop job as he could sit on big fluffy, satiny, purple cushions and could afford a comfortably sized and padded saddle for his bike.

Jack expressed his sympathetic understanding, aware that haemorrhoids could be painful and suggested he could lend the archbishop a wire brush, if he would like. He thought for a bit, chuckled to himself as a mental picture was conjured, 'Of course, we could always send him Aedd.' And Jack rolled up, and added by way of explanation of his hilarious joke, 'Poopey can sit on his head, as good a wire brush as any Brillo pad,' which, to Jack, was astonishingly funny, though to the others it was just astonishing that Jack thought this funny at all. Pimple did ask what a Brillo pad was, which was considered truly funny; the staff would generally wash up for the Pimples, you see.

Mandy looked at Cecelia with a degree of sympathy. She certainly had her work cut out for her, of that Mandy had no doubt and she was not just thinking about sexual synchronisation, swimming, or scouring of the pans.

'Okay, let's get serious,' Samuels said and Jack and Pimple laughed, then jointly they harrumphed. It seemed Samuels truly did want to get serious. 'Lord Pimple, it may be that we will need you to speak to your uncle for us. It hopefully will enable us to circumnavigate some of the praying and bureaucracy that seems to surround the Church hierarchy, cut through the red, or is it purple, tape?'

Pimple could not stop laughing and he showed hitherto unappreciated spook field skills when he swayed so that Cecelia's right hook, the strength of which we had previously attested to, missed and, as a consequence of her follow through, she found her head in an embarrassing, though titillating, in a synchronised swimming manner, position upon Pimple's lap, not that Pimple seemed to be objecting and he did mention that side breathing was important when swimming the front crawl.

PETE ADAMS

Before any additional rebuke could be forthcoming from the gorgeous Cecelia, Samuels stepped
in to halt both the anticipated physical and verbal re-
posts. 'Pimple, do you know who I am?'

Pimple thought for a moment and sloping his
head, he responded quizzically, 'Mr Whippy?'
Pimple giggled like a small child and Jack and Mandy
just had to join in. It was funny because Samuels had
a thick mop of white hair that waved energetically
like the surf on Bondai Beach and also had the appearance of a *Carpigiani* ice cream cone.

Cecelia looked at Pimple and considered him either a natural wit, or an innate dimwit. She went with
the latter postulation and wondered if it was too late
to reconsider her life choices, but knew that in her
heart, Pimple was the man, or at least, soon to become
a man with her assistance, for her.

Pimple, encouraged by the warm smile he had received from his dearest lovely Cecelia, added information he considered essential background,
unappreciative of the fact that he was in point of fact
the background, as had previously been established
by MI5 and, and establishment background to boot.
'Well, he isn't really my uncle. It's just what my
Auntie Edith used to tell me to call him, when he
stayed over and curiously this always occurred when
my real uncle, Lord Arsekins of Applecrumble, stayed
over in London, at his club, Poncenbey's, don't you
know, for he has a peculiar bent for hairdressing.'
Pimple cut off his illuminating discourse and stared at
the Samuels *Carpigiani* whipped hair and imagined it
with a flake, crushed nuts and chocolate sauce. Tittering, Pimple carried on, 'Many in my family do enjoy
excessively a bouffant, don't you know?' And he

chuckled more vigorously, he was thinking of squirty cream atop apple crumble, in a bouffant manner, we have to imagine. 'My bent, however, is for embroidery, of course,' and he smiled, ducked and dived, but it was all to no avail as Cecelia got him a pearler as he righted himself. Samuels thought she would be good in the field and he was probably right.

Mandy tittered, Cecelia looked at *her* Pimple with a renewed affection, tinged just with a bit of humour at her prospective life partner's naivety and Jack and Mr Whippy rollicked in their seats as they guffawed knowledgably. They had just been offered the lever they might need to get information from the Church of England, to bring them fully on board with VI6, if they were not already, and all inadvertently offered by the archbishop's pseudo nephew. A bonus, Jack loved apple crumble, but with custard and none of the Poncenbey's bouffant squirty cream, shite. He knew the club. He knew of its radical evangelical underground hairdresser reputation and, apart from Claudio the Italian Cutty Sark parrot, he had no liking of the members, though he thought he might do well to renew his friendship with his old apostolic bricklaying chum Derek sometime soon. He had in mind building a garden wall, after he had dismantled the old one that is. Jack was good at dismantling but recognised he may need some expert guidance on the remantling, as was evidenced by the crooked and sloping mantelpiece that had, taking pride of place, the Papal Blessing that Mandy and he had been awarded (see *Ghost and Ragman Roll*), nailed down, so it didn't fall off.

Jack looked at Mandy, curious. She had that funny look he liked so much, but sometimes such

looks came with danger signs he had yet to comprehend fully. Her head was sloping, like a mantelpiece;
did she want to see him horizontal? Did she want sex?
Or did she want to knock him flat with her well
known haymaker? 'What?' he asked, leaning back in
his chair out of haymaker range, thinking also he
might like a ploughman's lunch as an appetiser before
dinner. Whatever you think of Jack Austin, he was no
fool (and I wrote that with a straight face, well just a
ploughman's cheesy grin and a mantelpiece slope).

'Very well,' Samuels interjected into the mirth.
'Pimple, perhaps you would be so kind as to contact
your Uncle Poopey for us, maybe with Jack, and en-
quire as to his knowledge of the Umble Pies, please?'

'I would be absolutely delighted, Mr Samuels. I
shall get on to it directly,' Pimple said as he made to
lift off his chair, but Samuels indicated for him to remain seated, so he sat back down with a thud.

'Perhaps, Jack and Mandy can brief you before
you make the call, Pimple, just so you will know how
to, er, word your enquiry, so to speak?' Samuels said,
rising himself now to take his leave and looking towards Father Mike (who actually was aware of the
Umble Pies, the Archbishop and, the Numpti and,
was already in touch with VI6, of course). 'Mike, you
will speak to the Pope for us please? Full SP if you
wouldn't mind? How far are they intending to go and
all that? Do they need us to act now, or later, and any
preferences?' Samuels knew Jack would converse
with the Numpti and Mike indicated he would indeed speak to the Holy Father and, at that, the department head of MI5 left as an orangey sky to the west
indicated the onset of dusk and shepherd's pie for
Jack; "Red sky at night, shepherd's pie for dinner," an

old English expression Jack gets wrong every time, though he does love shepherd's pie, provided the shepherds had been taken out because the crooks are like fish bones and, he later suggested to Mandy they might have this, with apple crumble and custard for their dinner? This time he was unable to dodge the haymaker; maybe Mandy was thinking of a plough-man's? Jack thought from the floor, feeling his fur-rowed brow.

Following the departure of Samuels, the mirth and good humour of the meeting soon returned, Jack slapping Mike's back, in a manly manner, which fooled nobody and Cecelia knocking Pimple for six, in a gentile womanly nudging manner. Mandy looked on. It seemed simple, what Samuels was asking, but she had known Jack, or is it Dick Dashing, for some time and this had shite written all over it. Dick was in this up to his feckin' neck. And was she excited?

Yes, Duck was; quack.

THIRTEEN

THE FLEA-BITTEN CLAUDIO SWUNG AIRILY ON HIS
perch, a gentle breeze from an open sash window offering just a little unaided momentum and, from his
strategic parrot station above the Cutty Sark bar, this
advantageous position, he kept a close eye on the
Twink mob. It amused the Poncenbey patrons when
Claudio spoke in fluent Italian. In truth Claudio's
English was not that brilliant, it was a sort of pigeon
English, but he was able to convey the *gisteo* to this
Council of Christ's Hairdressers, which included of
course, Lord Arsekins of Applecrumble. Not a main
protagonist and, if the truth be known, he was just an
amateur hairdresser, but he had influence in the right
places and a penchant for bouffant ice cream. He
could be used. There existed pictures, some with
flakes in unmentionable places and crushed nuts.

The Priest-Finder General watched the entrance
door to Poncenbey's in White Horse Street. He was
aware of the council that met in this club and aware
of their agenda. A dyed-in-the-wool, dogmatic, religious hairdressing conservatism, but what concerned
the priest-finder more, was how much they knew of

the Pope. Were they aware that the Pope wasn't the Pope and, if they were, how would they react?

The priest-finder pressed himself against the wall, his mission covert, but visibility did not bother him. Liberato Zondo's apparel gave the appearance, if he appeared for you, of being not inconspicuous. He wore a black silk shirt that hugged so tightly it was possible to pick out a rib or two from the emaciated cage that resided below. His legs also displayed the bones, especially the knobbly knees, adorned as they were in skinny, shiny, black, drainpipe trousers, just a tad looser than tights and these trousers gripped the ankle so the bump stuck out to complement the knees. He had black extended winkle-picker shoes that curled ever so slightly and he wore an all-consuming black cloak. The spooky ensemble was completed with a wide brimmed black hat that shadowed a pasty skull like face, which in turn was shaded by an immense hook nose. He had the look of *the Phantom Flan Flinger of Olde London Town*. Yet, extraordinarily, people passed him by and gave him not a second glance, as if he was invisible, which he was. He was the Magus of the *Illusionati*.

FOURTEEN

THE NEXT MORNING IN THE PORTSMOUTH Cathedral rectory, there was the usual hubbub. Mrs. Owseyfather, the stout housekeeper and keeper of the bishop's Guinness and Dogs Bollix Ale, was busy preparing breakfast for the priests and a separate morning repast for the bishop, who ordinarily isolated himself in his side of the big house. The other side of the massive (if you pardon the Catholic pun) rectory accommodated two priests and a deacon and then, there was Father Mike, with whom even the bishop was wary, and this priest without portfolio wandered within the rectory wherever the fancy took him.

The two priests and deacon sat around the breakfast table waiting to be fed by the comfortably plump, no-nonsense housekeeper who, just as the telephone rang, crashed down a dish of scrambled eggs and a wodge of toast, stacked irregularly on a chipped plate. As she departed the table, she gave a friendly clump to the back of the head of Father Mac, 'Get the phone, you Jock neap,' she said, and went back to her kitchen sink and menial life of dominating the priesthood.

Father Mac, in turn, ordered the deacon to get the

phone. It was the order of things after all, hierarchy still meant something in the Catholic Church and meant even more in the cathedral rectory, albeit seemed not to matter a jot to the enigmatic Father Mike and this view of Mike, was about to be further compounded.

'Good morning, Cathedral rectory,' Deacon Chas answered and the gathered onlookers watched as the cleric began to quiver and stumble over his words. Mrs Owseyfather turned to see a usually cocky and confident deacon stumbling and stuttering into the phone. She went over and snatched the phone from the now dribbling cassocked excuse for a man.

'Yes,' she said, 'who?' and she listened some more. 'Pope who?' Mrs Owseyfather's mouth began to gape also, then she regained control. 'Pope Siderney eh? Yeah Jack Austin, you're fucking hilarious. Now, I have a lot to do, so be a dear and fuck off.' She hung the phone up and turned to the stunned tabled priests. 'Tell that prat Father Mike, when he eventually gets out of the bog, where...' and she looked at a nonexistent watch, '... he has been for at least half an hour, that his moronic mate just called pretending to be Pope Siderney,' she said. She returned to the kitchen sink and plunged her hands into the washing up water, lifted one of her meaty fists out and flicked soapy water at the seated priests and guffawed. The priests sat in drenched high dudgeon, the housekeeper's jokes wore a little thin sometimes.

The phone rang again.

Priests and deacon looked at each other, covered up to prevent being splashed again, just as the bishop surprisingly walked in. They stood and Mrs. Owseyfather got them with half a washing up bowlful.

'Well, is anyone going to answer that?' The Bishop broadcast, aggressive in tone.

The priests and deacon slowly shook their heads, which sent tiny splatters of *Fairy Liquid* bubbles on to the bishop's purple shirt. The splatter looked like one of those pictures a psychiatrist shows someone and says it's a butterfly, when it is obviously two dogs rather attracted to each other and having a go.

'Don't look at me, I can't stand that fucking tart, Jack Austin,' Mrs. Owseyfather responded, threatening some additional bubbles to a bishop, whose face was colouring to match his shirted regalia. The bishop was a man who had led a cloistered life and the brazenness of the housekeeper's language and manner sometimes embarrassed him and left him often not a little unnerved, though comfortably reassured he had settled for a life of singular celibacy.

Eventually the bishop relented and answered the still ringing phone. 'The rectory, Bishop Finger speaking.' The bishop listened for a while, coloured even further and then managed to just get a few words in edgewise. 'Look Austin, shove off, there's a good chap,' he suggested, then hung up and went across to place his breakfast order with the housekeeper, who had omitted to call and ask what his eminence wanted to eat.

'Mrs. Owseyfather, you forgot to take my breakfast order and I have a lot to do today,' he said, a tad nervously. He was wary of this big bosomed and fulsome woman who wore a flowery patterned apron and a matching turban on her head, despite not being of the Sikh persuasion, though she was a good finder at hide and seek, as Bishop Finger knew only too well when he tried to dodge his turn at the washing up.

The housekeeper turned to the bishop, who visibly shrank back into his cassock and mumbled incoherently; a prayer? Probably, and he began to wish he had been wearing his crash helmet mitre, a modern design of bishops' headwear formed in *Kevlar*, which would stop a bullet and even the mop stick from an irate housekeeper, but played havoc with the hair, they were worse than the traditional cloth mitres. It was the sweat, you see, it had nowhere to go and so it lacquered itself to the strands of hair that would stick up in a point and be the devil to get to lay down afterwards.

'You've got a lot to do?' Mrs. Owseyfather commenced her response and began immediately to wind herself up into the full rebuke. 'Legs fucking broken are they? Too bleedin' high and mighty to have breakfast with us in the kitchen, are you?' The housekeeper's response was under way and Bishop Finger cowered some more. 'Bit behind on your prayers are yer, you woolly woofter? What shall I do, stick a broom up me arse and sweep up while I run meself ragged looking after you precious holier-than-thou gobshites, shall I?' And then she barged past the bishop, forcing him to inadvertently take a seat at the plebian churchmen table, while the *Hagrid* housekeeper answered the phone, ringing irritatingly, again.

It was hard to say, as the housekeeper always displayed a countenance of mysterious womanly exasperation, but the Deacon thought Mrs. Owseyfather was a tad miffed and this may have come over in the tone and manner with which she answered the call.

'Yes?' She listened, 'Not, Jack Austin, you say and that really is an Italian accent? Hold on,' and the housekeeper left the phone swinging and bouncing against the kitchen wall on its curly springy cord while she went to the bottom of the stairs and shouted up to Father Mike, still in the toilet: 'Oi Mike, yer tosspot. Phone call for yer.'

'I'm on the toilet,' came the distant thundering and echoing reply, like this would come as a book of revelations to the housekeeper.

'Your time is up number 666,' she called back, snickering. She liked Mike, 'Come and answer the dog and bone, yer faggot (In which observation she was correct, and Mike was not at all ashamed of being a gay priest, indeed boasted of the fact, though he was celibate, of course; "Backs to the wall, chaps," Jack would say).

"Who is it?' Mike called back, undisturbed by the vehemence of the housekeeper's call; he liked her.

'The Pope,' she replied.

'Pope who?' Mike called back, the hint of a chuckle.

'Hang on.' Mrs. Owseyfather said to herself and she went back into the kitchen and picked up the phone, obviously listening to someone speaking on the end. 'Do I sound like Father Mike to you? No, he's on the toilet and wants to know Pope who?' She listened, 'Okeydokee,' she said and dropped the phone to bounce and swing by the wall again.

Back out in the hall she called up to Mike, 'It's Pope Siderney and he said to...' and she relayed the message in a mock-Italian accent, '...wipa yer arsoleh and getta downa to the phonah,' and this all seemed to amuse the bulky housekeeper, as she scratched beneath her turban and then t'other end to attend to her not insubstantial bottom crack.

The bishop passed by. 'Bit of dirt in your eye,

Mrs. Owseyfather?' The bishop rather daringly enquired, though on his starting blocks, ready to make a run for it, 'And I'll have scrambled eggs and coffee in my study, please... yerghh...' The strangled final repost faded as the housekeeper scurfed the Bishop by his hood and redirected him back to the kitchen with a not particularly subtle boot up the eminent Bishop Finger bottom department.

'Table, now, yer doziness,' she ordered.

She could hear the flush of the upstairs toilet and the waggle of the loose doorknob. Nothing ever got fixed in this Cathedral she thought to herself, even Jesus on the wall in the kitchen was held up by a hope and a prayer and a couple of injudicious, though quite appropriate nails and, in all of that, she included the fucking priests, except for Father Mike of course; he was lovely.

Mike appeared, adjusting his trousers and his sticking underpants that in his rush he may have pulled up a bit too hard, as he descended the stairs. 'Mrs. Owseyfather, what on earth would we do without you? I should probably take this call in the bishop's study. May I have a pot of tea, toast, and scrambled eggs, please?'

'Of course you may, Father darlin',' the housekeeper said, patting Mike on his bottom, to send him on his way, while at the same time pinching the pants and giving them a pull, 'and when you have a moment, let me have your pants. I will soak them and put them in the wash for you. You must have had them on for a fortnight now.'

'Mrs. Owseyfather, you are a diamond indeed,' Mike replied as he disappeared into the study, adjusting his trousers and wiggling his bottom as he closed the door. She returned to the kitchen.

'May I have some scrambled eggs, toast and coffee now please, Mrs. Owseyfather?' the Bishop asked, as polite as he could, while demonstrating that he was still in command here, but more importantly, was being a good boy, sitting nicely at the table.

'In a minute,' she replied, 'I have to take Mike's breakfast and tea to him. He's speaking to the Pope in your study.'

The two priests and the deacon splurged their own scrambled eggs and toast as they could not contain their energetic laughter, but that soon halted as the bishop got in a Brahma of a stare that would scare the bajeezers out of any cleric, but not a sturdy housekeeper of mammoth stock. Mrs. Owseyfather batted the Bishop around his un-mitred head for luck. She was a superstitious woman and who wouldn't be, given that she worked with this load of holier-than-thou tosspots, excluding Father Mike, of course, he was a holy gobshite but lovely with it.

———

'Papa Siderney, eh, whatsamattawivyou,' Mike said as he picked up the phone and settled into the Bishop's comfy office chair, feet up on the desktop.

'Mike-a, you sona-of-a spuda (it was a mistake many pontiffs made, Mike O'Brien, so he must be Irish, but Mike wasn't, except Jack and he liked to quote *Father Ted* dialogue and enjoyed cod Irish, especially on Fridays), what tooka you so longa to getta to da phone?' the Pope asked.

'I was inna da bog Siderney, reading that booka

you sent me, 500 *Funny Prayers*, you remember?' The Pontiff clearly did and they exchanged views on various favourites with Mike saying he had only got as far as two hundred and forty three and the Pope recommended that he read two hundred and fifty seven, a personal favourite. A favourite of God as well, he was able to assure Mike as clearly he had run it past the relevant deity and received an amused appreciative response. God was known to be a bit of a card, but you try and tell that to *Zealots Inc*.

Mike looked forward to his next visit to the thunder box, 'We're having a curry tonight Siderney, so I will probably get to two hundred and fifty seven tomorrow morning.'

The Pope laughed and said they had a copy of the book in all of the Vatican toilets. It was required reading. 'So, whadda you want?' the Pope asked. 'Your e-maila seemeda to suggest eet wasa urgent.'

Mike became serious. 'We have an issue in this country and we believe it might go farther afield also, into other countries, though we need to confirm this.'

Before Mike could continue, the Pope reacted, 'Is this about the Umble Pies?'

'It is,' and Mike could not disguise his surprise, though he shouldn't and he didn't, in case the phone was being tapped. It happened, and he should know.

'Why be you surpriseda, did you thinka you woulda be the only onea phoning me to check if we have senta da pies and didn't Olive Doyle briefa you?'

'She did, but so many pies and is it not just you. I think we may be getting some radical reaction within the church cliques?'

Pope Siderney hemmed, indicating he was aware. 'Simply put, Mike, don't aska. I have appointed a

Papal Investigatore, you know heem, I zink. Liberato
Zondo, a very capace magus sacerdote from Maggior-
ino. He maya beeena ina touch, as I also ask heem to,
how you say indagare, investigate the claims from the
St Winifrede's madre superiora, who has a been
hounding me about miracloli in Portsmouth. The
sciocca mare wants St Winifrede's convent and school
declarata a well holyo and pellegrinaggio, pilgrimage
site. Keep an occhio on St Winifrede's Mike and particolarmente, zee madre superiora. I sensea she may
be in cahootes with the Holy Barbaras of Sevilla; per-
hapsa you could sabotaggio her pattini a rotelle, her
roller skates?'

Mike chuckled, mainly because he was always
amused at Siderney's piccione Inglese, pigeon English, but needs must in the world of VI6 and he reassured the Pope he was already keeping a close eye on
the convent. He mentioned the press coverage that
the incident of the resurrected dancing nun was getting, although the intelligence the mother superior
was considering the Barbaras was news and not a
little disconcerting. The last thing Britain needed was
a roller skating Spanish Inquisition; nobody would be
expecting that.

The Pope continued, 'I mayabe need to send a
Padre Zondo to have a parola tranquilla, zee quiet
word with ze nun, Winifrede? Not to esagerare,
overdo this butta to build it up lentemente; a quanto
pare. Apparently, she has not stopped danza since a
getting her capo, head, back, and zee madre thinks she
may be posseduta,' Pope Siderney laughed at that,
Winifrede being possessed. The Pope was,you recall,
a *bit of a papal card*.

After the mirth St Petered out, the Pope remained

quiet, and so did Mike, but the Pope eventually lost that particular battle of nerves. 'Va bene, okay Mike, I will push things on and tornare a voi, get back to you. Will you be in Londra and will you be taking that feckin' suaora, nun?'

'I believe I will. I will meet with Olive at Westminster cathedral, she can take the nun. I have already summoned the mother superior and her dancing nun to meet the Cardinal of Westminster,' Mike answered, 'and tell the cardinal to keep his nose out, please. He's more of a hindrance than a help.'

The Pope agreed. 'Now, if you willa scusi-me, I need to get back, we are watching the Tutti insieme appassionatamente, *Sound of Music* in a minute, it'sa my favorito film.'

'I love that film too, though I think it would have been better with *Barbara Streisand* as Maria,' Mike answered, knowing the Pope's view on *Barbara Streisand*, that she had too big a nose. 'Tell me, Siderney, what would you do about Maria?'

The Pope chuckled in Italian, 'Wella, I wouldn't let her go up in zee montagne so much and particolarmente on her own and I would switch her to a ordine silenzioso and, keep her away from a my le tende, curtains.'

Mike joined in with the Pope as they laughed. 'Okay Sid, be seeing yer, arriva derche.' They said their goodbyes and Mike hung up, still chuckling and settled to sip some tea and enjoy his breakfast, though his eggs were cold.

———

Poopey was apparently still praying, maybe he needed to, Jack thought, but not really believing it. Jack was a non-believer, except in the Church of Egypt, where he denied everything and he was good at that, De-Nile being the core faith of the C of E, North African Continental breakfast division; the church of the Holy Croissant (not Crescent as that was a street in Bath, in the UK).

FIFTEEN

Headline in the *Sun*, a tabloid newspaper
*HAVE YOU SEEN THE ARCHBISHOP OF
CANTERBURY?*

FOLLOWING THE AMAZING ANTICS OF THE
*resurrected and reheaded dancing nun Winifrede, of St
Winifrede's Convent, Portsmouth, there are now concerns for the whereabouts of the Archbishop of Canterbury who is reported to have disappeared. He was last
seen wearing a white cloak with gold, silver and green
embroidered funny patterns and a matching, silly,
pointy hat. He is said to have departed from the cathedral on his bike to get a haircut yesterday, late in the
afternoon and has not been seen since.*

*The housekeeper said she was not worried at first
as he had left his shepherd's crook beside the front door,
in the corner, next to his cricket bat and light sabre and
he rarely left his crook, bat and sabre for more than an
hour or so. The archbishop is thought to be a bit batty
as well as a bit of a card.*

Police found the cloak and mitre in a ditch beside the main A2 road from Canterbury to London. The housekeeper later confirmed that the Archbishop's lime green spandex cycling shorts and coordinated Lycra cycling shirt, which has the logo, "Jesus prefers Sturmey Archer Gears", written on the back, were still in his wardrobe, but his Famous Five outfit was missing from his dressing-up box and, a bottle of ginger beer in the pantry had also gone missing. His hair shirt was nowhere to be seen, but, "This often goes missing – hair today, gone tomorrow" she said. The housekeeper is known to be a bit of a card as well.

The broadsheets went with:

ARCHBISHOP OF CANTERBURY MISSING

The religious world is waking up to tumult this morning. The miracle of the resurrected nun, Winifrede, from St Winifrede's Convent in Portsmouth, who is reported to be ballet dancing and has not stopped since regaining her head and life's breath. And now the Archbishop of Canterbury has reportedly mysteriously disappeared. Police could offer no explanation as to the cleric's whereabouts after finding his cloak and mitre, which the Archbishop was last seen wearing, discarded at the start of the "Pilgrims' Route", home from Canterbury to London.

The archbishop was known to be on his bike, an old dark green, former police constable's cycle of the nineteen-fifties era, with a shopping basket on the front, "A personal favourite of the archbishop", *the archbishop's housekeeper said. 'He would keep it in his bedroom and often I heard him working on the Sturmey Archer gears and pumping his tyres, so to speak, late into the night."*

He is thought to be dressed casually, though in a nineteen fifties manner, "A little like William Brown", the housekeeper went on to say.

The archbishop's close friend, Ginger Flowerdrew (thought to be a pseudonym), said he had not seen him and there had been no secret messages at their hideout. Our reporter checked also with Violet-Elizabeth Bott, real name Susan Doko, who spoke with a pronounced lisp when she told our reporter: "I haven't theen William for thumb time". She had also checked their hideout and he had not been there for the past few days, and if you didn't believe her, she said she would: "Thcweam and thcweam and thcweam until she was thick".

———

'Well, that accounts for that,' Pimple said the next morning, sitting around the breakfast table and reading the newspaper.

'Accounts for what?' Jack asked.

Jack never read the newspaper, he said it was because he couldn't stand the Magnets who manipulated the news, but Mandy knew he just liked her to read it to him; newspaper reading was admin.

'Poopey has gone missing,' Pimple replied, rattling the newspaper and displaying the bold headline so Jack could not miss its wording.

Jack recoiled as if he was having Kryptonite

thrust into his lap. 'Where's Mandy?' he asked, just as she walked down the stairs.

'What is it?' she enquired, having already guessed Jack needed the newspaper read to him, but she never tired of tormenting her husband, in a loving way, naturally.

Jack nodded to the newspaper, now being displayed to Mandy by Pimple, 'Poopey is missing,' Pimple answered, not realising that being admin she could not only read but also comprehend sensationalist journalism.

'What's up?' Cecelia appeared, looking gorgeous in a pink flowery chiffon housecoat that opened just enough for Pimple to observe, in a dirty old man, leering sense, her sheer nightie below. The siren of the news desks sashayed to Pimple so she could massage his shoulders while reading the news article herself; she knew her Pimple, you see.

'It's err, ah-hum, er, thingy Poo.' Pimple replied, already completely distracted, in a pleasant and tantalisingly way, as Cecelia used her perfume cloud to stun her man momentarily, as would a spider paralysing its prey, so that she might best steady Pimple's hands and read. It worked. See, told you she knew Pimple.

The telephone rang and Jack generously answered it as Mandy had now joined Cecelia and the stupefied Pimple to read the news article herself.

'Jim,' Jack said to the phone, then commenced waving it around like it was a sparkler and said to everyone, 'it's Jim.'

'No shite, Sherlock,' Mandy replied, a little irritated as she was now into the depth of the report in the *Guardian*.

Jack was stunned into silence, a quite rare event that generally only ever occurred when he was faced by his beautiful wife in a state of semi-undress, or she was telling him off. So, as Mandy's dressing gown had opened inadvertently, revealing her own nightie, Jack was momentarily distracted and, if you added the picture of sex-bomb loveliness of Cecelia and also taking into account the perfume cloud that had traversed the table and was now surrounding the sideboard where the phone resided, then expecting Jack to return to his normal world of the living dead any time soon was, not unreasonably, doubtful.

Mandy finished reading and was distracted herself by the insect like gabbling that was coming from the dangling telephone receiver. The metre of the chatter was getting stronger and higher pitched and Jim Samuels, for she recognised his busy bee voice immediately, was resenting being dangled by the Lone Dangler. She strode over and took the phone from her husband, who leaned into her advance in an unsubtle pretence of making the handover to administration a more proficient exchange, but really it was a clumsy effort to look down the front of her nightie. He never tired of the view, breastscapes being one of his favourites in the art world.

Mandy sighed, took the phone receiver and bonked Jack on his head with it, in an area where she was aware he had fewer bumps. 'Ow,' he said, and satisfied with his reply, she spoke to Jim Samuels.

'Jim, good morning.' She listened, 'No, I have just read it and not told Jack yet. I think he saw the headline but, as you know, he doesn't like to spoil the surprise for himself.' She listened some more, for an extended period and a frustrated Jack leaned over the table and rattled the newspaper, still in the stunned grip of Pimple's hands. Cecelia had disappeared to the kitchen to put the kettle on. Jack knew that it would suit her, she looked stunning in almost anything. Jack tittered to himself, realising he was quite amusing, especially to himself and he knew this for a fact as Mandy often told him to keep his jokes to himself. See.

Mandy looked across the table to her husband, irritated he should rattle a newspaper at her and titter, so she leaned over, stunning him with a cleavage peek and then bonked him on the head again, and into his largely ineffective, jumbo, taxi door ears, 'What were you laughing at?' she shouted.

'What?' Jack replied, smoothing his two new bumps.

Mandy went back to Jim. 'Have they got a tail on Pope Siderney?' she asked, and listened and then said her goodbyes. (Mandy had forced Jack to tell her all yesterday evening on pain of no cuddles – so he had told her, but whether it was all, she could not be sure and, she had accidentally cuddled him so, as a consequence, he lost his train of thought and became a bus conductor).

Jim was off to Downing Street where there was to be a meeting. Cabinet Office Briefing Room A, referred to as *Cobra*, the room where the government crisis committee meets to coordinate a response to any national emergency, for example, the custard may be cold on the Downing Street apple crumble, or someone wants to invade. It is similar to what the Americans call the *Situation Room* and this one, in England, was nicely situated in the basement of Number 10 Downing Street. It had no windows but the televisions were dressed as mock windows with frilly pink net curtains that could be drawn if there was anything interesting on the telly. There was a TV remote controller, known as the conch, and this enabled the PM to fast forward the adverts from the various arms manufacturers as invariably they watched world events on catch-up.

SIXTEEN

In Committee Room A, in the bowels of number 10 Downing Street, the members of Cobra, senior politicians, both government and opposition, high-ranking military personnel and civil servants, sat patiently awaiting the arrival of Mackeroon and Blogg, PM and deputy PM, who had had a prior meeting to be briefed by Jim Samuels from MI5. As the double doors opened, the members saw a stern looking prime minister enter, followed on his heels by the puppy dog deputy and, a short distance behind, the wolf in sheep's clothing with ice cream cone hair, Jim Samuels.

Everyone stood and then sat following a casual gesture from Mackeroon, who remained standing. 'I am going to hand this meeting over to Dr. Samuels, who will brief us all on the latest Umble Pie developments, the disappearance of the Archbishop of Canterbury and news that suggests the Pope might also have mysteriously vanished.'

The prime minister remained standing and, for effect, he effected his statesman-like pose, a recent habit he had acquired and he had even been caught watching old film footage of Winston Churchill. Heaven help us all, Samuels thought as he ignored PM Mini Winnie and started to speak, nodding for Mackeroon to take a seat and, for the frilly pink net curtains to be drawn, to reveal a composite set of TV screens and an electronic White Board.

The Cobra attendees looked as if they had been smacked about the head by a soggy haddock. Something fishy was certainly happening and not for the first time since the news of the Umble Pies was revealed, it was squeaky bum time. The central TV displayed BBC twenty four hour news with a breaking news strap line:

POPE MISSING, ARCHBISHOP OF CANTERBURY still not found... Resurrected nun still dancing, head remains firmly attached... police say the CEO of Godzilla, who had received a Humble Pie, was about to reverse his company's position on fracking, it is confirmed...

The *strapline* was running below a news item on how the populace of England were more and more taking to wearing plimsolls. Resident footwear pundits appeared to suggest a connection that the nation's feet were deteriorating due to the neglect caused by the deepening austerity measures and, the relative affordability of the gym shoes. A suggestion also that if the trend continued there would be odour issues contributing to global warming when the weather was hot and the air still.

'Bollocks,' the PM said in response to the news item on the Cobra telly, looking down to his own black plimsolls that he wore around number 10 because they were so comfy and he could also run up the stairs quickly if the Labour leader or the milkman called. He would pretend not to be home. It was something Mackeroon was good at, being a slimy hider, lessons learned as a fag at Eton or was it a dog end? It is sometimes difficult to tell at these elite schools, although important life lessons were learned at these top public schools, such as buggery, cold showers and of course, divine arrogance and the right to rule.

Jim Samuels replied, while fiddling with the conch and looking down at his own highly polished black town brogues. 'Not bollocks. However, we are not here to discuss austerity footwear but the disappearance of the Archbishop of Canterbury and now, seemingly, the Pope. And finally, the people seem to be rallying around this dancing nun. They see it as a sign things need to change. You recall I mentioned that we expected a sign? The TV changed and the split screens showed pictures of the Pope, the Archbishop and the Numpti of Cairo, as well as a blurry image of the dancing nun.

'Is this linked to the Umble Pies?' The home secretary, Dai Zeeze asked, as he turned his ankle and glanced down at his diamanté leopard-skin, kitten-heeled town shoes for the fashionable discerning man about town. No plimsolls for him. It was thought that he ran in these shoes also, though not away from the milkman.

'Umble pies, linked, yes. The nun, we're not sure and we are as yet unclear as to the, what's and why's of all that is happening there. My man spoke with the Pope shortly before he disappeared and I have yet to debrief him, to find out what was actually said and whether anything could be read in-between the lines to suggest a planned disappearance.'

Samuels already surmised that there was and knew he needed to pump for more information from Olive and then Jack Austin, maybe via Amanda. He will ask her not to cuddle him so quickly this time. He knew also that this Pope continually harked on, and on, about mitre hair, a bit like helmet hair only more pointy and, Samuels knew also that the place to truly sort this was London, the resident specialist being Twinkle Friseur, barber to all the high ranking clergy, C of E, RC and Church of Egypt, except the Numpti had Fez hair, some considering this far worse as it bunched, which was not quite so modish as pointy. But was this where the Vicar of Christ and the Archbishop were heading, to London? It would certainly make sense and not just coiffeurly speaking. Olive Doyle had also been conspicuously tight-lipped, which he had put down to her overt fondling of Bong's private parts, but maybe her head had been elsewhere, upon reflection, and Samuels smiled in a double-entendre manner.

Samuels was aware that the Numpti of Cairo, the formal head of the Church of Egypt, was already in London. He had slipped in under the radar, arranged for by MI5 and more specifically Jack Austin, who was of course a member of the Church of Egypt, though sometimes, when he was a little peckish, he would pop into the Portsmouth Roman Catholic Cathedral for some bread and a dropeen of holy *Dogs Bollix Ale*. Jack wasn't a wine lover and neither was Jesus, apparently, who preferred ale, *London Pride* and, if that wasn't available, then the next best thing was the *Dogs Bollix*, Jack would tell people, elastically knowledgeable, (he meant having an expert knowledge in ecclesiastic matters – though he did stretch the truth often to suit his personal narrative).

So Samuels tentatively had a direct link to Archbishop Poopey, via Pimple. The Pope via Father Mike and the Numpti via Jack Austin, though that was a dubious Egyptian link at best and, if you were to ask Jack, he would deny it. Denial (De-Nile) was the core faith of the Church of Egypt, as well as wearing ordinary clothes by those people who ordinarily wore a uniform. The Church of Egypt was known, after their traditional flowing ordinary robes, to favour fashions from ordinary nineteen fifties Britain. Was there a link between this and the *OLD* team and the DaDa fashions? Samuels never pretended to know the entirety of what Jack Austin was up to, but it would be a reasonable guess and, if you sought confirmation, Austin would deny it, as would the Numpti, naturally.

SEVENTEEN

Liberato Zondo bided his time outside Poncenbey's. He waited for his update following the meeting of the *Council of Christ's Hairdressers*. Claudio, the VI6 parrot intelligencer, squawked the Poncenbey's low-down in Italian, via the open sash window, recounting the hairdressers' increasingly volatile agenda. The Italianate parrot talk was incomprehensible and highly entertaining to the assembled seven, known only to a few, to be the radical wing of Christ's Hairdressers; *The Jesuit Coiffeurs*.

Derek understood what was being said, he spoke a little Italian, enough anyway. His dad had been the Cardinal of Westminster's bricklayer back in the day, the reason why Jack Austin arranged for him to get the job as Poncenbey's steward, that and he looked good in Speedos. Not that this look appealed to him, Jack had argued to a salaciously grinning Father Mike, who was not averse to wearing Speedos beneath his cassock during mass from time to time. Derek would pass as a bricklayer, yes, but as a *God's Caretaker*? This was another question that was in the realms of hope more than anything else, but Derek had his own secrets and he was confident.

———

There were times when Poopey, who was the eldest of six children, resented his Dad's stock-in-trade expression, "Always be prepared", and his father had walked his talk, literally. When the police came a-calling at their East End of London terraced home, Poopey's dad was prepared enough to be able to show them a clean pair of heels. The only problem was the family had never seen him again and, as a single parent, his mum had been of no use, either. She had to raise the five other kids. His abiding memories were of a house suffused with the smell of the copper stewing nappies, boiled cabbage and cat wee. As the eldest son, Poopey was expected to provide, and that would be in the tried and tested East End way of villainy; you can generally make the hours to suit, you see.

But Poopey, William Archibald, at fourteen, had not a crooked bone in his body and so he appreciated being taken out of the criminal embrace of his East End of London family and enfolded into the clutches of the Church of England, eventually to be whisked off his feet into a parochial school where they saw something in the young Archibald. They coached and moulded him for a career in the church. Not only was Poopey a child with above average intelligence, but his street savvy gave him an edge over other boys of his age and, add to that a silver tongue and handsome countenance, he was soon mixing with the great and the good (especially Pimple's aunt, it would seem). He was comfortable as much with the hoi polloi down the

market, as he was in the Church of England's hierar-
chical and rarefied circles. Post hoc, as he used to like
saying, he made his way up the Church ladder, which
was appropriate in some way, as his father had been a
window cleaner when he wasn't using the principal
tool of his trade to get in and out of other people's
houses, nicking things.

Poopey's dad, had he been around, would have
been proud of his son, for Poopey was prepared and
had been for a little while now. He knew what was to
happen. Things had been a long time in the planning.
He knew what he needed to do. He knew the allotted
tasks that would fall to him because of his position
and he had issued missives to all of his cathedrals, to
thence be sent on to the smaller churches and onward
to the people. It was to be a nationwide gathering and
they would know when to gather, for there would be a
sign. His bike was in good nick, the Sturmey Archer
gears oiled, axles greased, tyres pumped, chain strong,
pedals firm, the shopping basket capacious and now
holding his doorstep bread, spam sandwiches, ginger
beer, emergency *Mars* bar and his well-thumbed and
read Bible.

Poopey was pleased at last to be taking direct action. As archbishop, William Archibald felt that despite the ever-present resistance from the church
establishment with whom he dealt daily, he needed to
mend the church's ways. He also felt he had a personal penance to exorcise. It was simple, he had seen
that the church had remained passive, had stood by
for so many years and watched the populace of England, the ninety nine per cent, be trodden into the
ground by the one per cent, the corporations, the career politicians in the pocket of the powerful, the

landed gentry, many of whom were a part of his church and sat in the House of Lords ruminating in an alcoholic haze of personal and institutional self-interest, aggrandisement and avarice. Revisions to the structure of government over recent years had just been peripheral tinkering. A sop to the people that had had no real effect. It was business as usual and Poopey, although he had risen on this almost relentless tidal wave of vested interests, knew he needed to do something. For too long, the institutionally narcissistic Church had neglected its people. It was time for change and things would change. The people would rise up, his only fear being the hurt this might cause but, needs must, and it was increasingly looking like the only way.

And why this personal penance? Well, he had stood by and risen in the church, enjoyed the trappings and comfortable lifestyle. He had his own crook, light sabre and cricket bat, even though it had been as clear as day to him what was happening; his raison d'être had been, after survival, a personal fulfillment. Furthermore, it was *his* people suffering, even more so within the interminable recession and unremitting austerity measures. The Government spin doctors rammed the message down the throats of the people that things were recovering. Well, they might be for a blessed few and he counted his church in that, but it was not for *his* people. The working class, and even the middle classes, remained well and truly under the cosh, limping from one week to the next, focused only on survival, living the hand they had been dealt and, believing what they were continually told, that they should be grateful, distracted from the reality by propaganda and endless banal TV programmes; the opiate for the rabble.

Unaware that head honcho cathedral caretaker Basil Jackson was listening in on his mea culpa moment, he had agreed his penance at the Canterbury tomb of Thomas Beckett who, in his ethereal reply to Poopey's pledge of atonement, had suggested the plan, the route and then, in a rather picky way, so typical of saints, suggested Poopey do penance for all of his extra-marital affairs. Now, this was a bit excessive of the saint, in Poopey's view, but he took it on board. Wouldn't you?

"Will no one rid me of this troublesome saint?" Poopey had mumbled, unaware Basil Jackson had heard and that his sect of Holy Caretakers viewed William Archibald as a troublesome priest. Basil had been commissioned that at the appropriate time, he was to assist the Archbishop in his final elevation in the Church of England; a martyred Saint. The Archbishop was to be executed at the altar of the cathedral. But when? Basil followed orders and figured he would have to bide his time and he followed as the archbishop left to go to his bike he had locked up by the pulpit, a regular thing. "Thieving bastards, you couldn't trust anyone around here", the archbishop regally told his flock.

So, with the caretaker looking on, Poopey showed the cathedral a clean pair of heels and made an *undetected* getaway, or so he thought, cycling along the old Roman Road of Watling Street, the route of the Pilgrims from London to Canterbury, only going the other way, home to London after a bit of guilt-ridden praying with Beckett.

The going was easy in places on part metaled

road, but on the country paths and rutted rural ways, the tough cycling conditions befitted his personal penance. The sweltering summer sun reinforced his act of contrition, sweat soaking into his hair shirt, lumpy and irritating beneath his powder blue, short sleeved shirt, tucked into his voluminous khaki shorts. His plimsolls, encapsulating his worn and holey white socks with potatoes at the end so his big toes stuck through, he knew, would whiff excessively.

He slept under the stars, comforted by his Bible and the continual ringing tone of his mobile, set for the *Treble Bob* peal; forward four, back two. He had recently changed the ring tone from his normal *Back Rounds*, bells ringing in order of pitch, treble to tenor, because he was known to have this on his phone and he did not want to be instantly recognised. He did consider the Whittington's change as a rather apt peal, but in London this might be too familiar. So he sought God's guidance and, through Beckett, He had suggested the *Treble Bob*.

The almost continual ringing he appreciated, though he studiously ignored answering. It was a part of the plan as he looked to see who tried to contact him. Who texted? Who was worried for their vested interests and who actually cared for his well-being? He was tempted to reply to Pimple, but Poopey knew Pimple's family were a part of the one per cent, screwing the country, even if they were not particularly aware as they had a lineage of ownership and inherited earnings that came naturally to the Pimple family. A divine right, they would assume, so much so they would never begin to question it. Poopey did concede, however, that Everard Pimple had a grain of conscience and this had been reinforced with his latest exposé work with Cecelia Crumpet, which had impressed the archbishop. It had not, however, received a favourable response from his council of self-interested advisors. He would return the Pimple call to brief him and his journalist partner as soon as he had safely entered London.

He entered the capital on the second day. He locked his bike to the railings of Southwark Cathedral and made his call to Pimple before he embarked on the short walk across London Bridge and into the City, the business district. Target number one. "And the Lord Spake unto me, follow the pies", he said to himself, quoting the scriptures; Proverbs, steak and kidney, chapter one, verse two, the King James version, with gravy.

———

Basil Jackson was not amused at the disappearance of the archbishop. He passed on his intelligence to his comrades in brown overalls. Basil considered (as he had been told to consider and he was, if nothing else, an obedient foot soldier caretaker) William Archibald to be a radical thinker, not what the church needed if the country was to be steered, in the *right* direction, by the *right people* with the *right and proper* moral compass.

Basil was instructed to pack up his broom and toilet plunger and leave Canterbury to meet up with colleagues, as well as representatives of other allied sects, in London. The Caretakers generally met at their formal headquarters in Shepherd Market, but those hallowed halls, well, two rooms above a café, were not for other groups. The Shepherd Market base was reserved for formal functions and the deliverance of disinfecting edicts, known as *Dettols*. No, when they met en-masse in London, they would usually select one of the larger membership London host establishments and, this time, it was considered that St Thomas' hospital would suit just fine, principally because it was just across the River Thames from the Houses of Parliament. Ideal, and things would be sorted, at least as far as the archbishop's responsibility in the Church of England and the House of Lords were concerned. How this would be resolved in the Catholic Church or the Church of Egypt, Basil could not begin to comprehend and, he was not even sure if his brotherhood, *The Caretakers of God*, should have allied themselves with *The Jesuit Hairdressers, the Bricklayers* and the *Coptic Orthodox Nile Synod* (The CONS). But, he had been told this was the only way and he had gone along with it, biding his time, and when the time was right, the *Caretakers* and their brothers, the *Electricians of Voltaire*, would resume their rightful place atop the hierarchy as protectors of all Christianity. God's chosen artisan sect.

Singular in their resolve, all of these groups had avoided any liaison with the *Barbaras of Seville* and who could blame them? It was reverently hoped that their mother superior, *Miss Babs,* would stay in Spain.

So Basil folded his tan dungarees and, along with his caretaker's ceremonial regalia, he packed the brown vintage, reinforced cardboard utilitarian suitcase that bore beside the latch locks the symbol of the Caretakers, an inverted broom standing in a bucket, adjacent to the double lightening symbol of the Electricians, and he made his way to Canterbury Station to take the train to London.

EIGHTEEN

GIORGIO SIDERNEY GRISSINI WAS NOT A RADICAL thinker, neither was he what you would call a down-to-earth man. He did not have his feet on the ground, and why should he? He was the Pope, for Christ's sake. To say Pope Siderney was a reactionary, would be to underestimate the dogged dogmatic Catholic fundamentalist he had become and, still was, except he wasn't, actually, the Pope any more. Well, he was Pope, but he was not poping, because he had been spirited away some time ago and, kept secure while a doppelganger, Fabio (Sid) Smith, had taken his place. It was one of the smartest moves ever made by Father Mike O'Brien and Mike knew this because his brother in all things dastardly, Jane Austin, Jack, or maybe Dick, as the name had begun to grow on him, had told him so. Except the doppelganger they had inserted was English and a bit toffee-nosed. But Fabio's mum had been Italian and so he could speak the language fluently. And though Siderney didn't particularly resemble the real Pope, this was a small matter that Father Liberato Zondo had sorted long before Sid took over the papal seat, which was a lovely chrome yellow with gold tasseled bits and a deluxe, comfy, purple sat-in cushion.

By degrees, and over what had been nearly eighteen months, Sid, as acting Pope, had eased back on the strict interpretation of the Catholic Church's doctrine and a new, more caring Papal guidance was emerging; proclamations that favoured humanity and not extreme Catholic dogma. Sid was aware of the ever-present threat from the various secret organisations that claimed to protect the sacred teachings of the church, but this audacious plan, the concept of Father Mike and Jane Austin, sorry, Dick Dashing, had to succeed. The ground was fertile. The populace was ready for what he hoped would be a bloodless revolution led by the churches of the world, Roman Catholic, and the two C of E churches of England and Egypt. It was a daring and simple plan, but there would be mantraps along the way and Pope Sid was aware of them all. He was aware of the risks and not sure if he was capable of surviving, but he trusted in the ever-faithful *Illusionati,* and, of course, Claudio. A lot rested on the flea-bitten wings of his beloved parrot.

Of course some people, especially those cardinals closest to the Pope, had their suspicions, but they could never prove anything. Zondo was the best. The enchanted veil he had cast was impenetrable and, who in their right religious mind would challenge the *Illusionati?* The *new* Pope knew also that if he maintained the cardinal gravy train, at least for the time being, then his identity would not be questioned to any depth. Zondo and Claudio had his back, which was a great relief to him.

And now the not-quite-apostolic likeness, following on from the vanishing act of Claudio, had gone on the missing list. He was presumed to be seeking the whereabouts of the papal parrot and, a barber to sort his mitre hair, but that had been two days ago. The Vatican had only just released the news. The last thing they needed was a line of Barbaras from Seville offering to ply their sanctimonious, questionably pious, roller skating trade at the Vatican, but unknown to the papal intelligencers, the Barbaras were not on their way to Rome, but to London, where nobody was expecting them.

———

Cue serious, dah, dah, daaaah Dada music – some of Stravinsky's best, The Firebird, especially for Claudio.

———

Ben Ali Aziz, known as Azzer to Jack Austin and Father Mike O'Brien, was Arch Numpti of the Church of Egypt. There were some, however, who considered it more important that Azzer was one half of the Egyptian flowerpot duo, Bill and Ben Ali Aziz and, both had arrived in London almost two weeks ago, though in different modes, both fashionably in conveyance and where they stayed.

Ben was settled, staying with Jack's sister Doris who had a little two-up, two-down, terraced house in Stepney, East London. Jack thought he would be safe there, discreet, secret. Bill was also incognito and staying at the Dorchester. Who of the two flower pot Egyptians had the best deal was questionable. The

Dorchester is one of London's finest hotels, but they could not match Doris's apple crumble and custard, a favourite desert dessert going back in Egyptian history as far as the Pharaohs and, some thought to have originated as a Nubian favourite, before it was brought back to England by Sir Sidney Carter's assistant archeologist, Jack (the sarcophagus) Austin. (Dick's great, great, great granddad, on his Egyptian mummy's side – though Dick thought he was a bit of a tosser and most definitely he was not a favourite of his great, great, great mummy, though he had to concede, he was a fair pharaoh explorer).

Culinary aspects to one side, the Dorchester was ideally located, just up from Buckingham Palace, where the Mall ran down to Trafalgar square and Birdcage Walk. This ran on to Parliament Square and, with Whitehall completing the third side of the triangle, Downing Street was encapsulated as the *eye* central in the triangle. Parliament was at one apex, Buckingham Palace at the second and Trafalgar Square the key third. The triangular symbol of the Illusionati was thus created and it was here that the planned culmination of Umble Pie would take place, successfully the churches hoped, with the enforced dissolution of the current parliament and government and, a new set of codes established, to be voted on by the people, for the people.

The triangle of religious ferment would then be set in the capital city. Other arrangements were being made in cities and towns across Britain and this would all be coordinated by a TV broadcast of the dancing nun, if all ran to plan, dancing in Trafalgar Square to music played by the Nuns' Orchestra, con-

ducted by none other than the non-nun, Bea Flat, recently resurrected herself and receiving modest
attention from the press, but not in the same league
or as celebrated, as Sister Winifrede. So secular and
godly sectors of life were represented, each with their
guiding light and those lights were women. It was felt
necessary for the light to be female as it was seen as
symbolically non-aggressive, healing, nurturing and
peacemaking. Incredible? Yes, it was, but sometimes
the simplest of plans had the most potency and, most
of all, it would all be unexpected. Any challengers
would not have time to prepare a defence other than
knee-jerk reactions that the churches and the DaDa
expected and hoped they were prepared for.

Though the heat on the streets of London was
building as summer took hold, it was not as hot as The
Numpti's native Cairo and he eschewed his flowing
robes, which would be sartorially and physically
cooler. He wore today his knee length Boy Scout
shorts, Cubs shirt with its sixer stripes that he loved so
much and in which he would dress up at home and
his new plimsolls, courtesy of Dick Austin. Plimsolls
were not always available in Cairo where they
favoured aromatically more acceptable open-toed
sandals.

Ben, The Numpti, was ready to leave, but still
looked into the mirror, continually fiddling with a
leather woggle that tugged loosely at his yellow-and-
green scarf and, after a while, he bid farewell to Doris
and stepped out, assured by Doris (as much a bozo as
her older brother) that he blended into 21st-century
London streets. He still wore his official fez, which he
acknowledged might be a little incongruous and this

is what Ben Azzer imagined people stared at. Jack had told him that if he took his fez off then they would stare even more and reassured the Numpti he knew an expert in fez hair. Azzer hoped so, because even in Cairo, the fez capital of the world, there was nobody truly proficient in the fez haircut department. So, people wore the fez continually, even to bed and when attending Brownies.

Bill Azzer also dressed in fifties fashions. He did not, however, like the scouting attire favoured by his more elevated brother. He preferred the *William Brown* school uniform, quite popular in Cairo among the Church of Egypt lower echelons, though some of his colleagues aspired to a Baden Powell attire with a wide-brimmed fez. There had even been a meeting of the Egyptian Synod to vote on whether the lower order of the Church should discard their customary robes in favour of British nineteen fifties schoolboy attire; the vote narrowly failed.

Bill had his instructions and, shod in his leather open-toed sandals with rattling buckles, like the spurs of a cowboy, he stepped out of the Dorchester hotel on to a bustling Park Lane. Bill set in action his part of the plan, which was to gather supporters in Hyde Park. It was agreed they would rent boats and hold their meeting in the middle of the Serpentine to avoid electronic listening devices. What could go wrong? But first he had a task. The Dorchester hotel had been chosen for his stay, the compelling advantage being not only that it was located opposite Hyde Park, but also adjacent to Shepherd Market. And this was the direction Bill took in the first instance, ignoring the ignorant posh jibes at his fez hair and unsubtle suggestions he should go to Twink's and shouldn't he be dressed as a cub or a boy scout. Determined, Bill Azzer took his seat at a corner cafe where he could monitor the various HQs of the sects, in particular Poncenbey's.

NINETEEN

Derek left early the following morning. He had work at Poncenbey's. Babs, Derek's wife, baked, pleased her husband had left, he did not approve of her sideline in pies. The local butcher had become suspicious of her regular purchases of considerable quantities of offal and so she went to her brother, a porter at Smithfield's, the London wholesale meat market, slap bang in the centre of the City, not that Babs saw the irony. Babs's brother now brought home increasingly larger quantities of offal as the demand for pies grew steadily and although she was pleased for the extra income, the neighbours had begun to complain about the "something offal" smell.

And still Claudio returned with orders for more pies.

She wondered what her husband would think of her. Was she losing it, taking orders from a seedy Italian parrot? She was unsure of her husband's view or even if he was aware of the extent of the parrot's influence. She worried also, not just for Derek's role in Poncenbey's, but how much he knew of what was truly happening. Babs knew her husband could be a bit dodgy in the brain department and she relied on Dick Austin and Claudio to protect her husband when it came down to it, as it inevitably would. Dick needed Derek to help him build a new wall as a part of his grand plans to landscape the garden to the rear of the Dick and Duck, Frisian Tun villa – so there was an incentive. She trusted in that, knowing also that Dick was more than a sandwich short in his picnic department, just like her husband and, as crazy as it sounded, it was exactly in times like this that you needed to surround yourself with loonies.

Babs was waiting on Claudio, pulling aside the net curtains, looking out of the front window, anticipating the arrival of the rag-and-bone man with his horse and cart.

(*In London, a rag-and-bone man collects unwanted household items and sells them on to merchants – rarely seen these days*).

The freshly baked pies were collected every morning, early, by Ted the rag-and-bone man, who dozed on his seat while Babs loaded the cart. The pies were packed into individual cardboard boxes and clearly labelled in English and Italian so Claudio could read them. Nelly, Ted's nag, showed only marginal interest in the stacking activity and wafting aroma, more interested in getting back to her cool stable for some hay and oats.

Babs often wondered where Ted, or more accurately Nelly, took the pies. God only knew, she thought to herself, quite appropriately when you think about it, aware only of the good money she was earning and the brighter future it held for her family.

She was not aware that the TV News was now reporting incidents of company policy being reversed here and there, as well as corporate officers making *mea-culpa* stands after receiving a pie. Currently it was only business news and so it went over the heads of most people, but not so the dancing nun. Winifrede had everybody in the country glued to their TVs and radios, anxious for news of the miracle and what would happen next. There were also pictures of the resurrected Bea Flat conducting the Nuns' Orchestra, along with news of a free concert being planned in Trafalgar Square, to be broadcast nationally and, sensationally, the dancing nun might dance while Bea conducted The Nuns' Orchestra.

Nelly generally knew her way around London, though even this experienced and knowledgeable horse was on occasion guided, which was just as well as Ted was inebriated most of the time and couldn't see his nose in front of his face, even if he'd had his eyes open and his bottle-end glasses on. So Nelly would trot off, negotiating the East End streets and on into the *Square Mile*, the City of London business district, while the snoozing Ted gave the impression of steering. Today there were pies to deliver in the City and additionally it was important that the PM and dep PM be *legitimately* delayed in Downing Street. This was Nelly's true mission of the day as the plan began to fall into place.

In the City, business people hurried and scurried, marginally frustrated by the plodding of Nelly and her cart. They were important people, or so they thought, but the rag-and-bone man was a feature of Old London and was tolerated, if only reluctantly. If these very important people, in their own opinion, spared just a few moments from their busy self-engrossed agendas to look up from the pavement where they avoided eye contact, and tore themselves away from mobile phones glued to their ears, then they might have been amused by the rag and bone man with a parrot on his shoulder, the bird calling out in a thick Italian accent and seeming to guide the horse; "Lefta here righta here, stoppa the lighta she isa red. Giddyuppa".

At various points, City messengers, lads often from the East End themselves, would appear from the service areas of the big corporate office buildings and take the pies, Claudio giving direction as to where and to whom the pies were to be delivered. Nelly was a bit slow but they had time; Claudio did not need to be back at Poncenbey's until just before lunchtime.

After delivering the final pie for the day, Claudio said his farewells to Nelly and flew to a small and seedy hotel behind Euston station. He had a message to deliver. Nelly knew the way home, even if she could be a bit dodgy with the traffic lights, motorists made allowances for this legend of the City of London. She would have her horse lunch and then, it was Downing Street in the afternoon for Nelly.

———

Cabinet Room A saw the reassembling of the Cobra team, thinned down this time to just the essential snakes. PM, dep PM, home secretary, leader of the opposition, head of each section of the armed forces and Tony Davenport from MI6. Davenport was there to introduce the worldwide aspects. Pies were being delivered all over the known Christian world, and Egypt, where they were generally ignored and thought to be another pyramid scam.

Brian Graveney was disgruntled for he was doing essential maintenance work in the committee room and had been dismissed. He worried if he had done enough. And, in his tan dungarees, he lugged his bag of tools away. He was the Downing Street caretaker, a part of the furniture and attracted no attention, not even from Jim Samuels, but Mabel was guarded as she passed a steaming hot pie to her boss in the corridor and tipped him about Graveney.

After placing the Umble Pie in the centre of the Cobra table, Samuels took his seat. Although everyone knew the pie was baked entrails and offal, the aroma was sublimely mouth-watering as lunchtime approached.

The lights unexpectedly dimmed.

Everyone looked around for an explanation, from each other and then from Samuels, who shrugged; he had no idea. There was a gentle whooshing sound, a breath of welcome cool air passing across clammy faces. The net curtains covering the wall of TVs, swayed and parted and as they ruffled mesmerisingly, a spotlight, seemingly from no visible electrical source, zeroed in on the prime minister and a second seemingly celestial beam picked out the aromatic pie. It was as though this pie, or at least the metaphor, was meant for the PM. Then, as quickly as the visual effect had manifested itself, so the light beams vanished and the table and room lights returned; normality resumed.

Mabel, picking up on her cue, entered with her tea trolley. 'Cooee, light refreshments,' she called out and, ignoring the stuffed shirts, she began distributing small plates as if she were dealing each member a hand in a game of poker. The committee members looked on in bemusement. Not so much Samuels. It was not unusual for Mabel to enter the secure room, she had clearance, but today she strutted confidently, her bearing demonstrating a commanding presence. This was not the ordinarily modest and demure working class charlady. The birdlike woman leaned over the table and cut into the pie, a series of equal wedges, which she then distributed. Each steaming slice oozed a rich, dark brown gravy and belched a sensual aroma of cooked offal and entrails into the stuck-up noses of government ministers, the military and mandarin monkeys. Mabel ordered them to eat, clipping the deputy prime minister's ear as she made to leave. 'And that's for the tuition fees, you fucking tosspot,' she said, and wheeled her trolley to the door.

'Mabel, come back this instant,' the dep PM commanded, though he looked as though he was adjusting his body position to contain a watery bowel movement as the tea lady returned and leaned over Blogg, a menacing sight, this incongruously robust, stick-insect woman, in a flowery apron and headscarf, minus only a fag dangling from her mouth and a rolling pin. She was prepared to take on the might of the establishment.

'Yes...' Mabel threw down the gauntlet.

'Err...'

'Cat got yer tongue...?' Mabel challenged the deputy prime minister, whose colour drained from his face.

'You can't talk to me like that.' Blogg managed to say, although he did not look confident and wondered if he should be in this job and, whether Mabel could in actual fact talk to him like that? Well of course she could and, of course she would and she did.

Mabel flicked Blogg's nose with her finger and thumb. 'You are a duplicitous tosspot... any questions?' Blogg searched around for his spine but couldn't find it. It was the yellow thing that ran up and down his back, connected to his sphincter, Mabel pointed out. Not for the first time, Samuels thought that maybe it was a mistake to have put Mabel in this job, but she was one of his best operatives and MI5 was now alert to the caretaker after feedback from Mabel. 'Thought not.' Mable said, 'Eat yer Umble Pie, sunshine and, if I might respectfully say, about time too,' and she looked around the table and everybody picked up their forks while she stared. Mabel's stare remained threatening until each and every one of them had eaten a mouthful of the pie.

Mabel left and, as the doors to Cabinet Room A closed, the squeaky wheels of the tea trolley could be heard disappearing down the corridor. Samuels made a mental note to ask Mabel to oil those wheels, but then he thought that maybe she knew what she was doing as he observed the noise grating on the frayed nerves of the attendees. Would they change? Would they apologise, mend their ways? Probably not. Did the beams of light signify something and, if it did, who had arranged for it? The caretaker? And, what did it signify?

———

Poopey made his call to Pimple before crossing London Bridge, heading to his first target, the London corporate headquarters of Ma-Santy.

———

Pope Siderney, who wasn't really Pope Siderney but Fabio Sid Smith, surfaced in a seedy hotel behind Euston Station. How come he drew the short end of the straw, he thought to himself as he shuffled and stuffed his robust frame into the tiny shower cubicle. He made a mental note to sort Father Mike as soon as he could, but making due allowance for his general slippery nature, it was by the grace of God, in the guise of Father Mike, to whom he owed this elevated pious station, not Euston, although there is something sanctimonious about this major London rail terminal. The plans were going well, too and, although he had heard that Bill Azzer had drawn the Dorchester straw, it could be worse. He could be staying with Jack Austin's sister Doris and he thanked God and Father Mike for small mercies.

As an ordinary priest, Fabio had oft been viewed as a radical, an agent provocateur, and this had held him back for many years in the establishment church. However, he had come to the attention of Father Mike, who felt the radical firebrand fitted right into the mould he wanted.

Even so, Fabio growled and mumbled to himself. He had given up a cosy rural parish, where his basic needs were generally well met, where he had plenty of time to dictate his revolutionary pamphlets and, although the relative opulence of life as a pope was desirable in theory, he had found it a little too rich for his comfort. Gradually, he had been reducing the standard of living for his papacy, establishing a more frugal lifestyle to be continued by future popes.

However, his principal annoyance, though he was comforted by being back in England, the birthplace of his father, was the loss of Claudio, his faithful and longstanding parrot companion. But needs must and Fabio understood. Claudio had explained it to him in Italian words of one syllable, like "eh" and "wot" and "bozo", and it was effective when Claudio spread his wings and shrugged his parrot shoulders. And, if Fabio was honest with himself, Claudio seemed pleased to be back to his old undercover ways. Fabio had helped the parrot through a difficult period of convalescence after a serious altercation with a set of pigeons in Piazza San Marco in Venice and that particular rebellion had been put down, but at a cost to the then VI5, and now VI6 (Papal intelligence on Foreign soil) parrot.

As Fabio emerged from the en-suite, like a cork from a bottle of wine, he could hear a tap, tap, tapping on the window. His mind drifted to the *Sound of Music* as he moved to the raggedy curtains dragged across the window. Not even Maria could make play clothes out of these, he chuckled as he tugged them apart and his heart burst with papal joy. The deprivations of the hotel were completely forgotten as he saw his parrot sitting on the window ledge, pecking at the window. He already knew the sash window was stuck fast behind centuries of paint, as his sweltering sleepless night could attest. There had even been a moment when he considered smashing the window but didn't.

'Claudio, mi belissiamo bambino,' Fabio said, slipping easily back into Italian.

'Eh,' Claudio said, spreading his wings, shrugging his parrot shoulders and nearly losing his balance on the window ledge. 'I thoughta I'd tolda you notta to call me that, it's a embarrassing,' Claudio replied in pigeon English.

'Whatsamattawivyou?' the Pope responded, already a tad fed up with his parrot, who looked like a slightly more colourful version of the raggedy curtains. Claudio must have had a long night and he felt immediately guilty. Christ, who'd be a Catholic? He promised himself a few Hail Mary's later and then felt better.

'What is it?' Fabio mouthed through the fixed glass.

'I'm outta of seed, dipsteeek,' Claudio beaked back a reply, chuckling to himself.

The Pope thought, what did he do to deserve a parrot with a sense of humour and then asked, 'What do you really want?' And Claudio said he wanted to make sure Fabio knew exactly what he was expected to do and to make sure he didn't mess it up like so many times before. Claudio looked exasperated with his pope, as Fabio recalled trying to nick some buns from the housekeeper, back in the simple days. What a catastrophe that had been! He again remarked to himself that celibacy had its merits and what was it with housekeepers to priests? Blaming the parrot didn't work, either, even though it was Claudio's idea.

Reassured that his pope knew what he expected of him, Claudio flew off to return to Poncenbey's. If he flew fast there might just be a little time for some seed, a packet of cheese and onion crisps and a *Cinzano Bianco* before the lunchtime gathering.

TWENTY

PIMPLE CLOSED THE CALL, LOOKED FIRST towards Cecelia then at Jack Austin, who guessed at the caller. 'Poopey?'

Pimple nodded, 'Yes.'

'Southwark?' Jack asked.

Pimple nodded again. 'He's just locked his bike up to the cathedral railings.' He swiveled his gaze to the gorgeous Cecelia, 'I have agreed to meet him with Ceeley after he has been to Ma-Santi and few other corporate offices.'

Before Cecelia could respond and ask what he was doing at Ma-Santi, Father Mike appeared having let himself in via the back door. He bounded in like *Tigger,* through the kitchen and on into the dining room. 'Whatto, everybody peeps,' the priest called, mimicking both the posh Pimple and the cockney Jack, before taking a seat and summoning some breakfast from the steaming Mandy. For a dipstick priest of dubious piety, Mike relied a lot on the goodwill of God to safeguard him, but it seemed to work.

'You know what,' Mike said.

'No,' Pimple and Jack replied.

'That bleedin' nun is still dancing, the soppy mare. Still, she's getting a fair bit of news coverage and you know, a movement is building faster than we expected.'

'Possessed?' Pimple asked, and both Mike and Jack nodded yes.

'Possessed... my eye,' Mandy responded, irritated. She flicked her head at Cecelia and the two women went into the kitchen to plot and, they might just make some brunch while they were there. Jack had started getting up later so he could have brunch, which he considered made him particularly avant-garde. He therefore skipped breakfast and then he could skip lunch, skipping being a part of his keep fat regime. That, and hopping, and go directly to tea, though this was often limping to the scones with a nutritional intravenous drip fortifying him. Jack struggled missing meals and wondered how the Yanks survived, eating brunch all the time and no breakfast. But Jack was nothing if not *aving-a-guard*, as he constantly informed Mandy.

'What is Olive Doyle doing about the nun? And more to the point, Pope Siderney?' Jack asked of Mike.

Mike smiled his beatific gobshite grin. 'She's going to ask Grace and Lilac, remember them...?' Jack nodded and Pimple shook his head, which didn't bother Mike but did mention that Grace was MI5 and Lilac a DCI at Scotland Yard. 'Well, she's going to ask them to get the prancing nun and bring her to Westminster Cathedral. The Nuns' Orchestra will be playing in Trafalgar Square with Winifrede dancing. Olive and I thought that this might fit well. Maybe we should all go up on the train.'

'Oh,' Jack responded, now distracted as the smells of brunch hit his nostrils that were far more effective than his ears, so he missed Mandy calling for him.

'On a train?'

'Yes Pimple, why?'

'Oh, nothing, Mike. I just thought it might be a bit obvious, a dancing nun in a carriage full of people?'

'It's okay; they'll put her in the guard's van.'

'The avante-guard's van, Mike. Oh, ow!' Jack followed up as Mandy flicked his head in a previously bump-free zone.

'I've been calling you.'

'You have?'

———

They wore stripy schoolboy pyjamas, some a washed-out blue and white, others a dull ochre or an insipid green stripe. Each wore a vibrant crimson fez, though one stood out. He wore a very tall fez, approximately three feet high, like a stovepipe top hat, only with loads more spiders' legs of black string hanging down the side than the shorter hats. The owner of this magnificent fez was Wahneferhotep, the Vizier of St Mary Cray, in Kent, and the leader of this radical breakaway Christian group of the Coptic Orthodox Nile Synod (the CONS: a form of reactionary, counter-revolutionary, Church of Egypt Tory party – not very popular in St Mary Cray, but they added a bit of local washed-out colour).

Hepzefa, the second in command and high priest of hair styles, ran a small and undistinguished hair salon in this small Kent village nestled beside the River Cray. The local people were accustomed to

seeing Hepzefa, early, every morning, way before
brunch time, come rain or shine, summer or in the
depths of freezing winter, taking his pyjama-clad dis-
ciple hairdressers down to the River Cray to act out
their rituals. They would wash their hair and then
their ritual rollers, combs, scissors and hair grips, to be
cleansed of their sins and bad hairdos in the blessed
water of the Cray; a river full of holy sticklebacks.
They would collect a small amount of these tiny fish
and take them back to the salon in a jam jar with a
string handle. The sticklebacks would be fed
throughout the day with the blessed dandruff of the
pharaoh. Remarkably, the fish thrived to be ceremoniously released the next morning. Unless, that is, they
were to be taken on a mission; like today.

It had become a familiar sight in St Mary Cray
and the typically British, tolerant residents, those who
were up that early in the morning, had become used
to seeing seven, sometimes eight skinny men, loosely
wrapped in schoolboy pyjamas, each with black-stub-
ble-encrusted faces, prominent cheekbones, poppy-
out eyeballs and relatively new plimsolls, cavort and
sand-dance their way to the river accompanied by
Tchaikovsky's Swan Lake. It was a rendition played
on Egyptian pot and pan pipes by a famous Nubian
recorder player; the recorder priest. This recorder
music had a choir of wailing Egyptians emanating in a
gentle waft of mystical music from a Cairo-ghetto
blaster carried on the shoulder of Kawab, high priest
of music and dance, who also did the shampooing and
dandruff zapping. This high priest of lyrical accompa-
niment leapt and pranced in a practiced manner in
front of his troupe, holding out in front of him the
Holy Jam Jar of Sticklebachus. It was his mastery of

the string looped handle that meant he never spilled a drop of the revered river water from the jam jar.

What looked like Swan Lake played out the morning after a particularly spicy Jalfrezi curry was in fact, a dissembled form of Japanese calisthenics, called Tabata, which was brought to Egypt during Eighteenth Dynasty, the Armani period. This period of ancient Egyptian history was noted for an influx of Italian fashionistas and Japanese tourists, some of whom stayed at the invitation of the Pharaoh. And, it was this form of ancient Middle and Far Eastern beating up that later became indelibly associated with King Fu of Nivea, a region in southern Egypt where the people were noted for their lovely complexions. The art form later developed as an ancient form of warm-up prior to a battle.

The steps of the St Mary Cray Cops were carried out in silence, just the eerie strains of the Tchaikovsky pot and pan pipes and the prerecorded wailing, as the disciples stepped and spun and crouched and, cart-wheeled, jete'd, and pretended to fire invisible assault rifles into the air, much in the style of Japanese pharaohs, as they made their way to the life-sustaining river.

The River Cray was England's anointed Nile. A river of holy stickleback fish, which the CONS would collect in their little fishing nets and put into the jam jar and, just prior to a battle, two of the tiny fish were ceremonially stuffed up the nose of the vizier, who then blessed them and snorted them into the sham-poo. It was like holy water, but it foamed and cleansed the unwashed hair of infidels. They would then be ready. They would fight them on the beaches of the Cray and the floors of the British salons.

These were the much feared reactionary, *Fishers of Men*.

Today was a special day, as Wahneferhotep, the vizier, was present. Today was to be a day of action. This was the day they had waited for and prepared for. Fed sticklebacks for, and stuffed them up the nose of the vizier for. Thus, they were ready, suitably trained and washed in the river and, following this ritual cleansing, they would return to the salon to have their hair done, the bit that sticks out the sides of the fez, before setting off to London, probably after brunch, which consisted of apple crumble and custard with snotty stickleback sprinkles, if there were any left over.

———

Heathrow and the midmorning flight from Spain touched down on time. They had no luggage, save for a carry-on *Samsonite* vanity case each and, one by one these cases were examined at customs. Special Branch officers had been warned to greet this plane from Seville and to especially look out for the seven identically attired women; nuns on roller skates. As the nuns glided to the customs desk, so each case was opened to reveal only the tools of the trade for hairdressers, a profession that their immigration forms declared the nuns to belong to. Orthodox Catholic hairdressers. They were nuns, but not following the strict discipline of the current Catholic Church, they were a reactionary religious cult. *The Barbaras of Seville*. Precious little was known of this group of malcontents, a regressive group of nuns, other than that they had distanced themselves from the recent teachings of the Pope. They had been responsible for the issuing of many counterrevolutionary pamphlets, calling for the Church to reclaim its parishioners and guide them back to the dark days of mystery and godly power. To righteous perms and Tory blue rinses, and each nun carried pictures of the Mrs. Mouldwarp, Margaret Thatcher, who had been, unknown to many, a *Barbara of Seville*. The former PM of the UK had secretly worn voluminous flannelette navy blue knickers when she carried out terribly caustic acts in the name of setting Great Britain back to the subjugating true faith.

The Barbaras were barbers but with a barbaric streak. They were a modern day incarnation of the *Spanish Inquisition* but on roller skates and they relied on nobody expecting them and, the people generally didn't. And so, in secrecy, the Barbaras plied their evil trade in the name of God, exercising deft skill in torture with their hairdressing tools, tints and perms. It is said that some people left the Barbaras' inquisition with hair that was too difficult to describe, such was the horror they had had to endure. A perm from Hades and marked out for life.

TWENTY-ONE

THE SEVEN *JESUIT HAIRDRESSERS* HAD MET EARLY
in Poncenbey's. Well, it was early for them. It was
eleven and some looked decidedly shabby for this
break of day, crack of their dawn call. Claudio would
be cut. They knew this. The CCTV had shown that,
over the past week or so, the bird had magically made
his escape via a mysteriously opened window. How
did the window open? The window was shut and
then, it was open. It wasn't Derek, whom they all had
first suspected, after all, who else could it be? There
was an expressed relief at the steward's innocence;
they liked Derek, even more so when he wore his tan
dungarees when unblocking a drain or assisting in re-
lieving members' constipation. Well they would, he
was well built if you got the drift and we are not
talking about a brick wall, but they would not hesitate
in disposing of him if they suspected he was batting
for the other side.

Derek had been reluctantly accepted into their
fold as a quasi-Caretaker of God, a functionary of the
new alliance between the Brickies and the Hairdressers. Not that Twink was comfortable. He was, if

anything, piously sceptical. It seemed also that Derek's wife, Debs, was not aware and had never seen him in his dungarees, except when they played games in the bedroom; Debs played Mrs. Overall. The Poncenbey hairdressers had no idea that he did bat for the other side. Derek was an opener in the Bricklayers' eleven and had even played at Lourdes, where he had hoped and prayed for a miracle as the England cricket team hadn't won an ecclesiastical test match in ages.

Before the club closed for the night, Claudio was always put back into his cage. A print cover of Mary Magdalene (looking uncannily like Margaret Thatcher) with a blue rinse bouffant hairdo and the Sistine Chapel as a background, was draped over the cage. However, when Porky covertly stayed over in the club the night before and, after Derek had locked up and left for home, Porky, who was, as his name suggested, an exceptionally fat, though gifted hairdresser and keeper of the holy Jesuit Doughnuts and *Haribos*, had crept into the lounge and, lifting the Maggie Sistine Chapel cloth, he had found that Claudio had disappeared. But how? He checked the CCTV, which the club members rechecked again that morning and there was no evidence as to how Claudio had made his escape. It was a mystery. Or, was it a miracle? After all, there had been a lot of those lately, not least a resurrected and reheaded dancing fucking nun. The Jesuit hairdressers kept an open mind.

Derek was in the kitchen preparing midmorning coffee, to be served with tiny almond puffs. These were a favourite with the Council of Christ's hairdressers and indeed his own religious clique of caretakers (but not the bricklayers, who liked Cornish

Pasties – the tiny delicate ones), who believed also that it was recorded that almond puffs had been a part of the Last Supper. They were viewed as a sort of petit fours, though there may have been more of them at the Last Supper, possibly thirteen, and maybe they had been quite big and on the far side of the table, just outside of artist shot. Henceforth thirteen had forever been an unlucky number for all hair stylists. The Caretakers were not superstitious, nevertheless, they were always suspicious regarding the number thirteen. But, it was the number two that caretakers were most wary of and many thought this was why they always carried a holy plunger and a bottle of blessed spray *Domestos*.

Derek was alerted of the council of war taking place that in all reasonable understanding of alliances, he should be a part of and he was astutely cognisant of the abrupt silence that greeted him as he entered the lounge to deliver the coffee and sacred pastries.

'Derek,' Porky slobbered through spittle-ridden chops, 'where ish Claudio?' White foam dribbled from the corners of Porky's mouth, making him look like an effeminate wild and rabid boar.

The steward looked bemused as he turned to the empty cage, the vacant perch above the Cutty Sark, then back to the council of radical Godly conspiratorial hairdressers. Answering the foaming Porky, 'I have no idea, Sir,' he said truthfully, but the council looked as if they didn't believe him. They were aware that the historic order of Christ's Caretakers considered themselves a notch above all other radical dogmatic religious groups. There were some who thought they were in actual fact, the very secretive and all-powerful *Illuminati*, whereas they were in

reality, the not-quite-so-influential, *Highlighti,* and
Twink dwelled on that thought, but was soon distracted.

'Eh, whatsamattawivyou? Iffayou don'ta believe
him, give himma Polly-giraffa test,' and at that rather
witty aside, Claudio, who had appeared from
nowhere and was now strutting confidently across the
floor from a door that had been previously closed,
rolled his wings and squawked a hefty guffaw that defied the petit form of the bird. The hairdressers looked
at the parrot with mouths agape. 'Closea your
mouthas, we areanotta a codfeesh,' Claudio said,
mimicking *Mary Poppins,* the Italian dubbed version
that they watch in the Vatican. It was a well-liked
film, second only to *The Sound of Music,* though
Claudio was convinced the Robin redbreast on
Mary's finger wasn't real and it sort of spoiled it
for him.

Claudio jumped on to the bar. 'Okeydokee, seed,
an agua minerale Dewek, per favore,' he placed his
order and hopped on to his perch, from where
Claudio assumed control of the meeting, as was his
perceived feathered position in the pecking order.
Claudio was wary, the atmosphere in the club was
tense, and those who understood the subtleties of
parrot plumage and body language would have noticed that uncertainty. Claudio sloped his beak. This
meeting was unscheduled. He was uncertain of
Derek, who was now wearing his formal tan dungarees and Claudio thought he might need to act sooner
and, now he was alerted. Was the Pope walking into a
trap? He squawked a message to Liberato Zondo, in
Italian, via the now mysteriously fully opened sash
window. Zondo acted on the Parrot's instruction and

headed in the direction of Berkeley Square and Twink's salon.

How did that window open? The barbers thought and then all said, but they soon folded into fits of laughter as the Italian parrot hopped off his perch on to the bar and danced a Mumbo; a rhythmic dance of Caribbean origin in 4/4 syncopated time, with a heavy accent on the second and fourth beats. A favourite of Italian parrots and Claudio rhythmically shuffled across the bar while Derek played the spoons. Claudio and Derek both thought, for their own various reasons, that this was a seriously dozy set of viperous zealot hairdressers. They could be so easily distracted, but he may just have underestimated the parrucchieres (hairdressers in Italian parrot talk, which is the Italian version of pigeon English).

———

Ben Azzer was accoutered in his *Famous Five* Boy Scout ensemble for the day. It was his favourite. Khaki suited his complexion and also reminded him of Linda, his best camel back home, and loved the startling contrast of his cherry red Fez. It was an important day and he wanted to look his best for the Ooh La Lovelies, DaDa. He would ordinarily wear his white flowing robes on a state visit, but this was not really a formal trip and he didn't care much what he looked like for the prime minister, the Pope, or the archbishop, for that matter. But, for Jack Austin and his wife, the Numpti had dressed with care. He knew just how important such matters were to the Austins, well, Jack, or Jane at least, or was it Dick?

He set off for Waterloo station to meet the

Portsmouth train, not realising he was followed by a troop of cavorting ballet dancers dressed in nineteen fifties, bleached out, striped schoolboy pyjamas and each wearing a red fez, one a very tall stovepipe fez with extra spider leg dangly bits.

———

Grace and Lilac had argued, which had almost become a norm in this very new relationship. But Lilac, who was ordinarily an assertive and strong police detective inspector in the Met Serious Crime Unit, had ceded most of the decisions so far in the relationship by dint of the fact she loved Grace. She did however, reassure herself that she was being conciliatory because of her wounded shoulder (*see - Dead No More – Rhubarb in the Mammon*). In this minor matter of travelling to Portsmouth to collect a cavorting nun, to be delivered to Westminster Cathedral, Lilac had been adamant. She was accompanying Grace, despite the soreness of her shoulder wound and, in mark of their love for each other, Grace agreed.

The funny thing was, Lilac thought it was she who would protect Grace, but so far in the relationship it had been the demure church-mouse, blue stocking who had done the lifesaving of her cop lover. And so it was, tooled up, they had taken the train from Waterloo and were now just arriving in Portsmouth Harbour station. It was to be a quick off, collect the nun and then in their railway guards' uniforms that Lilac thought suited Grace inordinately, shut Winifrede in the guard's van. There they would keep her safe, and at Waterloo, the Ooh La Lovelies, DaDa, had arranged for transport to the cathedral, (what could go wrong?). Well, Jack, Jane, Dick had arranged the transport, for one thing...

Zondo had worked the miracle of obfuscation as expected, and the twirling nun, still attired in stiff pink tutu and lacy pink brassiere over her black habit, the lower part tucked into her navy blue flannelette knickers to allow freedom of movement for her skinny legs, appeared almost out of a mist. Well, it was a miasma of sorts as it was the Ooh La Lovelies DaDa team of Pimple and Dick, dancing around the nun by way of a distraction and, miraculously, the other passengers at the Portsmouth Harbour terminus looked on bewildered only because there was music of sorts, a discordant screeching, which was Jack Austin whistling what he thought was Tchaikovsky's Canoe Lake. The bewilderment was not so much the dancing, as it was not unusual to see ballet at this station, but, cavorting to a whistled theme from *Bob the Builder,* was.

Everybody boarded, Grace and Lilac steering Winifrede, who was looking decidedly frayed at the edges, into the guard's van, while the DaDa and Father Mike hopped into a normal carriage.

'Does she never sleep?' Grace asked of the disappearing Father Mike, 'and how would you know?'

Mike stopped mid step, 'Yes, intermittently. I've not seen it, but apparently her legs wobble a lot in tune to Tchaikovsky's Sleeping Bertie.'

And so it was they were en route to Waterloo, London's busiest rail terminus.

Nelly arrived back at her stable and got stuck into her nosebag of oats and a refreshing bucket of cool water. It was going to be a long afternoon and she needed to be revitalised and on her mettle. Aware also not to let her master get too plastered, she had knocked over his bottle of stout. She needed him just on the brink of comatose. Nelly was determined not to let Claudio down. As a horse not overly fond of birds, especially the pigeons in London, Nelly quite liked Claudio – he wasn't half bad for a wop bird.

Claudio, on the suggestion of Dick DaDa, had asked Nelly to meet the Ooh La Lovelies DaDa, Lilac and Grace, and a nun, from Waterloo Station after taking the Numpti to Downing Street. Confident in the horse, whom he liked for an animal with four legs and no feathers, but worried about whether the rag-and-bone man could remain sufficiently compost mantas (Claudio had learned a lot of his malapropism English from Jack Austin, the dozy bird. All falling into place for you now is it? Good, back on yer 'eads).

TWENTY-TWO

Poopey waited patiently in the luxuriously cavernous lobby of *Ma-Santi*, the global conglomerate with fingers in many worldwide pies, all very profitable and not many for the benefit of humankind. But what did that matter to a corporate machine engineered for profit only?

Today, though, the archbishop was interested in only one pie.

'I'm sorry, who did you say you were?' a snooty receptionist with too much eye make-up asked.

Poopey was not to be dismissed so easily and recognised a fabricated posh accent when he heard one. 'Where you from, sweet'art?' he asked in his indigenous cockney accent, long time buried as he had risen up the ecclesiastic ladder, but it was still there. It is said this is what attracted Pimple's aunt; she liked a bit of clerical rough trade.

The receptionist was taken aback, but smiled. 'Beffnal Green,' she replied in an equally demonstrative cockney cadence.

'Know it well,' Poopey replied, noting the young lady's nametag and giving the receptionist a broad smile, one of his best, and the girl melted in his presence. 'Thelma, darlin', can you let the PA to Jock Mannford know that William Archibald is here to see him, please.'

The receptionist smiled at the personal recognition, even though she hated her name. She telephoned up to the PA of the big boss and let it be known who was in reception for Mr. Mannford. She paused, looked back to Poopey and, with a growing frown asked, 'Do you have an appointment?'

Poopey replied, equally unvarnished, "Don't need one, sweet'art,' and he waggled his head but skipped the cheeky wink.

The receptionist conveyed Poopey's response and after a moment replied, 'I am sorry, if you do not have...' she was halted in her reply by a patrician hand gesture that brooked no question.

'Tell the PA to ask, did Mr. Mannford enjoy his pie?'

The receptionist passed on the message and hung on the phone for what had to be a stultifying two minutes, before coming back with the question she had been asked to convey, 'Who did you say you were and who are you with?'

'I'm William Archibald and I am with the Church of England,' Poopey replied, and Thelma in turn relayed the information.

'Church of England?' Thelma came back, as instructed.

'Yes'

'If you can wait here please, Celeste will be down in a moment to meet you, Mr. Archibald,' Thelma replied, indicating by waving the phone that Celeste was the PA she had been talking to.

After a suitably long time, to indicate the importance of the person he wanted to meet, Poopey looked up, reacting to the clack, clack, clacking of stiletto heels across an expansive marble floor. He saw slinking toward him a prim-and-proper slender lady, dressed in a billowy silk blouse and pencil-slim skirt, tight blond hair scurfed back into an uncompromising bun with a complementary taut grimace.

She presented herself, stiff and erect. 'Mr Archibald?' She snootily enquired, patronising the unknown guest.

Poopey stood from his uncomfortable, though stylish, chair and stretched out his hand, which confused Celeste; Poopey's hand was upside down. What was this handshake? She thought. Was she about to be introduced to a mason and what would her boss think? Was her boss a mason and, how should she respond?

Poopey reacted to Celeste's confused look. 'You may kiss my ring,' he answered, still holding out his hand to the querulous stylish woman, wiggling a finger that sported a gold ring with a ruby stone. He suggested Celeste should get on with it as he didn't have all day and his arm was aching.

Celeste looked at the pudgy hand and sparkly ruby ring and shucked her façade. 'Fuck off,' she replied and, in case Poopey didn't understand the words, Celeste's body gesture conveyed the sentiments equally forcefully.

'You swear at the Archbishop of Canterbury?' Poopey responded, allowing himself a cheeky grin.

'Fuck off,' Celeste said again. She was not a woman to be messed with.

Now Poopey's grin widened. 'Tell Mr. Mannford

the Archbishop of Canterbury asked if he enjoyed eating his Umble Pie and, when he is ready to speak to me, he should place an advertisement in the personal column of the Times saying, "The head of Ma-Santi has eaten of his Humble Pie. He is sorry and will make amends", and then we can talk about what he can do in reparation. Do you have that, Celeste?'

'Fuck off, your fucking holiness,' Celeste answered, no chuckling, a manner she reserved for dealing with street loonies. 'You're a fucking loony and I'm not kissing your shitty ring, now get out before I call security and have you thrown out...' Celeste halted her fruity rebuke in order to respond to Thelma who was shaking a newspaper at her, and pointing to a picture of the Archbishop of Canterbury, who bore a remarkable resemblance to Mr. Archibald, except he had a silly pointy hat on in the picture, but it was most certainly the loony in reception. Both women could see that.

By the time Celeste had gathered her wits, Poopey was already departing through the revolving door. She called after him but to no avail as Poopey jumped into a cab.

'Shit a fucking brick,' Celeste exclaimed, and Thelma agreed with her.

TWENTY-THREE

A RATHER CIRCUMSPECT MANDY SAT ON THE train with her DaDa team. She was dressed appropriately in an Ooh La Lovely manner for London, although the mode of fashion selection had not been without its difficulties.

In the morning, after an early brunch that Mandy called breakfast, Jack and Mandy had discussed the role they would be expected to play today. Well, Mandy discussed their role, Jack was more concerned that his infamous *Morecombe and Wise*, voluminously baggy khaki shorts, had gone on the missing list again. He particularly wanted to wear them to London. Mandy continued discussing the plans, not wishing to get into a debate about where she might have hidden the shorts that made her husband look even more ridiculous than normal, the baggy elongated legs of the shorts being so wide in circumference that whenever her husband sat down, he inadvertently gave all and sundry more than a passing glimpse at his naughty bits. Eventually, Mandy produced the shorts. She knew she would and wondered why she ever hid them. Jack would always make such a fuss and she always would concede, though one day she swore to herself, she would chuck them into the sea.

Jack smiled his victory smile and slipped on his shorts, the legs of which came just to his pimply knees. He twirled to demonstrate his sartorial elegance and the ensuing draft of excess cloth ruffled the bedroom curtains.

'Come on, yer big pansy,' Mandy said as she exited the bedroom, 'I can hear Pimple and Ceeley downstairs.'

Jack pursued his wife. 'You don't think I'm a pansy do you?' He called, running after her and bumping into her back as she stopped mid-landing. 'I suppose you fink that's funny,' he said nasally.

Mandy could never stay irritated for long with Jack. She smiled, he responded with his victory grin, and her irritation returned.

She chuckled to herself as she observed him laid back on the train seat.

'What you laughin' at?'

'You, yer dipstick, in those feckin' shorts. Tuck the legs in.'

He did, but most reluctantly. It was hot and he had just managed to elevate his legs sufficiently to capture the draft from the open train window to achieve a substantive cooling, efficacious effect, much to the horror and amusement of the other passengers. Father Mike had seen it all before and frankly, he was not impressed and commiserated with Mandy.

———

Fabio, the Pope not Pope, dressed as required, in smart and elegant fifties mode, a pale cream shirt and silk paisley cravat, burgundy cardigan, unbuttoned as it would be hot on the London streets, cream billowy linen slacks belted with an old school tie, and tan brogue town shoes. He was edgy as he left his hotel room. He knew his task and, although it was nice to see Claudio, sometimes the controlling nature of his bird got on his papal tits and, as he descended the narrow rickety stairs of the rickety hotel and passed the seedy reception desk with the seedy reception clerk, who needed to shave and clean his teeth eighty three times a day, he thought to himself, was Claudio his parrot or was he Claudio's pope? He already knew the answer to that as he recalled Father Mike had told him, one day, that the papal parrot had suggested the plan. The big idea they were about to execute was thought up by his parrot? But he was uncertain if the bird had not been in cahoots with Dick? Cahoots? That was an owl, wasn't it? And so he was doubly suspicious.

Was Fabio nervous? Yes, of course he was. If this went wrong, everything would unravel, his doppelganger papacy and the whole plan to revolutionise the thinking of the mainstream churches, and if it did, would people believe him when he said it wasn't him but the parrot?

Fabio had to admit he was a tad clumsy and, after Claudio had left the Vatican, mysteriously, or so it had been reported in the Vatican Times, Fabio had been decidedly more clumsy, dropping the ball many times, which included the papal football match when he had played in goal against a Jesuit eleven, who, if he was honest with himself, took the game far too seriously. Fabio played in goal as he was the widest player and they needed a miracle to stop the ball going in. It was his innate clumsiness that worried him now as he walked, criss-crossing the streets, zigzagging his way to the West End of London and Berkley Square. He tried hard not to be offended by the jeers from passers-by commenting on his pointy hair. Well, at least that would be sorted if nothing else today, he thought, as he paced steamily to keep his hair appointment with the Twink Friseur, Tonsorium.

By and by, Fabio arrived at the salon. It was a converted old brick workshop and stables situated in a back street. An out-of-the-way mews. An expansive plate glass screen crossed the front facade where there had once been timber gates and upon the shop front was a stuck-on sign, set at a jaunty angle, saying "Special Today, Helmet, Fez and Mitre Hair sorted".

Nervously, Fabio pushed open the plate glass door and entered to be greeted by a chorus of "Ooh Ooohs" from a team of identically attired stylists, all in stripy city boy trousers, figure hugging, white collarless granddad shirts, and prancing in pristine-chapel white plimsolls. They were white but had tiny pictures of floating cherubic angels blowing trumpets on the toes. Apparently, they are an exact copy of those worn by Michelangelo when he painted ceilings for his dad's decorating company.

'Ooh, Allo,' Fabio was addressed by a receptionist. The name tag said Simone, a beanpole man slimmer than the rest and he greeted Fabio as he flounced out from behind the marble counter. 'Ooh, I say, that's a bit pointy,' said the receptionist as he signalled to his attendant colleagues, indicating Fabio's mitre mullet. 'Bev, love,' he called out to a burly looking chap in a singlet vest, revealing a hairy torso and arms plastered in tattoos depicting hairstyles through the ages, clearly a standout stylist as he had his own manner of attire. 'May need your help here. If I'm not mistaken, we have a serious case of mitre hair,' and he looked at Fabio. 'Cleric, are we, darling?' Fabio muttered back a yes and Simone gently stroked Fabio's cheek, followed up with a playful slap. 'Could do with a decent shave as well,' Simone added and, looking down at the papal hands in a disparaging manner, Simone sighed, 'and those nails have not seen a chiropodist for a while, I'll be bound,' and, kissing the air with a fruity raspberry, Simone offered a reassuring declaration so loud, the Queen in Buckingham Palace was probably comforted. 'Don't worry, sweetie, we can sort you out, but it may take all morning and the A team.' He scratched his bottom and, with the same two fingers, whistled, then shouted, "A team", and from behind a Chinese screen, two more barbers appeared, each again identically attired in the city boy uniform, except they had tan leather builders belts circling the top of their stripy trousers. The belts had loops and pockets containing combs, brushes, scissors, hairdryer, cheese-and-onion crisps and what looked like a pistol, a *Walter Matthau* point something or other? As a doppelganger Pope, he was not up to snuff with guns.

Simone noticed Fabio looking at the gun. 'Ooh, don't worry about that, sweets,' Simone said, fondly pinching the papal bottom. 'We sometimes get a bit of trouble from our clients,' and then suggested Fabio might like to avail himself of the facilities before they got to work.

Fabio did, and not a moment too soon.

TWENTY-FOUR

THE DADA TROUPE SETTLED AS THE TRAIN smoothly and speedily whooshed towards London. Mandy wanted just to get on the train, but Jack and Pimple had been hopping all morning, practising for hopping on the train and then arguing who had won the game of hopscotch they had been playing on the Frisian Tun street, while Mandy and Cecelia selected their outfits.

Jack had chalked his hopscotch grid on the pavement outside his house, much to the chagrin of the poncy middle class neighbours, except for the admiral who lived down the road, who wanted to join in, but had to wait his turn. He then showed his sailor boy temperamental nature, as the Ooh La Lovely girls were ready to go quicker than Jack had anticipated. To ameliorate the admiral's sour puss, Jack loaned him his special flat stone, making the retired matelot officer promise to post it back through Jack's letterbox after he had finished playing. Jack had assured the retired mariner that, if he blew on the stone and whispered the required number, before casting it, it would land just where he wanted and then it would just be down to how good he was at hopping. Hopping, he went on to say, was something you needed to practice. Jack knew this, and now Pimple did, and this was why the two of them practiced hopping at the station, which conveniently screened the spiralling sister Winifrede and, after handing over the prancing nun to Grace and Lilac, Jack and Pimple hopped on to the fast train to Waterloo.

The train was due into London just before midday. It would be just a short horse and cart ride to the Savoy hotel, via Westminster Cathedral, Jack had said, to an unbelieving Cecelia and Pimple. Mandy looked knowingly at her husband. Was there a grain of truth in this? She thought. She would have to wait and see but did take solace from the fact he had not said they would hop to the Savoy. In London, they were due to meet Samuels for a spot of lunch at the Savoy. Jack said he didn't eat dog, though he loved a savaloy sausage and chips after a few pints. Mandy calmed her husband and told him that a spot of lunch was just a posh Savoy expression for having a light lunch, not eating *Spot the dog*. Mandy thought this would calm her husband, who loved dogs, and, up until quite recently, had been inseparable from his border terrier, Martin, who now lived with an orphan child, supporting the girl emotionally in the manner Martin had previously done with Jack.

Jack, however, was not to be pacified. He now argued he was not settling for a light lunch. It had been ages since brunch and then it would be ages before tea.

Mandy sighed, suggested he needed more hopping practice and mentioned how cooling this could be for the undercarriage, now that they had closed the carriage window. She continued chatting amiably with Cecelia as the train sped on towards London and Pimple and Jack chugged and hopped up and down the aisle, then argued about who was the better. Mandy umpired saying that Pimple was the better hopper but Jack was the best chugger and after ruling that chugging was a more accomplished skill than hopping, Jack finally appeared satisfied.

———

Fabio had been shaved within an inch of his life and had *Nivea* massaged into his hands and into his newly shaved puffy cheeks. He felt like screaming and still no show of Twink Friseur, which was the reason for his visit, that and the mitre hair, which seemed to be coming along nicely, even though at first it resisted the initial level of cut. Mitre hair is notoriously stubborn, ask any clerical hairdresser of merit.

'Think we may need something extra strong,' Bev said casually to Fabio, then called out, flicking his head demonstratively to the lofty ceiling. 'Ooh-oooo,' he shouted, not listening to any response from Fabio, who was desperately seeking information as to the whereabouts of Twink. '*Harmony,* dear, dogmatic strength please,' he called, and another hairdresser called Jules appeared with a locked *Samsonite* case. Bev retrieved a key, attached to a looped string around his neck that had, up until now, nestled unobserved in Bev's chest rug. Jules raised the case as Bev lowered himself and the key, inserted, twisted and the case popped open with a noise similar to the breaking of a vacuum. And I know what that sounds like, which is why I never Hoover in my house.

Bev took an aerosol canister from the case and shooed Jules away with a flick of his spare hand, which held a comb, scissors and a cigarette card that depicted a pope from years back. This was a pope who had removed his mitre to be photographed, revealing an enormous and stubborn looking mullet point. Bev looked at the card, looked at the *Harmony Dogmatic* hairspray and signalled for a photo to be taken of Fabio. Jules returned with a camera and snapped away, while Bev twisted, turned, pirouetted and flounced with his hands as he considered his next move. He hemmed. He looked beaten. He picked out his phone from his utility belt, herred a breath on the screen, gave it a quick polish on the bum of his trousers then pressed a speed-dial number.

'Twink luv, we have a serious case of Papal Mitre hair. I have the *Harmony Dogmatic*...' he paused, listening, 'no I've not seen the fucking parrot,' and Bev stamped his plimsolled foot in irritation. He had a much more serious problem than a missing bird. He thought he had the missing pope in his chair who had probably the worst case of mitre hair he had ever seen. Bev continued to listen to a haranguing Twink, realising that patience was needed sometimes when his boss was on a rant. Twink went on to explain, in a most descriptive and blue manner that Claudio had been dancing for Twink and his associates and then, out of the blue, had received a phone call and flown out of the window. Bev didn't like Claudio, or birds in general, but knew how much the capture of the bird meant to Twink and his religious confederates and, if Claudio was in London, then the Pope would not be far behind and here he was, in Bev's chair. Bev expressed sympathies and offered up some platitudes,

'Claudio always comes back though, doesn't he?' It seemed to do the trick and Bev closed his call, cued up his phone and the photos of the Pope and emailed them on to Twink.

They had to wait. The tension was papal-able as there was now a crowd of hairdressers and beauticians gathered around Fabio's mitre Mohican, humming and erring, tutting and pouting.

Jules stepped in, he had to defuse this situation that experience told him could blow. It was a coiffeur powder keg, 'Cup of tea, sweeties?'

"Oooh, lovely", came a collective response, and the crowd broke up to partake of refreshments, and Bev breathed a sigh of relief. He fingered his pistol. He thought about shooting the Pope, which would certainly solve the hair crisis and a few other matters, but decided against it. It was Twink's prerogative to decide the fate of this renegade pontiff.

TWENTY-FIVE

NELLY HAD WAITED FOR MORE THAN AN HOUR for Claudio, but the parrot had still not appeared. She decided to drop the Numpti off at Downing Street and then trot on to Waterloo. Nelly knew the way to Downing Street but rarely went south of the river, but didn't worry, the mainline terminus would be clearly signposted. Even so, the mare was nervous, and it showed as she deposited stuff that would be capital for the capital's roses as she approached the Downing Street gates.

Elevated way above the police cordon, sitting on the cart bench seat, Numpti Azzer announced himself, saying he was here to speak to the prime minister and deputy prime minister. Nelly and her cart remained stationary, while the perceived driver zizzed in inebriated oblivion. The security guards were ready to let the rag-and-bone man in as he was a regular at Downing Street, the Mackeroon's generally had a load of old shite to dispose of, and regularly; old worn out policies and so on, but the guards were not sure who Azzer was? An Arabic looking chap in fifties attire, blue plimsolls, and a bright red fez. They were alerted because the blue plimsolls did not go with the pale green checked shirt tucked tightly into beige baggy shorts. He looked like a big Egyptian boy scout, but it was the green checked shirt that mystified them. It rang out as odd to the stiff paramilitary policemen oft referred to these days as the *Plebs of Downing Street* (Plods)

'Tell Mr Mackeroon and Mr Blogg that the Grand Numpti of Egypt is here to see them, please,' Azzer said loudly and in a naturally authoritarian manner that came with his, up until now, unknown status as the head of the Church of Egypt, though he fiddled nervously with his woggle.

Well that did it, the slumbering, ever attending press photographers leapt into snapping action. The horse and cart with a pissed driver and a boy-scout eejit in a fez raised no interest until Azzer's announcement and now, this command was being reinforced by a parrot who spoke with a distinctive Italian accent, as it alighted on the shoulder of the rag-and-bone man.

'Eh, wottsamattawivyou, why you no opena gates?'

The guards, if they were up until now reluctant, opened the gates in response to the authoritarian parrot and Claudio called "giddyuppa" to Nelly. She trotted into Downing Street, turned the cart and stopped beside the famous door, to allow the Numpti off and then proceeded on her way back out.

The guards allowed the horse and cart to exit and Claudio said he was mosta exceedingly oblige-dah as he flew off to the centre of Whitehall and, taking up a commanding parrot stance, his right wing extended, he halted the traffic to allow Nelly ease of passage on to the busy Whitehall thoroughfare. He alighted on the rag-and-bone man's shoulder and Nelly with Claudio trotted on to and then across Westminster Bridge towards Waterloo station.

———

'I can't see why we couldn't get a cab to the Savoy, and you,' she added, pointing to Sister Winifrede, closely guarded by Grace and Lilac, 'stop fucking dancing, for Christ's sake.' Jack sensed his wife felt confident she had a reasonable point, having also pointed out to him, as the horse and cart drew up beside the Waterloo station taxi rank, that the cart was filthy and they would probably get splinters in their bums and, as a throwaway afterthought, she mentioned it would take ages. Sometimes Jack wondered if he had inadvertently married a dozy cow and a woman with no sense for the occasion and appropriateness of transport in certain situations.

'No, I haven't got any sense for appropriate modes of travel,' she responded to his thought and she poked Jack in his belly. She felt her finger go in and continue travelling towards her husband's centre of gravity before it could travel no further and miraculously, her hand sprung back out. 'And that's for thinking me a "dozy cow".'

'Did I just speak me thoughts, darlin'?' Jack asked unnecessarily, and was about to reinforce the logic of his argument, when two rapidly trotting ponies and traps skewed to a halt and seven roughty-toughty Arab looking men with thumping great hooked beaks on charcoal faces, dressed in stripy schoolboy pyjamas and red fezzes, leapt from their equipages and, extending their arms as if they were children on a play battlefield, they began mock-spraying the area with machine gun bullets. This all accompanied with the appropriate schoolboy sound effects as they danced and pranced around the Ooh La Lovelies DaDa team. Lilac and Grace closed ranks in order to protect Winifrede.

The extraordinary thing was that, although there was no evident weaponry, there was in fact real damage from the make-believe bullets and pretty soon the thousands of people who were all arriving to gather in Trafalgar Square to demonstrate for Winifrede and the revolution she danced for, (there is no way news of a dancing nun arriving in London can be kept quiet), were diving for cover as glass shattered and signs splintered and fell to the floor.

Pimple leapt into action and pushed Cecelia, Mandy, and then Jack, to the ground as the invisible bullets strafed several black cabs, their drivers slumping as they pretended to be hit. They did not stand a chance as they often had film companies filming on the cab forecourt and knew they had to play their part, assuming that their guttural death throes and the machine gun noises made by the pyjamaed assailants would be edited in, and actual bullets and sound effects inserted by the special effects team. People pretend screamed and scattered back into the station concourse in a very convincing panic, patting their hair and straightening their attire, looking for the cameras, hoping their bums would not look too big and they would look good on the film when it was released.

Out of the tableau of carnage, a powerful beam of light pierced the now smoky shadow of the cab forecourt and picked out the Ooh La Lovelies DaDa. Jack realised immediately what was happening and, rolling across the forecourt, he pushed Mandy and then Cecelia, after they had just clambered upright, out of the beam's seemingly magnetic grasp. He swerved back to release Pimple from the tractor beam's grasp, but too late. Pimple writhed in patent agony, his piercing wail cutting through the silent movie pandemonium. Jack cried out Pimple's name and Cecelia screamed from the tarmac floor, but her wails were soon muffled when a swirling thick, black, turbulent cloud, descended and churned energetically, eventually enveloping the whole scene before it condensed into a small tornado that extinguished the light and focused itself on Pimple, Cecelia, Mandy and Jack, who were sucked into the air and after a short time were able to fall gently to the ground and roly-poly away.

The blackness that engulfed Pimple allowed no sight of what was happening to him, but, as the cloud faded so it could be seen that Pimple was vertical, feet lifted off the ground, and then slowly, gently, he was lowered to the taxi concourse and laid out. He was still. He showed no vital signs. A dribble of blood oozed slowly from the corner of his mouth. Winifrede danced beside him and all of a sudden shrieked a virago wail, slowly, guttural at first, growing in pitch and modulation and loudness as the visage of Winifrede morphed into a hag. The nun's head was witch-like with festering pustules as if it had been buried underground for some time and dug up and the beldam swung into action, swirling, leaping, and scything her way into the pyjamaed ballet terrorists.

Almost as soon as it happened so it ended. The pyjamaed COPS limped away. Those who had fallen in action were lifted by their hobbling comrades and raised back on to their ponies and traps and, in silence, no clattering of metal horseshoes, they scarpered. No need to mess with the loony nun and in the distance could be heard the modulation of the two-tone police sirens.

Mandy raised her head from the tarmac, shook it to blow away her confusion and watched the pyjamas making their escape into the midday London traffic.

'Blimey, did you see that,' Jack said to Cecelia, who had seen nothing of the action other than a face full of pavement. 'Those were super-dooper trotting carts. I've always wanted one of them and, the horses wore plimsolls. No wonder we didn't hear them coming. Cunning!' He shook his head in acknowledgement of a clever plan well executed.

'Help me up, dipstick," Mandy commanded from the floor to a still recumbent Jack, though he was propped on one elbow so he could watch the departing pony traps and the arrival of the SBS. 'SBS?' Mandy shouted over the increasing noise as the crowd regained their composure, returning from the station concourse and expressing their horror in a general, multidirectional, panicked, chicken run, some effecting overacted limps and serious wounding, in case the cameras were still rolling.

Jack looked stunned by his wife's energetic rebuke of his spoken thoughts, but loved it when she spoke sweet nothings to him. And so, generously, he considered in the circumstances, he responded that he would pick her up just as soon as he had checked his bottom department as he might have poo'd in his underwear, which had been clean on last week. Mandy sighed as she rose under her own steam, aware that, as her husband had such a large bum, the inspection could take some time. She looked on in amazement as the approaching police squads, all in plimsolls, began dancing, their truncheons twirling in synchronised unison, as they pranced and twirled, eventually to end up in a line in front of the DaDaists and, linking arms, did a *Tiller Girl* routine of high kicks and linked rotations. After a minute or so of convoluted manoeuvres, they eventually came to a kneeling halt and a head flick in unison, the large swirly Ostrich feathers on the top of their helmets exaggerated the flick, which signalled an end to the police routine.

The crowd applauded respectfully before they made their way on to Trafalgar Square. A uniformed inspector, with a pink tutu circling the waist of his blue uniform and a matching fuchsia plume, tied with string to his inspector's cap, stepped from the serried ranks of the Metropolitan Police, Special Ballet Squad. This was the famed and feared SBS, sister organisation to the SAS, Special Artistes Service.

The inspector introduced himself to Jack Austin in the traditional SBS way, 'Allo, allo, allo,' and with his arms folded behind him, he gently bent his knees and rose upright again. It was SBS secret squirrel code, loosely interpreted as hello.

Jack knew the appropriate response, he had learned this at spy school, not that he learned much else as he had sat at the back, but he remembered this bit. 'What's all this 'ere then?' he said, which Mandy noticed was received with a nod of approval and another bend of the knees from the twat prima-ballerina copper.

Mandy looked on in wonderment as the inspector and her husband hugged, stepped back and danced like Sugar Plum Fairies around each other, high fiving like disabled Morris dancers and eventually finishing with an extended raspberry to each other and another hug.

'Wally, Wally, 'ow yer diddlin', old son,' Jack said, brushing himself down, his brushing having no discernible effect on the now grimy, previously ill-fitting and tending to shabby, clothes and especially the huge shite shorts. He turned to Mandy to effect an introduction. 'Sweet'art, this is Chief Inspector Wallace Wallace, we call him Wally-Wally,' and Wally Wally stepped up and embraced Mandy and, after a long hug, that felt like a fortnight to Mandy, he held her shoulders with extended arms, eventually tugging her in twice for a kiss and raspberry on each of her now flushed cheeks. If I am not mistaken, Mandy had just been inducted into the brotherhood and sisterhood, and caninehood (in case Martin the border terrier is reading this, which he might have been as he had recently acquired some reading glasses), of the SBS.

'Oi,' Jack said, 'yer filfly tow rag, get orf me missus,' and the inspector and Jack shared a knee-jerk guffaw and extended back slaps that eventually saw Jack, the cotton candy, pansy-arsed leader of Ooh La Lovelies DaDa, on his knees. Wally-Wally, it seems, was a strong man (a common mistake, ballet police are not wimps, but extra strong, like the mints).

Mandy gave Jack the stare as he raised himself from the ground, still in almost uncontrollable hysterics. The fixed glare from his wife was enough to curb Jack's enthusiasm so he applied his attractive grin. He knew Mandy liked that grin.

Wally-Wally ignored Jack and spiralled to Pimple, who was still prostrate and giving the appearance he was spilling his life's blood. 'Lord Pimple!' Wally-Wally exclaimed, and Pimple rallied a little, felt his chest and his mouth and looked at his hand. It was covered in blood. Pimple knew he should get up and do a bit of the Hokey-cokey, it seemed an appropriate dance as he had never had classical dance training and so would probably make a fool of himself with ballet. In his youth, he had focused mainly on knitting and embroidery. He had his Boy Scout badge for that, but he was now preoccupied with the fact he could not move. He choked and coughed more blood.

Cecelia screamed, 'Heeeelp!' and she flopped on to her Pimple.

Pimple managed a polite though weakening enquiry of the inspector, pushing Cecelia to one side. 'Does the B in SBS, stand for Boy Scout? Because, if it does, I may be your man?'

Wally-Wally managed a feeble chortle as he looked out for the ambulance, but knew it would not get here in time. It didn't, and Pimple took his last blood soaked breath, a choked whisper to Cecelia to say how much he loved her and a reassuring platitude. 'Don't worry, it'll be all right,' and his head slumped and nestled into the folds of Cecelia's most intimate naughty lady parts. He breathed his last breath, and it was a Brahma.

Jack leaned over the now sobbing Cecelia, looked at Pimple and announced, 'Yeah, he'll be all right, and that was a brilliant last breath,' stunning everyone, including Wally-Wally, who had known Jack for many years, but even for him, this was a mega eejit statement. He knew things had just got serious.

TWENTY-SIX

THE DOWNING STREET STEWARD GREETED THE Grand Numpti and let him pass through the shiny black portal into the grand entrance hall of the British seat of power. He wiped his plimsoles on the mat that said "welcome" in English and "fuck off" in Russian, and immediately hop-scotched on the black and white chequered tiling, demonstrating to anyone who was anyone, and especially those in the know, that he was not to be messed with. After he had got to ten, he spun and made to set off on the return leg, so to speak. Azzer kept his fez on as was his right, he did adjust it after he had got back to the start as it had become a little unbalanced and he tipped his head to acknowledge a rather formal man.

'You are the Numpti of Cairo?' The gent asked, in a clipped military and rather patronising manner, seemingly unimpressed by the Numpti's evident skill at hopscotch.

'The Grand Numpti, yes, I am.' Azzer replied, equally stiffly, miffty for a Numpti, who were generally known for their placid demeanour as well as camel coats for when it got cold at night in the desert.

The steward leafed through some papers on his clip board, looked at Azzer and appeared satisfied. 'You have no appointment with the prime minister but fortunately Mr. Mackeroon and Mr. Blogg were only playing a game of snakes and ladders before prime minister's question time in the House. They can spare you fifteen minutes.'

I need only five minutes,' Azzer announced formally, which was not actually true as he wanted to keep the PM and dep PM in Downing Street. If the Numpti's nose had not been so unfeasibly large anyway, the doorman would have noticed he was telling fibs and that at any time his pants could catch fire. 'Always providing they can keep their mouths shut and just listen,' Azzer added in a stern, though still placid manner and then he bowed, to indicate the introduction and any conversation was over and that the military man should convey this message to Mackeroon and Blogg. 'Clogg, Dog, or whatever was his name,' he added.

The steward turned on his heel, a military three-point turn as opposed to a military two-step which was reserved for informal visits, marched off, and shortly, as he was an officer in the midget military, he reappeared, stared up and steered Azzer into the office of the prime minister.

———

Olive Doyle, mother in VI6, sat with the mother superior from St Winifrede's in the nuns' refectory attached to Westminster Abbey (it was a legacy of when the Abbey was Roman candle just before the fireworks of Henry the Eighth, and still exists for the use of Catholic meditation and eating). Olive had been annoyed at first that this forceful nun had barged in on her interrogation of the dancing Sister Winifrede, but it was the way that the big penguin had asserted her authority that suggested to Olive the woman was acting not on her own initiative. This had Holy Barbaras written all over it, and she considered that if the mother superior had thought to claim the dancing nun as her own saint, the Barbaras might wish to usurp this claim and set up a base in Portsmouth. If the Barbaras achieved this, the church would find it difficult to challenge if they had a saint batting high up the order for them.

So Olive let the scene play out, to learn what she could. She had already tipped off Father Mike that the Barbaras were active and, might already be in London. If this was the case, it could spell trouble for them, especially with the hordes gathering just up the road in Trafalgar Square. Olive had heard that already the crowds were surging into Whitehall and the Mall as the numbers grew. She had arranged for a rostrum to be set up on top of the steps outside the National Gallery for the Nuns' Orchestra, and the sound system would convey the music way down to Parliament and along Birdcage Walk to a distant Buckingham Palace. Olive had also been informed that masses of people were congregating in other major towns and city squares throughout the country, filled with people sick and tired of austerity and bearing the brunt of the financial crisis, a crisis brought on by no fault of their own and that is before they got to losing so many of their human rights under this government. Big screens were being erected and the Nuns' Orchestra's performance would be relayed and everyone hoped Winifrede, the inspiration of this modern-day peasants' revolt, would make an appearance and dance for the country – the concert was already being called, *A Very British Rite of Spring*.

Meanwhile, in the nuns' refectory, Sister Winifrede was still dancing, twirling and squatting, sticking her leg out and wobbling it. Olive Doyle watched, despairing as she sat chewing on a doughnut and stroking the private parts of Bong, her now formal fiancé. Bong, head bowed, looked to his fly region, to the deposits of sugar and raspberry jam. He wanted to say something and then he wanted to say nothing to the love of his life and was starting to think, as the raspberry jam began to drip down Olive's muzzle, that he was not comfortable in the cathedral refectory. But he could not contain his excitement as Olive continued to consume more sugary confection, which exponentially increased the fervour of her fondling, in proportion to the resultant sugar rush, the parts that Olive had recently declared belonged to her, now.

Olive displayed no apparent sense of vacillation or embarrassment. She was preoccupied in her thoughts that maybe this fucking miracle of the resurrected dancing nun, though expected and even planned, might have a downside as Winifrede seemed to be unable to stop dancing. Furthermore, the mother superior from Portsmouth appeared keen to claim the nun for her convent. Or, was it for the Barbaras? Olive had noticed a pair of recently refurbished Jacko skates in the mother's *Bob the Priest* rucksack, and she was now more than ever convinced she had a cuckoo in the nest, and she didn't mean Winifrede, who was obviously cuckoo. How would this influence the plans for the day? Her experience told her never to underes-

timate the power of the Barbaras and she resolved to
despatch Zondo to Shepherd Market as the Barbaras
would surely rally the Shepherd sects to roller skate
behind their banner.

Ordinarily there was a rule of silence while in the
refectory, except for the current postulant who was
obliged to read the football results and religious texts
during mealtimes and, it seemed that this lunchtime
the novice, Sister Margot, read from this week's *Ballet
Times*. Not religious, many might think, but then you
would not be dancers and classically trained and, had
you been, you would understand and, I suggest, the
next time you meet *Darcy Bussel* out of *Pride and
Prejudice*, you ask him.

The order of silencio was waved away by Olive as
she questioned Winifrede. 'Can you remember anything?' Olive asked, taking her chance at a question as
Winifrede pirouetted nearby. Olive was already fed
up that the task of questioning Winifrede had fallen
to her, while she knew the real action was going on
outside, in the streets of London and not far from
where she sat. The centre of London theologians and
the Ooh La Lovelies DaDa were all on red alert. She
had also learned of the carnage at Waterloo Station
from Grace and Lilac when they delivered the nun,
shocked, battle-scarred, but still dancing.

'I thought we were supposed to be silent?' An out-
of-breath Sister Winifrede suggested to her mother
superior, who sat contemplatively stroking the bristles
on her chin as she plotted and schemed. She had already agreed to secure formal adoption of the sainted
dancing nun, preferably as a martyr and, martyred by
beheading being her preference, for the Barbaras. St
Winifrede was to be her passport to fame and glory in

the roller-skating inquisitorial order, who at this very moment she knew were skating their way to Shepherd Market.

The mother felt exhilarated as she responded to the irritating nun, wishing she would up and die soon so she could get the martyr process and eventual sainthood applications under way. She had already filled in the martyr forms and had them concealed in her rucksack, next to her Jackos, not realising that Olive had purloined the papers, scanned and sent them to the Vatican and to Father Mike, who was with the Ooh La Lovelies DaDa, after which she had returned them to her holy bag.

'Oh fuck that,' the mother replied. 'I make the rules, so tell me all,' and big mum penguin dismissed Olive's frown, returning the glance in full measure, demonstrably looking at Olive's hand and the rhythmic movement it applied to Bong's naughty bits, and then a flick of her eyes to indicate she had noticed also Bong's rather gormless visage.

The mother superior smugly returned to the focus of her attention, she had questions that needed answering in order to complete the sainthood application form. She sat poised, her writing hand ready to take notes in her especially commissioned, sainthood book.

'Well,' Winifrede said, as she danced to the mother superior, trying to think of something that might satisfy big mum whilst not truthfully being able to recall anything, 'there was a bright light.'

This was good, Mum thought, always good to start with a bright light, and she scratched this down in her holy book.

Olive couldn't help but be intrigued and for a moment, ignored Bong as he seemed to collapse and sprawl across the floor in what had to be another miracle; *The Jam Doughnut Ecstasy of Bong*.

Winifrede began to recall some events, not sure if it was just some memory of events unfolding, or the fact it had gone dark in the refectory and a laser light from out of nowhere focused on her. The postulant ceased her reading in order to focus on the miracle unravelling in front of her eyes, a writhing giant with jammy flies, apparently caught up in some religiously ecstatic vision and, a ballerina nun, on tiptoes in pink plimsolls tied with wide fuchsia ribbon bows, highlighted in a celestial beam and recounting to everybody the story of her transcendental benediction as she danced.

The mother superior was a little irked that the supernatural beam had not chosen to highlight her, but that could be flipped when she wrote up the account. She thought, maybe two beams.

Winifrede continued as she leaned on the edge of the table and did some barre exercises. 'I was setting up the orchestra chairs and sat for just a short while to run through my part and to pencil in the fingerings for the second violins.'

The mother superior interrupted. 'I couldn't give a rat's arse about the orchestra and fucking fingerings.' She stopped mid-sentence and thought for a while, looked at Olive and coloured. She cleared her throat to disguise her embarrassment, 'Er, what fingerings would these be?' A butter-wouldn't-melt look was on her face.

'The fingering and bowing patterns for the violins, so that the second violins were all in accord,' Winifrede replied, but was interrupted again.

'Yeah,' Mum said, 'skip the fingerings. What happened next?'

There was now complete silence in the refectory, all the nuns intent to learn of the miracle.

Winifrede exhaled in frustration, her ragged breathing becoming quite noisy, but she curbed any retort as she whizzed to the end of the room and back again, pirouetting all the way. Winifrede was familiar with the regime of obedience and the hierarchy, but was pleased she had dispensation and was allowed to dance and talk.

'Well, I sat and began playing a piece of music I thought celebrated God. I know not from where it came, but it was soft and lyrical, and a voice came unto me and said, "It's a Bird Going Up by Vaughan Williams, yer dipstick, and I'm just gonna take yer 'ead off for a bit sweet'art, carry on playing, it's lovely", Winifrede said in a passable cockney accent. (Does this mean God is a cockney? Well, that's a turn up for the bleedin' Bible). 'And, the next thing I remember, I was watching myself from the conductor's rostrum, still playing The Lark Ascending, but headless, and I sensed someone doing my hair,' and Winifrede patted her head. She plumped and prodded the new hair style, rather pleased with it, and would look in the mirror if she could only stop dancing.

'Fuck me gently,' Top mum said, as she scribbled the amazing account. 'Bird going up? Could you play it again?' she asked.

Winifrede wanted to shake her head but was still wary as to the security of her neck, so answered, 'I don't think so, though I suppose I could try, if I could only stand still and had a jeffing violin.'

Mum shouted at the still stunned non-orating postulant. 'Oi you, Margot, or whatever your bleedin' name is, go and get a fiddle and hurry up about it.' The postulant picked up her skirts and dashed to the cell block and as she departed so the atmosphere seemed to get darker and the beam stood out more brilliantly. The atmosphere, already of miraculous charge, was further energised.

Winifrede continued dancing, a bouree, Olive suggested, and was not mistaken. It was a quick French dance at double time and in the fifth position on releveé, Winifrede's plimsolls tightly together and, with quick moves, front foot and then the back foot moved quickly in tiny steps, as if the ballerina nun needed to find the lavatory, tout suite, or would that be en-suite?

The postulant returned with the bishop's best violin and, as Winifrede passed by and on the second attempt, she was able to give her the fiddle and, on the subsequent pass, hand her the bow. It was as if another miracle occurred. Winifrede stopped dancing, lifted the violin to tuck under her chin and a beautifully soft and elegiac melody ensued for a few moments and then the sister collapsed and died, her head lolling to one side.

'Oh, fuck me, not again.' Olive exclaimed.

'Thank Christ for that,' the mother superior said, grabbing her pen and holy book, unable to disguise her displeasure at the need to rub out some stuff in order to rewrite the ending.

But was this the ending? (Have a quick look and see how many pages are left).

————

The postulant, in a state of despairing frenzy, once again ran from the room screaming out that the dancing nun was dead. Well, as everyone knows, a nunnery, even one attached to a Church of England Abbey (and some say more so because of the Protestants), leaks like a sieve. It was not long therefore that the news was out and being broadcast across the country, but most especially in Trafalgar Square where there was patent disappointment as the huge crowd groaned. But, there was still the resurrected conductor of the Nuns' Orchestra, admittedly a classical orchestra conductor and not a working-class bus conductor, on the 229 to Galilee, but where signs were concerned, multitudes generally took what they could. Multitudes know you have to follow something, and pretty soon the crowds across the known country, following the lead of the Trafalgar multitude, were baying the name, "Bea Flat, Bea Flat, Bea Flat." as if requesting the return of the conductor for an encore, or maybe a return ticket. Or, she just needed pumping up?

TWENTY-SEVEN

'Do you like my hair, Aedd darling?'

Aedd was scared for his mortal soul, but did think he should like Bea's new hairstyle, say that it suited her, and so he nodded. 'Yes, sweetgums. It looks divine,' embarrassed, using the word *divine*. Maybe Bea's head repatriation was something of a miracle, Aedd thought, which was more than he could say of the hair-and-scare-em new hairstyle, and then, back from the dead and, calling me "darling", with a bouffant that erred more on the maniacal conductor than a controlled elegant coiffure. But, Aedd had to admit, it did suit her, in a frenzied way.

They had just finished rehearsing in the great hall of the National Gallery, prior to taking to the stage for their first scheduled performance. Bea could hear her name being chanted by the crowd and it seemed to her that all of her musical dreams had come true. This is what she had always wanted in her life. She thought of Aedd. He was just there, a mild ginger irritant, but every maestro needed someone to pick up after them and Aedd might just fit the bill.

'What is it, Aedd?' Bea asked, responding to

Aedd's gawping countenance. That was not unusual, but his mouth had remained open longer than was normal.

Aedd answered as best he could under the circumstances, 'Er, er...' that should do it, he thought.

'Er? Is that all you have to say?' Bea was controlling her temper. Aedd could get right up her nose on occasions. What was the matter with him? She thought for a moment and then said, 'What is the matter with you, Aedd?' See, told you that was what she was thinking.

Aedd remembered Jack Austin's confidential discourse on women, when they were having a pint in C&A's, and how sometimes women look for more than just a nod, which would be as good as a wink for a blind bat and, sometimes more than just one word answers. Extraordinary beings, women, Jack had gone on to explain. Although technically, "Er, er," was two words, and, he had screwed his face up when he said it, which could be construed as a knowing wink to a blind old bat, Aedd sensed a more detailed answer was called for? So he screwed his eyes tightly, turned three times, didn't spit, though he should have as Jack had insisted that Indian Egyptian Gods required a little gob, and he summoned the spirit of Heptep and patted the map of Egypt he had in his miniature *Compendium of Maps, Modern and Ancient* in his back pocket. He then answered. 'You do realise you were reported dead, that you had been decapitated? Though I have to say, your hair... is that a Beethoven?'

Bea punched Aedd in the arm, playfully, although Aedd's facial response would have said to anyone else that it was a haymaker (if you forgive the hairdresser remark). Combined with her baton nearly poking his eye out, he was naturally wrong-footed, but Bea missed all of this as she preened, patted, and pushed the back of her hair. 'Yes it is, thank you and, I have to say, I think it suits me. Ideal for the performance of a lifetime, but how this happened I have no recollection and what are you talking about "dead"? Now, take me to that broom cupboard and take your trousers off,' and she nodded her head to where Aedd presumed there was a broom cupboard. 'You Irish Welsh streak of piss you, my throat is feeling better and I'm as horny as anything. A quick fuck before I go on would set me up a treat.'

Aedd wondered if he should get his compendium out and point to the horn of Africa as they passed on the way to the broom cupboard, wherever that was, just beyond the Faroe Islands. Not the ones in Egypt, they were over the other side of the world and had just been patted in order to summon Heptep and, he was no expert, but his luck might have just changed. Good old Jack, Jane, Dick – he certainly knew women, Aedd thought to himself.

———

The chairman of Ma-Santi, Jock Mannford, invited his personal assistant to step into his office. He was busy, but distracted, irritated that someone claiming to be the Archbishop of Canterbury had called on him and suggested he should eat humble pie. Mannford was a small man who had an uncompromising nature. He had heard it called *small man syndrome* before now, which he dismissed as nonsense, but those who worked for him knew this not to be the case. He also favoured employing vertically challenged people. So he looked normal, people presumed. He was vain and his large office had mirrors, many of them, and frequently he would glance at himself in order to admire his powerful captain-of-industry image.

But with this countenance of arrogance and power, came a less obvious, though equally prominent, if you knew where to look, strong steak of self-preservation, and that streak, was yellow and ran up and down his spine, behind him, so he never really saw it. He had read about the Umble Pies in his magnate magazines, *Making Loads of Dosh*, and *Rolling in It*, and he was conscious of the metaphor and also aware other powerful heads of businesses had received a similar pie. It was thought these pies came from the church hierarchy. Some CEOs, who were of the Catholic persuasion, had received pies reportedly from the Pope. Arabic companies, even those with Muslim faith leaders, received pies said to be from the Numpti of Cairo. And now he had a pie and, had also had a visit from the Archbishop of Canterbury.

To say Jock Mannford was wary, or concerned, would be to underestimate the inconstancy of the streak of spinal scaredy custard. He had spoken on the phone to many other corporate leaders. He was not alone in his fear, for it is a common fact that these powerful men were bullies and, bullies did not like it when they were confronted and more especially, when they had something to hide. Some who had spurned their pie had had mysterious accidents. And then there had been the very public death of the CEO of Godzilla, the fracking company, but he had been about to commence a mea-culpa act; Odd? Were there two factions operating? It is the nature of a cor-

241

porate bully that they have rarely any concern about the fairness of their actions, or consideration for others. They were, and Jock Mannford was a classic example, sociopaths, and they considered themselves outside the demands of society's norms. It was all about profit, regardless of the consequences to the environment, particularly pertinent in Jock's case. They had no feeling for social justice or fairness. How could you if your focus was on maximising profit?

Momentarily, Jock thought about the reports coming in thick and fast of serious accidents, deaths even, of equally important people in the corporate world in the City of London. Civil servants, some of whom were in his pocket, were also declaring mea culpa after having received their umble pie. Jock saw this as a plague of pies and confessions. Politicians throwing themselves on the mercy of the electorate, paying back expenses and blaming someone else. "It wasn't me, Guv, honest. Just following orders."

Mannford thought for a moment. He would never be cowed, but how to wriggle out of his predicament is what preoccupied his thoughts.

His personal assistant, looking on, was starting to feel nervous. Her boss had turned white as a sheet, a china white face with sprouting broccoli purple cheeks. Mannford was planning his excuses, running through a list of his employees he could blame. Maybe he could curb his galloping greed for a few weeks? Yes, he would need to put on a show of contrition if he were to survive, for it was clear that whoever was orchestrating this campaign was ruthless enough to bring him and his fellow greedy bastards, down. Kill them even, but this was not what worried Mannford. In his corporate life, he had always known that for one pressure there was generally an equally powerful counter pressure, or in this case argument. This was orthodoxy. In the various Christian churches and other religious establishments, he had become aware that not everyone supported this recent diametric swing in promoting a caring leadership. Self-interest would always out. Jock Mannford knew this only too well, and the church was not unlike the corporate world. It had its self-interested people and organisations, those who had a vested interest in maintaining the status quo.

The difficulty Mannford had was deciding on which side his safety and security resided. The Church, one presumes, in its recent guise of the caring society, would not resort to violence to achieve their aims. However, they might not be averse to publicly shaming him and his businesses, and had more than suggested this was among their weaponry. However, the alternative, the orthodox people, were his kind of people and they could be ruthless. He knew also that some were not averse to a bit of physical persuasion to get their own way. Hadn't he resorted to this occasionally, to get *his* own way? For the good of the company, of course. For the overall benefit of the bottom line, naturally, the shareholders, and this was how he justified his actions that ordinary people would be jailed for. But such calling to book didn't happen in his world. The bankers did not get jailed for what they had done to bring down the financial systems of the Western world. They were supported as an absolute necessity for the future of a capitalist society, as a natural course of events. So it was also with the big corporations. They were needed and they needed to be strong, so that they could sustain the people in work and make their products. It was the trickle-down policy that Mannford had so readily promoted, knowingly and, frequently chuckling to himself that, in reality, it was only the crumbs from the table that tumbled down unequally. Mannford restricted those crumbs, naturally; they were his crumbs, after all. The people always had to be hungry, wanting more. Not sufficiently sustained to grow in strength, or in numbers, in order to challenge the status quo, but most of all, they had to be grateful for what they got.

So, what to do? He was aware of the crowds gathering in the centre of London, and across the country, apparently. 'This dancing fucking nun, and the conductor, for heaven's sake,' and he chuckled at his own little joke, further confusing his PA.

Well, Mannford had already anticipated his pie, as you would expect. He had already trailed a more humanitarian policy for his company, not that he had any intention of keeping to this policy. However, it had been seen by some fellows in the City of London as a weakening of his and his company's stance and he had received warnings a lot less subtle than a pie. However, these were his people and these people knew he would be grifting. Wouldn't they? He had noticed a lot of activity with the office caretakers lately, not unexpected as he had reported problems with the electrics in his suite of offices.

Celeste had lost a lot of her bravado and for the first time worried her boss was having a heart attack. She addressed Mannford while taking a sideways glance at the Umble Pie, central on the conference table, steaming and giving off a mouth-watering aroma. 'The archbishop left, sir, but he made it clear you should reconsider your company policies, not those recent palliative messages, but to declare a new direction at a press conference, today. I believe he considered your discreet trailing at the recent Guild-hall dinner as not substantial enough. The humble pie is a metaphor. I'm sure you see that...'

'Never,' Mannford shouted, interrupting Celeste and quite frightening her.

And as she stepped away from her manic boss, the natural daylight in the room dimmed and a beam of light illuminated the pie. Celeste backed further away, a little shaken. She looked up, swung her gaze to the light switches, but she already knew there was no spotlight on the ceiling, and no controlling switch in the room.

Jock Mannford stuttered a response, himself a little taken aback by the inexplicable darkening of the room and the laser-like beam of light, but he took things of this kind in his stride; he was arrogantly convinced of his invincibility. It was probably a facility he had not known about until just now.

'I hope you told the archbishop he could go fuck himself, Celeste?' he chortled. Would this be a strong enough response to satisfy his orthodox fellows?

Celeste waved a scroll of paper that had been handed to her by the archbishop after she had indeed told him to fuck off and that she wouldn't be kissing the bloated tart's ring. Celeste recounted the story to her boss and Mannford chuckled, picturing the tableau and quite enjoying the thought. Celeste waved the tube of paper, secured with a red wax seal, seeking permission to break the seal and read. Mannford nodded to indicate she should read it to him. Celeste broke the seal with her index finger and unfurled the paper. It curled back again so she laid it out on the table and pinned the corners down with nearby weighty reports of profit and the consequent death of the environment and, just then, a second laser beam illuminated the scroll. She read: *"Ma-Santi has policies that neglect the welfare and sustainability of the world and, the people within. Ma-Santi is driven by corporate greed and this is criminally irresponsible. This must stop immediately or the consequences will be dire for the company and you personally. You have been delivered an Umble Pie and this should be seen as more than just a metaphor, but a stark warning. The world is in danger because of you and your company's actions. This is the eleventh hour and you have until eleven am to telephone the number below and declare that Ma-Santi will be changing completely their corporate strategies. You have this one chance only."*

Celeste and Mannford both glanced at the clock on the wall. It was five minutes until eleven. Celeste copied the telephone number down and handed the piece of paper to Mannford, who memorised it, screwed it up and targeted the ball at the waste basket. 'Well, seems I have no choice,' he said as the clock ticked toward the eleventh hour, though he was still considering all of his options. How to declare what is wanted and how to renege on it later. His main worry was, would his fellow sociopaths concur? Well, of course they would, but would they realise what he was doing? Would they recognise his strategy and, as the clock rolled over to eleven, so another spotlight beamed on to Mannford and he jolted in pain. He convulsed, his hair, such that it was, frizzled and smoked and after a minute or two, the spotlights on

Mannford and the pie ceased shining. Daylight returned.

Celeste gripped her nose, the smell of burning flesh made her feel sick. She looked on, amazed at what she had just seen. She walked over to her smoking boss but could already see he was dead, electrocuted was her guess, and she would have been right.

TWENTY-EIGHT

THE AMBULANCE ARRIVED AT THE WATERLOO taxi rank, Sister Winifrede having already been whisked away to Westminster Abbey. The paramedics set up drips and were carrying out CPR, (*clever para-prancing round*), it did not seem to be working, but still they danced as Pimple was lifted into the ambulance and it departed, nee-naaing, blue lights flashing.

'Where you taking him, mate?' Jack asked of the paramedic as the man packed up his dancing pumps and folded away a lovely flowing skirt that had coordinated beautifully with green fatigues, and put them in the saddle bags of his bike.

'St Thomas' Hospital.' the medic replied. 'It's the closest.'

'Right,' Jack said and, turned to Mandy who was trying, unsuccessfully, to soothe the sobbing Cecelia. 'We can pick him up later, or I can get him a message to meet us at Trafalgar Square. What do you think?'

Mandy did not know what to think. About what had just happened, how stupid it was and yet, how serious it had been, and more importantly, about her husband, who might now have completely lost it.

Cecelia continued wailing.

'Okay. I'll get a message to him.' Jack said, just knowing he was having a calming influence on the women in his life. Jack was good at calming women who, he knew from experience, could get as little upset at times, not realising he was the one who generally gave them the vapours, which in extreme cases became more like an attack of poisonous gas.

Mandy sideswiped Jack and he teetered, but did not fall. He was pleased with this, because frankly, he was not very good at teetering and although he would not admit to it, he was so bad at teetering he would, more often than not, fall. She watched her husband teeter and wondered why Jack teetered, knowing he should have fallen and then, she had her answer, he was getting his phone out of the almost bottomless pockets of his billowing shapeless shorts.

Jack looked at his iPhone, it had a cracked glass. He raised the phone to his ear, shook it, it still had that familiar rattle. He handed the phone to Mandy who turned it on for him and passed it back. Jack hit loads of buttons and shouted at it, 'St Thomas' hospital?' Nothing, so he shouted again. Still nothing. He looked towards Mandy and she shook her head in wonderment, which Jack read as, don't be daft she was admin, so he handed the phone back to Mandy and said, 'St Thomas hospital please, sweet'art, quick as you can.' While he waited, he looked around at the make-believe carnage, whistling a lovely tune that for the life of him he could not identify, and was thus surprised to find himself teetering, though not so expertly this time. He fell.

'Fuck off, I'm not admin.' Mandy said to her husband as he strived to lift himself off the ground. 'And, it was Doctor fucking Who you were whistling.' Slowly he lifted himself up, quite pleased with himself, albeit a tad injured, as he had noticed Mandy was making the call and he now knew what he had been whistling, but, for the life of him he had forgotten again. Such was life as a big roller he thought. Mandy handed him the phone and, for health and safety reasons, he ignored the Mandy death beam stare, hoping it would not morph into the Vulcan death grip. He responded to the squeaky voice coming out of his phone.

'Hello, St Thomas' Hospital?' Jack asked unnecessarily as the ant on the end was repeating the fact that she was. 'All right, all right, keep yer girdle on,' Jack said to the irate ant. 'I was wondering if Thomas was there,' and Jack rolled up at his incredibly witty aside, went back to ask for the mortuary and was greeted by the dialling tone. Swaying to avoid having to teeter, he handed the phone back to admin. 'Get her back for us, babes, and see if you can get one with a sense of humour this time, please,' He looked again at the carnage of the station forecourt while he tapped the theme from Dr Who with his best tapping foot, his right one, as this foot always remembered what tune was being tapped.

Mandy sighed, considered bashing her husband but just recently she had noticed he was mastering his teeter and sway and wondered if Mike had been giving him lessons. Mandy was aware that in the Catholic seminary you learned about ducking and diving, which she presumed included teetering and swaying. She got the hospital back on the line and gave the phone to Jack, who was momentarily stunned as he looked down the deep cut blouse of his wife. She prodded him with a pointy finger and he teetered into action.

Such are the amazingly anaesthetic qualities of Mandy's breasts to her eejit that he just took the phone and completely forgot to fall over. 'Thanks, luv,' he said and then addressed the new hospital telephonist ant. 'Mortuary, please.' The hospital ant was obviously confused as Jack repeated his request twice and each time escalating in tone and noise level. Eventually he was put through, 'Dead Fred, is that you?'

Mandy was surprised at her husband knowing the mortuary attendant, but then knew she shouldn't be as he seemed to know everybody. She then heard him arguing with Dead Fred who, it seemed, contended that Dead Fred wasn't his name and Jack saying he should get it changed then, by dead pole. Jack rolled up laughing and went to go back to his call but got only the dialling tone. Jack sighed, 'Blimey, some people just can't take a joke.' He handed the phone back to Mandy.

'St Thomas' Hospital?' She asked, trying unsuccessfully not to laugh.

———

Bev opened the salon door and stood aside. Claudio fluttered in and took up a position on the reception counter and, with his spare wing, he brushed the comb on his head. He had always disliked his top feathers and wondered if his mum had not had a fling with a macaw. It would explain a lot.

Bev flounced back and addressed the parrot, 'Yes, luv, what can I do for you?' Bev could already see the unruly feathers atop Claudio's head, and also knew the parrot and knew to be wary of what he said, but now, as he looked towards Fabio and back to the mitre feathers on Claudio, he thought he had some information he could share with Twink. This had to be the Pope's parrot and, if he was also correct in his surmising, the man sitting in the chair only a few metres away with his head under the hairdryer setting the manipulated Vatican Mohican, was the missing pope.

Fabio could not miss the arrival of his parrot as he looked into the wall mirror through the visor of the hairdryer. He had been briefed by Claudio to not react as this would give him away and, for the time being, the papal Parrot needed Fabio to be Pope Incognito the fifth.

TWENTY-NINE

THE CARETAKER CHRONICLE, CLOSELY ALLIED TO The Barbers Bulletin, both electronic political pamphlets, buzzed. The telecommunication reporting:

Is the Pope the Pope?

Is the Pope a pretender pope and not the Pope at all?

So who is this other pope if he's not the Pope?

Who is this dancing nun and has she actually stopped? Is she now really dead? Will she start dancing again and will her head fall off?

Is she actually dead? Again?

Is resurrection becoming a new trend in the church?

The conductor of the famous Nuns' Orchestra is reported to have miraculously turned up reheaded and although short a second fiddle, the stand-in not quite up to lamasery muster, the orchestra would meet its playing commitment in Trafalgar Square. This might not be a good idea.

The mainstream media, TV and newspapers,

were full of the religious conundrum. A missing pope. A missing Archbishop of Canterbury, although he was reported to have apparently visited Ma-Santi headquarters in the City of London, mysteriously, and was said to have handed over a church canon to the PA of CEO, Jock Mannford. He had then departed and, moments later, the chief executive had been electrocuted. There was also the Arch Numpti of the Church of Egypt, seen modestly and humbly crossing London on a rag-and-bone man's horse and cart, being delivered to number ten Downing Street. There was a picture, which admittedly had focused on Claudio. What was that all about? The government press officers were being tight-lipped. It was being reported that the dancing nun had again dropped down dead, exhausted, and had been taken to the Mortuary at St Thomas' Hospital, just a short distance from Westminster Abbey, where she had been dancing for members of the cardinal's clergy, in the Catholic bits of the Abbey.

Mandy picked up a newspaper in the reception area of the Savoy hotel, scanned the religious news and relayed the gist to Jack, as was her administration newscaster lot in married life. Jack took it all as normal and ruminated on the salient points, like, where are we having this spot of lunch and he needed a wee. To be honest, Jack was a little irritated. What should have been a pleasant horse and cart ride across Waterloo Bridge and down the Strand, had been spoiled for him by the constant wailing of Cecelia. All of his platitudes, meant in a kindly way, that she should not worry and they could nip back to the mortuary and pick Pimple up later if she was so concerned, seemed to fall on deaf, grieving ears.

There were times when Jack just did not understand women.

Mandy clumped him.

'What?' Jack said.

'You.'

'Me?' Jack was the picture of innocence; ugly, but innocent.

'Yes, you.'

'What have I done?' He looked down at his trousers to make sure he had not wet himself whilst ruminating. It can happen, ask any cow.

Mandy set about explaining to him about his insensitivity. She skipped the horse and cart journey, to tell him he was also a deaf twat, which to be fair, Jack knew, but never admitted to if he ever heard anyone say this and, she pointed out that they were now being addressed by the hotel concierge. Jack jumped when the concierge tapped his shoulder. (Told you he was a deaf twat). Mandy chuckled and felt immediately guilty as she took in the wretched look of Cecelia.

'Excuse me, Sir; can we do anything for your friend?' The concierge, whose name tag said he was Bill, was looking directly at Cecelia.

Jack recovered his posy. Mandy thought he meant poise and mentioned this to Bill, but having said that, she thought he did look a bit like a bunch of dead daisies and definitely had cauliflower ears.

Jack addressed Bill. 'Look, Gill, I'm here to have lunch with a Jim Samuels and don't worry about her...' he flicked his head towards Cecelia, '... her fiancé's just died, but it will all be okay in the end, except I'm feckin' Hank Marvin. I've not had anything to eat since brunch.' And at that Jack beamed, having scored, he thought, a significant point in impressing

Gill that he had brunch, and not just elevenses. He continued, 'And, I'm getting a bit of an 'eadache, what with her crying an' that.' Jack added, displaying his empathetic side. 'Haven't got any parrots-eat-em-all, 'ave yer, mate?'

'Pathetic side more like. You're a dozy twat,' Mandy reacted.

Jack thought Mandy was being a little intensive and should understand that he would be hungry and had even suggested elevenses on the train, but of course he had hopping and chugging practice to do, which Mandy had helpfully pointed out as the food trolley passed by.

'Insensitive,' she said, correcting his thinking.

Cecelia let out another wail, and Jack considered asking Gill if he could find them a soundproof booth for lunch and Cecelia wailed some more, so Mandy bashed him.

'Did I speak me forts?'

'Yes you did and, you can be so intensive at times. I don't know what I ever saw in you.'

This shocked Jack, as you would expect, but there were plenty of mirrors in the hotel foyer to reassure him he was still a handsome man, knowing also that his wife could be quite shallow at times, and his physical appearance was number one in her things she liked about him.

Mandy slapped her forehead.

Jack looked at one of the mirrors and he was definitely mystified. He examined his wife's forehead, he could not see a squashed fly that he was prepared to remove for her, just to show there were no hard feelings, and was even tempted to eat it unless he got something nourishing soon.

The hotel reception pantomime was interrupted by Jim Samuels, who calmed the concierge who seemed to take exception to being called Gill. Bill stepped back, accepting the authority exuded by the MI5 psychiatrist.

'Jack, please, enough.'

Jack drew his finger across his mouth to indicate it was truly zipped, then quickly unzipped it. 'Come on Jim, I'm starvin',' and then speedily re-zipped. He looked towards Mandy and she acknowledged he was a good boy and Jack smiled, not realising that his mouth became a little unzipped because of it and some tiny noises came out, nothing that anybody should really worry about, mainly revolving around how feckin' hungry he was. He harrumphed and, putting a comforting arm around Cecelia, which was just a way of Jack resting it as he had been doing a lot of waving lately and, by way of multitasking, he steered the tragic figure of extraordinary beauty, apart from red eyeballs, to the dining room, following Jim and Mandy.

Jim directed them to a table in the corner with a glorious view across the gardens down to the Thames. Jack pointed this out, but Mandy spoiled it for him by telling him it was only a picture on the wall. It was all the same to Jack and he further commented on what a beautiful day it was and funny how all the people out of the window wore mediaeval costume and stood still a lot.

Mandy derred, read the note under the black and white etching. It was a picture of the Savoy when it was the Duke of Clarence's residence, back in the day. She knew a bit of history and recalled it was before he betrayed his brother the king, Edward the something or other, but could not be sure. Maybe she would ask Gill on the way out? He might know.

Cecelia said she was not hungry and grizzled a bit more. Jack thought this was an improvement on wailing and suggested she still order as Jim was paying, and he could eat hers if she was not hungry. Cecelia clumped Jack and, for the first time since the demise of her Pimple, she felt a little better.

Jack thought also it was nice to see she was over it now and Mandy clumped him. Feck me, he thought, a man can't win around here and Jim leaned across the table and flicked his head. 'Shut up, Jack, and listen.'

Jack did shut up, but only because the waiter had brought the bread rolls that he noticed were warm where the hotel cat had been sitting on them. Jack blew away any stray fur, and with his knife, scooped up all the butter in the dish and smeared it on a tiny part of his roll. 'Oi, Pedro, some more butter per favour.' Jack had noticed that the waiter was Mexican, although he did wonder where his sombrero was. The waiter said he would bring more butter, in what Mandy was certain was a German accent; Herr Pedro?

Jim Samuels quietened Jack. 'Jack, settle down and tell me what you think is happening and, what we need to do about it. Mackeroon and Blogg will be with the Numpti by now. I hear prime minister's question time has been cancelled as Whitehall is chokka with demonstrators, as is Trafalgar Square, Parliament Square and the Mall, so the PM, dep PM and the Numpti are going nowhere. You say the Pope is having a haircut and the Archbishop seems to be visiting all the corporate headquarter buildings in the City of London and, in his wake, many of the CEOs are either going *mea culpa* or snuffing it. Some dying just after they have declared their company policies will change. I have to say, this is not what I expected. I expected people would be pleased these companies were announcing a more humanist approach to their business and, if so, why are they dropping like flies.'

Jack had his nose into his bread roll, sniffing loudly, was that the cat's arse he could smell?

'Jack, please,' Mandy admonished her husband, who she knew was often put off by cat bottoms; he was, after all, a dog man. He even looked like one; a pug. Jack demurred and told them he might as well sample the Mexican dancing beans (olives) as lunch had not arrived and, he was sure his bread roll tasted like cat shite. Mandy stopped him from summoning Herr Pedro.

THIRTY

ALL HELL BROKE OUT IN THE SALON AS CLAUDIO
jumped on to the Harmony hairspray can and
squirted it past a smelly candle on the reception
counter. A big jet of flame burst into the hall-like
salon and set alight the net drapes that flounced down
as prissy hairdressing station dividers. The nets were
reminiscent of clouds and these clouds now flashed
lightning and rained down flame and fury upon
Twink's cutting crew.

The Pope grabbed the gun from Bev and shot him
in the leg. As Pope, he had no desire to kill anyone,
but to maim wouldn't hurt, well it would, but it
wouldn't kill and not him, see. He had to get to the
door but Bev had limped there and was stopping him,
menacing with an M25 or some type of motorway
machine gun, Claudio was not sure, except it was
pink, so it was probably one belonging to the Kalashnikov Ballet Company. Bev was looking menacing
with his blue-rinsed hair and bloody leg. The Pope
shot and killed him. Well, he wasn't really the Pope,
was he?

Claudio steered the Pope, still with rollers in his

hair, out into the street as flames began to lick the pavement. The glass shop front exploded and shattered fragments carpeted the road, the blast knocking the Pope over and the stuffing out of Claudio, who soon recovered and barked at the Pope to get up and stop mincing around and crying. (He was good at dog impressions, did them all the time in the Vatican). The Pope did recover and followed Claudio as his Papal bird headed out of the mews and turned toward Berkley Square, both ducking and diving as shots rang out, bullets chewed into brickwork and ricochets pinged off lampposts.

Just as they neared Berkley Square and the relative safety the public space offered, out of the blue, a set of roller-skating nuns swept into their path and, with deft use of battery-charged supersonic hair driers, the Pope and Claudio were knocked back and swamped. They were captured, prisoners of the Barbaras. What would happen now?

———

Lilac kissed Grace. Despite the seriousness of events occurring around them, their powerful new love continued to surface, frequently preoccupying both women. They were in the anteroom of the mortuary of St Thomas' Hospital, as requested by Olive Doyle and some cowboy called Dick Austin, who had said he was MI5, Gumshoe Department. Grace knew of Jane Austin as she was MI5, but thought he had retired, not realising he had only flounced a bit; there is a world of difference.

The waiting area was a small room that tried very hard to be bright but respectful, mock windows with

flowery drapes, plastic flowers on woodgrain lami-
nate-topped coffee tables, dark blue PVC seats that
squeaked and farted as you sat on them and a black-
and-white chequer board tile floor. If, for some extraordinary reason, you were indeed comforted by the
décor and ambience, the distinct smell of carbolic
would wrench at your nostrils and scorch your throat
as the all-pervading scent inveigled its way to agitate
your stomach.

Lilac and Grace, however, were preoccupied, in a
lovely way and did not notice the tall skinny man
standing by the double doors to the autopsy room,
dressed like a shiny black drainpipe with a floppy
wide-brimmed hat atop a hooked nose that cast no
shadow from the flickering fluorescent lighting. Of
course, Grace and Lilac would not recognise Liberato
Zondo, the Priest-Finder General, even if they could
see him, which they couldn't, and not because they
were otherwise engaged.

'This is quite sexy, isn't it?' Lilac said suggestively
to Grace.

'Lilac, we're in a mortuary.'

'Well, not quite in a mortuary and we are all
alone.' Lilac flicked her head toward a cupboard and
headed for it, opened the door and stepped inside
with Liberato Zondo, not that she was aware of this.
Grace soon followed and the appassionato grew
rapidly and then eased back as the cupboard developed an eerie red glow and, at the point of acute embarrassment, Zondo revealed himself.

'Fuck!' Lilac said, snapping her head back and
banging it against the cupboard door, going ouch as
Grace grabbed her. She screamed again, 'My fucking
shoulder, Grace.'

'Language, Lilac,' Grace and Zondo said together, except Zondo said, "Lingua Lilla," and they looked at each other, a smile appearing in the corner of Grace's mouth and a rare look of fear upon the face of Zondo.

'Zondo?'

'Si' Zondo replied to Grace, but his gaze was focused on Lilac, who, although carrying a shoulder injury, looked as if she was about to let fly with a series of kung fu moves that would cause serious injury. So he disappeared again.

'Where the fuck did he go?' Lilac shouted.

'Lingua,' Zondo said, thus revealing his invisible appearance enabling Lilac to get a side kick into the priestly crown jewels, that he had never used, but now were no longer in pristine chapel condition. The priest finder general reappeared, this time crouched and clearly in some pain. 'Donna di tits di Cristo senora,' he squeaked.

'Language,' Lilac and Grace said in unison.

'A thousand pardons, ladies, mille scuse, signore,' Zondo replied, correcting his English and Italian manner of conversing, standing more erect, though appearing as though the cupboard had developed a stifling atmosphere, which Grace and Lilac agreed upon, so they stepped out into the waiting room.

'Zondo? You are Zondo, aren't you?'

'And you iz Grace. I 'ave 'eard so mucha abouta you,' the priest, who looked like the phantom flan flinger of Olde London Town, said, acknowledging his identity while staring at Lilac.

'What's your problem, face ache?'

'Lilac, please.' Grace admonished.

'Well.'

'Well, what?'

'Just well.' Lilac looked at Zondo, 'Oi, knob 'ead, got a carrot up yer celibate arse, 'ave yer? Never seen two women kissing?'

Zondo coloured again and Grace stepped in to relieve the discomfort of the Magus. 'So, I take it a lot of the mystical stuff is down to you?'

'What?' Lilac exclaimed.

'You heard, Lilac,' and she turned to face the still red faced priest. 'Lilac, let me introduce you to Liberato Zondo of the Illusionati. Straordinario Eccezionale, mago; stregone, genio parte del programma che aiuta l'utente a eseguire una funzione efficiente, in other words, the Vatican's magician, or sorcerer, a part of the Vatican programme that helps to perform a religious function efficiently, to nudge things along a bit, so to speak. The Illusionati perform extraordinary and exceptional acts. What, in the olden days, would have been called miracles.

THIRTY-ONE

LONDON IS ARGUABLY THE HEART OF BRITAIN. IT
is certainly the capital, the decision making centre
and holds the decision making institutions. It is the
power base for the establishment and that establishment, by way of the established grapevine, had been
informed that the *People* had been inspired by Sister
Winifrede and, to a lesser extent, but no less seriously,
by Bea Flat, apparently a bus conductor. But it was
the dancing nun who had become the shining example, illuminated as she was shown in all of the papers,
by a shaft of brilliant light, dancing and not stopping.
Formal news of the demise of the dancing nun had
not been released as yet. Although rumours were
spreading, it was generally not known, and Olive
Doyle and Jim Samuels wanted it kept that way. At
least until they had worked out what to do. Olive had
said the Vatican had sent Liberato Zondo of the Illusionati to the mortuary, but that had meant very little
to Samuels. Jack Austin had asked for Olive to pass
his best wishes on to Libby, he liked her and that
wasn't an illusion, he had said.

And so, as Jack had predicted and Olive had encouraged, the railway tracks, like veins into the heart of the country, were currently channelling trains full of people into the capital city to demonstrate. Pilgrims, inspired by Sister Winifrede and further energised by the announcement of the resurrection of Beatrice Flat, the conductor of the Nuns' Orchestra, who had been requested by the Vatican, Canterbury and Cairo, no less, to play for the people in Trafalgar Square.

But a caretaker at St Thomas' Hospital had recognised the nun, the pink netting that formed the tutu over the habit, tucked into the nun's navy blue flannelette knickers being a dead giveaway. He broke the news, and this spread like wildfire and noticeably, the inbound protesters were deflated, as news was displayed on their phones, but, committed to their journey into town, some solace offered and taken in the knowledge that Bea Flat would still be conducting the Nuns' Orchestra in Trafalgar Square.

———

News of the leak was telephoned through to Jim Samuels by Olive Doyle, not that it had any effect on Jack Austin. He just said it would be all right and the next resurrection might be even better. He always thought second resurrections were somehow better than the first, which could always be seen as a fluke. Anyway, Jack was finishing up Cecelia's Savoy special, egg and chips with spam but he was distracted and further irritated when a shadow loomed over their table. Jack didn't look up, he'd seen the copper enter the hotel dining room just now and he couldn't take a chance that the grieving

Cecelia might change her mind about him eating her grub.

'Are you the people who were at Waterloo Station just now?'

Uh oh, Jack thought, and then said, with a mouth full of chips and spam. 'Wof all out nit?'

'What?' the police inspector replied.

'Wof all out nit?' Mandy explained to the policeman, chuckling to herself and immediately feeling guilty. Blimey, who'd be a Catholic? But Cecelia let Mandy off as she laughed as well and Samuels joined them. The tension had been broken, but not for the copper.

'I fail to see the humour. We have two dead bodies in the St Thomas' Hospital morgue...' He didn't finish as Cecelia immediately burst into tears.

Jack jumped up and, spitting chips with little bits of spam, he said, 'You, tosspot, you've set the silly cow off again,' and the silly cow mooed some more and Jack sighed. What do you have to do to be asthmatic around here, everyone's so intensive.

'Yes,' Mandy said, 'you are insensitive and did you mean empathetic, not asthmatic? So, Jack, please, think about Pimple,' and at that, Cecelia was set off again.

'Fuck!' Jack shouted, and made everyone jump, including the copper who ordinarily would have considered himself a hard nut and not a scaredy cat. He flinched more than jumped, but Jack was bombastically loud and also spluttered chips and spam into the inspector's face.

'What, Jack?'

'Mandy, we've forgotten Pimple.'

Mandy looked confused. Nobody had forgotten

Pimple, except maybe, upon reflection, Jack, 'How so, Jack?'

'This is no time for Japanese, Mandy,' he said and tutted, while flicking his fingers at the copper, who reacted as if he was not used to having people flick fingers at him, either. This cop was on a steep Jack Austin learning curve.

'Phone, you tosspot, mine's got a rattle. It might be a virus snake.'

The policeman was stunned and even more bewildered in that he complied with this loony's request and handed over his phone and then, watched as the grotesque one eyed epsilon hit all the buttons, looked at it, hit more buttons then shouted. 'St Thomas' Hospital, the morgue, please.' Jack waited, listened, perplexed. Nothing. He had even said please.

'Shall I ring the hospital for you?' The copper asked, applying a supercilious grin.

'Yes, please,' Jack and Mandy said in unison and, handing the phone back, Jack mentioned he had already pressed some buttons and reminded the inspector that he should ask for the morgue.

The inspector cancelled all of the gobbledygook on the screen of his phone and speed-dialled the hospital. He was soon put through to the morgue and looked at Jack as to what next? Following Jack's instruction he asked for Dead Eyed Dick. The inspector held the phone away as a tirade from a mortuary attendant with no sense of humour, barraged his plod ear, saying it was Fred, then paused for thought.

Jack flicked his fingers again, summoning the phone. He would take it from here, and the copper passed the phone over. 'Hello Fred, it's Jack here, although funnily enough, in my gumshoe persona, I'm known as Dick.' Jack looked up and expected to see a sea of amused and impressed faces, but didn't. He did see a steaming policeman, a frustrated Jim Samuels, a distraught Cecelia and, his wife just had her hand over her eyes with her head tilted backwards. Jack thought she'd never see the ceiling if she kept her hand like that and might have mentioned it, if the hastily received rebuke from his wife was any guide. No sex tonight he thought, thinking Mandy must have a headache.

'I do have a headache and it's you. Please get on with it,' and she tilted her head to the phone as Fred the-dead-eye-dick ant, was squeaking to get Dick the dipstick dicktective's attention.

'Hi Fred, Dick here again,' and Mandy swore she heard a large sigh from Dead Fred. 'Look, you have a Lord Pimple in with you, and, unless I have misunderstood all what is happening, a baller-feckin'-rina nun. Whatever you do, don't start the autopsy, and if you put him in the fridge, make sure he's wrapped up nice and warm, there's a good Dead Eye.' Jack thought that was it and handed the phone back to DI Plod, who demonstrably had to pacify the mortuary attendant.

Just then Wally-Wally turned up, nodded recognition to the other Met inspector and then to everyone sitting around the table. He took the phone and spoke slowly, to make sure Dead Fred got the message. 'Hello, you have just received instructions. This is Inspector Wallace from SBS and you should have also been talking to, or if you hadn't you soon will be, Grace Church and Detective Chief Inspector Smith of the Yard, please do as you have been asked and as they direct.' He looked up to Jack, 'Anything else, Jack?'

'Yes, tell him he will be visited by a priest, one Liberato Zondo, and he is to allow the priest to give Pimple the last rites.'

Cecelia whimpered.

Wally-Wally passed on the message, hung up and returned the phone to Inspector Plod, looked at Jack as he pulled a chair up for himself and one for Plod. 'Okay, Jack, what's occurring?'

Jack smiled, flicked his fingers again and summoned Pedro the German waiter. 'Ve vil haff zee appfel crumble unt zee custard, and make it znappy, vee hav to getanzee a body from zee charnel house mein mush and then, we go to the concertbaumstuff down the road.'

———

Liberato, Grace and Lilac entered the autopsy room just as Dead Fred was putting down his phone. In front of them they could see laid out on stainless steel tables Winifrede and Pimple, both dead as doornails.

Fred put a hand up to halt their entry and to offer a jobsworth rebuke about them not being allowed into his domain, but was immediately caught mid verbal assault by an intense beam of light that also paralysed him. Dead Fred could see what was going on around him but could not move a muscle, his dead eyes remaining focused on the two women, who appeared not to be able to keep their hands off each other. The other person was an extraordinary-looking tall gent, dressed like a skinny black plastic bin bag, with a big hat. He took in everything and was further stunned as

Liberato flared his big black shiny cloak that transformed into a dense black cloud that settled over the two corpses.

As the cloud dispersed, sucked up by the autopsy ventilation system, it revealed Pimple sitting up. stretching and yawning, as though waking from a deep sleep, except it had been a short and apparently shallow death.

'Gawd blimey, guv,' Pimple said to the still paralysed mortuary attendant and, swivelling off the shiny stainless steel table and swinging his legs to the floor, he switched his gaze to the now not quite so stiff, stiff nun, as her previously stilled plimsolled feet began to twitch. 'Strike a light sweet'art,' Pimple said to the now animated formerly dead nun, 'fort you were bleedin' brown bread?'

Lilac looked at Grace and they both looked towards Liberato. He looked down at the slick polished floor of the autopsy room, was that a hint of colour tipping his china white cheekbones? Was the Illusionati sorcerer embarrassed?

Yes he was. 'Oopsah eh Pratolina,' he said in a flourishing Italian (whoops a-daisy). 'E fottuto dat uno fino (fecked that one up)'.

'Yeah, wot he said, and I couldn't 'arf murder a cup of Rosie.'

'He's gone all fucking cockney,' Grace said.

'Lingua,' Liberato said.

'Lingo,' Pimple said looking directly at Grace, trying to recall who she was.

'Yeah, Grace, language,' Lilac said.

PART THREE
A MURMURATION OF PLEBS

THIRTY-TWO

'YOU HAD BEST STAY HERE, SIR,' THE AIDE MORE than suggested to the prime minister.

The PM brushed the aide aside; he wasn't about to go out, least of all into a baying mêlée of the great unwashed just for prime minister's questions in the House.

As is normal, the House of Commons debating chamber was packed for Question Time and, although they were unaware it was to be postponed, they did know they would be stuck in the House for the duration. MPs and their entourages had been advised it was too risky to go outside. The fervour of the crowd was, at best, unpredictable, especially for Tory MPs, who were considered red rags to a massive herd of bulls all dressed in black hoods. Why the hoods? It was thought it was out of respect for Sister Winifrede, their inspiration, or like a monk's hood? Some were beaked, rather like mediaeval plague doctors' masks. The crowd swayed this way and that way as they chanted. The movement varied like radio waves as the amplitude fluctuated. The collective appearance was that of a murmuration of starlings as the crowd energetically oscillated, each anonymous individual following another and this swirling mesmeric moiré of black dot patterns was filling Parliament Square and all the way along Whitehall to Trafalgar Square and down the Mall, filling the ceremonial road all the way to Buckingham Palace, where the guard had been re-inforced.

For the police looking on from elevated positions, the effect was hypnotic and the sight did not stand extended viewing. This had been the reasoning for the masks, as well as anonymity, and the semblance of a mass of like-minded people. The peasants were rising up, here and across the country, for the hoods had been distributed nationally and all demonstrators wore them.

Stuck in the chamber, MPs debated the actions outside, not least the dancing nun, who, they were re-lieved to hear, had stopped dancing and finally expired.

As far as the PM and dep PM were concerned, the crowds choking Whitehall were not baying, they were peaceful, civilised, just a lyrical repetitive chanting for a new world as they swayed in unison. The merriment changed gradually to an incessant, groggy, sigh of sadness and, the movement slowed as the news of the dancing nun dying again was ab-sorbed. And then, the swagger returned – there was still the resurrected conductor Bea Flat. The crowd clung to this scrap of inspiration as if it were the last vestige of hope for a true democracy, for a new way of life for the people. It was a mixture of grief and mourning but, most of all, hope. Hope for a new dawn where the rights of the people would be paramount. It was a vision that had taken a grip of the whole country, and those who had considered eschewing, as opposed to chewing, their Umble Pie rapidly reconsidered their position.

The British were known as a peaceful nation of tolerant people, but as many in the past had found out, they will be pushed only so far, after which the mouse will roar, transmuted. The British Lion incarnate. Governments and even the monarchic line had for more than two hundred years lived in dread of a people's revolution and the PM was being informed that throughout the land, masses of plebs had taken to the streets. Peacefully at the moment. Was this Britain's *Velvet* revolution, *A British Spring*?

Mackeroon took his latest in a long line of telephone calls he had fielded all morning from captains of industry, City-boy bankers and big players, looking for action from the prime minister. More than a few suggested that this was what their donations paid for and, not for the first time that morning, Mackeroon regretted his policy of cuts to the police and the military. They would be no match if the crowds turned nasty and all reports were suggesting this crowd was rigidly resolute. The establishment wanted action to defend what they considered their morally and righteously proclaimed rights. The government, in whatever guise, needed to put down this peasants' revolt, and in a manner that would teach the plebs a lesson they would not forget in more than a few lifetimes.

'But we have already seen off the dancing nun,' Mackeroon suggested down the phone, hoping he would be seen as a ruthless leader, a man of decisive action, which is what he knew he was expected to be. It was what he had been inserted into number ten to be, even though he knew he had nothing to do with

277

the final demise of Sister Winifrede. He listened dutifully and attentively to his telephonic lecture, unable
to disguise his fear as he was instructed to assure each
caller in turn that the resurrected conductor would
meet a similar fate, preferably before the concert was
due to start. The crowds had to be subdued. Subjugated is what was meant and the PM and dep PM
knew this as they discussed telephoning MI5 to make
the necessary arrangements, in the national interest.
Needs must, for the greater good and all that.
Mackeroon's posture became more erect,
Churchillian, as he prepared to defend his country by
putting down the people, not on the beaches, but on
the streets.

By coincidence, as he finished the final call, the
PM and dep PM were informed that Dr Samuels of
MI5 was on the line. Mackeroon accepted the call
and history would record this conversation as the telephone call that *joined the dots*.

––––––

'Oi shut it!' Lilac regressed to her natural cockney wit.

'Oo me, mush? Shut your own bleedin' norf an
sowf or you'll get a bunch of fives so far down yer
frote I'll be able to tickle yer bottle an glass.'

'Language, Lord Pimple! You as well, Lilac,'
Grace admonished both verbally and with an accompanying combative face.

Lilac had seen that look before and shivered with
a sexual frisson that she had only recently realised she
enjoyed. 'Have I been naughty, Grace?'

'You have, Lilac, and when we get home...'

Grace grinned salaciously and Lilac squirmed in

anticipation, but realised she had to think and also had to get Zondo back on track. The magus stood in the corner of the mortuary, completely visible, murmuring to himself that he had never made a mistake before.

Grace knew that prima-donna wizards often needed the occasional boost in morale. 'Liberato, darling,' she began and the papal wizard turned his head, 'that was a lovely bit of magic, wasn't it, Lilac?' She looked for support from Lilac and got it.

'Yeah, skinny, totally brilliant, especially how you turned Pimple from a posh dead knob into a galloping cockney,' and she giggled, then froze under Grace's stare.

Grace turned back to the black beanpole. 'Liberato,' she said, softened her voice a little more, addressing the man's puppy dog eyes, 'you are such an amazing magician.'

Zondo muttered an interjection: 'Magus.'

'What?' Lilac and Grace replied.

'Magus, it's magus, I'm a Papal magus,' Zondo asserted.

'Oh, fuck off, you ponce.' Lilac expressed what she thought of magi, Papal or any other sort, for that matter. She didn't even like *Harry Potter*, considered him a weaselly ponce with National Health glasses. She much preferred *Hermione*; well, she would, wouldn't she?

Grace brought things back on track. 'Zondo, what I am trying to say is that you are a wonderful fucking papal sorcerer, isn't he, Lilac?' Lilac dutifully nodded, still pissed off with the narcissistic cry-baby magus divo, and might have mentioned it, including that she also thought he was most definitely a ponce, and

Zondo cried some more, and Lilac kicked him up his bony rabbit's bottom and he stopped.

'Look, sunshine, if you're such a bleedin' ace mage-fucking-us, you can magic Pimple better later on, okay?' Lilac shrugged her shoulders, waved her best supplicant hands about a bit, and turned on her best charm, which did not fool anyone, especially Grace, but it did fool Zondo (some magus he was – but of course he was currently a sulking magus).

'Si, si. I can, can't I,' and he looked at Pimple.

'Right you are, guv. So let's get this apple sauce and pony show on the frog and toad, then.' Pimple replied, heading off to a nearby corpse of a bloke who, although resurrecting a bit, did not look at all well and, he took the man's telephone from him as it was ringing. 'I'll take yer dog and bone, mate.' He stopped it ringing, pressed a load of buttons, then shouted at it. 'Jack Austin, get me Jack Austin.' He thought for a bit, 'Dick Austin, get me Dick... yerk.'

Lilac yanked Lord Pimple's collar and nicked the phone from him, dialled Jack Austin the Dick. 'Hello, I thought this was Jack Austin's phone?' She listened. 'Okay, can you pass me to him, Mandy, please, it's Lilac.' She turned to Grace, Zondo and Pimple, while she batted the resurrecting man demanding the return of his phone back down on to his stainless steel table, telling him if he didn't shut his trap she would make sure he stayed deceased and, behind her hand as if it was a secret to be kept from the not well looking fellow, she whispered to Grace to explain who had answered Jack Austin's phone. 'It was Mandy, Jack's admin,' she said.

Jack came on the phone and she briefed him on where they were and the current status of the various dead and resurrected. 'What? I 'aven't a clue about hairstyles, what?' She looked at Winifrede. 'Yes it's lovely, a lot like Bing Crosby in the Bells of Saint fucking Mary, now what do we do, tosspot?' She asked. Listened, then hung up and passed the phone back to the newly resurrected chap who had now swung his legs off the table, worried that this aggressive cockney sparrow might indeed insert his phone up his bottle and glass, wherever that was.

This new chap was talking posh and wondered why everybody stared at him, not realising he spoke as Pimple ordinarily would.

'Well?' Grace asked, ignoring the Pimple-speaking doppelganger. Lilac looked at her lover's *Rita Tushingham* hair, she thought it beautiful and adored this woman and wondered why she did not tell Jack Austin this. 'Lilac?'

'He said to go to the House of Commons through the secret tunnel under the Thames and Winifrede should address the House of Commons.'

'Okay,' Grace replied, 'where's the secret tunnel?'

Lilac shrugged her shoulders. 'Fucked if I know, it's a secret. Is this Jack, Jane, Dick, feckin' Austin all there?' And she made like she had a screw loose in the side of her head.

'Lingua' Zondo said.

THIRTY-THREE

JIM SAMUELS FINISHED HIS TELEPHONE conversation with the prime minister just as Jack Austin ended his call with Lilac. 'She's a bit fruity, that Lilac girl, ain't she?

'Pots and kettles.' Mandy said under her breath so everybody heard and enjoyed the jest, except Jack, who looked askance that his wife would consider he had a bit of a mouth on him and especially that he might look like a kettle. 'Well you're always spouting on,' her coup-de-grace, and she left it there.

Dr Samuels brought the informal meeting around the Savoy lunch table to order.

'Brunch.' Jack responded.

'What?' Samuels asked, knowing he should have ignored Jack and carried on. Will he never learn?

'It's brunch, Jim. Will you never learn?' And Jack smiled his beatific smile that he knew the Pope would like when they meet, hopefully later that day and, he ran his fingers over his mouth in order to commit the facial gesture to memory, which he promptly forgot as the Archbishop of Canterbury cycled in, brakes squeaking as he pulled up to the table. Leaning, he stuck his archbishop leg out and sat back in his comfortably sized and luxuriously padded, purple satin bishop saddle.

Jack jumped up, his ungainly tree trunk legs bashing the table, causing the tea, coffee and juices to spill on to the pristine starched white table cloth, but things like this would never bother a prima-donna dipstick. All just collateral damage to Jack. 'Poopey.' he called out as if the archbishop was on the other side of the world.

'Jack,' Poopey acknowledged, as the others gathered up the overturned cups and saucers, glasses, and reassembled the scattered cutlery. Samuels waved away an agitated waiter. "Oh, have I missed lunch?' Poopey enquired politely.

From the frenzied activity of tidying and mopping up the table, everyone, including DCI Wally-Wally, intuitively and collectively replied, "Brunch", and Jack leaned back with his hands on the small of his back as if he had just finished cleaning up his mess himself and it had exhausted him. He smiled the smile, the angelic one, the one he was saving for when he met the Pope beatifically, but it was good practice on an archbishop. He had a passing thought that maybe he could become a saint, as he fingered his mouth as would a blind man feeling for the first time someone really ugly (well, Jack was half blind), and he just knew it was a saintly smile. The Pope would love it, but would Claudio? Still, Poopey approved, so bugger the papal parrot, he thought.

'Who's Claudio?' Mandy asked, nodding to confirm he had spoken his thoughts, 'And, I'm sure the Pope will like your Holy Gobshite grin... so, Saint Jack, Claudio?'

'The papal parrot, dozy. Cor blimey, don't you know nuffink? I fort everybody knew Claudio.' He stopped there because not only was it clear to him Mandy had never heard of Claudio, or even that the Pope had a parrot, despite the white smoke when Claudio was elected Parrot to the Pope, but his wife had that look that ordinarily common sense would suggest he run away, which he would commonly do, if he hadn't been frozen to the spot in startled fear.

'That's one of the things I wanted to say.' the Archbishop interjected, having rung the bell on his handlebars of his Sturmey Archer hub-geared steed. It was a Triple Bob peal and it saved the day for Jack. 'I've had a secret squirrel message from the Order of Caretakers, but it is actually from a Brickie you know, Jack. You installed him in Poncenbey's, or so he says?'

'Derek?' Jack replied, and the archbishop nodded.

'Derek?' Mandy asked, and Jack saw that it wasn't one of her throwaway asides that he so often missed and, when he was brought up straight, he would argue that he thought she had thrown that one away. This strategy did buy him time as Mandy was generally confused, but she would quickly throw that away and be back on track, but in that time Jack could usually think of something.

He did think of something. 'Did the Pope get his mitre hair sorted?' It was a reasonable question and one the Archbishop pondered, as he also had a lot of difficulties with mitre hair himself, although some judicious use of gel usually sorted it for him, but it made a mess of the rim of his silly pointy hat.

'I believe he did, just before the shoot-out at the Twink Friseur salon in Mayfair. I am told it was carnage but that is not the main thing.'

Jack looked at Poopey and sighed. 'Have the Pope and Claudio been taken, because that'll throw a spanner in the works.'

'What? What spanner, and in what works?' It was Mandy again.

Blimey, Jack thought, she don't 'arf bang on, but unfortunately spoke and she clipped him around the ear so as to avoid all the bumps on his head. She was always considerate like that, because she loved him, Jack supposed.

Jim Samuels was nodding in agreement with Mandy's question and seeking an answer from Jack, a look that Jack missed of course as it was a direct stare that he met with his saintly grin, not realising Mandy had in mind his martyrdom. What was the question again and, would he be Saint Jack, Saint Jane or Saint Dick? Jack ignored their throwaway comments, ducked, prudently as it turned out, and carried on talking to the archbishop as he had remembered what he was saying now. 'And what are you not telling me? Obviously they were taken to Poncenbey's, that would be logical, or why else would Derek be messaging you? What else is there, Poopey?'

Now, that did stop all major assaults that were planned on Jack's eejit person to speed up his martyrdom and beatification, and all eyes swerved to focus on Poopey.

The archbishop took his time before imparting the bad news and sighing, as he leaned on his handlebars, 'I am sorry to say, I think I have been rumbled by the Caretakers and this may even come from my own Cathedral precincts... but...'

'What else?' Jack pressed.

Poopey offered an expression that suggested he

should have seen how this would all pan out. 'The Pope and Claudio were captured by seven roller-skating nuns.'

Jack took a deep intake of breath and blew it out slowly as he sat down. It was as if he were a big fat balloon slowly deflating, the noise and the exaggerated wrinkles on his face a worried reminder of just how old and how big an eejit he was. But right now he was clearly a worried eejit, 'Sheeite.'

'Jack? What is it, darling?'

Jack looked at Mandy and then at Jim, who seemed equally mystified and thence, biblically, he looked unto the head of the Church in England to announce the dire facts and how their day had become, not just difficult, but nigh-on impossible and, just maybe, they were on the slippery slope to failure.

'Poopey?' Samuels asked.

Poopey screwed up his courage, swung his leg over his saddle and, in a practised manner, flicked the sprung metal stand and parked his bike. He knocked an elderly lady off a nearby chair, blessed the chair, then the prone woman, who cursed in reply as he swung and spun the chair mid air as if it were made of matchsticks. He had found a holy strength from somewhere and, as he sat, as though riding a horse with his arms folded on the back of the chair, so he also deflated, cupped his hands over his head as if to ward off the devil and the now rising harridan, he said unto the stained brunch tablecloth. 'The Holy Barbaras.' He looked up, worried faces stared at him across the bomb site of a table. 'They're here.'

'Here?' Jack asked, clearly horrified, but you had to know how to look through all the ugly bits of his face to see that he was horrified.

Mandy commentated on his looks and people appreciated it. 'He's horrified,' she said. Mandy tempered her desire to bash her husband and spoke softly to him, 'Jack. Who are the Holy Barbaras?'

He looked up and Mandy mentioned to the table as a throwaway aside, that his face had now changed from horrified to sad, and then had morphed to one of resolute preparedness to fight. As she reported on this she saw the next change in visage and sank back herself and deflated her own balloon. He was preparing to die for this cause. She knew he had always wanted a civil insurrection to get the country back to the people and, all of these arrangements, she had already surmised, were dreamed up by her husband and maybe Father Mike, knowing also he would want a peaceful handover and then a Mandela-style truth and reconciliation commission. But these Holy Barbaras, whoever they were, had obviously scared the bajeezers out of him.

'Jack?'

He looked up at his wife, 'Yes?'

'Please, and Umble Pie?'

He nodded. 'Sit, and I will tell all.'

And everyone ignored the fact they were already sitting and waited for Jack to spill the Umble Pie gravy.

———

Everyone looked at Zondo, including the newly resurrected and extremely posh and toffee-nosed corpse, who turned out to be Bernie. More shocks came as Bernie explained how he had been Black Rod in Parliament before he snuffed it. He had eaten an Umble

Pie in the posh-knob restaurant, in the House the night before and, he was not in the least humble about it, he said, but also mentioned that it did smell lovely and, probably because he had tried to trick the pie, it had turned in his stomach and eventually killed him. He could see this now, 'The power of hindsight and resurrection, I imagine,' he said. 'Anyway, I'm repentant,' he declared, through a smirking visage, grateful, but particularly irked as he had not finished his dessert of apple crumble and custard.

'It'll probably be cold now, Bernie,' Lilac said, matter of fact, knowledgeable in such matters of heat dissipation in apple crumble, even if it had had a cloaking of piping-hot custard. Though, to be brutally honest, she was more au fait with rhubarb crumble and custard (see *Dead No More – Rhubarb in the Mammon*), 'and it can get cold in the dessert at night,' she concluded with a pearler of a joke that only Grace tittered at.

Zondo reacted, as a normally invisible Papal magus, he was distinctly unnerved when people stared at him. He considered his nose too big. It was as if he was from Nose City and not the Vatican City. 'Why eez you all looking me?'

Grace answered, still mindful not to hurt the eejit's feelings. 'Well, as a very accomplished magus, we thought you might be able to magic up the secret tunnel into Parliament for us?'

'Secret tunnel, do you mean the one under the Thames to Parliament?' Bernie asked, body still jerking, unable to believe he had just been resurrected and, with a newly acquired plum in his mode and manner of speech.

Zondo was relieved, the attention had moved to Black Rod, Bernie.

'You know the tunnel, then?' Grace asked and Bernie nodded.

'Okay, so where is it?' Lilac asked, nicely for her.

'It's a secret, it would be more than my life is worth to let you know its whereabouts.' He stopped, thought about it, looked at Zondo, who looked ready to throw a spell, then disappear, and probably to get his nose fixed. Bernie reconsidered. 'Okay, follow me,' and they did.

THIRTY-FOUR

A SEVERE LOOKING SAVOY WAITER, MOVING AS IF he had a carrot up his backside, tripped a loose bow-elled light fantastique (which should have alerted the gathering around the brunch table, if the big red fez didn't, but it didn't). He danced up to the inordinately messy table, nonchalantly leaned over and let down the tyres of the archbishop's bike. He ahemmed, startling Jack who was distracted listening to the hiss from the bike tyres and wondering if it was him. He sniffed the air, the hint of puncture repair kit from his youth, so it wasn't him. However, the shock of the intrusion from the befezzed and schoolboy-py-jama'd waiter, with a crusty five o'clock shadow, caused Jack to spill the scalding hot gravy over his in-ordinately clumsy hands and, as a consequence, he dropped the gravy boat, in order to blow on his hands and it crashed on to Mandy's cup of coffee. The china shattered. The table cloth was now a complete write-off.

The waiter tutted and, all things considered, this is not the sort of thing you should do to a temperamental gobshite spook eejit, and Jack reacted. Mandy suspected something was about to happen, because her husband was scared.

'Oi, you feckin' tosspot, don't you tut at me. What are you? Fucking Egyptian or something?' The waiter affirmed he was Egyptian as he stripped his red waistcoat, that matched his fez, to reveal fully his striped schoolboy pyjamas and, under the shiny dome on the silver tray he revealed a pair of ballet slip-on plimsolls, that he immediately donned, after he had flung the circular discus like tray, as if he was *Odd Job* in *James Bond*. Jack ducked but it got Wally-Wally who immediately fell from his chair gripping his stomach.

Jack clambered across the table and, as he made his way to the man he now recognised as a member of the Coptic Cops, Jack's delicate size thirteen clodhoppers tripped over the salt cellar and he fell flat on the waiter, rendering him unconscious and considerably flatter.

Just as Jack was looking who to blame for putting the salt cellar in his way, so the dining room was thrown into greater chaos as it was invaded by more ballet-dancing Coptic Cops and, Wally-Wally was knocked back down again by a flying Sphinx. As Jack looked to see if Mandy was angry with him for knocking the salt over and, as he leaned to get some salt off the table, another flying Sphinx missed him and got Wally-Wally, as he began to raise himself yet again. Jack, being superstitious, emptied the salt from the salt cellar and casually threw it over his shoulder, fortuitously a direct hit into the eyes of Heptep who, blinded, was unable to dodge the salt cellar that Jack had decided to throw for additional luck, and this hit Heptep in his temporarily blinded, though well-seasoned, eyeballs. In the confusion and desire to rub his

Egyptian peepers better, he dropped his jam jar of sticklebacks onto the table and the tiny fish made a bid for freedom and ended up lavishly splashing around in a pool of orange juice and gravy, seemingly quite content.

From below the table Wally-Wally, thinking he might just stay down for a while, phoned to summon a rescue squad, which he managed just before Jack fell over a writhing Heptep on the floor and flattened the SBS, DCI. 'Sorry,' Jack said, not convinced Wally-Wally had heard him.

Samuels was up, Mandy was up, Jack and Wally-Wally were down, but getting up, both groaning, just as Father Mike strolled in and immediately went on to his toes and spiralled in for the coup-de-foie-gras, a lawn mower *corpulent du ballet* move, scything through the Coptic pyjamaed crew, felling them like skittles. Jack, sensing safety, managed to tread on them all as his contribution to the annihilation. He later said it was a brilliant strategy on his part, but Mandy later found out he had rubbed his eyes to stop himself crying and had inadvertently rubbed salt into them. The rest is, as they say, made-up history.

The Special Ballet Squad police arrived to a scene of chaotic dining room carnage, flattened Coptic pyjamas and fezzes strewn everywhere, tables upturned and Jack going around picking up salt cellars, throwing salt over his shoulder. The last thing he needed today was bad fucking luck, he said to anybody who tried to stop him, which included the restaurant manager who was now bathing the salt out of his own eyes. The SBS officers removed the ballet plimsolls from the Coptics and they were effectively immobilised and ready to be arrested.

'Telephone Bill,' Jack said blindly to Mandy, who appeared to resent being told what to do by a salt-ridden eejit.

'We can sort the domestic bills out when we get home. You need to focus, Jack. Do we need to rescue the Pope?'

Jack looked perplexed, which Mandy, an expert Jack watcher, missed, thinking the screwed extra-special ugliness was simply as a result of salt in his one eye, but she did respond to his flailing arms as one of them knocked the restaurant manager over, the second missing Mandy only because of her experienced Jack, dodgy arm, dodge.

'Jack, sit down.' Jack sat, and so would you if you knew Mandy's rep. 'Now, what are you saying?'

Jack answered: 'Me dot, ah hah, et bone et zee Bill, mush... et don't eh knock it all back at once, ah hah...'

It was Jack's famed frontier gibberish, which fortunately Mandy had mastered, as he spoke it a lot when he cried and, as he cried a lot she had had a lot of practice. She understood Jack wished for her to telephone someone called Bill, but clumped him for calling her "mush".

'It's not frontier gibberish,' Jack managed to say quite clearly.

'So you don't want me to phone fucking Bill, then?'

'Yeah, I do.'

Mandy sighed and wondered, not for the first time that day, what she saw in this feckin' eejit, but knew she had to pursue the question in order to extricate herself from this current Jack Austin minefield. 'Sorry, daaaah-ling,' she simpered in her melt-Jack-the-eejit voice. He duly melted, 'What language was it you were speaking then, dearest lovely Mr Darcy?' She'd brought out the Pride and Prejudice big guns and Jack was done up like a kipper. Mandy fodder.

'Pirate,' he said.

'Pirate?'

'Yes.'

'What about fucking Pirates?'

'Pirate talk.'

Mandy lamented her lot but followed where Jack, her Sparrow, led. 'Oh, I see.' She didn't, but truly didn't give a toss. 'Who is Bill and what is his telephone number?'

Jack applied his olde sea salt grin, screwing up his one eye that still had grains of salt lodged in the wrinkles and, Mandy was immediately appraised of the situation. It was his sea salt, sea dog, countenance, and made the obtuse Austin link to the salt cellars. She barked in pirate, 'Ah hah, woof.' Jack smiled and she saw the lovely look in his one red-rimmed eye. It was his sea-puppy-dog love for her and she melted, and immediately resented his melt look. 'Jack, tell me now or so help me.'

She'd said enough, and never let it be said that Jack, Dick, Jane, Austin, was slow to catch on, because he had caught on, however, he was notoriously slow in ducking, and Mandy managed to flick his pirate taxi-door ear.

'Ouch. What's that for,' he asked, truly not understanding a woman's frustration with a man, and who can blame him for not understanding? Because he put no effort into understanding and the reason for that was that he thought, erroneously as you might understand, that he understood women as a natural way of things. In other words, understanding women came naturally to him. As natural as speaking his thoughts, so Mandy flicked his largely ineffective ear again, because she was irritated that he thought he understood women, when clearly, he didn't understand her, his wife. He couldn't understand why she had flicked his ear, so she flicked it again, only a little harder this time. Now, if you understood women, you would know that they sometimes have a tendency to build up their ire in gradual steps. Jack understood this, of course, but never managed the ducking that should accompany this comprehension.

'Bill?'

'Ben,' he replied rubbing his sore ear.

'Ben?'

'Bill's brother,' His ear was feeling better; it was really his pride that had been flicked.

Mandy sat back in her chair, scanned the room, and took in the havoc that she was used to seeing, having been with Jack for some time. She realised that had she thought this through, she would have expected this to happen if you had breakfast in the Savoy with her husband.

'Brunch,' he said, and Mandy flicked his ear again.

So, like a teacher dealing with the pupils at the back of the class, she regrouped and put her question into words of one syllable. 'Who are Bill and Ben? And please do not say *Flower Pot Men*, and why do I need to phone Bill?'

Jack smiled at his lovely and very patient wife and, she needed this patience, he understood, being a connoser of women, because sometimes she could be a little slow on the uptake. 'Ouch!'

'I am not slow on the uptake, it's you slow in the brain department. So, who is Bill?'

'The Numpti's brother.'

'The Numpti?' She was calming, but Jack's danger synapses were on red alert. He covered his ears, which he struggled to hear out of at the best of times and thus, he missed the next part of Mandy's question, which was, "Why phone Bill?" He took his hands away, which upon reflection, wasn't his smartest move of the day, and asked Mandy to repeat what she had just said.

"Ouch, ouch, ouch." A rhythmic response to Mandy repeating the question while emphasising the singular syllables with additional ear flicks, but he did manage to convey to Mandy that Bill was Ben the Numpti's brother, and he was positioned in Hyde Park with an Egyptian camel cavalry posse. Jack said he might need them to go into Shepherd Market and rescue the Pope and Claudio from Poncenbey's and, most particularly, from the Holy Barbaras who might be torturing them at that moment.

Now she understood, and pressed for more information. 'The Numpti is holed up with the prime minister. Wasn't that your aim?'

'Yes,' Jack replied, and considered leaving it there, but there was an inquisitorial look on his wife's beautiful face that reminded him a lot of the Holy Barbaras and their Spanish Inquisition. Their famed beauty, incongruous alongside their notorious torture techniques, and then his mind drifted to being tortured until he confessed all, which, being a cry baby, scaredy custard, would generally be forthcoming almost before he had sat down.

'More,' Mandy asked, clicking her finger and

thumb in a threatening manner, suggesting she would go straight for his weak points if he held anything back, knowing also this could be anywhere on his cotton-candy, pansy-arsed body (see how she can wind herself up – and if you knew women as Jack Austin does, then you would understand that this is a natural feminine reaction to inquisitorial questioning of a feckin' eejit fella).

Jack told all.

THIRTY-FIVE

CLAUDIO STAMPED HIS ONE FOOT UP AND DOWN on his perch above the Cutty Sark bar. His other foot was tied down, his wings secured behind his back with a cable tie and he was silenced with duct tape on his beak. Duck tape! Claudio was mightily offended. The Pope was tied to a seat in Poncenbey's lounge with his mitre pulled right down over his face, which would do no good whatsoever for his mitre hair, recently so expertly redressed.

Derek wore his formal Caretaker's beige overall coat with the duck-egg-blue badge and insignia, over his Bricky's formal leather lederhosen. He served drinks to the Council of Hairdressers. The Holy Barbaras had freshly squeezed lemon juice, which suited the sour faces of the Spanish-Inquisition hairdressers. There was a synergy between the two groups. However, it was pretty clear the Barbaras ruled the roost, and they insisted everyone dilute their drinks with holy water, with an olive on a stick, reputed to be from the Mount of Olives. The stick and the olive. The drink was known as a Dirty Mountini, and it is finally set alight as the petroleum gases vented off the *Holy Fracked Water*, vials of which were always carried by the nuns in special panniers attached to their *Jacko* roller skates.

Through the eyeholes cut in the mitre, Pope Siderney looked at Claudio, who responded with a feathered shrug. He had no idea how they were going to get out of this one, and had not a clue where Liberato Zondo was.

———

A still sulking Liberato Zondo was last in the line, following Lilac and Grace, the cockney Lord Pimple, and a twirling, dancing Sister Winifrede. They were all traipsing after Black Rod Bernie, who now had a spring in his step and, anyone who has ever been resurrected would recognise that feeling, but Bernie's sense of well being had been further enhanced by a now superior posh voice. He had, courtesy of Zondo, replaced his previously estuarine accent that he could never disguise and felt had always held him back.

Coincidentally, it was this *spring* in both step and sense that was emerging among the people of Britain. The people had recovered from the shock that the dancing nun, the inspiration of this rising-up of the British people across the whole of the country, had finally popped her ballet plimsolls and would soon be pushing up holy daisies. Their faith was now transferred and instilled in the Nuns' Orchestra Conductor, Bea Flat, following the announcement to the crowds in Trafalgar Square and beyond, via the telly media big screens and the tinterweb, that Britain should Relaxacat. Bea Flat was still resurrected and would conduct the Nuns' Orchestra in a performance of Stravinsky's *The Rite of Spring* at six that glorious evening in Trafalgar Square. The country waited in awe, rapturous at the rebirth of democracy, of civilisation even. A new order where social fairness had been promised and not a politician's promise, either, but one made by a dead dancing nun and a resurrected conductor and, promises don't come much better than that.

If the crowd had any feelings of spiritual doubt, the announcement had been made to the people by the Welsh-Irish beanpole boyfriend, with the hint of a Bristolian twang, of the confirmed resurrected conductor. This, in itself, was thought to be yet another miracle, as the voice seemed detached and emanating from an ethereal ginger cloud, but, it turned out that it was just an ultra-skinny Aedd Murphy standing behind the microphone stand with only his thick, rusty *Brillo* pad hair visible and, when he stepped aside and leaned across the microphone, the crowd could not hide their disappointment. This did not bother Aedd too much as he had become used to being a disappointment throughout his life. You would never have guessed he was descended from a great Irish King, except when he drank his tea from a saucer and, a Welsh miner hairdresser with a fondness for masculine personal hygiene.

The scene was set in London's central Trafalgar Square and the country waited as the crowds sang, *If She was the Holy Girl in the World*, a song that had been adopted by the great British populace in memory of Sister Winifrede.

Bernie waited for the others to catch up while Winifrede danced around them. They gathered like a group of tourists standing in the gloom of a subterranean corridor stuffed with pipes and services, with no sign of a tunnel door, all waiting upon pearls of wisdom from their tour guide.

Sister Winifrede danced to the front, laid a gentle hand on a pipe, to take support and waved her other hand like a bird taking off, bent her knees and while straightening and extending to her full height pointing and standing on the tips of her plimsolls, she called out in a croaky tired voice, 'Give us a sign, oh Lord.' She pushed herself off the pipe to reveal behind her a bit of cardboard that had written on in black felt tip pen, "DOOR", with a little arrow and there it was, it was a sign. Sister Winifrede had once again shown the way, although Bernie did say he knew where the door was and was using dramatic irony to milk the situation theatrically.

Sister Winifrede spun like a helicopter and her outstretched hands whacked Bernie on his Black Rod head; another sign? So they followed the directions of the arrow and within six feet there was a door that had secret tunnel written on it, another sign, but this time in a different colour felt pen, moss green.

'Here it is,' Bernie said unnecessarily, and he opened the door.

A foul odour puffed from the dank and dark tunnel. Liberato, holding his nose in a magical way, stepped forward and magicked a set of light bulbs along the walls of the secret tunnel. They stepped inside and, with a whoosh of whistling smelly air, the door behind them closed and disappeared.

'Fuck that,' Winifrede said, dancing in a crouch as though she was en-route in a prima ballerina way to a dying swan. The tunnel had only five feet of head-room at the top of a vaulted ceiling. Jettying was completely out of the question.

'Lingua,' Zondo said, admonishing the miraculously reheaded sister, and gestured for Bernie to take the lead. Some of the old confidence was returning to the Vatican sorcerer, but only for a minute, as it was spoiled by Lord Pimple's remark that it was "Bleedin' taters (potatoes in the mould – cold) down 'ere and pen and inks," a sad reminder of Zondo's recent fallibility.

The tunnel sloped steeply down, presumably to get below the Thames, levelled as they passed under London's river and, began to rise equally sharply at the other end, where, as you would expect, there was no fucking door, which Lilac announced as bleedin' obvious.

'Oi, Zondo, get your wand out and magic us a door pronto tonto amigo.'

Zondo duly obliged. Nervously he waved his hands about, which caused his flowing black cloak to agitate the smelly air, but fortunately a door revealed itself, swung open, and they made a mad dash for Parliament and the Clean Air Act.

———

'For the love of Ada, Jack, give me Bill's telephone number.' Mandy was waving her phone around and the look on her face suggested that on the next pass, should Jack not provide the number, the phone would be inserted where Jack's sun didn't shine, not that he was worried about this, considering himself an all-round ray of sunshine.

'I don't know the number.' Jack replied, rapidly to defer any precipitous action by his wife that may render her phone inoperable for the rest of the day.

Mandy sighed. 'Then how do you usually contact the Numpti's feckin' brother?'

Jack gestured for Mandy to pass him the phone, emphasising that he wanted it in his hand and she passed it to him. She watched as he pressed loads of buttons and then shouted at it, 'Hello Bill? Bill, you there... Bill, for fuck's sake.' He then pressed a load more buttons, put the phone to his ear, listened and then shouted at it again. He was getting quite irate; this call was urgent.

Samuels tapped Jack on his shoulder and made Jack jump.

'Jim, don't do that, can't you see I'm on the dog and bone.'

Samuels was not to be deterred, he took the phone from Jack and returned it to Mandy and, struggling to hold back a full-on laugh, handed Jack his own phone. 'It's Bill, for you.'

Mandy guffawed when Jack offered her his smug grin, as if to say, told yer, all you had to do was press buttons and shout. There was nothing to this admin lark and Jack put his stopping the traffic hand up to stop any incidental passing traffic and, there had been quite a bit in the dining salon while also stopping Mandy from interrupting his call. Mandy simmered, but decided it might be best to listen in on what Jack said to this numpty, Bill.

303

'Bill, you mounted up and ready?' He listened and clearly received the reply he wanted. 'Okay, get your boys down to Poncenbey's in Shepherd Market, they have the Pope and Claudio...'Jack paused and put on his serious face and the crowds of people engaged in clearing the mess in the Savoy Dining room, stopped what they were doing to laugh at Jack's face. 'What?' Jack asked, unable to understand the looks on the people, and why they should be looking at him? He'd only come in for a quiet brunch... and thus the speaking of his thoughts broke the stolid curiosity with another barrage of laughter.

Jack ignored them; he sometimes had to ignore people in order to get on with the serious stuff in the world and this, elicited an even more energetic roar of laughter, which, and as you would expect of a consommé spy, he paid no mind. 'Bill, mate, watch out when you get there, the place is full of fucking Holy Barbaras and they could play merry hell with yer fez if they get their hands on yer.' Satisfied he had got the master plan under way and Bill and his Light Camel Brigade had been duly warned about the Barbaras, Jack settled back, flicked his fingers like his wife would, but not around his ears, and summoned a waiter.

Out of the debris, a waiter appeared. 'Yes Sir?'

'A cup of Girl Grey splosh for me and monkey tea for me babes 'ere,' and he looked at Mandy who nodded that a cup of tea might be welcome just about now. Jack nodded towards Samuels, who was busy getting strawberry jam off his phone, 'Give the Jack and Jill to him,' and then he laughed. 'Bill... oh blimey, bill,' he said and looked at Mandy babes, who seemed confused. He explained, as he so often had to with his jokes: 'Jack and Jill, bill, Bill,' he said, and she pretended she understood him and he was satisfied that she did understand him, because he understood women and their understanding looks, understandably.

THIRTY-SIX

THE NEW BLACK ROD, DRESSED IN HIS BLACK finery, looked a lot like Zondo, except Rod wore knickerbockers and not drainpipe trousers. There was nothing glorious about them, though his red nose did look like a cherry on top of the ice cream Knickerbocker Glory, whereas Zondo was a particularly skinny magus. Rodney, (a curious coincidence that Black Rod was called Rod) was a tub of lard. Bernie's replacement met the crew as they climbed the stairs from the basement in Westminster Palace, intent on entering the House of Commons chamber.

Black Rodney stood in front of the motley crew, raised his formal rod, which was black, and instructed them all to halt, to stand where they were. He called for their passes, when all of a sudden, he recognised dead Bernie and then, the dancing nun, who could not stand still even if she wanted to. Black Rodney went as white as a sheet. 'Bernie,' he said in wonderment.

'Rodney. I see they made you the new Rod then.'
'Er yes, er... is that the dancing nun?'

'It is Rodney.'

'Bernie?' Rodney was looking for an explanation of not only how the nun got here, but also how he had died only a day ago and was now standing in front of him as large as life, though not so black. Bernie was attired in a sober grey suit, double-breasted.

'Rodney, you need to let us into the chamber.' Bernie asserted.

'Can't do that Bernie.'

Bernie knew Rodney was a jobsworth and had been made his deputy only as a favour to some big-wig. And here he was, floundering and trying to assert his presumed rank and power.

Bernie took the Rod from Rodney, brought it up hard between the legs of the jobsworth Rod, and while he folded over and cupped the Rodney crown jewels, which by coincidence, he is also supposed to protect and, squeaked his complaint from the floor where he writhed. Bernie indicated for the crew to follow him. He marched off and they followed, Sister Winifrede spinning and twirling, up steps, then down, in front and then behind, until they reached the House of Commons where she marked time while Bernie raised the Rod and banged hard, three times, on the chamber door.

The Commons Chamber was full as it ordinarily was in anticipation of Prime Minister's Questions, which had been cancelled. The doors had been sealed in order to protect the MPs better from what was being described as an unruly mob outside. This was the debate that was in full flow, discussing the peasants' revolt, and this came to a sudden silence in response to the thud, thud, and thud. The Sergeant of

Arms, the officer in charge of the MPs' arms as well as their legs, rose ceremoniously, as he was expected to do if ever Rod knocked, demanding the attention of the Commons.

All eyes were on the sergeant as he paced stiffly to the door and gave the formal response. 'Hello, who is it?'

Bernie gave the formal answer, 'It's me, Tom. Open the fucking doors.'

The sergeant bowed to the doors and, with both hands took a hold of each leaf and stepping backwards, pulled the doors wide open and was immediately knocked over as Sister Winifrede pranced in, swirly twirling, advancing as she jete'd up to the formal mace, grabbed it with both hands and, raised it above her head and danced around the floor. She now had the *formal* attention of the House, as was her right, bearing the mace.

The MPs sat in awe. They knew who this was. Sister Winifrede's picture had been on the telly and in all the newspapers. The stories of a resurrected nun, a stiff pink tutu and pink brassiere on top of her black habit, which was tucked into her holy flannelette navy blue knickers, as is the habit of the Order of Ballerina Nuns, not that Sister Winifrede was a member of that order, or nobody would have batted and eyelid.

The MPs watched, mouths agape, the nun was still dancing. She had only gone and bloody resurrected herself again and there was fear plastered all over their faces. What did this mean? Was this a sign? The sign they had been told to expect, combined with the Umble Pies and the peasants' revolt outside and across the country. What did this signify for the powerhouse that was Parliament and, most importantly, the establishment, their establishment?

The members were not to be in wonderment for long as Sister Winifrede was about to explain, and all eyes focused on her as, ever so slowly, her dancing eased and she slipped into a trance-like state. She stared like an eastern mystic with ping-pong ball eyes. After a short while she stood still, mace aloft and the watchers thought she was about to die again. But she didn't, she spoke to the House from in front of the Speaker's chair, her words conveyed by Zondo, although no one knew this, except Grace and Lilac, who had a shrewd idea.

The hush in the chamber was powerful and symbolised an announcement of serious import and it was to be thus as the sister remained still, for the first time since her first and latest resurrection. She turned her head to the Tory government benches and officiously, with a trace of an Italian accent, she said, 'You are notta in power, you are a inna office and, thata office does not entitle you to wielda zee power over zee people. You are a here to server zee people and, currently zee people are a suffering. So, you are notta doing your jobba. The people cannotta accept self-serving politicians.' She swung her head to the Opposition benches, 'Anda, thisa includes politicians of all colour and belief. You servea zee people and, if you cannot a do that, then you deservea to be removed from zis powerful and most responsible position and, today, zee people remove that power from you. Zee people, they remove you from office.'

This event was of course broadcast to the nation via Parliament TV and relayed to the big screens in Parliament Square, Trafalgar Square, along Whitehall and the Mall, and across the country, but within the precincts of Parliament, the public response was never more so potent. The nun's announcement was greeted by a resounding cheer that grew steadily in volume and could be heard clearly within the insular chamber. The MPs were left in no doubt as to what had just happened. The people had taken back power, but what would happen to them? The metaphorical, *Madame la Guillotine*?

There was a rumbling of shock, which soon turned to righteous indignation and a return to the braying idiotic nonsense so typical of this supposed mature debating chamber. A chamber where rarely does a debate with serious answers take place. Zondo materialised from nowhere and, with a puff of purple papal smoke, the politicians were frozen where they sat, or stood. They had no choice but to listen and watch as the Pope's sorcerer appeared and then disappeared. Zondo was beginning to feel a lot like himself again and Sister Winifrede recommenced her berating of the state of British politics and the curse of career politicians.

In the meantime, Bernie had escorted Lord Pimple into the House of Lords where already, what was happening in the Commons, was being greeted with astonishment and had even woken some of the slumbering lords and ladies, as they were addressed by a man they recognised as Lord Pimple, but this errant Lord spoke like a street tyke.

'Oi you bleedin' load of toffee nosed twats, listen up or I'll trot you down to the guillotine where most of you self-serving, up-yer-own-arses, fucking bastards, deserve to be.'

Well, this got their attention. It was bound to as,

for time immemorial, the powerful of the land, the entitled, had feared a revolution such as took place in Paris not much more than two hundred years ago. Now, here was one of their own, threatening just such a fate for them if they didn't listen. So, they listened to the modern-day Pimple-Nell.

Pimple, in his new crude manner of speech, vocalised a similar argument to that which Sister Winifrede was giving in the House of Commons. Where his ability to speak these words and, where the words came from, he could not say but, all of a sudden he was granted a new eloquence, albeit cockney in parlance. He had found an intensity of argument that made his pigeon chest puff out with pride. He believed in this stuff. He felt it truly and, after a short while, Zondo released Pimple to orate of his own accord and he did so, most eloquently.

———

All that was happening in the House of Commons and now the Lords continued to be broadcast, despite the BBC trying hard to disconnect the live feed, but nothing would work for the engineers. The roars of approval from the people persisted, resounding and reverberating from Parliament Square and along Whitehall. After Winifrede, Lord Pimple's speech was transmitted to even greater acclaim. The second chamber was collapsing and Lord Pimple called upon its dissolution to form a second, but elected, chamber.

———

The newly re-established quiet and accustomed decorum in the Savoy dining salon was only interrupted by the slurping of Jack, drinking tea from his saucer. He had in mind some crazy notion, Mandy told everyone, that he was descended from the Kings of Ireland, and all was explained. Everybody knew the Kings of Ireland drank their tea from a saucer.

Cecelia had remained in a grief-stricken stupor. The grieving fiancée of lord Pimple had hardly moved as chaos and carnage reigned around her statuesque seated form, all of which Jack considered quite considerate of his nerves that were a little on edge. He had to pour the Girl Grey tea into his saucer himself, blow on it, himself, to get it to the correct sipping temperature. Mandy, it appeared, had gone on strike.

All of a sudden Cecelia's wailing recommenced with hitherto unheard of gusto as Pimple's speech was relayed on the television. The sound had been down and so everyone had missed the dancing nun addressing the House of Commons. Cecelia shouted, 'Pimple,' and it was right in Jack's ear and, although he is notoriously deaf, he did hear Cecelia's wail. As a consequence his head splashed down into the saucer and the tea spilled, which was not an unusual occurrence this brunch time in the Savoy, but what irritated Jack more was that the tea had ruined his quiff that he had got just right after all of the brunch shenanigans. Jack, Jane, Dick, was most particular about his hairstyle. Well, the bit at the front, as everything else, out of his sight, fell under his religious precepts of denial and baldness, in a monk manner, not that he could see this.

Mandy turned to the TV and then back to Jack to

look for an answer. 'Jack, leave your hair alone. Look, it's Pimple.'

Jack was never one to be told by a woman what to do, well, he was, it was just he never remembered that he always did as he was told. He just grunted, 'I told you so', and went back to remodelling the front of his hair.

'Jack!'

Well, that got his attention all right and now everyone around the brunch table looked at him, which he assumed was because his quiff looked lovely and he grinned his tea-laden brimming smile. He was now in a more cooperative mood.

'Yes, Jack, your quiff is lovely,' Mandy said, knowing you had to give to receive.

Jack brimmed some more and then deigned, in his regally Irish manner, to answer. 'Yes, well I did tell you he would be okay,' and now, as he looked at a shocked Cecelia, he feigned being emotionally upset, 'but, would anyone listen to me? Noooo, they wouldn't and, I imagine Sister Winifrede has addressed the House of Commons by now? Time to get down to Trafalgar Square, I think. He looked at his hair and a pimple on his wrist, where most people had a watch, and said, 'We should have a word with Bea Flat and Aedd, maybe get the concert going as Winifrede will want to dance her way to Trafalgar Square. It's Stravinsky's The Rite of Spring, you know, and she's one of my favourite composers and, of course, I used to be a ballet dancer.' Jack stood, stretched, rubbed his ear that for some reason felt bruised, which he ignored as he tap-danced and whistled the Rite of Spring.

'Is he whistling the Rite of Spring?' Samuels

asked Mandy, 'Only it sounds like *Bob the Builder* to me.'

'It is *Bob the Builder* but it's all the same to him, and *Stravinsky*,' Mandy replied, thinking a stroll down to Trafalgar Square and a concert might make a nice peaceful end to the day, that in all terms holy to Jack, had been more chaotic than usual. But, at least Winifrede had been resurrected again, and Pimple was okay. Cecelia had calmed considerably and was wanting to meet up with her fiancé. They made to leave. All Mandy had to do was calm Jack, whose recently elevated and joyous mood had been holed below the water line by the Savoy manager who wanted to know where to send l'addition for the damage. Jack looked at Mandy, suggested the Tory party and mentioned to the manager that Mandy was admin. Mandy directed the manager to Jim Samuels who began to write a little note that hopefully would amount to a get-out-of-jail-free card.

Mandy looped her arm into the crook of Jack's elbow, and together they sashayed out of the hotel and on to the Strand, turned left, and already the noise from Trafalgar Square was beginning to deafen. 'Blimey the crowd is noisy,' she said to Jack.

'What noise?' Jack said in reply.

She sighed and looked lovingly at her deaf feckin' eejit with the Girl Grey quiff, whom she inexplicably loved so much, put aside his idiotic scheming and looked forward to a peaceful classical music concert and ballet.

It was lovely walking down the Strand, she thought, except for Jack singing *Let's All Go Down the Strand* and shouting to the rooftops: "Ave a banana." They were the only words he knew, but he sung those with tremendous and voluble enthusiasm, being a lover of both monkeys and bananas, which drove his wife bananas at her monkey-spanner husband. But, in no time they closed on to the crowded square. The people thronged, their attention seemingly focused down Whitehall to Parliament where the big screens were showing things happening. But what?

THIRTY-SEVEN

THE CAMEL CAVALRY HAD BEEN ANONYMOUSLY taking the waters of the Serpentine. At least, they presumed they were anonymous as they were all attired in *Just William* or *Boy Scout* nineteen fifties attire that Jack Austin had assured them would blend in. When asked about the camels in Hyde Park, Jack looked at Bill as if to intimate he was stupid, which Bill wasn't, but he thought Jack might be. However, Jack had reassured Bill that camels in Hyde Park would draw no attention whatsoever, especially if they all wore fezzes. The Camel Corp, officers and men, wore a fez, as did the camels, only they had holes in the side for their big camel ears, in the style of King Charles the second. Or was he a cavalier?

And so they had assembled, suitably attired for a lovely spring day, and awaited their orders. They had already familiarised themselves with the street maps and how to get into Shepherd Market and on to White Horse Street and, thence on to Poncenbey's, for it was expected that would be their point of attack. Questions from the curious asking what they were doing dressed like eeejits in fezzes, and why the camels, and should they not be drinking out of the Serpentine, all dissipated as the crowds thinned, some to get to TVs, others to Trafalgar Square, to see what was happening. Rumours abounded that the dancing nun had been resurrected again and would, after all, be dancing in the square in front of the National Gallery.

Bill took another call from Jack and, as instructed, he called his brother Ben, the Numpti of Cairo, still holed up in Downing Street with the prime minister and his deputy.

———

As the Numpti ended the call, so the PM concluded a conversation with the leader of the house, telephoning from Parliament. The Numpti could see the PM was not just displeased with the news he had received, he was seriously concerned, and his white Greek yoghurt cheeks tinged red as he received the knowing stare from their formal guest.

'You had your chance with the Umble Pies, but, as anticipated, you refused to respond to the clear message. I believe you have just been informed that Parliament has been suspended and the *People* have taken *back* power. Is that so?'

The PM nodded to the Numpti, turned to his deputy and explained all that had happened. He picked up a remote controller, pressed to draw the net curtains, pressed again to put the telly on and the news was repeating the address to the House by Sister Winifrede. In a split frame, it showed a picture of Lord Pimple's spiel to the Lords. The broadcast went to live feed and showed the legion of the proletariat

317

and commoners surging to the Parliament gates when, inexplicably, the throngs parted, as if in reverence.

A roar could be heard even in Downing Street, amplified on the TV. A massive crescendo that all of a sudden became an eerie silence. The PM, dep PM, and Numpti watched as eerily the cameras zoomed in. Nothing happened, there was just an air of expectancy. The skies darkened. The ceremonial doors opened to present a black hole. Then a powerful beam of light materialised, made brighter because the darkened interior and the blackened sky. The hush was patent. Portending what? It was difficult to say, the nun was there, in the spotlight, but dead still. Was she dead again? The PM hoped so, but he was to be disappointed. Sister Winifrede slowly and most elegantly lifted a leg, straightened it to almost the horizontal. People would later remark on the startling creative contrast of the delicate ballet moves, counterpoised with the brazen pink Tutu, stark against the black habit and the beam of light making the navy blue, flannelette knickers, stand out right royally. Winifrede spun on the tips of her plimsolls and the crowd, in a paroxysm of hope and joy, cheered. This was their nun. The *Peoples'* nun, and the tumult increased in fervour as she jete'd out of Parliament and, as she hit the fresh air, the sky brightened and a scriptural shaft of sunlight highlighted her dancing path.

The crowd parted more in awe than curiosity, as if the hand of Moses had reached down out of the clouds and parted the congregation. Of course, it wasn't Moses but God and, God had done this before, so he knew what he was doing. It was the Red Sea, all over again. Quiet. The crowds still. They observed and, close on Winifrede's heels followed the also recently resurrected, though just the once, Lord Pimple, now being hailed by the People as the *White Pimplenell*. Pimple was a major figurehead in the British Revolution, more so, since he had broken ranks with the aristocracy, his accidental birthright, but most importantly, the establishment.

The hush in the crowd became a hum of shared murmurs throughout Parliament Square, up Whitehall, and the now chokka Birdcage Walk, back to Buckingham Palace. There was informal partying on the green swards of St James's Park, below the big screens. This was a joyous day, being likened to the end of the Second World War. Hope. A better future. The end of the bad times.

The dancing nun was exiting and coming to greet the crowds having just dissolved Parliament and, as if by magic, which was not too far off the truth as Zondo had regained much of his confidence, the crowd parted to form a long channel from near the Houses of Parliament all the way to the far edge of Parliament Square. It was a sort of Red Stream. It was presumed God had gotten a bit fed up with the Red Sea as he was running out of fish, and like a gently undulating sound wave of respectful murmuring, a path all the way up Whitehall to Trafalgar Square was slowly formed, like collapsing dominos. There was no need for police barriers, no need for any law enforcement, this was the *Peoples'* show.

Just then, the front doors of Westminster Abbey opened and, in the hush, a pizzicato clip clop, clip clop, and the TV cameras cut from the front doors of Westminster, to the doors of the Abbey and, like another miracle, a horse and cart, immediately recognised as the famous rag-and-bone man of The City of

London, emerged. Mystically, along the Red River, it made its way to meet Winifrede and Lord Pimple, as if the horse was doing the guiding as the driver was in a coma. A celestial trance was the explanation, TV commentators offered, not realising Nelly knew what she was doing and was following Claudio's instructions, though the parrot should have been there, but wasn't.

Sister Winifrede, twirling, leaping, ducking and diving, accompanied by a stately Lord Pimple, effing and blinding beside her, made their way to the gates of Parliament. As if cosmically choreographed, they were met by the rag-and-bone man's horse and cart and, to the wonderment of all who looked on, which by now was the whole world as events were broadcast internationally, Zondo, unseen by the crowds, plied his trade. The pirouetting nun rose, unaided, elevated, and hung suspended in mid air, motionless, milking the awe of the crowd like a religious drama queen, before she stepped on to the cart and jete'd to the back bar that was the seat for a totally inebriated driver. She grabbed the back of the seat, turned elegantly sideways, bowed to the crowd and began a series of stationary ballet moves.

The crowd looked on in reverence and slowly, a rippling sound made its way through to Parliament Square. It was like the reverberation of a sound wave, but this time it was the eloquent strains of the Nuns' Orchestra who had struck up the Rite of Spring in Trafalgar Square and, the horse and cart moved off and, clip-clopped in time to the music. All along the parted Whitehall throngs, the ballet of horse, nun, and Lord Pimple, who was mainly scratching his arse, but in tune to the music, the divine cart journeyed.

The journey of a new *People's Spring* began. Winifrede prancing and jettéing all around the flatbed cart, occasionally treating the awestruck crowd with balancing moves along the rim of the wagon. She sometimes appeared almost to float. Witnesses later swore the nun did float, that her ballet plimsolls did not touch the dray at all.

And so the TV cameras, the crowds, and the world, watched as Sister Winifrede made her way to Trafalgar Square on a simple and honest, humble working man's conveyance of a rag-and-bone man's cart. The crowd began to call out, "Any old iron, any old iron... any, any, any old iron," as Nelson's Column became like a moral lighthouse, steering the future of Britain away from the rocks of subjugation, and into a better way of life. A rebirth. *A Rite of Spring*.

———

The Camel Corp mounted up in what was becoming a deserted Hyde Park, and their route across Park Lane into the back streets of Mayfair and thence to Shepherd Market became clear and unencumbered, as the usual mêlée of people in this part of the salubrious West End, found bars and cafés to watch TVs and events as they unfolded. But soon their attention was drawn to a befezzed camel cavalry charge into this Mayfair village, the resounding and echoing whoops and battle cries from the Church of Egypt soldiers of Denial, accompanied now by the howling Dervish Muslim Sect of the whirling and twirling camel brigade. The tiny and tight streets of this Mayfair village echoed and reverberated to the passion of righteous rebellion.

The camel charge was temporarily halted as the road became blocked by a motley crew of fez men in schoolboy-striped pyjamas. This militia of stickleback-bearing crusty middle-eastern warriors, looked as though they had already been in a war that day, which they had. The battle in the Savoy was already being dubbed, *the Savoy Sally Battle*. Not that Sally had been in it, nor even the Salvation Army, who had been relegated to handing out plimsolls to the soldiers of the *British Spring*. These exhausted soldiers of the River Cray were soon dispatched by Bill's expert camel corps, the writhing forms of schoolboy pyjamas scooped up by a patrol of policemen who saluted the camel corps on their way to Poncenbey's, deep into the Mayfair village.

However, the furore of the battle alerted the Barbaras and, skates on, they formed a defensive barricade across the narrow Whitehorse Road. All of a sudden, the street was clouded in a purple haze that disguised the entry of Liberato Zondo into the club and, as the cloud dissipated, it was obvious the Barbaras had not been distracted from seeing the camel formation in the square ahead of them. The head Barbara, known as Miss Babs *the not Merciful*, called her six fellow nuns of the Inquisition, to commence skating, slowly towards the village square and the line of the Light Camel Brigade. Slowly the roller-skating pace picked up as the Barbaras wielded curling tongs and the most dangerous and feared thinning-out scissors of holy repute. They cried, "Jesus perms for ever," as they skated, now, full pelt, toward the camel corps who advanced, steadily increasing their pace and calling back shouts of De Nile, denial, and how none of this could be happening and, it would all be right in the end. These stirring battle cries, steeped in the history of the Church of Egypt soldiers and boosted by confused Dervish cries, rallied the officers. Now they picked up their pace to engage the speedily skating nuns, the little wheels on their Jacko skates a blur, metallic sparks flying out behind them making their manic stares and berserking coiffeurly battle cries even more scary.

At last the camels and nuns engaged in a fury of hairdressing equipment and the feather boas of the light brigade, causing the nuns to laugh as the Church of Egypt soldiers, dismounted, and engaged in hard to hand tickling and hairdressing. Fezzes were knocked off and, skin and hair flew, as the Dervish hairdressers did what they did best, twirl and curl, with not much care as to the styling. All that could be sorted later, a classic denial, but just as it looked like nobody would survive, Barbaras, Dervish or C of E soldiers, a squawk could be heard, louder than anyone in Mayfair had heard before from a parrot, stunned the combatants and, Zondo froze them in statuesque form.

It was like a tableau from mediaeval Egypt. A renaissance sculpture of a frenzied battle, frozen in time. There was a spooky hush all around as the Pope stepped from Poncenbey's, and the crowd who had left their cafés and pubs to watch the unfolding events on their doorstep, witnessed the papal book of revelations. They ooohed and aaahed and dropped to their knees. The Pope was sans mitre and, he had wonderful hair, not spiked up like a Mohican mitre cut, but soft, and wavy and, mysteriously still staying in place as if held there by celestial *Harmony* lacquer.

The Pope walked into the middle of the sculpture

of conflict and spoke to the multitudes gathered. 'Today has seen power returned to the people. We have ended the grip of terror from the Illuminati and their soldiers of enforcement', and he waved a hand over the Barbaras. 'We will now begin to rebuild a *Society* that is fair and just. People will be held to account and, if they confess their evil deeds and repent, they will be forgiven.' He looked directly at the Barbaras and nodded to a purple cloud that cleared to reveal the Phantom *Flan Flinger of Old London Town*, who, it has to be said, looked a lot like Zondo. However, Zondo had handed the reins of the Holy Magus to the London Flan Flinger, in order to go off to Trafalgar Square, as Sister Winifrede's cart was nearing the National Gallery.

Flan waved his emaciated and black silk clad arm and, the tableau of conflict returned to living form, only now the arms, and legs, were laid down. The soldiers of Egypt embraced the Barbaras as they removed their skates and discarded their hairdressing tools, so symbolic of their historic devilish interrogative power.

THIRTY-EIGHT

THE CURIOUS THING WAS THAT, AS SISTER Winifrede was transported, dancing her way up Whitehall, all six hundred odd MPs and some four hundred very odd Lords and Ladies, followed, dancing vigorously as the strains of Stravinsky wafted to the ears of the purple-clouded Liberato Zondo, now very pleased his powers had returned.

This, was his greatest ever achievement as a magus d'excellence. A troupe of former power mongers, dancing ritually to entice the dawning of a new era, and then, the gates of Downing Street opened and Mackeroon and Blogg, PM and dep PM, appeared in plimsolls, tartan socks, no trousers, fully clad in body suit and tutu and they commenced ballerinaing their way to the top of the line, to tail just behind Winifrede's horse and cart. They arrived just as Nelly let loose a charmed cloud of foul air, followed up in short order by a Holy inordinate amount, a mound of magically holy horse poo that the power magnates all danced in as if enjoying being brought back down to earth, in among the mulch and mire of ordinary folk. The fertilizer for the *Roses of Britain* to grow again but this time healthily.

And so the line of ballet-dancing, defrocked dignitaries followed Sister Winifrede's rag-and-bone-man chariot and, as it approached Trafalgar Square, so the crowds again parted, and a natural forum presented itself in the form of a sculpted stage-set; the National Gallery steps.

To the north, the paved apron in front of the National Gallery held the Nuns' Orchestra. Bea Flat's conducting rostrum, just edging the wide, expansive steps that led down to the piazza that divided the two pools with their energetic central fountains seeming to reflect the mood of exhilaration. To the south, sentinel to the goings-on, and with a view down the Mall to Buckingham Palace, down Whitehall as well as to Parliament Square, and along the Strand, where Jack and Mandy were skipping their way to observe the concert and ballet, stood Nelson atop his column. This diminutive admiral, steeped in the history of the glorious days of the British Empire, no longer visible as he was shrouded in a purple haze. Today was not about Empire. It was not about conquering. It was about the *People*, for so long suppressed, subjugated, now to be reborn.

Jack steered Mandy down William the Fourth Street, behind St Martin-in-the-Fields, mentioned to Mandy and Jim Samuels that he loved concerts there and was really looking forward to the ballet. They told him to shut up and to explain where they were going.

'Through the Portrait Gallery,' he said, puffing a bit as skipping like a monkey with a banana can take it out of an old fat man. 'There's a picture there of a woman that looks just like my mum, only she's got this big wart on her nose and a frilly collar.'

Samuels stopped Jack. 'Do you mean the portrait of Oliver Cromwell?'

Jack stopped bananaing and thought for a while, as a puffed-out, fat monkey would when deciding which tree to swing on next and, wondering if his red bum looked big in his monkey suit, then he had it. 'Yeah, that's right, Olivia Cromwell.' and he carried on, singing, "Let's all go down William the Fourth Street to see Olivia, 'ave a banana..." and so it went, to the tune of *Bob the Builder*.

The traffic was at a standstill in Charing Cross Road. They crossed with ease to enter the Portrait Gallery and then to get lost, but Samuels knew the way and soon they were through and outside the front portico of the National Gallery, standing behind the Nuns' Orchestra, who had moved on to play the light lemonade anthem for the reported Camel Corps success. It was Cherrryade by Ripsyercorsetsoff.

'Now what?' Samuels asked of Jack, but it was clear Jack was miffed as he straightened his lips in order to not let his secret plans out.

'What secret plans,' Mandy asked. Jack checked his lips, mystified that they should let his thoughts out. 'What is the matter with you? You're behaving like a spoiled brat.'

Well that did it, Jack never liked being likened to a bat. 'I'm not a spoiled bat,' he said, and he meant it. 'I wanted to show you the picture of my mum,' and he stood resolute, arms folded, lips straight, but still leaking his thoughts. 'I think it was my mum, it might be my Aunt Nellie who had a spot on her belly that may have been a wart... ouch!'

Mandy had flicked his ear again. She had taken to doing this as she wanted all the bumps on his head to have a while to go down, and she also thought he looked funny with cauliflower ears. 'Jack, shut up muttering, and tell us what to do now, please.'

'You can't tell Stork from mutter.' Jack replied, too late to realise that his lips had un-straightened themselves and in their new wonky shape he had spoken, 'Oh well,' he thought, but spoke.

'Jack.' It was Samuels, but equally could have been Mandy.

'It was my Aunt Nellie. Anyway, Sister Winifrede should be making her way up Whitehall now, a short stop to pick up the PM and dep PM.' Jack's phone went. 'What's that?'

Mandy rummaged through Jack's trousers which made Jack completely forget where he was and what he was doing, and then he remembered, this was why he got married. Mandy was brilliant with admin and remembered important things, like, what he was going to do and often this came with a bonus of having his trousers rummaged, which, if he wiggled, which he was very good at, it would mean his naughty bits often got a little fondle.

Mandy answered the call for Jack, who had a beatific smile on his face, if you could see past the ugly, which Mandy was practised at and could see she would get nothing sensible out of him for the time being. 'Hello,' she said into the phone, and then listened. 'Okay, I will tell him.' She listened again and then closed the call saying, 'Pharaoh and out to you to.'

'Numpti?' Jack asked, by way of an aside from looking beatific. He knew he was good at being beatific; sainted, he thought.

'Yeah, St Dick, and he says that Mackeroon and Blogg have joined the process... what procession, Jack?

And Jack nodded his beatific head towards Whitehall and from the height of the Gallery steps, Mandy and Samuels could see a procession behind a horse and cart being driven by a vagrant, appearing to be in a holy coma, and beside him was Pimple, lording it, and Sister Winifred prancing on the flat bed of the cart behind. They watched as the crowd parted to allow the horse and cart and its procession into the square, just a hint of a wobble from Winifrede as the cart negotiated the kerb, before it processed, swerving sedately past Nelson's purple-clouded column. It passed easily between the pools and fountains to arrive at the bottom of the ceremonial steps where it stopped. It was here that something additionally miraculous happened, on this generally miraculous day of miraculous events. Jack told Mandy he needed a wee.

Mandy looked at her husband in amazement. All this happening and he wanted a wee? 'Go back into the gallery, there are public toilets. And hurry back, everything is kicking off.'

Aedd reappeared, he having completed his task of earlier announcement and relieved he could just watch events unfold and, of course, watch his wondrous and voluptuous resurrected Bea, and he ducked and dived so he could keep looking at her as she conducted away, her upper lady bumps wobbling in a most seductive way as the orchestra played with increasing fervour. The main event was imminent.

Mandy flicked her head. 'Go with Jack please,

329

Aedd, and make sure he washes his hands, comes straight back and doesn't go astray.'

Aedd looked as if he didn't want to go and, just for a minute, you could see the Irish warring ancestry in his face. This soon changed to the Welsh miner masculine hygiene face when Mandy gave him the stare. It was such a stare that even Jack wondered if he really needed a wee after all, as he put his hands to his bursting willie, so he absolutely needed to go and he had better hurry as he also needed to play his part in this rebirth of his country.

THIRTY-NINE

SISTER WINIFREDE FLOATED OFF THE BACK OF her cart and began immediately dancing around the raised plinth that edged the fountains. She stepped lively on to the plaza, separated out the MPs, lords and ladies and they became just a part of the crowd and, as she continued, dancers from the Royal Ballet, just out for a picnic from Covent Garden, up the road, swirled on to the plaza. There was a rapturous applause and it was at this precise point the orchestra struck up, for the second time, Stravinsky's Rite of Spring.

The men separated themselves from the women dancers and encouraged a reciprocal action in the nearby crowd, sorting young and old and slowly, as the music phrasing progressed, a perimeter was formed and the ballet dancers lead the way for the people, the young people of Britain, in their *Adoration of the Earth*. All of this was seen and cheered on by the huge crowd that thronged the square, who watched proceedings on the big screens. A similar reaction played out across the nation, in cities and towns, the people reacted in appreciation of what they were seeing, not able to resist dancing themselves.

And then, everything halted. A stunned silence as the ballet-dancing men threw themselves on the ground and the men in the crowd followed suit, in *Adoration,* as Sister Winifrede passed by them, to disappear into the company of women who had gathered on the ceremonial steps. The silence continued as the orchestra took a breather before commencing the second and final movement; *The Sacrifice*.

The orchestra started with a haunting modulating melody as the purple haze from atop Nelson's column spread like a thin diaphanous cloud across the whole square, hovering just above head height. The dancers remained motionless. There was no sign of the dancing nun. The crowd was hushed in anticipation, looking up from the square at the screens now so bright in the gloom of the purple haze. A laser light pierced that murk, down from Nelson, who now looked a lot like Flan Flinger, and all Londoners knew of his reputation and, there was a chill in the air. It was fear.

The laser ignited a bonfire that had appeared from nowhere, and mystically, the crowds to the western edge shuffled apart on a gentle wave of what appeared at first to be chuckling, but was in fact, mystical tittering. Now everybody could see on the big screens, a ghostly figure making his way through the crowd. Was it a ballet dancer from Covent Garden because, as he started to come into view, the man, who was generously proportioned, it had to be said, a body gelatinously contained in pink tights, a vest with huge armholes and a stiff netted pink tutu, strutted, proudly, his legs extended on each stride, plimsolled toes pointed.

As the music evolved into a crescendo of thumping, rhythmic chugging, like a steam train building speed, there was a cheer as Jack, being a Dick, pranced out like Jane, with whirls and twirls and the orchestra strings suggested high-pitched swerves as Jack accentuated this with his fluid moves, pointing to Flan Flinger who now hovered above him. He danced and spun around the bonfire, the music rhythmically pounded and, with a swipe of his hand, Zondo, from behind the orchestra, amplified the sound so the music from this fabulous orchestra, albeit with a substitute leader of the second violins, resonated and echoed off the enclosing buildings of Trafalgar Square. It was a huge sound, evocative of the magnificent miracle being played out for the whole world to see.

Mandy, watching on the screens, sighed, 'He was just going for a wee... what happened?' And then she laughed. What else could she do as her husband, the eejit, made a bigger eejit of himself, but she could see his face as one of the cameras zoomed in, red from exertion but deadly serious in an ugly way. His whole life had built to this very moment and Mandy now worried. Would he survive? Did he want to? Did she want him to?

All eyes were on Jack as he danced toward the National Gallery steps when out from the crowd of young women stepped Sister Winifrede, and Jack, in his poncy pregnant donkey walk, led her to the bonfire. The youths in the throng, accompanied by the

Royal Ballet dancers, crowded around the dancing nun as she gracefully skirted the blaze. Zondo and Flan Flinger floated nearer, to a big Oooh from the crowd and Zondo took Jack by the hand and led him, flapping his other hand and prancing like he never did relieve himself in the public toilets in the Gallery foyer, to a side spot. His part was over for the time being, as was Zondo's.

The music rose in a massive crescendo of brutal excitement. The pace and tempo of the dancers responded as they rose and encircled Winifrede who was now, ironically, a blinding, whirling Dervish and, as the music climaxed, so Winifrede collapsed, exhausted and she died, (again). The men and women dancers shrank down to a hunch, not knowing what to do. The music shuddered and then with a tinkle, (not Jack, he had actually been to the toilet) it ended.

There was an eerie hush as Jack reappeared. Respectfully, the crowd remained silent and, slowly and ceremoniously, Jack commenced stepping out, heading towards the prone form of Sister Winifrede. The nun still at last, a final repose.

Mandy, standing close to Jim Samuels and Cecelia, could be heard speaking under her breath. 'Oh no, it's his poxy Swan Lake,' she recalled it from the Napoleonic Fort in the Solent (*see Kind Hearts and Martinets – Cause and Effect*).

As Jack reached the dead nun, so he lowered himself and he gathered her into his arms. The sound of his sobs and the rustling of her habit and her pink netting, tickling his nose, could be heard across the square and, in an act of communal contrition, the crowd could be heard to weep.

'Oh Christ, he's bloody crying.' Cecelia hugged

Mandy, who was weeping herself. Cecelia was strong, maybe she had cried enough today and was now just so pleased her Pimple had come back to her and then, she thought, where the hell was he? Just as he appeared by her side. And then she wept, the floodgates again opened, as she let Mandy go and hugged her fiancé.

Jack leaned over the nun and, in a respectful and kindly gesture, the crowd could see his fingertips close Winifrede's eyes. He reached into the front of his tights and brought out his handkerchief and dabbed the face of the, fortunately, dead nun.

'Oh Jack; put that filthy rag away.' Mandy said to nobody.

And then Jack made to lift Sister Winifrede and, across the square could be heard: 'Fuck me sweet'art, you're as 'eavy as bleedin' Jumbo the feckin' elephant.' And, as Jack struggled to lift her the crowd tittered, their spirits somehow rising, a sense of rebirth of freedom, of joy, of hope made real, it was later explained.

'Oh no, Jack, your back. Please don't strain it.' Mandy again said to nobody.

Zondo stepped in with both hands outstretched and Sister Winifrede's body rose up and into Jack's waiting arms. The sorcerer lowered her so Jack took her weight and could carry her.

'Fucking Ada, Zondo, can't you just waft her over to the altar?' There was a collective intake of breath at Jack's cursing, or was it because the conductor's rostrum had miraculously transformed into a simple, rectangular altar. The purple haze evolved into a purple and gold trimmed altar cloth. (The stone is still there to this day, and will be tomorrow and forever, and is known as, *Winifrede's Lump of Stone* and is revered every bit as much as the Tomb of Thomas Beckett in Canterbury).

Jack struggled with the weight of Sister Winifrede though he knew not to complain to Zondo. This was the final sacrifice, his having to struggle with the body to the altar. If he could get there and lay the nun out, the ceremony would be complete and, as if sensing just this, the crowd reacted by humming the tune that had become, in just a few days, the anthem for the dancing Nun: *If you were the holy girl in the world.* Jack laboured. The humming increased in volume, which was fortunate as it disguised a lot of his effing and jeffing and complaints about his bad back, but slowly he made it, climbing one step at a time, in groups of four, and then a landing. Four times he did this before he reached the National Gallery summit. He staggered behind the altar and, with one last effort, he raised the body of Sister Winifrede to the crowd and there was a tumultuous response that reached a crescendo as he laid her to rest upon the altar.

The crowd silenced as Jack looked at them and Mandy sidled up. 'Well done Jack, can we go home now, please...?'

But Jack had one more thing to do and then his lifetime's work would be complete and he told his wife so. She stepped away and let him have his head, just a quiet mention that he was a feckin tow rag, just so he did not get ideas above his station, or bus stop, when he got home.

He looked up and the crowd silenced in reverence. This man was known. Known for his bravery and his sincerity, as well as for being the country's biggest, fattest and ugliest dipstick. But, they silenced to hear what he had to say.

'The blessed Winifrede has shown us the way. Through her guiding dance, the country has been taken back by its people, no longer to be controlled by the few, but by the many...' and he paused, '... it is done. So be it.'

THE END

But what of the DaDa Detective Agency? Do they slip back into the quiet and pleasant idyll of retirement in Frisian Tun? It was noted in the papers, after they had settled that Amanda Austin, Duck, often had her fingers crossed; arthritis, Yuppie quotation marks, or, crossed for luck, because that would be my guess and I would be right, because I write this stuff. So, that is 650 points to me, which makes me the winner:

The third DaDa Detective Agency book:
A Blood Sport
Wigs on the Green
by
Pete Adams

AUTHOR'S NOTE

The Rite of Spring – the metaphor.

I have always admired the music of *Stravinsky*, and it was during a performance of *Rite of Spring* that my mind focused on the analogy to life today. The need for rebirth, not for the old systems to be reborn, but for something truly new. For the *People*. A society where social justice and fairness predominate – if you do not dream of a better, fairer world, you cannot expect to achieve it. If you do not wish for something, you cannot strive for it.

The concept behind *The Rite of Spring*, developed by Roerich from Stravinsky's outline idea, is that after various primitive rituals, celebrating the advent of spring, a young girl is chosen as a sacrificial victim and dances herself to death.

Extract from the *Ballet Encyclopaedia* – with my annotations:

Part I: The adoration of the earth: The curtain rises to reveal young men and women in separate groups. Their surroundings are primitive and dominated by the dark forces of nature. At first the dances are light-hearted, but they slowly change to have more aggressive and savage movements. The young men take possession of the women and carry them off stage. A fight ensues, until a wise old man makes peace. There is a stunned silence, the men then throw themselves on the ground in worship, rise again, and start an even more frenzied dance.

To me this was confusion, a lack of purpose, a seeking of a return to the only thing they knew, even if life was patently tilted against them – is it wrong to seek something better and, who, could provide that, not realising that the power for change lay within... within the People. The powers that be fear the poor probably more than the poor fear the powerful. Someone once said, "... never underestimate the power of a small group to effect change, in fact, it is the only thing that has ever effected change."

Part II: The sacrifice: The young women are standing on the stage near a fire. One of them will be chosen as a sacrifice to the earth. The chosen one stands alone after a mystic dance and the young members of the tribe gather around her and dance in a *crescendo of brutal excitement*. Finally, the chosen one joins them and the dancing grows more and more violent until it climaxes and, the chosen maiden falls, exhausted, and dies. The men then carry her over to the sacred stone and fall prostrate; the rite is over.

We will never know what we can achieve until we challenge what is unfair. We were born to dream and not to be enslaved by one person's idea of what is good for us. After all, this ballet, The Rite of Spring, was notoriously received with aggression and vilification and only later admired and appreciated. It was the fact that Stravinsky and the dancer Nijinsky had challenged the traditional, the norms, and had shown that there was an alternative to the barbarism of that age (demonstrated belief and courage) – I see a similarity with the way our world is today, still run on a code developed in the 17th century, a code that benefits the few, the one per cent, relegating the ninety nine per cent to scrapping over whatever "trickles down"; not very much, and told to be grateful for what they have.

Rite Judgement – Umble Pie is a sequel to *Road Kill – The Duchess of Frisian Tun*. It can be read as a separate novel but a reader may get more enjoyment if they read *Duchess* beforehand, maybe the *Kind Hearts and Martinets* series of five books as well. In the DaDa novels, I wanted to take characters that have had key roles in some of my previous books and bring them back, along with a new cast, to take part in a surreal, or at least a quirky, plot – I in *Rite Judgement*, The DaDa Detective Agency pit themselves against the establishment.

Author comment:

I feel that sometimes to make a point, a writer has to exaggerate, make his plot and characters a little (and this may be an underestimate) larger than life. I hope that at the end of this book, where I deliberately twist into a DNA spiral, the real and the surreal narrative, the events in many of my previous novels may seem less fanciful and, may even make sense, beyond the elemental story – the direction however, the conclusion, is mine alone, and I will continue.

Dear reader,

We hope you enjoyed reading *Rite Judgement*. Please take a moment to leave a review, even if it's a short one. Your opinion is important to us.

Discover more books by Pete Adams at https://www.nextchapter.pub/authors/pete-adams

Want to know when one of our books is free or discounted? Join the newsletter at http://eepurl.com/bqqB3H

Best regards,
Pete Adams and the Next Chapter Team

Rite Judgement
ISBN: 978-4-82410-771-8
Mass Market

Published by
Next Chapter
1-60-20 Minami-Otsuka
170-0005 Toshima-Ku, Tokyo
+818035793528

1st October 2021

CPSIA information can be obtained
at www.ICGtesting.com
Printed in the USA
LVHW020322031121
702257LV00018B/1423